A
BEACON
OF LIGHT

THE LONG ROAD HOME, BOOK TWO

AN AMISH ROMANCE

LINDA BYLER

Good Books

New York, New York

A BEACON OF LIGHT

Good Books books may be purchased in bulk at special discounts for sales promotion, corporate gifts, fund-raising, or educational purposes. Special editions can also be created to specifications. For details, contact the Special Sales Department, Good Books, 307 West 36th Street, 11th Floor, New York, NY 10018 or info@skyhorsepublishing.com.

Good Books is an imprint of Skyhorse Publishing, Inc., a Delaware corporation.

Visit our website at www.goodbooks.com.

10 9 8 7 6 5 4 3 2

Library of Congress Cataloging-in-Publication Data is available on file.

Print ISBN: 978-1-68099-740-8
eBook ISBN: 978-1-68099-797-2

Cover design Create Design Publish LLC.

Printed in the United States of America

CHAPTER 1

To approach the home of her childhood after all these years was no small thing. Engulfed by the raw fear of rejection, the panic of being turned away with nowhere to go, her mouth turned dry as her heart drummed in her thin chest.

A wisp of a girl, budding into womanhood, her blond hair was caught in a ponytail, and her long coat hid any curves her blouse and calf-length skirt might have revealed. The lack of a covering rode like an uncomfortable nakedness on her head, the blue of her coat a neon signal of having divested herself of her Amish heritage. She had shucked the plain clothes just as she had rid herself of Melvin Amstutz and his hypocrisy. She had fled his home, but not before he had robbed her of her girlhood, her innocence, and her faith in the plain way of life in Arkansas.

Would anyone believe her if she even found the courage to tell of what life was like under Melvin's roof?

The home remained as she had kept it in her memory, perhaps with a fresh coat of white paint on the German wood siding of the house. A square two-story, unadorned except for the rectangular windows with small panes, the putty newly applied, the front porch with only the gray wooden box that contained the supply of fuel for the great range in the kitchen.

The bare branches of the maple trees thrust their black fingers toward the lowering gray sky, as if to warn her away, beckoning her silently to retrace her footsteps, forget about any hope of warmth or welcome. She stopped when the frenzied barking of a large dog reached her ears, followed by a low guttural growl.

She clutched the small black satchel, her breath coming in short gasps as a black and brown mongrel appeared from beneath a hedge that bordered the house. She saw the hairs lifted on the scruff of his neck, shuddered to see the great slavering mouth open and close with each frenetic burst of sound.

But she stood her ground. What did she have to lose? To be consumed by this unfriendly animal might well put an end to her existence on earth, an existence that had felt like a dark void since Clinton's death.

She watched. The dog was there, at her side, the low growl silenced as he sniffed the hem of her coat. She did not meet the fiery eyes, neither did she stretch out a hand to touch him, but held her breath as the long matted tail began a whisper of back and forth movement.

"Hey dog," she whispered.

There was no sign of life from within the white house. No parting of white muslin curtains or lifting of the green roll-down shades, no door flung open to reveal a welcoming face.

She stepped forward tentatively, the dog stepping aside to allow her to advance. She took this as a positive sign and made her way to the bottom step of the porch. The dog looked up, whined. Slowly she lifted one foot, then the other, until she found herself at the door, trembling. She drew down her top lip to catch the shaking lower one, lifted her hand, and knocked.

Immediately, the door was pulled open from the inside, the latch releasing like a explosion to her overwrought senses. She was face to face with a young woman dressed in the navy blue of traditional Amish dress, a white apron tied around her narrow waist, a large pleated head covering drawn forward over her ears, her face impassive.

"Hello."

She opened her mouth, but only a croak emerged. She cleared her throat, said hello in a small voice barely above a whisper. She met the curious gaze from the brown eyes, but lowered her own too quickly, guilt washing over her as she realized how unrecognizable she must be.

"We don't help tramps."

"I . . . I am not a wanderer."

"What are you then?"

"I am May. Merriweather Miller. I believe this is the home of my grandparents."

The woman's mouth went slack with astonishment, the brown eyes opened wide in disbelief as her two hands came up.

"You're . . . you're Eliezer's girl?"

"I am."

"May."

"Yes."

"But . . . you're in English clothes. Where are your real clothes?"

"I don't have them anymore."

"Are you excommunicated? Should I be speaking to you?"

"No, I never joined the church in Arkansas."

"Goodness gracious! I'm Nettie. Nettie Troyer."

May was bewildered. Was she supposed to know who she was? It had been so long; she was sure there was a dizzying array of cousins and new marriages, babies born, families moved to other locations, deaths and sicknesses. Her face revealed her lack of understanding, the shame of her years of absence.

"But . . . this house. It is the house of my maternal grandparents, is it not? Solomon and Mattie Amstutz?"

"Yes, but they both died. Solomon of typhoid and Mattie soon after. Fell asleep in her bed and never woke up. We bought the house. Aaron Troyer is my husband. Remember Aaron?"

May shook her head.

"Well, come in. Rex, move. Let her in. He's such a bossy dog. Thinks he owns the entire Amish community. Come on in. Bring your bag."

May was weak with relief, tears close to the surface, the hunger roiling in her stomach like a ravenous animal. The walk from the bus station had used up most of her remaining strength, the sleepless night adding to her exhaustion.

A small child peered curiously from the doorway, her hand to her mouth, the thumb inserted securely. Her small black covering covered her head, leaving May with a wrenching nostalgia, memories of her mother drawing a comb through her hair, expertly braiding and pinning the blond tresses, before pinning the *s'glay schwottz coppley* (small black covering) on her head.

She followed Nettie to the kitchen table, sank gratefully into the plain wooden chair she drew out for her, then crossed her hands in her lap.

"Well, since you are not excommunicated then, I suppose I won't have to shun you. According to the *ordnung* (rules) of the church, I can get you something to eat and join you at the table. It's only three o'clock in the afternoon, which is fine by me. Aaron won't be home till later in the evening. Come, Esta, come away from the door. Here, get your thumb out and say hello to May."

A wail from an adjoining bedroom took Nettie down the narrow hallway to reappear with the fattest baby May had ever seen. His face was as round as the moon, with small brown eyes hidden in rolls of flesh, his fingers waving like small sausages. Nettie sank into a chair, propped the large baby on her lap, and told May he was a *glutz* (heavy child).

May smiled, unsure what the proper reply would be.

"So, tell me your story."

May felt her face drain of color, felt the hopelessness of telling this friendly normal young woman of her own dark and bitter past.

If she spoke the truth, she would be turned away, marked forever as an *ungehorsam* (disobedient) or worse. The deep shame and sorrow of her years with Melvin and Gertie had to remain buried under a layer of denial, a truth that would cease to exist. She was capable of holding it inside; her courage would disintegrate it eventually, grind away at the horror of it until there was nothing left. No one would need to know her darkest secret, and certainly no one would ever find out about her illicit love with Clinton. She would never speak of it, would never marry another, could never love again.

Her ravaged mind and body was her own, and no one would ever again trespass on her own flesh and blood.

All this accosted her in the form of outward hesitation, a trembling of her mouth, a bewildered, evasive look.

Nettie's eyes narrowed.

"Oh." Quickly, May recovered her composure. "Oh, there's not much to tell. My . . . my . . . you know, my parents were drowned that spring. Eliezer and Fronie Miller. And . . . well, you might remember. My grandparents were old. Not, you know, capable of keeping my brother and me. The rest of our *freundshaft* (relatives) had homes and many children. Mouths to feed. Times were hard after the . . . well, during the war. So they all agreed Melvin and Gertie, our uncle and aunt in Arkansas, would be the best choice, the way he made a success of growing cotton in the Mississippi Delta."

"Were they good to you?"

"Yes, oh yes. We grew up in their care."

"How come you left them?"

"Gertie passed away, and Melvin became ill. I was taken in by an English family who led me into the world."

"And your brother?"

Here May lost her courage, her train of thought, her suave ability to make up a believable tale. Her long dark lashes swept her cheeks, two blushes of color appeared on her thin white cheeks, and she drew a shivery breath.

"I don't know."

"What do you mean?"

"I . . . he left. I don't know where he is."

"Hmm. Why did he leave?"

Thick and fast, the questions came then, till May was exhausted in body and spirit. Truthful to a fault, this was indeed a treacherous road, one to be navigated without the hindrance of the blackest secret.

Finally, she asked to use the outhouse, was pointed in the direction of the back yard, relieved to find Nettie occupied with setting out a block of Swiss cheese, a paring knife, homemade bread and butter, with a small dish of canned apricots.

May swallowed the rising saliva, felt the greedy glitter of hunger in her eyes, could not butter the bread quickly enough. She fell on the entire slice without breaking it in half, stuffed it into her mouth in a way that caused alarm in Nettie, who said nothing but wondered when this girl had last eaten anything.

When the husband, Aaron, returned, there was color in May's face, strength gained by the simple food, and courage to face the man of the house. Tall, well built, with a shock of unruly hair that sprang away from his face, he was given to a bashful curiosity, but being a man of few words, he allowed his garrulous wife to fill in the details without his comments upsetting her flow of words.

"So what do you want from us?" he asked finally, changing the toothpick from the right side of his mouth to the left.

"Uh ... well, nothing, really. I knew this was my grandfather's house and thought they might take me in, but I will move on if you direct me to my relatives' homes."

"And your relatives are?"

"You know, Aaron. S'alsa Abe. Danny Miller. There's Robert Amstutz and Henry Mast."

Aaron nodded. "You know none of them will take you in like that." His jaw jutted in the general direction of her blue coat, which hung open now to reveal the white button-down blouse and the plaid skirt.

Nettie raised her eyebrows, then nodded her agreement.

"Well, yes. You're right. I know how they are."

May's frightened eyes met Nettie's, the realization that some things remained the same, no matter the span of years or the mixture of joys, pain, or sorrow that moved down from one generation to the next.

Her *freundshaft* had been unwilling to take in the two orphaned children, and would certainly not accept one gone astray, a black sheep who had been misled by the world, decked out in a blue coat and no head covering, a sure sign of her wanton nature, her refusal to bow to *gemeinde ordnung*. Here was a heretic, one who the Bible would require them to cast out, to have nothing to do with. The way she was dressed was the way she was judged.

"Then, you mean nothing has changed." She could not conceal the deep disappointment in her voice.

"Not hardly."

May swallowed, facing the unknown future with the stark knowledge that she would have to grovel at someone's feet, to prostrate herself, beg and weep and whine. The world was not hers to experience, with no job, no money, no means of surviving from day to day without someone's mercy or belief in her blight. She felt the hope of being taken in by her family slip through her fingers like some diaphanous cloth. She had always bolstered her sense of neglect by telling herself her family really couldn't have taken them in, when times were hard. They had wanted them, really, but couldn't do it at the time. But no, it wasn't that. She wasn't worthy of their care then, and she certainly wasn't now.

"She could wear my clothes," Nettie offered.

May smiled, a small attempt at normalcy. "If I could spend the night here, perhaps I could start out in the morning, if you'd be kind enough to give me directions to one of them. The one you think most likely to receive me. I will work as a maid for room and board."

"I'm sure you will," Nettie said kindly, and Aaron gave her a knowing nod.

SHE FOUND HERSELF walking along the cold, dusty road, a set of directions clutched in her hand, a warm breakfast of fried mush and puddins in her stomach. There was deep woods on either side of her, here in this hollow where the road dipped close to a winding creek. The forest floor was carpeted with a dense layer of browned leaves, the red and gold of their former glory having been broken down by decay. Birds twittered from branch to branch like busybodies, telling each other about this girl's travels. Woodpeckers drummed in the dying trunks of trees felled by lightning, slurping up the hibernating beetles and moths with their extraordinary length of sharp tongue. Squirrels peered from the top branches, their flat bushy tails balancing the precarious position as they swung from one thin perch to another. The gray clouds were still the color of polished pewter, but there was an occasional sighting of an irregular streak of blue behind them.

She heard the rattle of a surrey drawn by a horse. The carriages here in her home state were built with the floor narrowed from the top, which left more room to make a short turn. She had not seen a surrey since her childhood, and was gladdened to see one come at a good clip down the opposite incline. She heard the scraping of the brake block against the back wheel, then the release of the handle when the team reached the bottom.

A cheery wave, the horse lunged into his collar, and the buggy was past in a split of gravel. Nothing unusual to see a young woman dressed in the traditional black shawl and bonnet walking from place to place, so she went on her way unhindered. If the occupant of the buggy would have looked closely, he would have seen the ancient moth-eaten spare shawl and the broken bonnet Nettie had given her. Sponged and pressed, it had turned into wearable headgear.

She'd helped her tremendously, allowing her a set of clothes, giving her hairpins, a white covering, with May's promises of paying her back as soon as she was able. It all felt so right, so good and solid and endearing, somehow. She knew girls who had left to join the mainstream, reveled in their freedom of dress and expression, and who was she to judge? For herself, however, there was a certain axis of her existence that had been righted, straightened, attached. It was a homecoming, a melding of her past with her present that strengthened her sense of who she was. A fortitude, really.

But the hardest part awaited—the introduction of herself to her forbidding relatives. She stopped, unfolded the scrap of yellowing paper, then nodded to herself. Yes, this was Branch Creek. She would turn left at the next crossroad.

There she would find S'alsa Abe, his wife Betty, her mother's step-sister by marriage.

Please God, please God. Her thoughts ran into a regular rhythm of beseeching Him to help her in her time of need.

Just a bed, enough to eat, a decent home, even without kindness. She didn't need much.

She walked on, found the macadam road, then turned onto a narrow country road that lay ahead of her like a long, fresh ribbon, turning neither left nor right, the fields falling away on either side with rattling stands of dry, rustling corn. Far in the distance, a wagon moved slowly along the outside perimeters of a cornfield, dark figures among the heavy shocks of cornstalks, ripping off the heavy ears, yanking down the husks and sending them flying through the air like yellow missiles.

There was the farm, then.

Tucked between a stand of pine, the barn was as white as the house. She saw a corn crib half full, a few sheds scattered at random, a barnyard, a cow and horse pasture, a black surrey parked beside the barn. It was a picture of everyday Amish life on a farm, with a few pigs producing fine litters of piglets, hens and a rooster in the henhouse, cows in the barn, plodding Belgian workhorses, a few hungry cats to keep rats and mice at bay.

May's heart swelled with a deep sense of homecoming. Surely here among her sainted relatives who worked the land, who were good and honest and upright, she could grasp the beginning of her healing. *Let it be, oh please, let it be.*

Again, there was no sign of life, but the dreaded barking of an untrustworthy dog was not there, either. Relieved, she wasted no time going up on the front porch, only to hesitate at the door. She felt the pain of refusal, imagining the act of being turned away, her head lowered, her mind racing to secure a clue about her next step.

So many trials, so many sorrows and setbacks in her young life, wouldn't it be fitting to be disappointed another time? She felt no courage or hope, only a tired acceptance of whatever it would be these S'alsa Abes would inflict on her. She almost smiled at the implication of a nickname. "S'alsa Abe" meant Salt Abe. As if he'd been salted.

A sense of humor, perhaps. Some former joke about salt.

She lifted her hand and knocked lightly.

When there was no answer, she waited, taking in her surroundings.

The porch floor was in need of paint, and there were mud-splattered rubber boots lying haphazardly along the wall. An old corn broom was propped in the corner, and the windows were covered in spider webs, the sills littered with dead flies, their bodies being slowly cremated by exposure to the southern slant of the sun. When there was no answer to her second tapping, she walked to the side of the house to find a very plump red-faced woman bent over a wringer she was cranking with studied concentration.

"Hello," May offered quietly.

The woman straightened, turned, and lifted bewildered eyes. May met her gaze. Chills raced across her shoulders and down her spine. She felt an inward quaking she could not control any more than she could control her breathing.

It was her! Betty. The only one of the relatives who had expressed regret. The one who had wrapped her in a warm embrace and told her she was terribly sorry, it wasn't right, but if this was what the family decided she couldn't go against it. She remembered a thinner, younger version of Betty, but oh, God be praised, it was truly her.

"Why, hello. Should I know who you are?"

May could not speak, could only allow her eyes to stay on this remembered face, remember the swell of her rounded bosom, the way her warm arms had flattened her own thin child's body. Those arms had crushed her to the scent of warm fabric and instilled a desperation to somehow creep inside of the woman's heart, to become smaller and smaller till she was no more.

She tried again to say her name, but was horrified to hear a rending sob emerge from her throat, horrified to feel the strength in her legs give way as she sank to the ground, huddled there with the black shawl spread around her like a blanket of sorrow.

"My goodness. *Do, komm komm* (Here, come, come)."

And still May found it impossible to rise to her feet.

She would later remember the smell of lye soap and the vinegar in her rinse water, the warm steam that rose from the water in the washtubs. She would remember the piles of soiled clothing, the fire crackling under the copper kettle hung from a tripod in the yard, the steam from the boiling water like a wet cloud.

In the house, children looked up like inquisitive rabbits, brown eyed and dark haired, then went back to their play. Every Amish home was filled with children, every house rang with the sound of them. Women bore them, fathers helped with raising them, reveled in their blessings, their quivers full of arrows from God, the way the Bible instructed them.

And Betty recognized May.

They talked and drank cups of sweet peppermint tea and cookies. The wash water turned cold, the fire fizzled into a pile of gray ashes with a few red embers like malevolent eyes, and still Betty plied her with questions, which May answered with evasiveness and near truths.

Yes, she was welcome. Why, of course she was. If Abe didn't agree, well, that was too bad. May had nowhere else to go, and Lord knew Betty had spent hours of guilt and regret, having sent those two off to Arkansas to Melvin and Gertie. She never could stand the man and she didn't care what May said, she guaranteed it hadn't been all roses, not with that cranky man and his lazy wife.

May told her, though, about the borrowed clothing, about Nettie helping her to become one of them with her clothes. Betty narrowed her eyes and armed her gaze like arrows.

"Now you can't tell me there wasn't something wrong, or you would not have left Melvin's house to live with worldly people."

How May hated that expression!

Who was "worldly"? Certainly Melvin had been in that category, with his hidden longings and the audacity to carry them out. She would always rebel against the labeling of who was deemed worldly. Wasn't there just a vast jumble of weeds and good plants that grew up together and it was God's sole business to sort it out? Plain clothes did not separate anyone from the world, if those clothes covered a body awash in sin.

"When you left, I was still pretty much a timid new bride, but believe me, May, it wouldn't happen again. Marriage changes a person. You have to have an opinion, have to stand up for yourself, else your husband and kids walk all over you. And that's the truth."

She finished with a resounding, "Yes, you are staying. You might have to sleep with Norrie, but you'll have a small room to yourself. Come. Come with me, and I'll show you around."

The house was a two-story farmhouse with four square bedrooms upstairs, a narrow hallway, chamber pots in need of emptying, dust everywhere, unmade beds and torn curtains. Betty sniffed, spread an open palmed hand across a bed and said resignedly, "*Ach*, that Isaac. Wet the bed again." With that, she heaved the flannel sheet and torn blanket out the window, flapped it a few times, then closed the window on top to let the urine-soaked bedding dry on the side of the house.

Seven children in ten years.

Betty laughed, propped her plump fists on her hips and said that was what happened when you got married. Kids all over the place. Abe was a good husband, but always busy on the farm. Always. She could sure use an extra pair of hands.

And that was how May found herself crying into her flannel pillow, tears of relief awelling up as if an artesian well had opened in her heart, the years of pain and betrayal leaking on the stained pillowcase, with quiet little Norrie sleeping a child's dreamless sleep beside her.

She had been accepted, had a home, food to eat, a family to call her own. She would work her fingers to the bone, would never complain, but show Betty what a dependable worker she was. Love for the assertive woman welled up, followed by a mushrooming appreciation of a structured Amish home. She would wash and scrub and clean, she would sing His praises forever.

And Abe seemed calm and docile, his weathered face wreathed in good natured grins of humor at his children's antic and his wife's endless tales.

Now if she could only find Oba and share all of this with him.

CHAPTER 2

OBADIAH MILLER RESTED ON THE HARD BENCH, HIS LEGS thrust forward, his hands deep in his pockets, and glared at the dull unpainted walls of the Greyhound bus station, somewhere in New York state. His shoulders slumped with the defeat that rode his body like a chafing, bitter thing. He had no destination in particular, although he wondered vaguely how many small towns he had combed with no real lead.

Clinton Brown might have been his sister's source of escape, but who could tell what had occurred from that getaway? The idea of May being with a colored man was hardly bearable, the childlike way she had about her, the trusting innocence, the sense of duty. He could feel her desperation, however, the need to remove herself from the Melvin Amstutz farm, and hopefully, the need to locate him, her brother.

His funds were running low, so he knew he would need a source of employment, but that, too, added to his bitterness. After working in a garage in Arkansas, he hated all mechanics and their greasy hands, hated the dank, oil-filled environment and the chugging automobiles that remained a complete mystery. He cringed at the thought of his lies, his inability to become one of them, no matter how much effort he put into it.

Raised in the Mississippi Delta, on his uncle Melvin's cotton farm, milking cows and resisting authority, his back crosshatched with the scars from whip lashes, he viewed the world through the lens of his painful past.

He was hungry, hadn't slept, and wrestled with despair and emptiness. If he could find May, he might be able to get it together, whatever "it" was. She had always brought him back from the brink with her soft voice, begging him to obey, to forgive, to remember God's love for him, no matter the trials they went through after the death of their parents, Eliezer and Fronie Miller.

He took out his wallet, checked the amount of cash, then turned his head to look out the door. Shifting his gaze away from any sign of friendliness, he scowled back at curious onlookers.

He got to his feet, picked up the black satchel, and walked out, pretending a destination.

The air was like a knife through his thin denim coat, and his ears tingled with the blast of wind that tunneled through the streets of the seedy little town. A neon sign from a large dust-encrusted window took his attention. Limp drapes sagged on an unwieldy rod, the words Lunch Special scrawled across a square of cardboard taped to the window. His mouth watered, the flow of saliva increasing as he swallowed. He couldn't be picky, not with the amount of money in his wallet, so he pushed his way through the oversized door that creaked on rusty hinges.

The interior was dim, the floor announcing his arrival with a few pops and squeaks as he made his way to the counter, straddled a brown vinyl barstool, kept his eyes on the container of sugar. He hadn't looked around, but he felt the emptiness, the lack of activity.

"Do for you?"

He looked up to find a young woman eyeing him curiously, one hand propped on the curve of her hip, her jaws working the chewing gum in her mouth with wet, sloppy rhythm.

"A menu?"

She pointed to the white rectangular sign above him.

Oba nodded, felt the embarrassment rise in his face.

He was hungry for anything other than another roadside burger, the odd mixture of gristle and questionable cuts of meat formed into a ragged patty filled with breadcrumbs, covered in ketchup from a bottle with too many refillings and no washing. Limp lettuce and rancid onion.

Chicken noodle for a dollar. Tomato and grilled cheese for two. Mashed potatoes and meatballs for three fifty.

He swallowed and ordered the chicken noodle. When it arrived, he found a blue vein floating on the greasy surface and called the insolent waitress.

"I'm not eating this."

He pointed to the vein, not meeting her irritated gaze.

A hand whisked the bowl away, but no other bowl appeared in its place. Oba took sips of his water, studied the menu, watched the paint-splattered and grease-speckled door to the kitchen. He found himself drumming his fingertips on the countertop, irritation rising to the point of anxiety.

Where was she?

He looked around, saw the cook lounging in a booth, a skein of yarn on the table, knitting needles flashing, her mouth pulled down in concentration. A corner booth contained an old man, gnashing away at some pile on his plate.

"Hey!" Oba called out.

There was no answer, so he turned to the cook with the knitting project.

"Could I have some service here?"

"S' matter?"

"I sent my soup back. There's a chicken vein floating on the top."

"Oh, come on. What do you think this is? Hollywood?"

"I don't like veins in my soup."

"Jeanie!"

The raucous tone brought the waitress, after plenty of time had elapsed, still chewing. She raised her eyebrows, leaned against the counter, crossed her arms.

"Give him his soup."

"There ain't any. He got the last of it."

"Give him tomato."

Oba brought his fist down on the counter, bellowing out his hunger and frustration. The sugar shaker rocked, a salt shaker fell over, spraying salt across the table.

"I don't want the tomato soup."

With that, he charged through the door to the street, still hungry and completely disgusted on top of it. He walked quickly, but was stopped by a burly voice calling him back. He turned, found the old man with the gray and white whiskers beckoning.

"Hey, kid. Come here."

Undecided, Oba stayed, kept his back turned. He heard rapid footsteps, imagined him quick on his feet for one so old.

"Hey, kid. Come on back with me. I'll buy your dinner."

He looked up to find the bluest eyes like polished stones from beneath brows as shaggy as a dog's coat, wrinkled like windswept delta loam surrounded by stiff whiskers the color of salt and pepper.

Oba said nothing.

"Come on."

He figured he had nothing to lose, and soon found himself seated at the corner table with a huge oval dinner plate piled high with mounds of potato and meatballs, a side of applesauce, the old man watching with knowing eyes as he forked the hot food into his mouth without speaking.

When he pushed back his plate and wiped his mouth, a plate of apple pie and rounded scoops of vanilla ice cream appeared at his elbow. He gave his benefactor a small grin.

"Thanks."

"You're welcome."

The old man slurped coffee, sat back, and waited till Oba was finished, then offered his name. "Jonas Bell."

"What?"

"I'm Jonas. Jonas Bell."

"Oba Miller."

"Yeah."

Jonas set the white mug on the tabletop, wrapped his massive, gnarled hands around it, and set his blue gaze directly into Oba's brown one.

"Couldn't help overhearing. I like your nerve."

Oba's eyes gave nothing away.

"I need you."

Oba gave a small belch and shifted uncomfortably against the booth.

"What for?"

"I'm going into the wilds."

"So?"

"I've been a hunter and trapper all my life, but now, after my . . . my companion died of influenza, I'm heading north. As far north as I need to go live off the land. I have all the skills. I just need a strong set of shoulders to help build, hunt, trap, fish."

Quickly, Oba cut him off. "I don't know about any of that stuff.

"You can learn."

"No, I was raised an Arkansas farm boy. Cotton. Cows. I hate the cold."

Oba was sullen now, and stubborn.

"You want more pie?"

Oba considered, but shook his head.

"If you were raised in Arkansas, what are you doing here in New York?"

Oba hesitated, then said, "Looking for someone."

Jonas considered this, raised his eyebrows, and said nothing. Silence grew between them as the older man gave the younger one time.

Oba sighed.

"My sister. She ran off with someone, but at this point I don't even know where to look for her."

"So what are your plans? Going back to Arkansas?"

"No."

"Where you going?"

"Nosy, huh?"

"Yeah, I am. If you have no roots, no job, no nothing, why not consider my offer? What's to keep you here?"

Oba gave him the benefit of a flat glare, the hostility that took the light out of his eyes. Jonas met the mistrust and anger head on, never flinching till Oba's eyes slid away.

"You don't want me."

"Sure I do. You have the look of a lost person, a vagabond, the devil-may-care attitude. You've seen some stuff in your short life. This will give you perspective. Survival is an art, a skill, and it makes anything else seem insignificant in comparison."

Oba picked at a thread on his cuff, wouldn't raise his eyes or respond.

"I told you, I need to find my sister."

"Does she want to be found?"

"I dunno."

"Look, this is a chance for you to learn something, to leave everything behind and start over. I really think you should try. What have you got to lose?"

"I told you, I hate the cold. I have no experience with snow and ice and crazy weather. I don't particularly relish the thought of being attacked by some loathsome animal, either."

"You won't be if you learn from me. Look, I don't have much money to pay your wages, but I'll keep you fed. You look like you could use some meat on those bones. And believe, once you get out in the wilderness, you'll find something bigger than yourself."

Oba cast a wary look somewhere in the region of Jonas's face.

"I don't know what you've been through, but it was something. If you feel better not saying, we'll let it go. Look, trust me, it will make a difference."

Oba could feel himself drawing away from this stranger, the resistance to advice necessary to stay in control. With freedom finally in his grasp, why would he allow someone to sabotage that?

"You don't know anything about me. So let it go. I'll be out of here and you can be a predator for someone else."

He was incensed to see a wide smile separate the bristly mustache from the whiskers surrounding it, a shaking of the thick shouldered to suppress a genuine laugh.

"Go ahead and laugh. You think it's funny. You're not going to get anywhere by making fun of me."

"I'm not a predator, okay? Quite the opposite. Look, I'll let you sleep on it. I'll meet you here in the morning around eight."

When Oba remained seated, Jonas wasn't surprised. He reckoned he had nowhere to go, so he waited without speaking.

The restaurant was busier now. The clatter of dishes, customers coming and going, everyday talk filled the small eatery, with everyone going about their business without giving them as much as a glance. Jonas shook his head at the waitress who returned with the coffeepot, then pushed Oba's plate to the side of the table before wiping his whiskers with the crumpled napkin.

"Well?" he asked finally.

"Well, what?"

"You can go."

"I don't have anywhere to go."

"I figured."

"You don't know anything."

"Do you?"

"Oh, shut up."

"Didn't mean to upset you. Look, this is an opportunity. Seems to me you could use a good opportunity right about now."

"I told you, I don't trust you."

"Do you trust anyone?"

"Yes. My sister. I can't give up on finding her. I would give my life to know where she is and whether she's all right."

"And that's a good thing, of course."

"I know."

"But your chances are slim, at best. You disappeared out of her life first, or am I wrong about that?"

Who was this man? He acted as if he knew everything, and Oba hated that. But something kept him from getting up and walking away. To place his future in this man's hands was risky, but so was everything else. He had no plan, no idea of what he would do next. To call on God to guide him was laughable. Oba doubted God's very existence, let alone His concern about his welfare.

So that was how he found himself sleeping in a dingy motel by the side of a humming highway, headlights crisscrossing the dark paneled walls, neon signs blinking through the window where the drapes did not quite meet. He was repulsed by the heavy snoring from the bed, disgusted by the odor of wet woolen socks and unwashed feet. Jonas hadn't showered or brushed his teeth, hadn't as much as opened the dirty leather pouch that must surely contain some clean change of clothing.

After he'd agreed to spend the night, they had barely spoken, for which Oba was grateful. And now Oba lay wide awake, mulling his past, his present, and what was to come. He remembered snow and cold weather from his early childhood in Ohio. He could feel the wet snowflakes on his cold face, smell the scent of sodden mittens brought to his face, his tongue stuck in a pile of soft snow. He remembered wet, cold feet, his mother clucking as she pulled off damp socks, draping them across the wooden rack by the kitchen range. In his memories, May was by his side, her cheeks like polished apples. He could feel his mother's soft hands, the swish of her skirt as she turned to shake the grate, his father's booming laugh as he viewed the rows of cold discolored toes. Piggies, he called them.

Mam would fry sausages in the cast iron pan, turning them expertly as they sizzled and sputtered, becoming brown and crispy, served with buttermilk pancakes and real Ohio maple syrup. They spent glorious moments of lingering around the table, his mother's tinkling laugh flavoring everything with love and security.

Then he thought of the awful day when he had to look in the plain wooden casket, her face white and still, her laugh silenced forever by the churning muddy water that had gushed down her throat and into her lungs, snuffing out the sound of her talking, her singing and breathing. His father's casket was beside her, his face the same waxen stillness, as cold as ice.

A deep pain brought a shudder to his inert form, the remembering as cold and cruel as the torrent of cold water that had taken his parents' lives.

Was he merely punishing himself by this relentless pursuit of May? Among thousands, millions of people, where could she possibly have gone? To remain among the Amish was one thing, but to leave the community and disappear among the mainstream of society quite another.

And especially if she did not want to be found.

She might as well be dead, just like their parents. Perhaps this Jonas knew what he was talking about. Maybe he needed an adventure to make himself feel alive again. But the thing was, he wasn't brave or courageous, and had absolutely no pioneer spirit. He'd never gone hunting, never shot a squirrel or a deer, the way Leonard Yoder's boys bragged about. Melvin Amstutz would never allow him to have a gun, or to spend hours in the woods hunting. He'd never even been allowed to go fishing on the river, like Arpachshad. Idle time was the devil's time, Melvin had said.

And so his thoughts ran wild, from one picture to another, a string of flashbacks like a disjointed reel that kept jerking back to May.

Sweet May.

All he could hope for was that she was safe, with someone she loved and who loved her.

He began to cry, soft hiccups and tears that ran unchecked into his pillow. He hated himself for the tears, hated his own weakness, his own inability to forget the past, to let go of May and the searing hurt of his parents' drowning.

So if he followed this Jonas Bell, would he become a real man, and not some sniveling schoolboy who wept into his pillow at night, hating Melvin but unable to do anything about it? Would the cold and the hardship of a life in the wilderness cleanse his cluttered thoughts?

As the night wore on, he became more convinced there was something in believing Jonas had been in that restaurant for a reason. Perhaps it was meant to be. But he'd have to have a talk with him about bossing him around. That simply wasn't going to work.

There was no light in the window except for the street light and the blinking neon ones that surrounded the area when he heard Jonas roll out of bed, cough, wheeze, snort, every imaginable sound coming from his throat. Muttering to himself, he got into his clothes without turning on the bedside lamp, then let himself quietly through the door, closing it behind him. Oba was given a merciful hour of early morning sleep before he was awakened by heavy boots kicking at the door.

"Open up, kid!"

Wide awake, he leaped to his feet, feeling wildly for his jeans.

"Come on!"

Another round of kicks.

Someone banged on the wall, yelled at them to shut up or they'd shut everyone up themselves. When Oba finally located his jeans, he wasted no time getting into them and fumbling at the door latch.

Jonas stood in the cold, holding two large paper cups, his eyebrows drawn over the blue eyes.

"What took you so long?"

"I had to find my pants."

"Puh. If that's how you're going to be, you're in for a surprise. God made us all, so there ain't nothing to be ashamed of. Once we get to the wilds, you'll forget about all that. It ain't important."

Oba took a long swallow of the bracing coffee, gave him a look that promised nothing. He thought of Tom Lyons in California, his gentle good manners and meticulous hygiene. He wished he was there now, in the balmy weather and beautiful home with good meals. He had left all that for May's sake, and now here he was, with no future, being drawn into a situation that was clearly dangerous, possibly even fatal.

And so his thoughts roiled between sips of lukewarm coffee that left a bilious taste in his mouth, an irritation at the nerve of this Jonas Bell to seek him out when he hadn't asked for it.

"I take it you aren't much of a morning person."

Oba turned, grunted, set his coffee on the bedside table to reach for his shirt, forgot his bare back that presented itself to Jonas Bell.

And Jonas saw. He saw the raised white welts, a testament to this boy's harsh past, but he had the wisdom to keep his mouth shut. Surely the young man had suffered more than he would admit, and there was no use pressing for details.

"I'm leaving this morning. Driving to the nearest supply store to get my finances in order. If you came to a decision, you're welcome aboard. If you didn't, then I'll leave you here."

And suddenly, Oba knew he couldn't deal with being left alone. He had no plan, nowhere to go, and not enough money to reach California and Tom Lyons, where he knew he would always be a square peg in a round hole. He would never quite fit into the family, the expectations they would require of him, the college education, the far flung quest to be a pharmacist. He could not imagine spending his life behind the counter of a small town pharmacy, just as he couldn't imagine being good enough to find a girl who loved him the way he was. Maybe he didn't even deserve to be a happily married man, a normal person who was capable of raising his own children, to belong to a community of caring people who accepted him in spite of his fractured past.

He picked up his coffee, took a long swallow, could hardly keep a grimace from forming. He didn't want to admit that this man had won.

"I don't know."

"Well, you'll have to know in a few minutes. I have to go."

"If I decide to stay, will you go alone?"

"Yes."

Part of him wanted Jonas Bell to leave, to get out of his sight and his mind. He wished he'd never met the guy.

"I tell you what," said Jonas. "Come with me, give it at least a few weeks, and if you don't like it I'll fly you back out of there and you can be on your way to wherever you're going again."

Oba stared straight ahead for a moment and then nodded his head, unwilling to agree out loud. He gathered his belongings and took a place in the passenger seat of the old station wagon. He watched Jonas turn the key, heard the snort from the cold engine, and for the first time in a long while felt a small rush of excitement.

CHAPTER 3

MAY ENTERED HER LIFE AT "S'ALSA" ABE'S, THE S'ALSA
standing for salt, meaning somewhere there had been a joke or an
incident about salt, so this was how he stood apart from the rest of
the Abraham Weavers scattered throughout Ohio. To be named by a
name from the Bible was a longstanding tradition, one that was upheld
by most conservative members of the Old Order Amish, so it was not
unusual to find three or four Abe Weavers in a few square miles.

Betty was soft and round, like her name, which was derived from
Betsey, which in turn had come from Elizabeth, the mother of John
the Baptist in the Bible. Betty conjured up warmth and coziness in
her name alone. May remembered her mother baking a concoction of
spices, apples, and oatmeal she called "Apple Brown Betty," a sweet,
warm dessert that tasted of baked apples and brown sugar and was
eaten with cold milk. When May called Betty by name, she felt all the
warmth and comfort of that dessert.

The house was not a large one, covered in wooden siding with the
paint peeling from the haphazard application of the now dried lumber. There were two windows on either side of the square dwelling, a
front porch, and a back porch that led to the large white barn, where
a menagerie of animals were housed in separate parts. A low henhouse, a pigsty, and a few lean-tos that sagged against various sheds
completed the homestead. This was life on a farm in the mid-1940s.
They had a small herd of cows was sufficient to make a living, a few

baby pigs to take to market in a crate on the back of the springwagon, brown eggs to sell to the housewives scattered along rural roads.

May was accustomed to hard work, had managed a house well, so nothing could take away from her enthusiasm to the do the best she knew how. She cleaned the whole house, a deep cleaning that changed the colors of the painted walls, especially in the kitchen where the enormous range burned year round, the smell of wood-smoke a sign of a warm house and a good cook. Betty urged her to take it easy, to slow down, but May was so determined to show her appreciation, she kept going in spite of a puzzling fatigue that constantly threatened to send her to the old hickory rocker.

In the evening, when the boys had finished their chores, the house turned into a wild kind of bedlam, children racing, yelling, crying, clattering toys and dishes until May thought she must surely go mad. Abe was an easygoing, laconic kind of husband and father, who could sit back with a newspaper and have children climbing all over him and never bat an eye. Betty could be stirring a pot on the stove, with one-year-old Becky tugging at her skirts and the baby pounding graham crackers into sawdust while screaming as if a monster was peering from the window, and go right on stirring as if nothing was out of the ordinary.

May learned to take care of the things she could, such as rescuing the baby when the squalls became unbearable, wiping up ignored spills, or separating two children who were beating each other up while both parents were engrossed in a conversation.

The weariness worsened, followed by a rush to the outhouse first thing in the morning. Finding it occupied, her stomach heaved its bitter contents into a lilac bush on the south side, before Abe greeted her with an embarrassed good morning while still buttoning his coat.

She was hungry, but the rolled oats and ponhaus turned her stomach. She cleaned plates and stacked them on the countertop, swallowed back the bile that threatened to send her back to the outhouse, felt the kitchen tilt crazily as waves of nausea threatened her stability.

If Abe told Betty about her sickness, Betty kept it to herself, but May thought Abe was a gentle, shy sort of fellow, one easily embarrassed being caught in the outhouse, so he might not have mentioned it.

After a month of hiding the weariness and fatigue, the nausea that sent her silently scuttling to the backyard, she felt no better, but was determined to keep her secret, determined not to bother the young family with her own silly health condition. She decided it was all in her head, probably a result of all she'd been through these past months. Sometimes it didn't hit you until you'd started to settle down.

One afternoon she found Betty watching her swab wearily at the kitchen linoleum. May stopped when her name was called.

"Yes?"

"Is something wrong, May?"

"No, just been a bit tired."

"Are you throwing up?"

"No."

Instantly, she regretted the lie, noticed the cunning look in Betty's face.

"But I've seen you."

"Only sometimes."

Betty narrowed her eyes. "May, is there a chance . . . ?"

"Of what?"

Betty could not bring herself to say the word, seeing the lack of comprehension in May's eyes. She realized May truly didn't know, didn't suspect anything at all. And yet Betty knew she had all the symptoms, had seen the growth that lifted the pleated apron.

"May, listen to me."

Emmie howled from her high chair, so Betty immediately went to her, grabbed a washcloth, and roughly wiped her face and hands before hauling her off to the rocking chair and opening her dress to allow the baby to feed.

May followed her to the remaining rocking chair, perched on the edge of it, and clasped her hands, still as innocent as when the conversation began.

"Did you tell me the truth about leaving Melvin and Gertie's farm?"

"Yes."

"Were you married to someone?"

Betty watched the light change in the beautiful brown eyes, watched them darken, the heavy lids lower themselves as a brilliant color suffused the pale, thin face. Slowly, the bright blond hair with the white covering wagged back and forth in denial.

"No," she whispered hoarsely.

"But were you with someone?"

Her lips were frozen, her mouth gone dry. For a second, Betty thought May might flee like a frightened bird, but she remained seated while the blush turned into a pale face, as still as a wax figure.

"May, I'll make this easier. Are you positive you aren't . . . aren't in the family way?" The last words were spoken in a conspiratorial whisper, her eyes going to the children playing on the floor.

"What do you mean?"

Clearly, May did not understand.

"That you might be expecting?"

May's eyes opened wide in disbelief as she struggled to understand. Then her hands fluttered to her stomach and stayed, her expression turning from understanding to shame, from shame to a fleeting hope.

"Is that why I seem to . . . why I grow? I can't tell you how much I wondered, but I have no knowledge."

"May, I want to hear the truth about your life. If you want to remain in this home, you must speak the truth. Do you realize your shame here among the Amish if you were unmarried?"

May looked around wildly, a rush of understanding and feeling washing over her. She pulled herself together quickly, the new knowledge that she was a mother seeming to mature her in an instant. *A mother!* She had new responsibility, new purpose. She would do any-thing for this child growing inside her.

"I'll go, Betty. I won't tarnish your name."

She would go. She would live in the caves of the earth, exist on wild game and herbs from the forest if it meant having Clinton's child. She would shoulder any shame, be forsaken by her remaining kinfolk, gladly carry ridicule for the rest of her days. Joy filled the empty places now, delight enveloped her entire being as she thought of bearing a child who resembled him.

Oh, that God had shined His mercy on her by allowing this!

"Tell me," Betty urged as she watched the transformation.

So May began, and the afternoon sun slanted toward the west before Betty sank back with an audible sigh, then rubbed Emmie's back absentmindedly as she tried to comprehend it all.

But not once had May allowed even a suggestion of Melvin's behavior to come to the surface. That was the only remaining thing not one person would ever know. She would go to her grave with it, and believe God would mete the vengeance, bring swift justice.

There was no other way for her.

"So this Clinton Brown is a negro?"

"Yes. He's . . . was lighter than some."

"How could you, May? It isn't normal. I don't believe it's legal. How could you go against God and the law like that?"

May bit down hard on her lower lip, reined in the hot words of denial.

"Betty, you don't understand . . ." She stopped herself before she revealed something she'd regret. Betty couldn't know the evil she had escaped when she left with Clinton. She would never know the sound of approaching footsteps or the shadowy dark figure at her door.

"Clinton Brown was a good man. He could no more help being born colored than you or I could choose to be white. In Arkansas, the people of color are everywhere. If Melvin or Gertie were half as kind-hearted as the sharecroppers who break their backs picking cotton for their financial gain, I would likely still be there." She hadn't meant to say that last part, but Betty hardly seemed to notice.

"But, May, that still doesn't make it right. This child will be born in sin. You were not married . . . and him as black as midnight."

"No, he was not. He was the color of caramel. Of dark honey. He was the most handsome man I have ever met. The sweetest and kindest. I don't care if he was purple or green. I will never be ashamed of our love. Betty, he loved me. He loved me so much. He would have died for me. He did die for me, going out to look for work to support us out in that cruel town who hated the black people for hatred's sake."

Here she suddenly turned calm, almost serene.

"You can make me go, Betty. But I will always be proud of my child and love him as much as I loved his father."

Betty sighed, looked off into the distance. Did she recognize a love such as this? She thought of her own dear, steady Abe, like a gentle, dying fire on a hearth, always there, always the same. Did some loves create a rushing firestorm, a height of great love that was extinguished too soon, leaving the recipient with only the remembering of it?

Or had it been love at all amid such sin?

Long into the night, she sat with Abe, elaborated on May's story as only Betty could, with Abe as steady as a good ship with a dependable rudder.

"It is strange," he said finally. Then he looked at his flustered wife with a level, wise gaze and spoke the one sentence that helped her make sense of all of it.

"How bad must her situation have been there at Melvin's for her to do something that drastic?"

"But she never said anything."

"They never do."

Betty missed his insinuation completely, and he didn't stir up the trouble of his forefathers, the young maiden's suicide, the burial outside the graveyard fence, the deathbed confession of his Uncle Enoch.

They said a white creature was still seen from time to time, swaying over her grave, and Enoch's family was known to be cast from one trouble to the next. But here was where Abe knew to let sleeping dogs lie, water under the bridge, never look back and uproot the sins of the fathers, of which there must have been plenty.

They came to a decision, to let her stay until someone began to ask questions. She would not attend church services until after the birth, at which it must be discussed with the ministry. They would stand by the bishop's decision, either way.

In the morning, Betty's lips were pursed, her eyes hooded. She served breakfast without May's help, watched as she toted the over-flowing basket of clothes to the kettlehouse. Her irritation was taken out on the little ones, slapping their hands when they got on her nerves. She told May to hang the towels on the south side of the clothesline, not the north, the way she had been doing.

May was up to her elbows in sudsy steaming water, a song on her lips. Even the nausea could not take away her deep sense of content-ment. She didn't care whether she stayed or was sent away. God had given her this gift in His everlasting love, and she would suffer any-thing He asked of her if she would be allowed to hold Clinton's child.

No matter that the people would snort and turn their heads to keep from looking in her direction. No matter if the bishop sent her away.

If God had gotten her this far, His grace would be sufficient.

And so she sang on.

She settled into a routine at Abe Weaver's, took Betty's suspicion in stride. The nausea dissipated, her strength returned as the lovely fall days settled into the short, harsh days of an Ohio winter. When the sun shone, Abe hauled manure from the barn, cleaned the pig-sty, and swept the henhouse. The cows grew fat from the daily ration of sweet alfalfa hay piled in the haymow like a great slippery moun-tain. May rose early, did her share of the milking, skimmed cream and made butter, drank cold buttermilk and mounds of oatmeal and potatoes. Her waistline increased, her cheeks filled out and took on the color of a ripe peach, her smile was quick and deeply sincere. The private blessing, the one between her and her Lord, surrounded her like the soft glow of a lamp. Over and over, she told herself, nothing was of any value, save this beloved child within.

She felt like Mary, wondered if they shared the same fate.

She knew she was nothing, knew she would never be able to hold her head high among her people, but so be it. She had a roof over her head, a warm bed to spend the night, food every morning, lunchtime, and evening, plenty of work to keep her occupied, so her heart was always grateful.

Eventually, Betty decided her chastening of May's behavior was sufficient and became her usual jovial self. She bought remnants of flannel and cotton to make sheets for the smallest crib, nightgowns for the baby, and a stack of prefolded diapers to protect the little bottom.

An old doctor came for a few checkups, was sworn to secrecy, and paid with a fine butchered hen before he took his leave. He muttered his way to his car about the sins kept buried from curious eyes, although he enjoyed his roast chicken immensely and didn't breathe a word to anyone.

May never left the farm that winter. When company came, she was kept in her room. She often read her Bible or knitted the tiny caps and sweaters taking on a delightful shape beneath her clicking needles. Gertie was the one who had taught her this skill. She often felt sad, thinking about the large, very overweight person she had become, embroiled in her own sense of misery and longing. Perhaps she had done the best she could. Didn't everyone?

She had not been like that when they arrived. In her own coarse way, she had shown an odd bit of kindness here or there. A new dress in town, a peppermint candy, an appreciation of a freshly baked cake. Poor Gertie, laid to rest in the loamy soil in Arkansas, the place she so despised.

May's hands plied the needles efficiently, the yarn draped expertly across her pinkie finger. Two pillows at her back, she rested against the iron headboard of her bed, her legs resting on another pillow, a quilt drawn over her rounded stomach to keep warm. At her bedside table, a kerosene lamp flickered, the wick turned high.

Downstairs there was talking and laughing, the oven door opening and closing, children shrieking with glee, babies crying amid the hullabaloo. It was Sunday afternoon company, a frequent occurrence at this house, and May never minded. She enjoyed the rare peace and quiet in her room, squirreled away like a forbidden fruit.

She had never found out if Betty and Abe had gone to see the bishop, and if they did, what answer had been given. She stayed, so she felt that was enough. Sometimes talks with the bishop were kept tightly guarded, and this was no different, she felt sure. Perhaps she would be violating the rules to bring up the subject, so she didn't. Sometimes she caught Betty staring at her with the most quizzical expression, but before she could meet May's returned curiosity, her eyes slid away like liquid.

She still went to the barn on frigid mornings, when the icicles hanging from the eaves were as thick as a man's forearm and the snow lay in great white heaps up to the windowsills. The quarter moon smiled at her, the stars twinkled and winked their friendly little verses to her, and the snow crunched underfoot as if it, alone, could tell her how many degrees below zero it really was.

Abe was opening water pipes that had frozen during the night, carrying buckets of boiling water from the house, grinning and humming under his breath, an affable soul in the middle of a freezing morning. Henry and Davey romped through the cold, crashed through the cow stable door to stand beside a fat, steaming cow, their teeth chattering as they pulled off their mittens to finish tying their black, leather shoes.

And May was reasonably happy.

THE QUESTIONS BEGAN at Ida's quilting, an event Betty had looked forward to for weeks, dressed in her green Sunday dress with the cape pinned neatly around her neck, her hair combed up over her head with care. She baked sour cherry pies with a delicate crumb topping, packed them in a roaster with clean rags to keep them in place, and left all the children at home in May's care. She took the reins from Abe who stood smiling beside the buggy, chirped to the steady brown horse with the long winter coat, and drove out the lane.

Oh, she was glad to have a day to herself, to be with women friends who would chatter about everyday life in the rural Ohio community, learn new recipes, the best way to render lard at butchering time, how best to bring a fever down, and who was dating whom. At church, there had been talk of a few cousins from Geauga County attending this event, and Betty looked forward to hearing news from the area.

She leaned forward, slapped the reins on the oversized rump, thought Abe should stop feeding quite so many oats in winter. This horse was lazy and much too fat. When she finally arrived she handed the reins to Davey, climbed down amid pleasant talk from the small man wearing manure-encrusted boots and a hat with a torn brim, and grabbed the roaster containing the sour cherry pies before hurrying into the warmth of Ida's steaming kettlehouse, eager to greet her friends.

"Why hello, Betty!" Ida called from her place at the stove.

"Hello, Ida!"

"Just take your wraps into the bedroom. There's plenty of room on the bed."

Betty heard the lively talk as she left the pies on the table, turned to divest herself of her shawl and bonnet, and stuffed the heavy gloves into her large coat pocket on the inside of the garment. No pockets were seen on the outside of the homemade outerwear, as that would not be *gehorsam* (obedient) to church *ordnung* (rules). And Betty was conscientious, obeyed all dress rules with diligence, her heart and mind sincere in being a true upstanding member of the church.

When she made her appearance, bright faces were lifted from the stitching, words of welcome as warm as the blazing fire.

She dug her favorite thimble from her dress pocket, found an empty chair, and exclaimed about the beauty of the quilt. Navy blue, gray, a deep red and green, a kaleidoscope of brilliant hues done in an intricate "Sunshine and Shadow" design.

"Yes, Ida pieced it herself. You know she does three or four every winter," Betty trilled, as proud as if she'd done it herself.

"Where are the little ones, Betty?"

Only a moment's hesitation, before saying she left them at home with Abe.

An awkward silence.

Finally, someone asked where the girl was. What was her name? May?

"Uh . . . oh, well yes, she's there too."

"Tell us about her. Is she okay? I mean, she was in church once or so, and now we don't see her anymore."

Rapid questions came like an assault, then, with Betty floundering to answer them in truth. Yes, she had been English, dressed in a skirt and blouse. No, she didn't know what happened at Melvin's. "Gertie passed away of a heart condition, you know."

"Well, they say Oba isn't with Melvin anymore, either. He's out in the world. I heard he's wild. Melvin couldn't handle him."

"It's just so *shaut* (it's a shame)," old Annie Mast said, shaking her head. "It seems when children are left after the death of both parents, they often lose their way."

"Ach, yes. And I always thought so much of Melvin and Gertie. So sincere with *gmayna ordnung* (church rules). I think this is why they moved to Arkansas," Edna Miller spoke up.

A loud "Pffft" from the corner.

"He moved to Arkansas for money. They say he's wealthy on that cotton with all the cheap labor from those black people. I never liked him. Gertie suffered plenty down there."

This piece of unadorned information was thrust above the quilt like an uncomfortable odor. No one but Clara would have the nerve to tell it how it was. Single, in her mid-thirties, tall, thin and outspoken. She had fiery red hair, a spattering of freckles, a nose with a champion hook in it, capable of holding up her round frameless spectacles. She was independent, spoke whenever and whatever she wanted. If folks didn't like what she had to say, well then, that was just tough. It needed to be said. She had a grudge against most of the human race, with men in particular, had never been asked for her freckled hand in matrimony and never missed it to be sure. As prickly as a horse chestnut, and as hard to control, she was Clara Yoder, take her or leave her.

But no one was more *behilflich* (helpful) than Clara. In times of sickness or a community disaster or tragedy, she was the first one to arrive, the first responder to a family in need. Bearing gifts of food, her wonderful casseroles or homemade wheat bread, freshly churned butter and jars of rhubarb jam, applesauce, or peaches, she was there, directing, organizing, in charge. She had a duty to carry out, and she did it.

The inheritance her father left her put her in the position of financial independence, and she kept a steady income by breeding and selling good solid driving horses, which she trained to be some of the most reliable horses around. She also owned a flock of extraordinary sheep, which produced beautiful wool that she sold for a good price. She placed no trust in a bank, but hoarded her money in shoeboxes stashed in a metal container and buried well in a secret cache. Only she knew where that money was hidden.

After Clara voiced her opinion on Melvin and Gertie, an awkward silence settled over the room. Betty's face had taken on some color, and a bead of perspiration appeared above her upper lip. She swallowed nervously, and was greatly relieved when Ida called them all to the kitchen where an array of cookies, cinnamon rolls, and doughnuts with fresh coffee awaited them.

Children ran underfoot, babies cried and were hushed, the conversation changed direction, and Betty breathed easier. She helped herself to a mug of coffee, laced it heavily with cream and sugar, put two doughnuts and an oatmeal raisin cookie on a plate, and sat down on a kitchen chair.

The first bite into a glazed doughnut was heavenly. That was one of the reasons she so enjoyed these gatherings. Such a variety of goodies to choose from.

"Ida, these doughnuts are delicious," she said, between mouthfuls.

"Well, I hope so. I got up at two o'clock to mix the dough, get my lard going. The cinnamon buns are the same dough."

"Really? Mashed potatoes in both? I know cinnamon rolls take them, but I never heard of doughnuts," Annie Mast was smiling, halfway through a cinnamon bun.

Betty eyed the elderly lady, thought she likely knew everything there was to know about yeast doughs and batters, and surely had said that to make Ida feel good. Bless her dear old heart. Certainly love grew in the elderly as Christ became more to them and their own desires and will became less. There was something to say about the accumulation of years. For a moment, she wondered if she should talk to Annie about May's predicament. But just as quickly, she realized it would never do. The old way was set in stone. No matter how much wisdom and compassion Annie had, she would still see May's situation for what it was: sin, and a disgrace to the community. And at this point, Betty would be guilty by association.

Once back to the quilt, Betty felt Clara's eyes boring into the top of her bent head like an auger, making it hard for her to concentrate. How much did she know? How much did she perceive?

Betty felt afraid. Afraid and condemned. They were going against *gmayna ordnung*, against her own conscience. There were sure to be consequences for keeping May hidden away like this. People would talk, tongues would wag, and their reputation would wind up in the dirt. They had always been God-fearing upright members of the Old Order who adhered conscientiously to the rules the bishop held forth twice a year at council meeting. How had she gotten so deep in this predicament? What had she done to their family?

A bolt of fear found its way into Betty's heart. Yes, there was something to say about upholding one's reputation, of keeping your good name intact. Some people might call it pride, but it really was only common sense.

CHAPTER 4

OBA SLOUCHED IN HIS SEAT, HIS HANDS DEEP IN HIS POCK-
ets, slanting a look at Jonas as the burly man dug into his hip pocket
for his wallet. He was sick and tired of sitting on this wide seat, sick of
watching the same scenery, sick of trees and snow and the open road.
He wished they'd drive into a snowstorm, be put out of commission
for a couple days.

Jonas rolled down his window, cranking away at the lever, muttering some sort of gibberish, the way he did most times. It was probably from living by himself too long, his mind half gone with the
loneliness.

"Yessir."

The gas station attendant had bent to peer through the window,
a heavy leather cap with sheepskin flaps down over his ears, a ring of
chocolate around his mouth. H didn't look old enough to be working.

"Fill 'er up."

"Yessir."

The cold crept in through the opened window. Oba watched
expectantly for Jonas to crank the window back up, but he merely put
both hands on the steering wheel and drummed the vinyl top with
both thumbs, looking straight ahead, his lips compressed, while the
gas nozzle spewed the fuel into the tank. Oba hunched his shoulders,
glared out at the endless level scenery, the dank gas station with the
filthy window, a yellow sign with SUNOCO in fat, blue letters. There

were no other cars or trucks parked in the gravel—only a green picnic table, a trailer, and a stack of used tires.

The youth came around to the front and sprayed a solution on the windshield before drawing his squeegee across it, his mouth pursed in concentration. He did a fairly good job, for a kid. Oba thought he should use it on his face, with that chocolate like a mustache.

"Arright. That's five dollars and twenty-seven cents." He held out his hand as Jonas deposited the money, said his thanks, and they were back on the road, Jonas humming low under his breath, his eyes keen, alert.

Snow was piled up on either side of the road, stretched for one blinding mile after another. An occasional red barn and white house rose up like a growth, a small group of pines weighted down by clumps of snow. Always north, always cold and wintry, Oba knew, with their destination filled with even more of the same.

Why, oh why had he agreed to this? He stuck his chin deeper into his coat collar, pulled his cap low enough to cover most of his eyesight, and drifted into a troubled sleep.

He was jerked awake by the sound of the old man's voice.

"You ready for a break?"

"What? Huh?"

"You wanna stop for the night?"

Oba looked around, the sun sliding below the horizon, laying a path of orange and gold across the glistening snow. The sky was a deep hue of lavender and purple, with navy-blue streaks mixed with orange and gold, the same color as the path. For one moment, the sight infiltrated Oba's senses, made him wipe his eyes to see if it was real.

"Pretty, huh?"

"Yeah."

"Wait till we get to where we're going. You'll think that there sunset is nothing. You are in for the adventure of a lifetime."

Oba didn't answer.

"Haven't convinced you, huh?"

Oba grunted.

"Watch for motel signs."

It wouldn't surprise him to have Jonas announce they would be spending the night in the car. But he wasn't crying uncle yet, wasn't going to show his need for a shower and a warm bed.

On they drove, night enveloping the car like a navy-blue blanket, the headlights parting it down the middle as they drove.

"Pretty rural," Jonas said. "Get the road atlas out of the glove compartment. Flashlight should be there. We're on 12 going north. That was Reedsburg about fifty miles back."

Oba found Michigan, Wisconsin, Reedsburg, then route 12. According to the map, another twenty or thirty miles would bring them to Black River Falls, hopefully a town large enough to have hotels, at least a room above some business establishment.

"Keep going. Black River Falls is about twenty-five miles."

Jonas cast him an appreciative glance. "Pretty good with that, huh?"

"What?"

"The map."

"Oh, that. Yeah. I can find my way around. I got from Arkansas to New York on the train. Traveled by bus, hitchhiked."

"Tell me again why you were in Arkansas."

"I told you. My aunt and uncle raised us. My sister and me."

"Why'd they do that?"

"My parents drowned. The creek took the horse and buggy." He stopped, a deep sense of regret washing over him.

"Horse and buggy? They didn't drive a car?"

"None of your business. Look, I don't want to talk about the past."

No, I guess not, Jonas thought. *Not with that back of yours and those dead, empty eyes.*

He drove silently now, his hands gripping the wheel. He hoped he hadn't picked up some juvenile delinquent, some seriously troubled kid who would be a genuine danger. To himself or those around him.

The man behind the counter at the Roadside Inn looked up from his paper, got grudgingly to his feet with a mumbled, "How're you?"

Jonas didn't bother with a reply, merely asked for a room, plunked down a ten-dollar bill, took the key, and went back outside. He turned left, found the proper door, and motioned Oba inside.

He was relieved to find scalding hot water rain in torrents out of the showerhead, clean washcloths, and fluffy towels. He scrubbed and soaked, ran his fingers roughly over his scalp, then applied more shampoo and started all over again. The mirror was steamed up, the tile floor slippery with moisture. He mopped himself dry, got into clean clothes, shaved, brushed his teeth, and felt like a new person. He plopped on the bed to slip into his socks, rolling his shoulders to release any remaining tension from the long car ride.

"Your turn," he said, eyeing Jonas with a hopeful expression.

"Ah, man. I hate to bathe."

"How come?"

"Waste of time. I'm a seasoned bushman. Seasoned as in spiced well, smoked, and dried." He laughed, a raucous sound not unlike a crow, or a hawk, the kind that let out a few short bursts of sound before flapping away.

Oba looked up sharply.

"Well, you stink." With that, Oba turned his back, suddenly embarrassed. Did his appreciation for hygiene make Jonas think he was weak?

Jonas let out another short clap of mirth. "You think I smell bad now, you wait."

Oba was hungry, but now he was ashamed to ask for food.

"Yep, Oba. You'll get used to it. You are literally a babe in the woods, a greenhorn, a newbie. You will have much more to occupy that little mind than taking a bath. But I guess it won't kill me to clean up a bit while we're here. If you have soap."

"There's some in there."

Oba left the room to check out the rest of the small hotel, and when he returned, Jonas was sitting up in bed, up to his chin in sheets and blankets, listening to a crackling radio show. "I thought maybe you left."

Oba just shrugged.

"Where'd you get that whitish hair?" Jonas asked abruptly, as he swung his legs over the side of the bed.

"My mom."

"Bet she was a pretty woman."

"She was."

"As blond as you are?"

"Yes."

"Your sister too?"

"Yeah, she's even blonder."

"Too bad about your parents. I'm sorry."

"What are you sorry for?"

"It's an expression. It means I feel bad this had to happen to you."

"Yeah. Well. You don't know what it's like."

"Maybe not."

They listened to the radio, fading in and out at times. They couldn't follow the story line anyway, so Jonas got up, turned the dial, and said it was time to turn in.

What, no food? Oba thought. His stomach puckered with hunger, growling out his emptiness every five minutes. They'd shared a package of saltines for lunch, washed down with water. That had been it.

Oba wasn't new to hunger, but familiarity didn't make the gnawing inside his stomach any easier to handle. Didn't Jonas feel hungry, or was that another sign of weakness in his mind? Oba wasn't about to find out. He didn't think he should have to prove his own toughness to Jonas, but at the same time he wasn't willing to risk being called a weakling.

So he lay awake on the floor of the Roadside Inn somewhere in Wisconsin, headed north to a land that simply smacked of danger, cold and snow, hunger and hardship. Perhaps this was some kind of test—Jonas's way of seeing how long Oba could go without a proper meal. The longer Oba thought about it, the more he wondered what exactly he was getting into. Was he prepared?

He thought back to the springwagon ride through the budding trees of Arkansas, that fateful day when he was eleven years old and his sister a year younger. Melvin had sat beside him, driving the horse, and May was on his other side. In all their innocence, they had trusted Melvin, trusted him and Gertie with the hopeful freshness of young children's minds. Still reeling from the death of both parents, they'd grasped at the thin lifeline of their aunt and uncle, kept a firm hold upon it until they both had to let go and fend for themselves.

Could the life he was heading for be any worse than the sting of Melvin's whip? He remembered Melvin's maniacal screams of disgust, the way he convinced Oba that he was weak, a mistake, incapable of doing anything right.

But after riding the rails with the rest of the clan of hobos, he had acquired a few skills, hadn't he? And Tom Lyons had tried his best to make Oba believe he was capable of excelling in life. Oba hadn't fully believed him, but his words had given him some hope. If he weighed courage on a scale with his failures, would it balance?

With a sinking heart, he realized his most intense failure was leaving May behind to fend for herself, and now, the inability to find her. Remorse coupled with cowardice was a debilitating weight, a burden that hung from his shoulders like a sack of the cotton he used to pick in Arkansas.

"Come on down, crystal river.
Come on down."

He could hear the sound of the sharecroppers' song, the sun hot on his back, the way the notes reached a haunting cadence in the still, hot air. There was soulful depth to their singing, a beautiful sound of hope and happiness that sent chills down his spine.

They'd often praised God, lifted dark arms to the sky, their eyes closed in reverence to their "Lawd." If he'd ever come close to believing in God, it was then. But the God they worshipped must not be the same one Melvin believed in, sitting in the crowded house where the congregation had gathered that Sunday, his doelike gaze lifted in tearful reverence as the minister delivered the message. That God was the same one who allowed his beloved parents to be pulled under the muddy waters, be tumbled along, their mouths open in silent screams.

It was better not to have faith in anything than to believe in a God who could be that cruel.

He drifted into a restless sleep, his empty stomach causing him to toss from side to side, thrash his legs, and dream of starvation.

But in the morning, he was rewarded with Jonas driving to the nearest diner and both of them eating the biggest pile of eggs, potatoes, sausages, and hotcakes he had ever seen.

Jonas explained that money was tight, which was why they had no dinner. A big breakfast was cheaper than a small dinner. They would need most of Jonas's savings to pay the man who kept the dogs while he was away and to buy supplies.

"Dogs?"

"The sled dogs."

"You mean, the kind you hitch to a sled?"

"How else are you going to get around in three feet of snow? I gotta keep enough money to outfit you, too. There's no way that coat and hat are going to keep you alive. You'll need boots, snowshoes, a parka with fur, woolen underwear, woolen socks."

"How many dogs do you have?"

"Seven."

Oba pondered this bit of information. He didn't particularly like dogs. The thought of seven of them to feed and get along with was a big frightening, but he drank the rest of his coffee, got up when Jonas did, and tried not to worry.

On through Wisconsin they drove, into Minnesota, and up into the Canadian wilderness. After crossing the border, the light turned gray, ominous, the sun becoming weaker and weaker, until there was no trace. The deep forest on either side of the road rose like sentinels of doom.

Jonas frowned, twisted the dials on the crackling radio, listened with brows drawn low, his mouth a hard line of concentration.

"Don't look good. Get out the map and figure out what's nearby." His words were clipped, frightening in their intensity. When Oba scrambled to obey, he said, "Not that one. The Canada one."

The light was poor, with the faded sunlight and the heavy pine forest, so he clicked the button on the flashlight and shone the thin beam along the blue, green, and red squiggles, like veins in skin.

"Nothing," he muttered.

"Has to be. Saskatchewan. We're on route 39."

Oba searched, shook his head. "At least a hundred miles."

"We're in trouble." He applied his foot to the gas, hunched over the steering wheel, with both hands gripping the top. Nothing to do but shoot for the nearest trading post or town as fast as possible and hope for the best.

It would take them two hours, maybe less. But here in the Canadian north, snowstorms could be colossal, wiping out roads in a matter of hours. Jonas checked the gas gauge, was satisfied with the number, watched the sky.

Oba shivered, stuck cold hands into armpits. "So what happens if a storm strikes and we're out in the bush?"

"Well, it depends." His voice hoarse now, he said no more. He shouldn't have taken the risk, driving this far north in the beginning of winter, but he had to return for the dogs, for his own sanity. He thrived in the wild, on his own conditions, on his own land, with his own cabin, guns, traplines, a cache of summer vegetables in the root cellar.

The darkness increased, the rough edges of pine forest blending into the threatening skies, the clouds like dirty wool, tumbling with the weight of unleashed snow and wind. Oba could feel the older man's tension and found he was pushing the soles of his feet on the floor of the old station wagon.

The first bits of hail bounced off the windshield. Oba looked sideways at Jonas, who muttered his irritation. The car picked up speed, shaking a little now, as the speedometer climbed.

"Keep your eyes peeled for moose or deer," Jonas said, low. "We hit one, we're both dead."

On they flew, the trees a blur, the dead foliage at the side of the road taunting their progress as they twisted and twined. The hail turned to snow and picked up momentum, assaulting the windshield of the fast-moving car and blowing across the macadam in a long, snaking, veil-like movement.

And still Jonas did not slow down. Oba's breathing was rapid, his mouth slightly open in fear and anxiety. They had another fifty or sixty miles to go. How would they get through a deep, drifting avalanche of this stuff?

The wisps of blowing snow on the road turned into a solid white, and still Jonas kept his foot heavily on the gas, his hands tightly on the wheel. When Oba could take no more, he asked Jonas if he didn't think it would be a good idea to slow down, and saw only a shake of his head, followed by a shift of his hands on the wheel.

"All we have is speed at this point. Once this snow gets too deep, the wind too high, we may as well forget it. So the way I figure, our chance of freezing to death is worse than slamming into a tree. Just keep watching for wildlife, all right?"

Oba thought he saw a dark object, opened his mouth, then closed it again. A stump. A fallen log. Oba's heart was in this throat.

The snow fell thicker, faster. The wind increased.

Jonas made a low sound as the car started to skid and he was forced to reduce speed. He was leaning forward over the steering wheel now, his eyes squinting as he strained to see the road. It was straight, with no significant incline, either up or down, so that was one thing. Oba didn't realize the importance of this fact, the woods on either side like a wake, falling away unevenly.

Oba was aware of being suspended in space and time, as if dangling from a gigantic hook, shoved along by an unseen force, the elements his only adversity. He was aware of placing his fear into the hands of Jonas Bell, who knew this was a serious situation, knew what it would take to keep the car on the road, and had assigned him one duty, the task of watching for any obstruction.

Everything was white. Everything was in motion, sweeping in from the north. The car was wallowing now. Oba could feel the rear wheels fishtailing. Jonas reduced speed again, but kept the wheel steady.

How long did they travel? Oba had no idea. He only knew his spine ached from the constant tension, and his feet ached from being pushed to the floor. And still they kept moving.

It was only when the car crept along, snow blowing on either side, like swimming in a long straight creek of snow, that Oba started to panic. There was no way this could continue much longer, with the deepening snow and the increasing wind.

There were times when nothing was visible, no pine trees, no road, nothing. If they were forced to stop, there was no way they could start up again until the roads were cleared, and who knew how long that would take?

"Oba, you better say a prayer. We're about at the end of our tether." Jonas's voice was surprisingly calm. He spoke as if he was merely making a statement, in the same tone of voice he might have used to announce dinner, or ask him to see the map.

"So what do we do?" Oba fought to keep his voice under control, to hide his fear from this brave man at the wheel.

"I just told you."

"I don't pray."

"You don't? It's high time you started. God is everywhere, even here in this place where it don't seem as if He cares. But He's here all right."

"You wouldn't pray if you know what I know." Oba struggled to see through the unrelenting waves of snow, thought if only he could find one yellow light, one A frame structure of a house somewhere in this godforsaken swamp of whirling white. "How many miles you reckon we've come?"

"I'd say close to eighty or ninety."

"So if we bog down, you think we have a chance?"

"Depends. You see, folks are thinly populated. No one else is out on this stretch of road in these conditions. I shouldn't have taken the gamble. Just figured we'd make Owens by evening."

"It is not dark," Oba said firmly.

"But I can't drive in this much longer."

Oba found it, the square of yellow light. At first, he'd blinked, swiped the back of his hand across his eyes, blinked again.

Then he yelled and pointed toward the light. Jonas turned the wheel sharply to the right. The car dipped and wallowed, then straightened itself before turning sideways and sliding to a stop near the warmth and security of the light.

They sagged, completely exhausted, and let out a whoosh of relaxing breath.

CHAPTER 5

BETTY KEPT HER HUSBAND AT THE KITCHEN TABLE FAR INTO the night, voicing her concerns. They had spoken to the bishop. His sage advice had been helpful, a voice of guidance, telling them to be patient, take a day at a time and see what came of it. If any member of the church brought a complaint, they would have to take it into consideration. He did not want an upheaval of the peace within the community, yet he didn't feel it was right to send May out into the world, where she could fare worse.

This had all been satisfactory, and they had driven home to the music of steel wheels on gravel, the horse's steady clopping amid the jingling of buckles and snaps on the harness. The night had been crisp, with white stars scattered like thrown rock salt against a black sky.

There had been no need for conversation, Abe's shoulder bouncing comfortably against his wife's rounded one, the buggy robe tucked securely around both of them. They counted their blessings, living in a secular community with elders who watched out for their souls.

But after the quilting at Ida's house, suspicion raised its ugly head in the community, and scattered seeds of rampant curiosity fed a pulsing vein of gossip, which in turn sent the most pious, conservative members to the deacon, Jacob Keim, who had not been exposed to any of this.

"She hasn't been to church at all."

"She's hiding something."

"She ran away from Melvin and Gertie Amstutz's farm and went completely English. Cut her hair and everything."

Then came the day when Ida came to visit her friend without warning and found May at the wash line where she'd dashed through the cold to hang a few wet tea towels, the brisk wind blowing her apron and her pleated skirt to clearly reveal her rounded belly.

The entire afternoon had been stilted, awkward, with much blinking and coughing, nervous tongues darting to wet dry lips, the tension in the room thick enough to choke both Ida and Betty. May crept upstairs softly, hoping desperately that this visitor wasn't the sort of woman who would cause Betty and her family any trouble.

Ida told Betty in no uncertain terms this was not going to work. An unmarried maiden carrying a baby? What was Betty thinking? By hiding May away like this she was keeping her from experiencing the consequences of her sinful choices, and thereby keeping her from repentance. She was living a lie, and surely God would punish her and her family for it. A red smear of color crept up Betty's neck, so struck by guilt and the fear of an exacting God she could barely breathe.

And so Betty told Abe that May had to go. She was not putting her good standing in the church in jeopardy, she would not go skulking around like some dog who'd stolen a bone. She hated, absolutely hated, being the object of gossip and ridicule. She'd always had a good name and planned on keeping it that way.

"But, Betty, I thought you said none of this would matter. You'd fight for her, regretted sending her out in the first place. When they were children."

"See, Abe. You're half in love with her yourself, or you wouldn't stick up for her."

"Whoa, here now. Don't start accusing me of anything like that."

"Well, she's as pretty as a picture."

"And you, my dear, are way prettier. You know I am the most faithful of husbands and will always be. But we can't send her out in cold weather."

"We'll find a place for her."

If Betty was truthful, she had nothing against May as a person. She appreciated her help, and had enjoyed her company. But it rankled too much to be ridiculed, judged, thought poorly of. She refused to be considered a liberal, someone who allowed a questionable person into their home. She enjoyed her status in the church, in the community, enjoyed being spoken highly of, a good mother, an example to the younger women, as well as the single girls.

Now that word was out, what would they think?

So she cajoled, wheedled her way into steady Abe's thoughts until he came to see it her way and agreed it was right to send May away. Betty had a long talk with May, who caught the insinuation at the first sentence and sat, bowed and defeated, while Betty kept up her one-sided ramble.

Finally, when she stopped for breath, May spoke in a voice barely above a whisper.

"So what, exactly, do you want me to do?"

"Oh, you don't have to do anything, May. I'll find a place for you. Abe said we can send you money every month. We're just not willing to go against church rules. You know, we don't want the deacon to have to come see us. This is simply too embarrassing."

She threw up her hands in an exaggerated manner, rolled her eyes to the ceiling. When nothing was forthcoming from May, she became self-conscious and reached for Baby Emmie on the floor, busily wiping the crumbs from her bib.

May exited quietly, went to her room, and got under the covers as the cold seeped between the loose panes where the putty had fallen away. She lay on her left side, tucked her delicate hands beneath her cheeks, drew her knees up, and allowed the sadness in her heart to overflow in a small, slow trickle of tears. She had no place to go except to the One in who she never failed to trust.

Oh Heavenly Father, Lord of all Lords, she began, her cheeks glistening with the steady rain of her sorrow. *You have given me this blessing that only You and I will ever understand, so help me now. Look down on Thy handmaiden and find me a place where I can be welcome. Guide me, show me the way, even if I can't understand. Give me courage, give me strength. Help me to understand Abe and Betty's viewpoints, help me to be tolerant and forgiving. They, too, are doing what they feel is right.*

She took a deep cleansing breath and felt the tension leave her body as she handed the one side of the yoke to Jesus, her Savior.

She drifted into a soft slumber as the cold crept in through the window. The baby cried downstairs as Betty rattled the stove lid.

SHE WORE THE shawl and bonnet Betty had given her, the heavy black coat with the sheepskin lining underneath, and a navy-blue dress. The brown satchel filled with the few belongings she owned was grasped firmly in her right hand.

"May!"

Astounded, Betty's eyes opened wide. "You can't just . . ."

"I can. I'm leaving, Betty. I don't want to bring disgrace to your household."

"But . . . where will you go?"

"I have a place I know will take me."

"Who? I mean, where? How did you learn to know anyone? You haven't been anywhere. It's cold. You can't walk. May, I wish you'd change your mind. It doesn't seem right. Why don't you just take off that shawl and bonnet and sit at the table. We can surely talk this out."

Betty was babbling now, nervously attempting to right some wrong she had not been aware of, till now. This couldn't be what she had meant when she had the conversation with Abe.

"Thank you for everything you have done. I'll always be grateful. Tell the children I said goodbye."

Her hand on the doorknob, she let herself out into the frosty morning with the sun creating sparkles like diamonds on the brown grasses by the roadside.

"May! May!"

The calls became weaker as she distanced herself from the Abe and Betty Weaver farm, the brilliant sunshine in her face and tears like diamonds dropping from her beautiful dark brown eyes. She turned left, toward the direction her senses took her, and walked sedately and with purpose. She knew there was a small town named Oakley and trusted someone, somehow would come to her assistance.

Her feet felt the sting of the cold first, then the tips of her fingers. She picked up her pace, hoping to generate more heat. She switched the satchel from right to left, and back again. An automobile cruised past, the occupants obviously curious. They slowed, backed up, and asked if she needed a ride. May did not want to trust a stranger, so she smiled, said no, she hadn't far to go. She breathed a sigh of relief when they moved off, then swung her arms as she walked rapidly.

She passed farms, a few houses, a row of corn stocks covered in snow, the tops filled with greedy blackbirds helping themselves to the corn. Melvin would have a fit, some lazy farmer not having his corn husked. Crows winged overhead, cawing loudly, and were quickly erased by a skittering of juncos flying close to the ground, pecking at leftover millet seeds before taking flight.

She was glad for the sheepskin lining of her coat, glad for the woolen shawl and her warm stockings. Betty had done so much for her, giving her dresses she had outgrown after the birth of seven children.

She would miss them all, especially Emmie, the baby, who was often handed from one child to another, everyone taking their turn, whether they wanted to or not. A large household for one so young, although Betty took it all in stride, loved her children, and did the best she could.

Her evenings with Norrie were precious now, the child accepting May in her bed as if she had always been there. May thought now of the verse in the Bible that said, "Lest ye become as little children, ye can no wise enter into the Kingdom of Heaven." The words of Jesus.

Children were completely without guile. There was no cunning, no hatred, no jealousy. Norrie merely stated her childish thoughts, her braided hair wound along the back of her head, her chin deep into the covers as she related the incidents of her day.

There would be much to miss now, much to ponder and remember. She had never been unhappy there, never wished to be elsewhere. Her life had been filled to the brim with kind, normal people whom she appreciated every day, always remembering to thank God for the kindness of this loving family.

As she walked, her legs began to ache, and her back felt as if the muscles were all drawing into a tight band. The back of her heel was being rubbed raw by the ill-fitting leather shoes, also handed down from Betty. She stopped to lift the heel from the shoe for a moment's respite, then continued on her way before realizing a painful blister had developed. Nothing to do but open her satchel and find a bit of cloth, a handkerchief to stuff into the back of the shoe.

She was bent over to open the satchel when she heard the familiar ring of running hooves and steel rimmed buggy wheels. She straightened, ashamed to be seen bent over, rummaging in a satchel like a common tramp.

Quickly, she picked it up, resumed walking in spite of the fiery pain.

The horse was small, a two-year-old, if that. His ear pricked forward and his head was lifted unnaturally high as he caught sight of her dark figure.

At first, she thought there was no surrey behind the horse, till she realized the young horse was pulling a light one-seated sulky, the driver's feet propped on the narrow dashboard, her headscarf a flaming red, her face very close to the same color.

The horse stopped, bouncing around as if on coiled springs. May stopped, made her way into the narrow incline beside the road, afraid she would spook the young horse who was obviously green broke.

"Come on. Get up there."

A chirping from pursed lips, a fleeting "Hello!" as the horse took off running, making a wide arc around her. May lifted a hand and stood to watch the young horse and driver keep the fast pace till they were out of sight behind a grove of trees.

She reopened the satchel, found a clean, flowered handkerchief, applied it carefully into the bend of her shoe, and was on her way.

Much better, she thought, grateful for the gift of a flowered hanky, another kindness from Betty.

As she walked, she began to wonder what would be expected of her after arriving in Oakley. Dressed in the conservative Amish shawl and bonnet might make it hard for anyone to take pity on her, wondering why the Amish did not take care of their own. She had no alternative at this point, the way Betty had mysteriously "gotten rid of" her blue coat and plaid skirt. Well, nowhere else to go but forward, trusting God to see her through. All she needed was one kind soul who would give her a place of employment, a bed to sleep in.

She stopped when she heard the ring of hooves on the hard macadam and turned to find the same horse and sulky returning.

"Whoa. Whoa now. Stop. You stopped before, and you can again. Whoa. Easy there."

Inquisitive eyes from the red face, but no smile of welcome, merely a nod in her direction.

"Who are you and why are you walking?"

For a moment, May was undecided if she should be frightened or just take the blunt question with good humor.

"My name is May."

The horse snorted, pawed at the macadam, pulled at the reins, the whites of his eyes showing as he tossed his head.

"Are you that May that lives with Abe Weaver?"

"Yes, I am."

"You used to live here, right?"

"I did."

"Your parents died and you lived in Arkansas."

"Yes."

"Why are you walking?"

"I'm . . . I'm on my way to Oakley."

"Why?"

May bit her lower lip, her heavy lids swept downward to eliminate the river's piercing, accusatory gaze. She shifted the satchel from one hand to the other, then swiped a piece of lint from her shawl. Somewhere, a dog began a low-throated bark. Another one answered.

"Uh . . . well, I need to um . . . look for a job. Perhaps a place to stay."

"What for?"

"I chose to leave Abe and Betty."

"You chose, or they put you out?"

"Oh, they didn't ask me to leave."

"You're lying."

"No. No. Well, not really. It was my decision."

The large chin protruding from the red scarf was pointed in the direction of a long, low building on a small grade uphill.

"See that?"

"Yes."

"That's my place. Meet me there? I'd pick you up, but this sulky only holds one. Come on up to my place, and I'll give you a rest, okay? See ya."

With that, she was off the minute she loosened the reins. May stood watching the flap of the brilliant red scarf.

What had she just said? Goose bumps covered her arms, chills raced up her spine. Come unto Me, and I will give you rest.

Is that what she'd said? No, not really. *But, dear Lord, is she You in a bright red scarf?* No Amish woman wore a red scarf.

Come to my place, and I'll give you a rest.

I feel Your Presence, sweet Jesus, May murmured as tears slid unchecked down her cold cheeks. Surely God would not answer before she even set foot in the small town of Oakley. She was not worthy of a love so great, so unconditional, when she stood here, on the soil of her *gehorsam* ancestors, tainted with sin and sorrow. She was soiled with every vile sin, thrust upon her or having chosen it herself.

Well, thy servant heareth. If this is the kindness I need, then I'll move toward it. One step, one hour at a time.

THE HOUSE WAS not an ordinary Amish farmhouse, and the barn was completely unlike anything she'd seen before. The porch was deep, with heavy pillars supporting the gable end, a small square dormer built into the steep roof.

Almost like a gingerbread house, May thought. Short and square, with long, low windows, the white curtains parted and tied at the sides. Wide plank porch steps, painted gray, with a gray milk box with red letters that said MILTON'S DAIRY. A fat yellow cat lay sprawled in the sun, as if he owned the milk box, the porch, everything.

May hesitated at the steps. The cat gave her a steady yellow gaze, then got to his feet to arch his back against the heavy post.

Still undecided, May looked toward the barn, wondering if the woman in the red scarf was still seeing to her horse.

The door was flung open.

"Come on in. My goodness, you have to be half frozen."

Gratefully, May stepped forward.

"Don't mind Ollie. He thinks this is his porch."

There was a whistling teakettle on the smallest kitchen range May had ever seen, and two mugs ready for the boiling water. The house smelled of soap, peppermint, and freshly baked bread. Everything was tidy, the wooden floors gleamed, and there were brightly colored rag rugs under every rocking chair along the front of the navy-blue sofa. Kerosene lamps sat on crocheted doilies. The chairs were metal, with iron crafted into a heart on the backs of them. A checked tablecloth covered the table, with a vase of greenery sitting on top. She noticed the wide porcelain sink with a tiny four-paned window adorned with a white ruffled curtain.

May could only rest her eyes on one adorable object after another, taking in the visual delights along with the cleanliness, the darling charm of this small home. It seemed as if it was only a dream.

"Here, give me your wraps."

Terrified, May's face drained of color. This would be the ultimate test, and she had to face it with courage. Slowly she undid the bonnet strings, her fingers beginning to tremble, then the shawl. With a deep breath, she unbuttoned the coat and handed it to the woman, who waited quietly without speaking.

"Just sit down. Make yourself comfortable. If you're still freezing, you can stand by the stove."

But May had seen the flicker of her eyes, the downward glance at her rounded waist, though nothing was said.

May sat down quickly, her knees no longer supporting her. The woman busied herself at the small counter by the sink. May heard a distinct gurgle of water, but the spigot in the sink was closed, which puzzled her, but she said nothing.

"Tell me what brought you back from Arkansas," the woman said, without turning her back. She was slicing something onto a white plate.

"It's a long, complicated story."

The woman didn't push her. "Oh, I'm Clara. Clara Yoder. I remember you as a child. You and your brother. Who could forget that sad accident, right?"

May nodded, her throat tightening.

"Well, no use starting out getting to know each other so bluesy, *gel* (right)?"

May could not speak.

"Look, I don't have to know why you came back, but I do have to know why you left Abe's."

May's startled eyes flew to her face.

"Why?"

"Well, I can see how it is with you."

May flushed scarlet, feeling alone, condemned, worthy of death.

"So if I'm not wrong, you're causing problems, right? Church problems. Your being here is not an everyday occurrence. I heard a lot more than you know. I've picked my battles, thought ahead, figured you'd be sent packing. Betty isn't gonna have her good name smeared by someone like you. I'm just surprised it happened quite this fast."

May was breathless.

"So how did all this come about?

May lifted miserable, condemned eyes.

"If I tell you, you'll send me away."

"If you don't tell me the truth, I will. If you dare tell me one lie about anything, I can't promise a thing. All I want is the real truth."

May's head sank lower. She felt weak with hunger and shock, felt her own cowardice like a hot iron. Slowly, she shook her head.

"I can't."

"Look, we'll get some hot tea into you. Some trail bologna and Swiss cheese. I made bread this morning and there's honey in the comb. You'll feel strengthened by a bite to eat."

"Thank you so much."

AND SLOWLY MAY found there was no condemnation with Clara Yoder.

When she began to talk, she flinched every time Clara opened her mouth to speak, waited for the tirade, the scolding she fully deserved. She would welcome it—it was right to be punished for all her transgressions. But the punishment didn't come.

How to describe the flow of healing? How could one woman in a red scarf, a nose like a hawk, and a spate of unbecoming freckles possess eyes of the deepest hue of compassion? She found an empathy she had not known existed in any human being's face. Words began as a hesitant drip, a hand to her mouth, wide eyes filled with fright and self-hatred. The drop turned into a trickle, and still there were many leaves unturned.

There were chores to be done, horses to tend to. May's eager offer to help was waved away, told there was no need.

She was to lie down and rest, cover herself with the crocheted blanket, take a long nap while Clara was in the barn.

But May was still reeling from the shock of being welcomed in to this liberal Amish woman's life. She was still unsure of the outcome, afraid of even the smallest kindness. How could she possibly rest?

So she paced. She lifted books, examined the covers, the descriptions on the back, laid them down, and wondered. Who was this woman? Try as she might, she could not remember a single girl named Clara in church when she was a child. Should she trust her? Did she have any choice?

May knew she didn't deserve this kind of welcome, didn't deserve to be put up in such an adorable and comfortable little home. Maybe it was too good to be true and it was only a matter of time before Clara changed her tune and sent her packing again.

Clara clattered back into the house, shucking outerwear as she charged through the kitchen, talking so fast May had a hard time following. The red scarf was snapped to rid the fringes of a few strands of hay, then hung over the hook.

"What are you hungry for?"

"Oh, don't bother. The bologna and cheese were plenty."

"No, we need something hot. I have some leftover chicken and broth. I'll make chicken corn soup with milk and hardboiled eggs. Noodles or rivels?"

"Noodles, if it is okay with you."

May struggled to compose herself, sitting in the charming kitchen, eating the flavorful creamy soup, saltine crackers, and tiny sweet pickles. The soup was so satisfying that she became very drowsy afterward.

"I have a surprise for you, May. I saw you go to the little house out back, which was all right of course, but let me show you this."

Her eyes sparkled mischievously as she flung open a door to a small room down a short wide hallway.

"A bathroom!" she chortled.

May took in the gleaming bathtub, the tiny sink with a mirror above it that Clara swung outward proudly to show off the small white shelves behind it. And the commode!

"Oh wonderful!" May said.

'Did you ever use one?'

"Yes, in New York. With . . . with Clinton."

"That's . . . Oh, yes."

May couldn't help questioning Clara about the bathroom being tolerated according to church rules, and was met with a shrug of the shoulders. "If they don't allow it now, they will soon. I'm probably the first one, but someone has to be. It's almost 1950. I have a radio, too, hidden under my bed. I listen to the horse races. Now *that* I know I'm not supposed to have." She held a finger to her lips. "I'm not hurting anyone. I enjoy keeping track of the best horses. Not that I bet on them or anything. I just like listening."

And May wondered what else Clara had up her sleeve. My, she sure sailed along with all sails unfurled, didn't she? Goodness. But who was she to judge? Much better just to be grateful, yet again.

CHAPTER 6

THEY WERE HOLED UP FOR ALMOST THREE DAYS. THE FAMILY welcomed them warmly, showed them couches to sleep on, and shared their meals. They didn't speak much, and what they said was short and to the point, but their kind hearts were evident in how they invited the men in with no hesitation.

Day and night the wind thrashed the tops of fir trees like bottle brushes, the snow skimming across the land creating drifts and caves with blue shadows, the landscape in constant whirling motion. It was only when the wind died down that they heard the muffled roar of the road-clearing equipment, gathered their belongings, said thank you, and got back on the road.

Oba had gleaned that they were headed to a place called Dawson Creek. An old friend of Jonas's had promised to keep the dogs while he traveled all the way to New York to take care of business. Beyond that, he figured if Jonas wanted him to know, he'd tell him when he felt like it. If he didn't ask Jonas too many questions, maybe Jonas wouldn't go prying into Oba's past, either.

They passed small towns, rivers, breathtaking mountains capped with low clouds, everything covered in the dazzle of glistening snow. The road wound in great curves with steep inclines and valleys. The trees were gigantic, clustered in great swaths of dense forest so thick and impenetrable he could not imagine trying to hike through them. He realized he was being introduced to a different world, with the very air around him cleansed and purified by the countless trees, lakes, rivers. The tumbling creeks held water so pure and clear he imagined fat trout in layers, hovering beneath tree roots and boulders.

He resented afresh the denial to accompany the friendly Arpachshad Brown, the black boy nicknamed Drink. He'd been invited to learn how to catch fish, the heavy bottomfeeders called catfish, that prowled the waters of the slugging Mississippi and fought stronger than a man. No, Melvin had told him. No. It wasn't good for a youth to have idle time on his hands, let alone spend it with that ne'er do well, Arpachshad.

The friendship had been loosened before it began, leaving Oba staring wistfully after the free-spirited boy with his fishing pole over his shoulder, a rusted tin can full of juicy nightcrawlers clutched in his right hand.

He broke the long silence with, "Do you fish?"

"Fish? You have no idea. We'll fish all the seasons, every piece of water around us. We fish to find food for the dogs. We dry them on racks, keep them in frozen caches, eat them ourselves. Sure we fish."

Oba said nothing, but felt redeemed, as if being kept from what he had desperately wanted to do had come full circle. *Take that, Melvin, I'll fish as much as I want and there's nothing you can do about it.*

As the car kept up its speed, the hum of the tires and the slight purr of the engine took its toll and Oba fell asleep, his head slanted to the side as the miles slipped away. Jonas kept his eyes on the road, with sideways glances at his young passenger, his face smooth and as relaxed as a child's. He wondered for the hundredth time what went on in his mind. What caused the flat stare, the deep blackness in the depth of his brown eyes?

Jonas was glad to have him and was eager to teach him life in the wilderness, an unparalleled existence filled with threats, trials, scrambles to survive, a wild beauty that would awaken his soul. He didn't pray, he'd said. Well, he would soon enough.

He'd lived along the Beatton River, him and Drucilla. Spent six idyllic years, with only each other and God's country, the seasons coming and going, bringing their own challenges, their own joy and appreciation. She had loved the "bush" as she called it, had been the best trapper and dogmusher he'd ever seen, but then, it was in her blood, being raised among the Indians, an orphaned trading post owner's kid. Not a drop of Indian blood in her, but she had taken to him and the skills of the Northwest Territory, never wavering in her resolve to make them both happy.

And for the thousandth time, Jonas felt the scalding remorse of not getting her out sooner, the sickness waning, his joy bursting, only to know the bottomless pit of despair when the fever raged back, her lungs filled with bacteria, the airplane landing on the river too late. The crackling two-way radio, her labored breathing, the intensity of his desperation.

Too late, too late. He heard the words in the cardinal's call, heard it in the flight of the snow geese, heard his own soul's heart-rending call in the bugle of the bull elk. He'd never get over losing Drucilla, his heart of hearts, his soul mate. And it was all his fault.

Yet, God was good. He had taken away, and had given him peace, but only after a time. His faith had carried him through, and still did. He could never hope for another woman who would truly love the wilderness, but he was fine with what God had given him once in his life. Perhaps he had sent the mysterious Oba as a service to him, knowing he, Jonas, needed a companion if he chose to go back. There was no other life for him—he could not begin to fathom living among crowds of people, working in factories and mills, grinding out a living that slowly corroded the joy humans were meant to contain.

Born and raised in the upper northwest of the state of New York, he had spent time in the military and afterward just wanted to be washed clean of all the atrocities one evil mind could accomplish against another. He tried to escape to the Yukon, but found all his demons traveled with him. But there was slow healing to be found in the heart of the spectacular rivers, mountains, and lakes.

He'd met her in the dining room of the Trader's Inn, that slovenly shack housing all manner of wanderers, derelicts trying to keep the thread of half-crazed miners and gold digger's lies intact. Kept as an indentured servant, carrying trays of food and drink, unsuccessfully avoiding lewd remarks and grasping hands, she'd been grateful to be taken away, and they married on the strength of hope and optimism.

He could barely travel fast enough now. He was impatient to be with the dogs, the huskies with light blue eyes, the inbred eagerness to run, their cries of anticipation as he prepared for a day's travel. Drucilla had loved the dogs and named them all, and so when he was with them, he could almost feel like she was there, too.

He glanced down at the fuel gauge, then to his surroundings.

"Hey."

Oba's eyes blinked, opened. He sat up, wiped the back of his hand across his mouth, glared at Jonas with his dark eyes that sent chills down Jonas's back.

"Get the map."

"What would you do if I wasn't with you?" Oba growled, all self-pity and childishness.

"I'd pull off the side of the road, open the glove compartment, get out the map, and find what I was looking for. But since you're here, you can do it."

There was no grin of good humor, no acknowledgment of having heard, only a hard bang of the small door to the glove compartment, an exaggerated sigh as he unfolded the map.

"Route 2. How far to Tupper? It's right on the Canadian line."

"No more than twenty, maybe fifteen miles."

Jonas nodded, hoped they'd have enough fuel.

But they didn't. When the car began to sputter, the gauge on empty, he said nothing, but after his speed decreased and the sputtering stopped, Oba turned accusing eyes to Jonas, who turned to the side of the road, stopped, and turned the engine off.

"What's wrong?"

"We're out of fuel."

"I'm not walking. You should have brought an extra can of gas. Why didn't you stop at the last town?"

Jonas felt his blood rise. Who exactly did this kid think he was?

"Then I guess we'll set here, cause I ain't going either."

"What do you mean?"

"Exactly what I said.

"You expect me to go? Uh-uh. Someone will be along."

"Step out then, see if you can flag someone down."

Oba yanked at the car door handle, slammed the door with unnecessary force, and walked to the edge of the road like an angry rooster. He waited. He shivered as the cold slammed into his denim trousers, crept up the back of his coat, raked across his exposed ears. He kept his back turned to Jonas, having no intention of showing any sign of discomfort. He was in a foul mood on account of his empty stomach, his gut roaring and fizzing with the stale crackers and half-frozen peanut butter they'd eaten for the morning meal.

He heard the steady roar of a logging truck, about the only vehicle on these roads. Snow lay in slushy piles, ribboned on the road like harbingers of death and destruction. A brake applied too fast, a wheel turned too sharp, the rig jackknifing and it was all over, he thought.

Here he comes.

Oba stepped out, waved a hand, a feeble flap of white that went ignored as the truck barreled past, throwing a sheet of dirty snow, cinders, and ice, all laced with a helping of diesel smoke. He leaped back, slipped, and fell on the seat of his pants. He got up in one lithe movement, his pride intact, and brushed furiously at his coat front.

Jonas rolled down the window slowly, stuck his grizzled face out the window, let out a braying laugh like a demented donkey. Before he thought of the consequences, Oba bent, picked up a handful of the dirty snow and hurled it straight into the grinning face, plastering it all over the unwelcome sight.

Next thing he knew there was a roar, a door flung open, and he was knocked to the ground, rolled into the snow like a piece of firewood. He found he was being straddled and squinted through melting snow to see Jonas above him, fist raised, yelling "Say uncle! Say it!"

Oba put up a good fight, he thought later. He kicked and squirmed, raised his head to bite, gnashed his teeth, screamed and yelled, but it was like being caught under a boulder.

"Say it!"

"No!" he gasped, and tried twisting and kicking with even more effort.

Of course he did say it, eventually.

They were both breathing hard, facing each other warily. Both were wet, cold, and ill tempered, and they had nowhere to go but back into the now cold vehicle. Oba yanked his cap off, shook it out the window, then threw it into the back seat.

Silence reigned, snow melting in tiny rivulets off eyebrows and coats.

"You gonna walk?"

"Are you crazy? I'm soaked."

Jonas shifted his gaze to the window. Finally his shoulders started to shake with merriment, but he struggled to keep his face sober, concerned.

"You know, that was plain stupid, running out of gas," said Oba, still mad.

"I know."

"Why'd you do it?"

"Look, kid. I'm not going to defend myself. If you're going to turn every situation on its head, and blame me for it, you may as well bail out now. If we're going to survive, it will have to be as a team. That is the first rule of survival in a place that will never offer anything for free. Every little thing has a price, and if you're not willing to give, then you just might not live to tell the story. I'm not joking, not saying this to pass time or for entertainment. You will have to learn circumstances will arise, and to sit there like a child, pouting and blaming me, is simply not going to cut it. We're wet, we're cold, we have two options. Walk, or get out and start a fire and wait for someone to help."

"Start a fire? Everything's covered in a foot of snow."

"Well then, I guess I'll have to teach the first lesson of the great Northwest Territory."

With that, he heaved himself out and went around the vehicle and into the trees that grew out of a steep incline. He began pawing at the snow with his bare hands, till he had a bare spot a few feet across. Turning, he motioned to Oba.

Oba shook his head. He was too cold to get back into the claws of that bitter adversity, the wind and cold that cut like knives.

So Jonas turned his back and continued pawing as Oba slid down in the seat to show he wasn't watching.

After a while, he had a crick in his back, so he slid back up and turned his eyes slightly to the right. He was amazed to find a crackling fire and Jonas standing with his hands held to the blaze.

Now where had he found anything to start that cheerful fire? Without thinking, he hoisted himself out and went to stand by the unbelievable warmth. He tried to keep his teeth from chattering as he watched the steam rise from the trouser legs, but he said nothing.

An old red pickup truck passed, slowed, turned, and pulled off the road. A dark-skinned man, wearing a heavy plaid coat and the biggest pair of rubber galoshes Oba had ever seen, got out and walked over, his expression showing no sign of friendliness or hostility.

"How you doing?" Jonas offered.

"Ran outta gas?"

"Yup."

Nothing more was said, but the man turned on his heel, lifted a chipped and dented fuel can, and inserted the nozzle into the station wagon. After a minute, he pulled it out and set the can back on the truck.

"Reckon that'll git you ta Tupper. Ain't but four, five mile."

"Thank you. How much do I owe you?"

He waved a calloused paw in a downward motion, turned, and waved a hand above his head, then stepped into the rusted truck and was back on the road.

Oba shook his head, amazed at the generosity he had just witnessed.

"His kind don't waste a lotta words."

"His kind?"

"Yeah. He's French. Lotsa them from the old logging camps."

WHEN THEY ARRIVED at Dawson Creek, it seemed to Oba as if Jonas became charged with a new energy, a visible brightening of his whole countenance. The town resembled every one they had passed through, with a fairly wide main street, stores with false fronts, streets arranged in blocks, with back alleys, a few houses scattered out into the surrounding forest. Snow lay in piles, some littered with gravel and cinders where the plow had upended the top of the macadam.

Pedestrians were scarce. If one came into view, it was a bulky figure wearing a thick coat and a dark-colored hood with a ring of fur around the face, when the hood was pulled up. If the hood was down, it was like a beaver or a silver fox slung across the shoulders.

Down a side street, past a few rusted sheds, and the car slowed, turned right, and rolled to a stop. The house was small, only one story, like a henhouse. Instead of the usual A frame, the roof was slanted, the highest part in front. It was covered in galvanized steel, the windows like unblinking eyes, no curtains.

Oba became aware of a cacophony of sound, a burst that bounced back against the windows of the car. The wooden door was flung open, the frame containing what he imagined a prophet in the Bible would have appeared to be. Not that he believed any of it, but raised in the Amish church, you heard plenty of stories about those old guys—every two weeks it was either Noah or Moses or Solomon.

His long hair was yellowish white, with a long, stringy beard, his face half hidden behind the unkempt growth sprouting from his cheeks. His clothes were the dark hues of the nondescript uniform of the northern wilderness—gray, brown, or navy blue, the frequent washing or the lack of it blurring it all into one.

Jonas was out of the car in a single leap, up to the door where a series of handshaking and shoulder clapping began in earnest. As usual, Oba felt the odd man out, alone, unrecognized, worthless. He was aware of the barking of dogs now, and the yelping and screeching jangled his nerves.

He looked up to find Jonas motioning for him to join them, the birdlike eyes of the old man watching him through the windshield. Every part of him resisted, but he stumbled up the wooden steps and allowed himself to be introduced to George and taken through the rattling, swaying door to a half-lit jumble of furniture and belongings.

After his sight adjusted to the dim interior, he became fascinated by the amount of what he perceived to be traps, hanging from pegs on the wall. Dozens of them. Fishing rods were stacked in corners, guns along another wall. There were knives and bows, skulls and horns, tin cans and cooking pots, newspapers, twine, firewood, and buckets of ashes, one with the potato peelings and another for garbage. There was a cast iron pan on top of what appeared to be a barrel with a homemade door, cherry red with heat.

"So this is Obadiah Miller."

The man let out a cackling laugh, the bird eyes opened wide, alert, taking in the sight of this angry, reluctant youth with a smooth face, hair the color of new wheat, dark, mocking eyes as lifeless as any he'd ever seen.

"I'm George. My last name is hard to pronounce, and it ain't worth nothing. So you're going into the bush, are you?"

Not with you, Oba thought, but inclined his head with only the slightest hint at a nod. George watched him, decided it best to leave this boy alone, and turned to Jonas. "The dogs are waiting for you."

Together, they went around to the back, the clamor of sound now elevated to a kind of hysteria. There was whining, yelping, and barking amounting to an almost unbearable level of noise, and Jonas and George were in the middle of it, hugging, patting, calling out names as dog tugged at chains, scrabbled furiously in the smooth snow to reach them.

Jonas laughed, happier than Oba had ever seen him as he called out the dogs' names, stooping down to greet each dog. George was in the middle of the bedlam, hauling out buckets, smiling, his eyes squinty with weathered lines.

Oba leaned against the tin house, wishing he hadn't come. The dogs were slobbering and howling, sitting back and whining when Jonas kept his attention on another dog. He had never understood the attraction from man to beast. Like mules or cows or slinking barn cats, they were all just animals, certainly nothing to be given this kind of affection.

So he leaned against the side of the house, shoved his hands in his pockets, and watched the ridiculous show.

Jonas stopped, motioned for him to join them.

He shook his head.

"Come on. You may as well. These dogs will be your closest friends for the next few months."

"I don't like dogs."

Jonas looked at George, incredulous. They passed a mutual look that was not lost on Oba.

"I don't have to like them!" he shouted. "No one is going to make me get pawed and slobbered on like that."

"All right, all right."

Both hands in the air, palms out in a sign of resignation, Jonas pulled himself away from ruffling the ears of the biggest husky and asked George if they could spend the night.

Oba remained at his post, allowing the two men to push past him. He waited till they both went into the house. The cold crept through his pants legs, around his ears, down the collar of his coat. He shivered, then lifted his eyes to the dogs. Most of them had lost interest, the chains dragging as they settled themselves back into the snowy bed, although two of them remained alert, their ears pricked forward, their eyes never leaving him.

He had never seen dogs like these. They were mostly gray and white, with patches of near black. Their tails curled up over their backs, almost like a flower, or some foliage that grew in perfect symmetry. Their heads were well shaped, with light blue eyes the color of stars, almost white, except on a few there was one shockingly blue eye and one brown one. He'd heard Jonas call them Siberian huskies. They were good-looking dogs, he had to admit.

Dogs were as necessary as a vehicle once you left civilization, of that he was aware. But these dogs weren't huge, the way he'd imagined. They were middle-sized, too puny looking to pull hundreds of pounds of food, gear, tools, and whatnot they would need for the journey.

One of the dogs sat back on his haunches and whined, his two front feet tapping the packed snow. He eyed Oba with two diamond-hued eyes, then tilted his head to one side, sitting very still as if waiting for him to make an overture. Oba just stood there with one shoulder against the corrugated siding and glared back at the dog. There was no way he would ever be wheedled into hugging those creatures. If Jonas wanted him to live in a cabin somewhere, well, he'd go, but he wasn't going to help with the dogs.

He threw the dog a contemptible glare before turning and making his way into the house where he found a chair and sat quietly, his eyes roving from traps to skulls to guns and back again.

A huge slab of red meat was flopped into a hot skillet, sending up a hissing sound and an aroma that made his mouth water. Conversation was lively, mostly escapades in times past, the far reaches of the bush planes in this day and age.

Jonas had told him about the small planes flying across the Northwest Territory, giving him hope of being able to return to normal life if things became too harrowing. "Normal life," as if Oba even knew what that meant.

He'd dangled above the chasm between the Amish and the English for years now. He no longer felt a part of the plain people in Arkansas, nor could he ever fit comfortably with any group he'd encountered thus far. In California, Tom Lyons had been kind, had given him a good start in the world, but what had he done but squander the funds on his dead-end search for May? He would never meet Tom's expectations for him of college and a girlfriend and basketball games. A person simply could not hide his plain upbringing, his lack of experience and ability. For all those years growing up, there had been no radio, no exposure to what was going on in the world. Up until recently, there had been a war raging, one Oba had rarely heard about until he left Arkansas. He'd been shamefully repressed living on the farm with Melvin and Gertie, then when he'd become a teenager, mercilessly assaulted with a mortifying attraction to girls, even dark-skinned ones with their smiling faces and thin cotton dresses who worked all day in the fields in Arkansas. He had no idea this was all normal, a part of ordinary life for any red-blooded young man, and so had been given to bouts of depression and self-hatred.

He felt suspended above reality, here in the dim trapper's hut, the yellow light bulb dangling from the ceiling like a malevolent eye, speaking of past failures and predicting a future chock full of the same.

CHAPTER 7

THE TREES WERE TAKING ON THE PURPLISH HUE OF PUSHING buds and the lawn was dotted with bursting yellow dandelions on southern slopes. The air was still chilly, but the sun warmed the small sitting room beneath the white oak tree. Beyond the oak was a backdrop of pines, the earth beneath them littered with pine cones and playful chipmunks. A warbler set up a melodious trilling, the delicate throat pulsing mightily as the song spilled across the yard.

A baby's cry was caught in the birdsong, the cry of need, of hunger and being loved. The sun caught the golden, caramel-hued contour of his cheek, the dusting of curly dark hair as soft as the new wool on a spring lamb.

May sat in the oak rocker, a soft blanket covering her lap, her face bent to her newborn, a son named Eliezer. He was named for May's deceased father, although she had wanted to name him Clinton, the father of her beautiful son, the love of her life. It was Clara who had finally persuaded her to pick the traditional name from the Bible. Clara knew she would need all the help she could get, if she planned on being accepted into the Amish world as a single mother with an *auslendish* (foreign) son.

Clara would sit and watch May with her son, trying to imagine feeling a love so great for any living being, newborn or not. She was amazed and a little bewildered by such absolute devotion to the squalling red-faced little creature with hair like a metal sponge.

The time and effort it took! The patience!

May was weak, tired, and getting no rest, and the stubborn little thing refusing to nurse. Beads of perspiration were popping out on May's forehead as she struggled to get the fussy baby to latch to her breast.

Clara snorted out her nose, thinking herself very lucky that she'd never have to go through such a trial. May knew how Clara felt, and it didn't bother her. How could Clara know that every ache, every pain, had been an exultation? She heard a cry of victory when the baby wailed. She heard rejoicing when he breathed, was enamored with the color of his skin and the perfection of his rounded head and shapely hands, his feet wide, adorned with five stubby toes. She saw Clinton in the shape of his eyes, the fullness of his beautiful mouth. She chortled as she bathed and dressed him, laughed when he woke, already impatient with his empty stomach.

She was so blessed to be there, in the irresistible little house with a comfortable bedroom, the heavenly bathroom, plenty to eat, warmth in winter. Now, with spring breezes coming through the smallest crack in the window, the sweet air filling the house with the scent of warming earth, new green buds as translucent as a dream, her soul was filled with soaring gratitude, and a great love for her newborn son, and for her blessed benefactor, Clara.

May was comfortably unaware of all that had transpired in the waning months of winter. As these things go, the feed man had spread the word from farm to farm. A young woman had been sighted at Clara Yoder's place, and yes, eyebrows raised and heads nodded meaningfully.

It was only a matter of time before Alvin Stutzman paid another visit to the deacon. The deacon was a man of few words and even less courage, so he sent Alvin to the bishop with his complaints. The two of them decided on an evening and went trundling down the road with a sturdy surrey and a spirited horse to have a talk with Clara.

She met them at the door, bristling with irritation and resentment. She got her coat, thought it best to leave the red scarf on the hook, and accompanied them out to the barn, not wanting to upset May. There was no need to get May worked up. What she needed was safety and rest—not to start worrying about the opinions of two pious men who would be better off keeping their opinions to themselves, thought Clara.

The kerosene lantern wick flickered in the cold wind as Clara stalked to the barn, ushered them through the door, and allowed the wind to slam it shut behind her. She set the lantern on a feed cart, crossed her arms, and waited, noticing the way the bishop, Atlee Mast, appeared waxen faced, his voice stilted, less than affable.

"Quite a few horses you have here," Atlee said to soften the inhospitable atmosphere.

"Yeah, well, I'm sure you didn't come here to talk about horses."

The bishop's mouth fell open in surprise.

Clara just waited.

Atlee regained his composure with a rumbled clearing of his throat. "Yes, we did in fact come for another reason. We need to know what's going on with May. Everyone is pretty worked up about all of this."

"Are they, though? Well, everyone will just have to continue, then, as I have no intention of putting her out. She's a young woman in need."

"But she has been caught in sin," the bishop reminded her. "They say she ran off with a *schwottza* (black man)."

If Clara had been a dog, every hair on her neck would have been straight as a toothpick, so rife was her indignation. To keep herself from spitting out her displeasure, she literally bit down on her lower lip till she tasted blood. She steadied herself, grasping the latch of the door behind her.

"And do you have any idea why she ran off?" she asked finally.

"She fell into temptation, I suppose. Promiscuous young women need to be brought to task. The way I understand it, Melvin Amstutz took them in out of the kindness of his heart, and both children rebelled."

Here Clara lost it. The wrongness of the whole sordid conversation was goading her like a red hot iron.

"You have no right to 'suppose' anything," she ground out. "May left out of necessity. Melvin Amstutz is not what you think. May has been through more than any human being deserves, ever. These things are not talked about, and anyway it's not my story to tell. But I will keep her and help her no matter what. If you want to excommunicate me because of it, then you go right ahead. But let me tell you something. If one of the members of this church is without sin, let them, just let them, cast that first stone. You know better than I do the story of the young woman caught in adultery." She felt too angry to say the precious name of Jesus. She was shaking now, had to clench her jaw to keep her voice steady.

Stone cold silence followed.

"So you are rebelling against authority?" the bishop asked coolly.

"I am, if said authority has no love or mercy. I must follow my conscience, which tells me it would be wrong to send away a young woman in need."

"Strong words, protecting a sinner," Alvin said, hard as nails. "Sin cannot come before God. He will not acknowledge her in such a state. She has been *behofft* (taken) by the devil and needs to be cast out with the unrepentant."

Clara was visibly trembling now. "You can't say this. May never joined the church, for one thing. Shouldn't we be trying to persuade her to do so, rather than sending her away to perish? And you have no idea whether she has repented or not. God is the only one who can truly know a heart, but I dare say hers is in a better place than half the people in our church who care more about their reputation than the lives of a young woman and her baby."

Alvin sniffed, his bent visage scowling with concentration as he shoved bits of straw with the toe of his large boot. "That is quite a speech, from a woman. I will remind you that you are the weaker vessel, meant to stay at home and ask your husband if you want to know spiritual matters, as the *Schrift* (Bible) expressly teaches us."

"Well, let me tell you. I have no husband, thank God, so if I want to figure it out, I have to do it myself. I have a pretty good idea that helping the poor, the needy, the sinner—whatever you want to call the rest of us ordinary human beings—is a good way to follow in the footsteps of our Lord."

"Well yes, but . . ."

"No, I don't believe there are any 'buts' here," Clara interrupted. "I've made my position clear. Why don't you all go talk about it some more and let me know where I stand as far as the church goes."

They'd left that night, in a flurry of cold wind and stray snow-flakes riding on the arrival of a full blown snowstorm, and she'd gone back to the house filled with indignation. She had no plans of backing down, absolutely not. Let them stew over it for a while. She doubted they'd actually go through with excommunicating her, but if they did, well, at least her conscience would be clear before God.

She let herself in the house as quiet as a cat, so May would never know about a word that had passed between them. Bit by bit, the tension seeped from her mind and body. Rather than fretting, she gave the whole situation over to Him who always knew best, asking God to work in the leaders' hearts, and in her own as well.

Suddenly she felt a bit guilty retrieving that radio out from under her bed and listening to the upcoming sale of a few of Kentucky's best race horses. It was getting to be a vice, this listening to the radio. She knew she was pushing boundaries by speaking out against the bishop and deacon about May like that, and she'd been right to do it. But it would be easy to start feeling self-righteous and like she was above *all* the rules. She'd have to be careful. So she left the radio underneath, although she bent to touch it, make sure it was there.

She hadn't heard anything for a month afterward. She'd driven her best horse to church, given the reins to none other than Atlee Mast himself, and marched to the house with her head held high. She couldn't care less who gave her the cold shoulder and who didn't.

As was usual among the clergy, much was discussed in quiet meetings without her knowledge of anything going on. The bishop asked counsel from a host of other church leaders, which caused a rift down the middle of a few meetings, but for the most part, the oldest leaders with the experience of the aged held sway over younger ones. And it was the young ones who usually held the harshest positions. A decision was reached, God's blessing was wished, and peace wound its way among the leaders. Some hearts were softened, and others were forced to submit to the decision despite their misgivings.

And Clara Yoder had another visit from the ministry, late at night, after May had retired to bed. They announced the result of the vote and spoke kindly and clearly of the decision to let her stay. For now, the church would have patience. They would allow a period of grace, and if May desired an application of membership, she would be allowed to join, but only if she bore fruit of the Christian life.

Clara said she had never seen a sweeter person than May Miller, one more appreciative of small favors. It seemed as if each trial only strengthened her, molding her into an even better person. The bishop had nodded, sympathetic, understanding.

"We are polished like gold, put through the fire," he said quietly.

They parted with feelings of goodwill, a renewal of respect, and on Clara's part, a renewed vow of obedience and love to her fellow men.

Infinitely grateful for the ability to keep May in her care without being excommunicated, her conscience grew stronger until she vowed to rid herself of the forbidden radio. She hurled the offensive thing down the privy hole, went back to the house, and subscribed to the *Horse Racer's Digest*, scribbling her name with a flourish on the bottom line. She stuck it in the envelope and marched out to the mailbox with a song in her heart. Yes, well, if it all came right down to it, she guessed you felt better if you obeyed the rules, and if you wanted to be Amish, you might as well do what you could. Although she wasn't giving up the red scarf any time soon. Just something about wearing it made her feel more alive. If God made cardinals, she didn't see why she couldn't wear a bit of red. Somehow that scarf made her feel as if she didn't have a big nose or an unruly bunch of thick red hair, not to mention the freckles dotting everything. Fine with her, God had made her that way, but still . . .

THE STERILE SOLITUDE of Clara's house was filled with the smell of Johnson's baby powder, of clean flannel diapers brought in on wash-day, of a smattering of tiny nightgowns and swaddle blankets hung on a wooden rack by the kitchen range to dry at the edges.

Clara cooked nourishing meals, turnips and carrots from the cold cellar, beef and potatoes, eggs and whole wheat bread and cereal. May's appetite increased, her cheeks blossomed with healthy color, and all her days were spent in deep and abiding contentment and praise to her Heavenly Father. She had never imagined such good-ness, such unabashed forgiveness and acceptance, a life lived free from repulsive feelings, guilt, or fear.

On days when her old demons would return to haunt her, she would pray, try to rise above the abyss of her past, but it wasn't always possible. Clara would know, when she came in from the barn and was met by a May without life, her vibrancy gone, her face drained of color, her eyes darkened by the terror of past memories.

Today, she sat beside the still, small form, took her hand and leaned forward.

"May?"

"Yes?"

"Are you having a bad day?"

"Only a little."

"How bad? Come on, just let it out."

May shook her head, bit down on her lip, before the gush of tears and the shaking, heart-rending sobs began. She groaned and swayed, held her arms tightly to her chest, her face tortured with remember-ing, afraid of unforgiveness and a headlong pitch into hell. Clara held her shoulders, blinked furiously at her own tears, and wondered what could cause this indescribable agony. She continued supporting her until she cried herself out. Finally, May sat back on the couch and breathed deeply, a sodden handkerchief twisted in fluttering fingers.

"I just don't know," she whispered.

"What don't you know?"

"If it was all my fault."

"What was your fault?"

May shook her head as a fresh sob tore through her lips. Clara sat back, stared into space. She told herself it was best to wait, let her speak when she was ready.

She thought of her own despicable years.

Finally Clara got up and put on the kettle, clanked the lid of the kitchen range, and thought she must find a way to keep these thunderous, defeating memories at bay. Her own words were as inefficient as a stale breeze.

"Come, May. I'm putting the water on."

May turned her face away, then went to the bathroom with heavy steps, like an old woman, her back bent as she swabbed at her cheeks with the handkerchief. Then she returned to the kitchen.

"Here." Clara set down the cup of steaming chamomile, pushed the honey jar her way. No use asking her to eat something when one of these times struck unexpectedly.

"I don't know, Clara," May said suddenly. "I just don't know. Why do I feel so overwhelmed with it all?"

"With what? You mean, running off with Clinton? Or was it his death or the times afterward?"

"I don't know."

A deep sigh, then a visible effort to pull herself back to the present, a cry from the bedroom where little Eliezer had been sleeping. May's face brightening as she hurried to hold him, to love her infant son with a fierce possessiveness. And Clara watched her go, and wondered.

THE FIRST WOMAN who dared come for a visit was none other than Abe Weaver's wife, Betty, bringing a casserole, a stack of newly sewn diapers, and a blue rattle to take along to church.

She viewed Baby Eliezer with the same gaze one would reserve for a two-headed calf, although she caught herself in time to comment on his healthy status and brown eyes.

May took it in stride, hadn't expected more, and thanked Betty for her kind gift. But Betty was obsessed with procuring information on whether she would be attending services with Clara in two weeks. She'd heard about the ministry bending themselves to May and her colored baby. And he was that, the color of dark honey, that broad nose and thick lips. What would become of him?

"So, are you planning on staying with the Amish?" she asked finally, when all her hemming and hawing brought no results.

May's brown-eyed gaze was lifted honestly, her eyes as clear and as liquid as spring water. "I am."

"Well, but, what about little ... uh ... the boy?"

Clara's hackles rose. "What do you think, Betty? We're going to feed him and bathe him and nurture him, after which he'll go to school and grow up to be a young man. Maybe he'll even share my love of horses."

"But ..."

"No, no buts. He'll wear a little round straw hat and denim trousers with suspenders like everyone else."

"But he's not really white."

There, she'd said it.

Clara looked at her with fiery eyes. "I'm not either. I'm red, in between the white spots."

Betty glared back at Clara, not finding this self-demeaning information humorous at all, and turned her attention to May. She asked if she'd had any trouble getting him started nursing. May answered honestly—a little, but he was doing okay now. Betty wished for a fortifying cup of tea and a few cookies, but when she saw none would be forthcoming, she took her leave, regretting that she had no firm answer on whether May and the baby would be at church in two weeks. She went home and told Abe something was a little off with that Clara, the high and mighty thing. She needed a husband to bring her down a notch.

Abe smiled to himself, wondering how any husband brought his wife down a notch, knowing this had been impossible in his own experience. When Betty got on her high horse, it was best to become increasingly dutiful or disappear altogether, the latter choice usually the best one.

He could imagine his wife's chagrin at the healthy baby's arrival, the church's acceptance of them. These days, Clara's kindness was being spoken of in quiet hushed circles. Whereas before Betty worried what people would think if May stayed with them, now she worried what people were saying about her having left their home.

Abe had always sympathized with May, now more than ever, but to disclose this bit of information to Betty was like throwing gasoline on fire. You were in too much danger of being burned yourself.

So he smiled, kept his peace, the way he always did. He was glad to hear the outcome of the ministers' meeting, glad to know love and mercy were alive and well. He had no doubt in May's ability to be a supporting member of the Amish church and wished her every blessing in the coming years. He listened to his wife's account of her visit with Clara, then got to his feet, clapped his hat onto his head, and thought it wouldn't be very long before the ground would be dry enough to get out the plow and the Belgians, his favorite job on the farm.

The dark days passed, and the brilliant spring sunshine became a healing antidote as May gathered strength after Eliezer's birth. Every day, she gazed into his darling face and murmured, "Little Clinton. Clinton." She wondered if Clinton was an angel, if he could look down and see his son. Sometimes he seemed very near, and at other times, she could barely remember his face, but always, she carried his memory close to her heart, her lips whispering words of love to the remembering of his life, their time together.

"We should call him Elly for short," Clara remarked one evening, as May sat by the sputtering yellow glow of the kerosene lamp.

May was horrified. "A girl's name? All Ellas are called Elly."

"Well, you know. Elly-ayser is the pronunciation, and Elly is better than Ayser."

May laughed. "Just call him Eliezer, like my father."

"I remember your parents. A better couple could not be found. And I remember you, as a child. You and your brother, Obadiah. Such beautiful children. The white blond of your hair is so remarkable."

"Yes, I suppose so. Same as my mother's hair." May lifted the baby to her shoulder, arranged the blanket around his shoulders, then spoke softly. "Losing my parents was very hard, but our life afterward was even harder. Sometimes I don't understand how our relatives could have been so cruel."

Clara nodded. "You know, Gertie was never a blooming rose. What I mean, she was the kind of girl no one would ask for a date. Like me. She wasn't very bright. An old story circulated among us that she was dropped on her head as an infant. Some say she never spoke a word until she was close to five years old, never got through school the way other children did. So when Melvin asked her, he was a sort of hero, everyone saying how Melvin saw deeper than the outward appearance, that he saw her good heart. And perhaps he did, I don't know."

May said nothing, her eyes veiled.

"She was obedient," May said finally.

"I imagine she was."

"In her own way, she loved the boys. Especially Leviticus." A sadness crept over May's features. "I feel responsible for those boys. I feel as if I left them to fend for themselves. I find myself praying for them every night."

"They are not your worry, May. God will take care of them."

May nodded, but the sadness remained.

"And Oba," she said suddenly. "I feel as if he died, although this not knowing is almost worse. He was so full of rage, unwilling to believe in God after we . . . he was mistreated."

"But he had the teaching when he was little. Perhaps that foundation will enable him to come back to God at some point in his life."

"I can only pray, right?" May asked, a kind of fleeting hope erasing the sadness in her eyes.

As THE DAYS went by, May regained her strength and began to help with the cooking and cleaning, allowing Clara to spend more time working with the horses. As the days turned warmer, May joined her sometimes when Eliezer slept in his small cradle, his dark head showing above the clean blankets covering his little body.

The days were alight with spring sunshine, breezes scented with the growth of violets along roads and fencerows, fat yellow dandelions with their brilliant yellow blossoms among the purple of the violets. The earth was changed into an explosion of green, buds turning into fresh new leaves, thick alfalfa and timothy grass growing with the nutrients from well-watered soil, rays from the sun adding the boost the fields needed. Farmers walked to the edge of their fields, chewed on fresh new blades of spring grass, and counted their profits. Sweating horses drew the one powerful blade of the plow through rich soil the color of fine mahogany, the lone man with his hands clenched on the slick wooden handles, staggering behind in the uneven furrow.

All over the Amish community, new life and fresh vigor was taken up each morning as men rose from their beds and went forth into the scented dawn to greet wobbly calves only a few hours old, or a sow with a litter of bumbling pink piglets, squealing and shoving their way to their food source. The metal milk cans filled with buckets of frothy white liquid from freshened cows; manure piles were leveled as the spreader sprayed it all over the old corn stubbles, ahead of the plow.

Women bent double, placed precious seeds in furrows drawn with the edge of a hoe, the frisky spring breezes whipping their wide skirts around their bare ankles. Little boys clapped their bow-shaped straw hats to their heads, their mouths open, laughing as they ran barefoot across new grass and soil not yet warmed by summer's sun.

In the evening, they would sit on the back stoop, a steaming granite dish of soapy water on the step below them, allowing their feet to be washed and dried before they scampered off to rest in their beds upstairs.

For May, standing at the fence, her arms draped across the top board, the scent of fresh soil and new grass brought sharp memories of her mother, her sturdy back bent over her work. When her mother straightened, she would watch the sky, her eyes following the cloud pattern, the ripple of heavy grasses, before telling May to come look at the bunnies, playing at the edge of the hayfield.

A sense of deep sadness overtook her at times, remembering the joy of childish things, the freshness of her innocence. She felt tainted, forever soiled, no matter how she clung to her faith in the power of Christ's forgiveness. She would always pay the price, carry the burden of Eliezer's birth, belong to a community while still being an outcast.

She never wanted to return to a world she never understood, the life of *die Englishy* (the English). For her, there was safety here among her people, in the rolling hills of Ohio, the birthplace of her parents, of her and Oba. She would merely need to accept her lot, prepare herself for silent ridicule and barbed glances.

But was it fair to Eliezer, her beautiful baby?

CHAPTER 8

Between them, they decided to stay in Dawson Creek for a month and let the worst of winter to blow itself out. George had no room for them, he allowed, but there were rooms above the old livery on Clark Street, which Jonas took into account, and they left one gray, cloud-scudded morning to see where they could be comfortable for a while.

He was in a jovial state of mind, joking and carrying on with Oba, trying to draw him out of his reclusive state. He walked with his hands in his pockets, shoulders hunched, the cold infiltrating every inch of his body. It seeped into his collar, his ankles, the tips of his toes. His eyes watered, his nose felt as if a hot iron was held to it, his cheeks on fire. This was a cold that could only be described as merciless, brutal, an assault on humans and animals alike.

The light of the sun was obscured by a thin gray veil of clouds, the wind moaning and hissing around corners of buildings, seeping into every crevice and lashing out as they walked by.

And to think those dogs were out in this stuff.

"Dogs are probably froze solid," he muttered, then wished he hadn't spoken, the way his teeth turned into painful lumps of ice.

"What? Speak up," Jonas shouted. "You're finally saying a word, and of course I can't hear it in this wind."

"The dogs," he yelled.

"What about them?"

"Frozen, aren't they?"

"No, not the dogs. They're built for this. They're insulated with two layers of fur, so many hairs nothing can get through them. They curl up in the snow, stick their noses in the warmth of their own bodies, and they're fine. They just need plenty of good dog food. Protein. Fish."

The apartment was disgusting, cold as a block of ice, with no furniture to speak of. Oba shivered in the cold smelly room, kicked at a tin can, and sent a paper bag flying in its wake. He eyed the cast iron radiator, green paint peeling from the filthy coils, the grease surrounding the apartment-sized electric stove, mouse droppings, and dead flies on the narrow windowsills. He'd been in some fairly cheap places, but this beat anything he'd ever seen.

"Ain't much. But it's here or nothing. I gotta have enough money to outfit you. The bush is not a place you can take risks."

"We can't live here," Oba growled.

"You wanna sleep with the dogs, go right ahead."

THEY DID LIVE there. They hoisted a couple of mattresses up the narrow stairway, borrowed blankets and pillows from George's ex-wife who was half Indian and who frightened Oba with her snapping black eyes. She reminded Oba of the ravens that flew over the cotton fields in Arkansas, their beady eyes swiveling from left to right as their rough-throated cries tore across the sky.

With a card table and two broken chairs, a set of chipped dishes, a few pots and pans, and towels and soap thrown into the box, they took up life above the livery. They'd swept, wiped off the grease, cleaned off the chipped windowsills, and settled in. The old radiators groaned and pinged their way to life, after which Oba felt the faintest warmth coming from the iron. After a while there was a gurgling, thumping sound, more pinging, and more heat.

Oba stood with his back to the sound, his toes as if in a cruel torture device that was clamped to all of them, his teeth chattering, his knees shaking with the misery of being so cold he thought he would never warm up.

But they had a place to sleep, some food in boxes, a table of sorts, and for all of it, he felt a fuzzy relief. It wasn't that he was turning soft and thankful—it was just good to be away from the dogs and George. He knew Jonas had business to attend to, which would leave him in solitude, a luxury he craved.

He trusted no one. This Dawson Creek place was crawling with shifty-eyed, slouching individuals who appeared to be half frozen all the time. Even the little children playing in the snow wore big parkas with fur-lined hoods, the heavy bristles around their faces as if they grew there. Oba thought you'd have to be crazy to choose to live in a place like this. He realized that might mean that he himself was crazy. But did he really have any other choice?

Jonas seemed to know everyone—business owners, shopkeepers, pedestrians—and he thrived on the affable greetings of old friends. He was always introduced as "Oba, my buddy," which did nothing to endear him to the many curious onlookers who were faced with a hot, dark glare of mistrust and anger.

With all the old man's talk about money running low, it seemed as if he unearthed a cache of it somewhere in this frozen land. He bought things almost every day. First came a gun for Oba, a long sleek oiled rifle with a gleaming wooden stock. He bought knives and clothing, boots and lace-up leather shoes with heavy soles. But for a coat, nothing would do except a parka made by George's ex-wife, which required a visit to her house on the outskirts of town.

It was twelve degrees below zero and windy when they began their walk. Jonas strolled along as if it was the middle of summer, but Oba was bent at the middle, his head lowered, shoulders hunched. He hated the endless squeaking of frozen snow, bit down on his teeth to be able to bear it. He would never get used to this frozen, inhospitable world, where everyone went about their lives as if the unrelenting cold was perfectly fine and dandy.

"Look at that!" Jonas stopped, held an arm out like some explorer, seeing a rare sight for the first time. "Just take a look, buddy."

Before them lay a vista of pure white, with swells and rolls of uneven terrain, fringed by dark pines covered in a thick layer of snow like white frosting. The sun created light and shadow, blue and lavender, the drifts of snow blown into perfect sharp-edged banks, the corners perfected by the ceaseless gale.

"You can't put anything like that in a picture."

Oba said nothing.

"You see that? God created that kind of beauty for our enjoyment, and don't you kid yourself. He designed some serious beauty in this great northern country. You wait till we get into the bush, away from all of this civilization. There, it's even prettier. You get up in the morning, and you can smell the ice and snow, the trees and the frozen water. Everything is pure, clean, amazing."

"I'm cold," Oba said.

They resumed their pace and soon came to an unpainted house not much bigger than George's residence, smoke curling thickly toward the sky, rusted cars half sunk in snow, fifty gallon drums, tires, and the usual posse of barking dogs.

"Git, git!"

The figure in the door was clad in brilliant red, like an oversized, chirping cardinal, her hands clapping to emphasize her words. She watched as Jonas bent to the dogs, running gloved hands across their ears, ruffling their necks, smoothing the sleek backs. Oba watched and still couldn't see why a person would have to go through all that to greet a dumb creature who didn't know the difference at all.

They finally stepped through the steaming warmth of the small hovel, the space mostly taken up by a red-hot cast iron stove, shaped like an egg, the stove pipe leaning crookedly into the ceiling, supported by a wire at the elbow. One good thump and the whole works could tumble down and burn the shack to the ground, Oba thought. She took their coats, hung them up, and gestured toward a small kitchen.

"So you need a parka," she yelled, clearing papers and plates, cups and spoons off the oilcloth-covered table. "Sit down, sit down."

"He's going to help me build a cabin, trap, hunt and fish. That life suits me just fine, and I have a hunch it will be the same for him, eventually."

"He don't look too happy about it," she shouted. Then she placed a fiery gaze in his direction, shook a brown finger, and said he better get a new attitude or there ain't no way he was gonna make it.

"Kids like you? They end up in jail. You can't go through this world with that kind of chip on your shoulder."

"Oh, now," Jonas said, trying to take the edge off, glancing uncomfortably in Oba's direction.

Oba sat sullenly, hating this blowsy, dark-faced woman, wishing he could say something, anything, to silence her. She reminded him of Gertie, the few times she'd stood her ground when Melvin disciplined the boys, the dark eyes with so much repressed wisdom, so much contained, that only a sliver of ill feelings could be allowed to escape.

"I'm not a kid," Oba growled.

"Sure you are. You're young and got no experience. This wilderness will wring you out and hang you out to dry. You ain't got any idea of what you're going to face out there. Me and George? We did it, for twenty-six years. Those were our good years, mostly because we had to get along to survive. I did most of the work. Hunted. Fished. You go into it with that look on your face, you ain't gonna survive."

Dark prophet, Oba thought. *What does she know? Loudmouthed thing. No wonder George won't live with her.*

"Good for you," he answered, mocking her in a taunting voice.

A tirade of words were hurled across the small, crowded room, raining down on his head with all the force she could muster. He sat unflinching, every cruel barb bouncing off. He was a seasoned receiver of these words, lashed by the sturdy whip meant to shape him into responsible manhood. Years of experience had taught him how to block out the words, shut down his mind until they stopped.

She refused to make the needed parka, said there was no sense spending her time on it when he wasn't going to last a day out there anyway. She threw his own light jacket at him and ushered them out the door and out of her sight. Jonas stalked ahead and said nothing.

Oba knew he had seriously overstepped some unseen boundary but didn't care. He waited for words that didn't come.

Back in the apartment above the old livery stable, Jonas lay down and fell asleep in an instant. Oba sat down hard on a kitchen chair, his anger subsiding, slowly replaced by a sense of having done wrong.

He got up, went downstairs and out on the street, and started walking to clear his mind. He stood at a plate glass window, saw the fur-bearing animals glaring at him through artificial glass eyes. He read the block letters on the window: HAMMER'S TAXIDERMY.

He backed away, then opened the door, curiosity getting the best of him. He was greeted by the silver tinkling of sleigh bells, a sound that brought immediate memories from his childhood. His father's laughing face, the scent of the woolen laprobe, the smell of leather harness and horse sweat, the *shh-shh* of the sleigh runners gliding across snow, coupled with the dull *thock thock* of the great Belgian hooves making their way through.

He felt the sting of emotion, arranged his face quickly before anyone would notice.

"Yessir! Do for you?"

The man was short, wide, built like a workhorse, his dark skin gleaming, his black hair combed up over his head, long in the back, greasy. His deep brown eyes were curious, but certainly not unkind.

"Just looking. Curious."

"You go right ahead."

So he did. Oiled floorboards creaked beneath his feet as he went from one animal to another. So these were the creatures of the northern wilderness. Marten. Mink. Wolverine. Fox.

"No wolves?" he asked suddenly, frightening even himself, having been lost in the interesting world of these fur-bearing animals. So this was how Jonas made his money. Caught these beautiful creatures in traps, skinned them, and brought them here.

"Not right now, no. Although I've done them. Tourist trade is slow in winter."

"So trappers bring their furs here?"

"No, no. Oh no. I get only a very small portion. Most of the pelts go to the tannery. The pelt place. They're sold all over the United States and Canada."

"I see."

But he didn't understand, not really. Who would buy these beautiful furs, and for what? It seemed a shame to end the life of these wild animals who were designed to live freely in the frigid wilderness.

A young woman came through the door, bringing cold air and laughter as if she wore it like a cloak. Small, dressed in the traditional furs, pulling off a stocking cap to free her long dark hair, she moved across the floor like a sunbeam, bringing light to the dark-haired man's face.

"Papa, I need two dollars," she said in a low, husky voice, one hand unbuttoning the fur coat, another shaking the bulky cap.

"Now why would you need that?"

"Mama needs baking soda and sugar. She's making a cake."

"In that case, I suppose I'll have to supply it."

She laughed, a low tinkling sound that gave Oba chills. He stared open-mouthed, oblivious to his surroundings. He watched the man open the cash register, heard the sound of the drawer opening, saw him give her the required amount, watched in disbelief as she bent to kiss his cheek.

"Thanks, Papa."

She turned, saw Oba. Their eyes met, hers surprised, his liquid with admiration and astonishment. She moved past him as she replaced the stocking cap, her laughter quieted, the sound of the sleigh bells the only thing he could remember as she passed through the door.

He'd thought he was over all that. It had been a long time since he'd felt attraction toward anyone, and he certainly didn't expect to be so struck by anyone living here.

But she was all brightness, fresh air, and laughter, as unspoiled as the pristine wilderness they had passed on their way from New York. He berated himself for his poetic, slobbery thoughts, felt the shame rise up in him. He told himself he was a fool and always would be.

THE WINTER DRAGGED on with frequent storms and gripping cold. Jonas went to care for the dogs every day while Oba hung around the cramped apartment and thought he would surely lose his mind. He read old newspapers, hunting magazines, anything he could get. Nothing seemed satisfactory or sparked his interest. He felt his body weaken, the lack of exercise taking its toll, numbing his mind, until he lived in a blur of sleeping and waking.

It wasn't that Jonas Bell didn't try. He asked him to accompany him each morning, tend to the dogs, but Oba always shook his head, hid his eyes from the question.

"Why not? You have to get out of this room. It isn't healthy, the way you hole up in here. You could make friends. There's always skiing and snowshoeing and dog racing."

This was always met with stony silence.

Had he taken on more than he was capable of? He couldn't understand Oba's lack of wanting to be in society, of trying to make something of himself. Surely the boy had some interest, some dream, a goal or a longing to be more than this unhappy recluse.

WHEN SIGNS OF winter's savage winds abated, Jonas became restless, packing and repacking his cargo. He slept fitfully, muttered to himself, snapped at Oba about nothing.

When Oba resisted in helping with the dogs, he wheeled around and stared at him with hot eyes.

"Look. I've had patience with you. I've kept my mouth shut all this time, but I'm telling you now. If you're not planning on cooperating with me, I'm kicking you out. Out. You'll find your own way back to where you came from. It ain't natural, the way you mope around here and refuse to try. You haven't made one single acquaintance since we're here. I'm giving you this one last order, and if you won't accept it, I'm done. Finished."

He was breathing hard, his chest rising and falling, his fists bunched up. For one sickening moment, Oba thought he was going to be hit in the face with those massive hands. But instead, Jonas walked out and slammed the door behind him.

Oba flung himself on his mattress, sick to his stomach with a nameless dread. Would Jonas do it? Send him down the road to fend for himself? The thought was chilling, literally and metaphorically. He had to shake off this sense of lethargy, summon courage, and get on with life. This waiting and not knowing what he would encounter in the coming months was almost more than he could fathom. It made him crazy, gave him too much time to think.

His dislike of the stinking dogs was the only reason he refused to help. He had no inclination of befriending them, and why did he have to? One sure thing was, he'd go in his own time, when he was good and ready, not one minute before.

He rolled over and stared at the ceiling, then got to his feet, his skin crawling at the thought of helping with the dogs. For a long time, he stood in the center of the room, battling his own will and what he knew would be required of him.

But he went, eventually.

He arrived at George's door amid the clamor from the dogs, lifted his hand and knocked, and was greeted with some degree of warmth and asked to sit with a cup of coffee.

He nodded. The whole place contained the scent of fish. Raw, frozen tomcod, dried salmon like slabs of bark. The dogs ate fish, crunching bones and eyes and guts. It turned Oba's stomach every time he thought about it.

And here George was, filthy sleeves rolled up, cleaning fish at the sink, his shirt splattered with shiny fins and blood, the smell overpowering.

"Hungry?" George asked, squinting at him through layers of leathery brown wrinkles.

"I guess."

"You guess?" cackling laughter from toothless gums, mustache disguised. "You wait, my boy. Once you're in the bush, you will know whether or not you're hungry. Actually, you'll just always be hungry."

Jonas looked up.

"Don't make it sound worse than it is."

"You thinking of bailing?" This was thrown over George's shoulder as he bent to his task of cleaning fish.

Jonas cast a sidelong glance at Oba.

"No. Why?"

"Wondered what brought you here?"

"Jonas said I have to help with the dogs."

"Don't know what keeps you away, anyhow."

"I told you. I don't like dogs."

"What else gonna take you into the bush?" When no answer was forthcoming, he turned around, dried his hands on a cloth, raised his eyebrows, and repeated the question. "There ain't no other animal on the face of the earth can take the cold, move faster and better, on less fuel than a dog. They're powerful, they're light on their feet, almost tireless. They're loyal, obedient, easily trained. What's your problem with them?"

"Shut up."

"What did you just say to me?"

"I told you to shut your mouth."

Jonas stood up, told George to leave him alone, the kid wasn't hurting anyone. He came over, put a massive hand on his shoulder, which Oba skillfully shrugged off, before sliding down in his chair, the usual stance that spoke of belligerence, self-hatred, and avoidance.

The fish were fried in a huge cast iron skillet, served with potatoes fried in another, the coffee cups rimmed in grease after each bite. But it was good hot food, and Oba found himself relaxing, feeling less animosity as he listened to the two old friends swapping tales from the bush. Oba gathered more information than he was aware of, his mind absorbing the expertise these men employed spending days tracking large game. Bear, caribou, or moose. It all sounded strange, otherworldly. How could a human being hope to keep up with a large animal that knew the terrain, knew every trick to rid himself of a predator? He decided most of the stories were made up, the exaggerated tales of two old men way past their prime trying to outdo each other with their lies. They couldn't fool him.

The old man whipped up a soft cake with frozen berries in it, called partridgeberry buckle. He cut huge squares and set them gingerly into bowls, ladled cream over the warm cake, and shoved the bowls across the table.

"There you be, friends. Nothing will make you sweeter."

It was delicious, warm and moist, with bits of sweet berry flavor bursting in your mouth. He watched George with a new respect, refilled his coffee cup and forgot about the fishy odor.

"So if you know all this stuff, why don't you go with us? Sounds as if we could use you."

Oba was taken aback to see the old man shake his head, a deep furrow appearing on his brow. His lower lip trembled as he squinted his eyes.

"You have no idea, young man. No idea how honored I'd be to accompany both of you. But I couldn't keep up, wouldn't be worth anything. I'd be unnecessary weight for the dogs, a burden to you while you're building. I've had my life there, for all those years, and I'm fulfilled. The only regret I have is Gina leaving me. I know the time will come when I'll need her, and she won't be here for me."

Jonas ran the tip of his finger around the rim of his cup, his thoughts elsewhere, then looked up suddenly.

"George, you're better off."

George nodded, sighed, then spoke through trembling lips. "I still love her, really."

Oba was amazed. These hunters and their mighty tales, sitting here turning to mush about past loves. Really?

He looked from one person to another, reliving all the shame of the feelings the young woman in the taxidermy shop had sparked in him. She lived in his thoughts, his dreams, filled his waking hours with a hopeful cross between misery and exhilaration. He remembered every sound, every word she had spoken in that brief exchange, the way her hair had swung like a silk curtain, the way she'd kissed her father's cheek.

Would he always go through life without the mystery of love? He had thought he would, had put all such longings out of his mind, until the bell above the door of the taxidermist's shop had jingled, and the ray of light named Sue had appeared. Not that he had a chance, but it was okay to dream.

He felt ashamed now, the way he'd mostly stayed in the apartment after the brief encounter, afraid he would run into her again.

And suddenly he knew that he had to speak to Sue before he left with Jonas and the dogs.

CHAPTER 9

SHE DRESSED WITH CARE, HER SLENDER FINGERS TREMBLING as she pinned her white organdy cape and adjusted the belt on the white apron. Her dress was navy blue, the most favored color for a Sunday dress, her covering white as snow. Her blond strands of hair were combed carefully, made to lie in just the right angle to portray a respectful adherence to the *ordnung*. Her breath came in short, hard gasps if she allowed it, so she calmed herself by taking deep breaths.

She swallowed a few bites of toast and went to feed and dress her darling baby. She had a small powder-blue dress and white pinafore prepared for him. Diapered and bathed now, she slipped the attire over his head, buttoned the apron, and turned him on his back, smoothing the dress down over his little legs.

She let her gaze take in the sight of him, the perfect contour of his cheek, the soft black hair so much like Clinton's. She loved the dress, loved the thought of dressing her baby boy in the traditional garb, one he would wear until he was trained, no longer had to wear diapers. Only then would she sew shirts and trousers for him.

"Dear Heavenly Father, stay by my side," she whispered.

Clara was in the barn, hitching her best black Standardbred to the clean surrey. May had found her to be meticulous about the appearance of her team, including the leather harness. The buggy had been washed until it shone, the wheels gleaming with cleanliness, the laprobes shaken and hung on the line. She had oiled the harness, washed the horse with the spray from the rubber hose attached to the hydrant by the water trough.

May stepped up, holding her black church bag over her arm, the baby Eliezer in the other. Clara tried to keep up a nonchalant banter, but both felt apprehensive about May's first appearance at church in many months. As they drew closer to the Dan Mast homestead, their faces became pale and tense. Clara's freckles stood out more than ever; her nostrils flared unbecomingly.

Clara drew back on the reins, called a firm *whoa*, and stopped the carriage at a proper distance away from the barn, waiting till a young lad came to take the horse, a service always provided for churchgoers.

"Morning," he said, greeting her in the traditional manner.

"Good morning, Davey."

She alighted, handed over the reins before waiting on May, who joined her on the ground. They looked at one another, taking courage, and walked to the house. They entered the kitchen, prepared to face the unspoken curiosity, the scrutiny that was inevitable. May kept the black bonnet and light black shawl on Eliezer as they shook hands with the women standing around the kitchen, then lay the baby on the table to divest him of his outerwear.

All conversation ceased.

She turned, stood tall and brave, a slight woman with blond hair and a big white head covering, her eyes as brown and shining as river stones, a slight smile on her face, holding the dark-skinned baby with the curled hair of another race.

What was there to say?

Slowly, conversation resumed. Shy children peeped around their mothers' skirts, some stepped out boldly to stare unabashedly. One three-year-old said clearly, "*Voss iss lets mitt sollot baby?* (What is wrong with that baby?)"

Hastily, the mother bent to hush her child. Voices were silenced, mouths pursed in righteousness. Here was evidence the end of the world would soon be here. A young woman with no husband, coming to church with a dark-skinned baby, as bold as day. Someone was slipping, and it was the soft-hearted ministers with back bones akin to a wet noodle.

Some watched May with genuine compassion, quietly impressed with her bravery. A few ventured a slight smile at the tiny baby.

Clara took her place among the row of women and motioned to May. May sat beside her, grateful for her calming presence. As the opening sounds of the first hymn rose and fell, she bit down hard on her lower lip to hold back the tears. It was so beautiful, this slow rhythm that swirled around her like a healing vapor. Her throat tightened with the unbearable homesickness, the longing for her pure childhood, her parents here with this group. She remembered faces, the old bishop, the one minister, but not the younger one. There was Aaron Troyer, with Levi Stutzman beside him. Her eyes fell to her lap, afraid of seeming bold.

Eliezer squirmed, grunted, and May knew he would soon want to be fed. She felt her cheeks heating up as she imagined making her way along the row of benches, all eyes boring into her. She lifted him to a different position, patted his back reassuringly, and breathed easier when he drifted into an uneasy sleep.

Clara slanted her a look. May gave her a small smile in return. Clara leaned over and whispered, "If you wait until he starts yelling, there will be even more eyes on you."

Clara hesitated, but when he began squirming the second time, she got up as quietly as possible and sidled down the aisle between knees and the back of another bench, hoping she would not cause a disturbance.

When she reached the back bedroom, she was relieved to find it empty and an old hickory rocker in the corner with a blanket thrown over it, waiting for her to sink into the comfortable haven.

She breathed a sigh, then bent to retrieve a clean white diaper from the small, square church *kaevly* (basket). The door creaked open, a round face appeared in the opening, the mouth in a perfect O of astonishment. Immediately the face withdrew and the door was pulled shut till the latch clicked into place.

As she changed the diaper, she told herself to stay calm. In time, things might change, and if they didn't, well, then, she'd still have Clara. She would not fall prey to self-pity. Rather, she would make the best out of an awkward situation and accept the fact that she was an outcast living among her home community.

The door was pushed open again, just as she had settled herself and Eliezer had started to nurse. She pushed at the diaper over her shoulder, certainly trying her best to remain inconspicuous. A mother she did not recognize came all the way through the door, carrying a sleeping child and deposited her carefully among the bed pillows before turning her back to leave. Her hand was on the doorknob and May's heart sank even further when the woman hesitated, then turned to face her. She took a few steps, crossed her arms, and said in a voice barely above a whisper, "May Miller?"

May's head was bent, her fingers worrying the blanket around Eliezer's dark head, but when she heard her name, she looked up like a frightened dog, ready to receive the first blow.

"If folks don't talk to you today, don't feel bad. It will take time."

"Thank you," May stammered.

"I'm Erma Stutzman. John Stutzman's wife. If you ever need anything, we're over along 250."

May nodded. She wanted to thank her again, but the obstruction in her throat would not allow it. She squeezed her eyes to keep back the unwelcome tears of gratitude. She had at least one person who wished her well.

She wondered if this was how Jesus felt when He healed the leprous men and only one remembered to thank Him. The one acknowledgment was more than enough. Let them all shun her for her shame, she could carry it if she had the support of Clara, dear Clara, and now this young wife and mother.

After Baby Eliezer was asleep, she pulled a blanket off the stack prepared for this purpose, the well-meaning housewife dutifully thinking ahead. Slowly she bent her back, laid him gently on the soft *budda nescht* (floor bed), then covered him with a crib quilt, before

tiptoeing silently past the sleeping children on the bed. She was closing the door very slowly when another middle-aged woman came
through the kitchen. May watched her, eager to make eye contact,
emboldened after the encounter in the bedroom, but it was to no
avail. The woman sailed past, all rustling skirts, swinging shoulders
and heavy-lidded eyes, disapproval in her wake.

She found her seat beside Clara, lowered her eyes, and tried to
concentrate on the sermon, but her cheeks felt flushed, her thoughts
scrambled, unable to shift into a normal sequence.

*Oh God, dear Father, am I doing the right thing? Will it be
too hard to raise Eliezer in the tradition of my parents? Help
me, guide me.*

Her heartbeats echoed in her head, a dull thud threatening to
turn into a full-blown headache. She closed her eyes, tried relaxing
her shoulders, felt Clara's sleeve against her own, and was comforted.

AFTER SERVICES, WHEN the women and girls bustled from kitchen
to the extended tables, carrying the traditional pies, plates heaped
with sliced homemade bread, jellies, butter, glass dishes of pickles
and red beets, May tried to remain as invisible as possible, shrinking back against the wall in an out of the way corner, relieved to find
Eliezer still sound asleep.

She would not offer assistance, ashamed of the line of men leaning against the wall, enjoying the camaraderie of lasting friendships
through the years. Children ran underfoot, were grabbed unceremo-
niously as they flew past an alert parent.

Huge bowls of bean soup were placed every ten to twelve feet
along the tables, with spoons stacked in layers beside them. Diners
would dip spoons into the hot, buttery milk-based soup, with chunks
of bread and white navy beans swimming together. No dishes were
used, only the large communal bowl of bean soup, with spoons rising
and falling as they ate, men at one table, women at another.

Clara stood before her. "Come."

Reluctantly, May left the safety of her inconspicuous corner, followed obediently, her eyes downcast, knowing everyone was watching, judging, thinking her a loose woman, or worse. Clara walked ahead, her head held high, the set of her jaw inviting one person to say the wrong thing, overstep boundaries she had set herself. Her eyes flashed with controlled impatience, her red hair bristled, and the set of her shoulders told them all to shut their mouths and look the other way.

The heads were bent in silent prayer, after which quiet conversation resumed. But where Clara and May were seated, the only sounds that could be heard were of lifted spoons, knives buttering bread, pickle dishes passing, chewing and swallowing.

May managed to eat a sliver of bread, a few spoonfuls of bean soup, before a child of about nine or ten years old announced in a clear tone, "*Sellot schwottz baby iss un gthasha* (That black baby is crying.)"

May's face felt as if it were on fire, then drained away to an icy coldness as she silently slid off the bench and made her way through the crowded house, into the bedroom where her baby was awake and crying. Quickly she bent to scoop him into her arms, crooning as she kissed his cheeks that were wet with tears.

"Poor baby. You must have been crying too long," she murmured.

Glad to be away from the table, glad to be here in the darkened shelter of the bedroom, May let out a long sigh of relief before she laid him on the bed to change his diaper. Thankfully, no one interrupted the procedure, so she sat on the vacant rocking chair to feed him. There were no babies or small children asleep on the bed, and for this, May was grateful again, and then berated herself for being the coward she was.

Would she always go through life afraid of the community's judgment? Would she always feel condemned, talked about in hushed whispers? But what was the alternative? Life outside the Amish community would hardly be easier, the presence of a white mother with a dark-skinned baby an oddity, cause for ridicule and jesting.

She felt as if she had chosen the easiest route, but after this first bitter church attendance, she wasn't so sure. Why didn't they have mercy? Would she always be picked apart, studied under the microscopic cruelty of gossip and evil surmising? She had done wrong in the eyes of the world, and now, the conservative group of plain people were left with what the eyes could see, the evidence before them in the form of her precious Eliezer.

But they didn't know the rest. They would never know why she had chosen to leave Melvin Amstutz, and so they would always believe it was because she had possessed a rebellious, ungrateful, lust-filled heart. The only hope May could have was the reality of mercy starting in one heart, spreading to another, until finally acceptance was possible.

Clara appeared at the door, saying it was time to leave, then bustled out again. As May bundled the baby in his little shawl and bonnet, she heard the rustle of skirts, plodding footsteps that came to rest beside her. Her hands were very still, her head bent as she waited for the scathing words that were sure to come.

"May Miller."

May remained very quiet, would not raise her eyes to acknowledge her tormentor.

"I remember your parents so well. Fronie would not have wanted this."

May waited, her eyes lowered.

"But he's here now, and for what reason we don't know. I hope you'll be taking instruction right away. Baptism is necessary for the forgiveness of sins."

"Yes," May whispered.

"I am not your enemy, you know. I will pray for you." A warm hand was placed on her shoulder. Shocked, May looked up into the kindest pair of eyes she could ever hope to see. Brown, like small buttons, in a rounded, aging face, topped by a scruff of unruly white hair.

Their eyes met, an understanding between them.

"You look like your mother."

"I do?"

"You surely do. Now go. Clara's waiting."

May stumbled down the steps and out to the waiting carriage, her belief in the decision she made only a bit firmer.

The high-stepping horse was eager to go, which took up most of Clara's strength and concentration as the buggy wheels flew along the gravel road, spitting pieces of stone into the fresh growth of dandelion and wild strawberries. May clutched little Eliezer under her light shawl, kept her comments to herself until the horse had settled into a steady trot.

"Whew!" Clara shook one hand, then the other, still holding back firmly on the leather reins. "So, how bad was it?" she asked, casting a sidelong glance.

"Oh, I don't know. I don't want to complain."

"You wouldn't."

May shook her head, bit down on her lip to keep her emotions in check. "Some days it would be so easy to drown, the way my mother did."

Clara gave her a sharp look. "Stop it."

There was no more conversation till they were both in the house, a small fire built in the cookstove and the kettle filled with clear, cold water.

May took off her Sunday covering, her cape and apron, loosened the belt on her dress, before settling into the rocking chair to feed Eliezer. She felt drained, weary into her bones, overtaken by a heavy sadness she could not name.

Clara was washing up in the bathroom, humming under her breath, the same exhilaration she always displayed after driving a strong horse that had plenty of speed. May envied Clara's carefree lifestyle, the independent spirit and ability to make quick decisions and never trouble herself whether they were good or bad.

She appeared at the bathroom door, wiping her hands on a towel.

"So what did you mean about that part . . . I mean, the drowning part?"

"Nothing."

"Come on. You shouldn't just say things like that."

"I know. It's just that life is so hard sometimes, and I feel afraid for my baby. Should I simply go away, take him into the world where dark skin isn't so shameful?"

"With a white mother? How is that going to be any better for you? You have me, May. How would you provide for yourself and him? No, you have made the right decision to stay. It will all just take time."

And still May was not comforted, the lines in her forehead deepening as the kettle began to whistle, steam rising in a narrow stream to the ceiling.

Clara got down the blackened aluminum kettle she used to pop popcorn, scooped a generous spoonful of lard into it, then slid it on the back part of the range. She added a cupful of small white popcorn kernels and waited till it began to sizzle, then shook the kettle vigorously back and forth.

A bowl of popcorn, buttered and salted, steaming cups of spearmint tea, and May began to talk.

"It's not all about me, Clara. It's him. Eliezer. How will he ever be accepted? What will keep him from being mocked for the rest of his life? This may sound ridiculous, but if he grows up, how can we possibly hope he will be able to marry an Amish girl? What if he remains an outcast? He won't fit in with the Amish, neither will he be able to be English. Today only cemented the fear I always carry with me. I was thinking perhaps the most logical thing to do would be for us to return to Arkansas, where there are so many dark-skinned people. He would be free to live life among his own kind, free to choose a wife without prejudice. I often feel guilty, leaving the boys. Ammon, Enos. And especially Leviticus. If I could lay down my life for my son, I would do that, don't you think, Clara?"

"Don't even think about it," Clara ground out.

"But . . ."

"No. No. Absolutely not. You are not going back there. You are not responsible for those boys. Melvin is." She stuffed a handful of popcorn into her mouth, coughed, choked, sending a spray of half-chewed kernels all over the tablecloth. She heaved and sputtered, wiped her eyes and slurped her hot tea, then wiped her eyes again with the back of her hand. "One day at a time," she rasped, clearing her throat.

May glanced down at her sleeve, flicked off a wet, white kernel, frowned. Clara began a sputtering laugh, then threw her head back, opened her mouth and let out a donkey bray of pure mirth. May smiled, then giggled, a hand to her mouth, before allowing the rolls of laughter to come up from the confines of her stomach.

AND SO LIFE resumed for May and Clara. Spring rains and sunshine brought forth the new tender green shoots in the garden, and the red mower clattered across the yard as May walked behind it, the baby nearby on a heavy quilt, his ears covered with a small bandana under his chin.

Out by the barn, Clara had a yearling horse on a long lead rope, circling him round and round as she called out commands. May stopped the mower, scooped up Eliezer, and went to the fence to watch. The horse was still coltish, gangly, his ears flicking forward, then back, waiting for commands, tugging uneasily at the rope.

"Whoa."

On he went, without grasping the meaning of the word. Again, Clara called out, and again, he went on trotting. Over and over, this was repeated, until the horse felt the pull of the rope, and hesitated, then stopped, for which he was praised. May stood by the fence, fascinated by Clara's confidence, the way she showed calm control around the most unruly horses. Sometimes, she understood why Clara had no interest in being anyone's wife, the way she did not find it easy to accept anyone's opinion, especially about horses. Completely self-sufficient, and proud of it, she moved through life with a sense of accomplishment that was a rare thing among plain people.

And May wondered about herself. Was she, too, ready and willing to admit she never wanted another man? Would she be able to eliminate her past, shrug it off like an unwelcome cloak, cherish Clinton's memory, and love again?

Her time with Clinton had been a heaven on earth. Love had obliterated the ugliness of life with Melvin and Gertie, she had blossomed like a flower in the fullness of its time. The dreariest day had been bright in his presence. To cherish and be cherished was God's design for a man and a woman, to love with pure hearts and God's blessing.

Had God given His blessing to her and Clinton? According to her upbringing it had been adultery—she had been adulterous, a sin according to the gospel. They had never married. And here was Eliezer. She looked down into the bright, dark eyes, set well apart in the caramel-colored face, and thought, how could she say it had been wrong?

But still it tormented her, this need to be forgiven.

She looked up as a buggy clattered on the gravel drive, the horse with his head held high, wild-eyed, flecks of foam flying off his soaked body, the harness coated with it. Instinctively, she covered Eliezer with the baby blanket, turned to go back to the house.

"Whoa!"

The horse was pulled back so violently, his mouth was open, his head thrown back, as he lowered his haunches in order to stop. A man May did not recognize jumped out of the buggy, missed the step completely, and yanked on the reins one more time.

"Hey!" he called out, his florid face with graying hair sprouting from under his hat like a persimmon.

May turned.

"Is that Clara out there?"

"Yes." She hurried away, left the man standing by the fence, lifting his straw hat to scratch his head, then nod to himself as he watched May's thin form with the baby in her arms. He watched Clara with an amused expression, waiting till she unhooked the lead rope and let the yearling back to pasture.

She strolled up to him, opened the gate and slid through, eyed his horse before turning to him. "Jake Weaver."

"Yep. Hey, I hear you have a few nice Standardbreds for sale."

"Not for you, I don't."

"What's that supposed to mean?"

"Exactly what I said. Look at your horse."

"What's wrong with my horse?"

"He's scared out of his wits, he's half dead with being pushed too hard. I wouldn't sell you a horse for a thousand dollars."

Jake's eyes narrowed. He sized up his opponent, deciding he'd never seen an uglier woman. Who did she think she was?

"Ain't nothing wrong with getting some speed out of a horse. This guy here loves to run. A good crack of the whip and he's gone."

Clara said nothing.

"Aren't you going to sell me a horse?"

"No."

Jake eyed her with suppressed anger, knowing it was his Christian duty to keep his impatience in check. But he wasn't leaving before he told her what he thought about harboring that girl with the *auslendish* (foreign) baby.

Clara listened, her eyes flashing sparks like the sparks from a welder's torch, her mouth pursed into a perfect bow, her red hair bristling out from her red scarf, her arms crossed tightly across her waist.

"And another thing. What you two women don't take into consideration is the child's future. I don't see how she can ever join the Amish church. Sol's Check's Amos told me your ministers are taking the wrong stand, allowing something like this. The church needs to stay pure."

"And who is to say what's pure?"

"Well . . ."

"You know, this is what's wrong in God's world. One thinking he's so much better than the other that he can have nothing to do with the one he considers lower than himself. You know Moses had a wife from Ethiopia. So what color do you think she was?"

"Now that ain't true."

"Of course it's true. Go look it up in Genesis. Go right ahead."

He shook a finger at her. "You mark my words. Nothing good will come of this. And you know whose fault it will be? Yours."

With that, he turned, took up the reins, jerked on them before climbing hurriedly into the buggy, doing a U-turn so that the iron-rimmed wheels slid on the gravel. Clara heard the crack of the buggy whip as he sped out the drive.

She was so angry tears clouded her sight, but she took a deep breath and steadied herself. He might be one bad egg in fifty reasonable folks, she reasoned, and tried to shrug it off, feel forgiveness. After which she bent to pick up a handful of gravel and flung it in his direction. She felt justified and marched into the house.

CHAPTER 10

His time at Dawson Creek culminated in one last, frantic rush to find Sue. Too many visits to the taxidermist's shop window brought narrowed eyes from Jonas, loud explosive sounds of mirth from George. Under suspicion and teased unmercifully, he finally took the initiative to walk into the shop and talk to her father, who glowered at him with a look that did not promise anything.

"I was . . . um . . . uh . . . wondering about your daughter," he said quietly.

A grunt, which could mean anything.

"Is she here today?"

"She's never here."

"But . . ."

"Look, you're one in a line of about a hundred young men. You look like you've been dipped in Clorox, so you don't stand a chance. I mean . . ." Here he passed a hand loosely over his own jet black locks, scowled at Oba, and hoped he'd leave.

When Oba stayed and did not shy away from his steady gaze, he sighed, pushed his chair away from his desk, and said, "She's not here. She went with her two brothers into the bush. They have a trapper's cabin along the frozen river. So don't bother me anymore. She's gone."

Oba's heart sank, but he nodded and headed toward the door like a sleepwalker. Well, so much for that. He was overcome with the usual amount of crippling self-hatred, that deep and electrifying shame of his own desire.

He felt sure he was teetering on the edge of a dangerous cliff, so perhaps it was a good thing to disappear into the wilds of this vast Canadian wilderness, to get away from foolish hopes and dreams.

He berated himself for his driven search, the fruitless forays into the shop where beautiful animals stared out of glass eyes, as dead and artificial as the man who was capable of making them. He hated her father, hated the animals, wanted to light the whole shop and watch it go up in smoke.

Why had he ever summoned the nerve to ask that stupid question? It just proved quite solidly that he was strange in a way he himself didn't even really understand. The rebellion and anger Melvin Amstutz had sought to whip out of him had only entrenched the roots. He knew he hated, knew the feeling of raw, acrid anger, and knew, too, there was no power within him to stop it.

He would accompany Jonas, go willingly, but Jonas would never, ever make him like the dogs, or obey him in all that he asked. Those two old men thought they knew everything, but they didn't.

THE SLED WAS longer and wider than he'd thought. It was made of wood, the runners as hard and smooth as stone, the fronts bent up like a toboggan.

George and Jonas were in a jovial state of mind, bristling with eagerness. They brought out so many supplies, Oba thought there wasn't a remote possibility of fitting it all on the sled. Dried fish, dried strips of beef, cornmeal, oatmeal, flour, lard, tins of coffee and tea, soap, nails, a change of clothes, extra long underwear and woolen socks, gloves . . . the list went on and on. The dogs strained at their chains, yapped, whined, pawed the snow, sent up a teeth-jarring cacophony of sounds that never ceased. Jonas went on working as if the noise didn't bother him a bit.

Oba leaned against the side of the wooden shack, his hands in his pockets, pouting. They hadn't asked him to help, so why would he?

Although he hadn't counted on being ignored. He kicked at the snow, cleared his throat, coughed, but for all the attention that got him, he might as well have been a post.

Jonas and George talked as they worked, reminiscing, laughing, lashing down the immense bundle. The sled was full, up to a man's waist, bound tightly with strips of rawhide over more skins. There was room on the back for one man to stand.

Suddenly it dawned on Oba, this fact of a one-person capacity. He hoped Jonas was good at walking. Oba had no plans of using his own two feet to find his way into the wilderness.

He had always pictured himself riding on the sled. The dog's harnesses were repaired, oiled, a long string of complicated leather that looked as hopeless as a jigsaw puzzle to him. No bridles? He was used to horses, creatures put on earth to move human beings from one place to the next—big, strong, sturdy beasts who were fully capable. These spindly-looking dogs looked like mostly bones and a thick growth of hair. He could not imagine any power or speed out of any of them.

That night was spent sleeping around the rusted drum George called a stove, their stomachs full of moose steak and sourdough bread with partridgeberry jam. Oba still felt ignored. He tried to figure out why they would not include him in the planning and resented the fact that the conversation mostly centered around dogs. He didn't know the dogs' names, although he gathered the lead dog was called Eb.

It was still dark when they rolled out of bedrolls, threw on their clothes, lit the kerosene lamp, and fried eggs in the grease from the moose steaks. Oba shivered by the crackling fire and turned his face away when either one dared speak to him. This thing could go both ways.

Finally George gripped his shoulder with a gnarly hand and told him he better cooperate with Jonas, that communication was every-thing once they got in the bush. His life could depend on it. Oba looked down into the whiskered face with dark crags and fissures crosshatching the leathery skin, the stubbles of white like the coat of an opossum in the cotton fields. The eyes were brown, sincere, his voice earnest as George wished him the best.

"Your heart and soul will be restored, young man. The wilderness will have its way with you. If you don't believe in God now, you will. You will." A faraway dreamy look softened his eyes. "I'd give anything to go with you, nothing I'd love more, but I know my time's almost up, the alarm about to go off. I'd have to ride on the sled, would never be able to keep up. So good luck, my son. You'll go with God, whether you know it or not."

Oba nodded and thanked him, surprised by the wave of emotions rising up in himself and determined not to let it show on his face. He looked to Jonas for instructions. When none were forthcoming, he stood aside and watched as the harnesses were brought out. The dogs pranced, whined, all bundles of eagerness as the harnesses were buckled into place, lines snapped to the lead line in the middle. Eb was, indeed, top dog. Silver and white, with a few black undertones, Oba admitted to himself that the dog was magnificent, standing about a foot higher at the shoulder than his subordinates. His eyes were the lightest shade of blue, his tail immense, curled up over his back.

One by one, the dogs fell into place. He heard Flo, Sel, Arnie. He was fascinated by the subtle control Jonas displayed, a word here or there, a patting of the head, a ruffle of ears, always the low monotone, "Good dog, good dog. Great, old chap. Hey, buddy."

When at last Jonas was satisfied with the weight distributions, sure the harnesses lay comfortably across chests and over shoulders, he looked at Oba, decked out in his brown parka, woolen trousers, and fur boots.

"Arright. I'm on the sled. You're running alongside."

Oba held back the gasp of indignation. "Uh-uh. I'm not running."

"You wanna go along? You'll run." With that, he stood on the sled, cracked a small pointed whip, and yelled a word that sounded like *shoosh*. "Hey Eb! Come on, buddy! Up! Up! Shoosh, there."

Eb leaned into the breast strap, his feet scrabbling till the remaining six took up the effort, got in line, and leaned their weight into it. As smoothly and effortlessly as if propelled by a strong breeze, the sled slid rhythmically across the snow, as sleekly as if it were coasting on its own. Jonas held on with one hand, waved with the other.

"Hey, goodbye, George! Goodbye! We'll see you in the great beyond!"

"Yep! Goodbye. Goodbye!" he answered.

Oba looked at George, saw the glint of tears on the old man's cheeks. He swallowed.

"You want to catch up? You best move along." And with that, the old man turned and walked toward the house.

Oba sprinted down the road, past houses and cars, curious onlookers, feeling absurd, some strange clumsy creature in a fur coat floundering after the dogs. He kept his eyes averted, heard yells and the barking of dogs. Ahead of him, the road was like a trough cut into the white snowbanks on either side, his goal the broad form of Jonas hanging on the back of the sled.

He was aware of morning sun creating light and shadows, blue pockets beneath drifts, fir trees with only a thin layer of needles visible, covered with a foot of fluffy white snow. His breathing was becoming labored, his sides aching as he ran. A slow panic gained momentum as he felt himself falling behind, the sled becoming smaller in the distance. He willed his legs to produce more power, felt the snowbanks drift by as he increased his speed.

The dull *bonk, bonk* of his boots, the heavy breathing from his mouth as the sun rose into the early morning lavender pink sky. His thighs began to ache, then burn. His calf muscles knotted painfully, as the hard breaths of icy air tore through his throat. He felt saliva rise like hot bile, and still he ran, propelled by the anxiety of losing sight of Jonas. Surely he would not be so cruel, to allow him to become lost? Or would he? A grim determination raised its fist, coupled with a strange sensation that he could run forever. His breathing was still coming hard and fast, but it was no longer uncomfortable.

Exhilaration replaced anxiety. He felt free, light as a feather as his feet hit the packed snow. The dark form disappeared as the road went downhill, and Oba increased his pace, running easily now that he had gravity on his side.

A raven called. Another answered.

Now he could see the sled and the dogs beginning the climb up a fairly steep incline. Eb was leaning into his harness, the rest of the dogs flattened as they heaved the sled up over, Jonas yelling encouragement.

And Oba began the climb, measuring himself, realizing he was closing the gap, but this would be the ultimate test.

He ground his teeth with the effort. His feet slipped out from under him and put him flat on his backside, where he lay for a few seconds, his chest rising and falling. Then he pushed himself back up and took off, using all his remaining strength to stay in sight of Jonas and the sled. He had no idea how long he kept running. Once or twice he had to stop and walk for a few paces, but as the yipping of the dogs grew fainter and fainter, he picked back up his pace. He had no idea that hours had passed like that. He went into a kind of trance, nearly forgetting his surroundings, his only focus the pounding of his feet and heart.

He almost ran into them.

They were stopped on top of the hill, the dogs lying in the snow, their pink tongues dangling from their mouths, as if they were laughing at him. He couldn't stand the sight of any of them. Stupid creatures.

"Hey, look who's here! You made it."

Oba dropped to the ground, his chest heaving. He was so furious he didn't dare look at Jonas or he'd smash a fist into his bright, cold face.

Jonas laughed. He had the nerve to raise his ugly red face and roar to the sky, his wide face with teeth yellowed with decay.

Oba was breathing so hard he couldn't speak, his head bent, his elbows on his knees. He was almost knocked sideways by a hefty smack on the shoulder with an immense palm.

"You did it, Oba, my boy! You passed the first wilderness test with all colors intact!"

Oba didn't lift his head, didn't acknowledge this moronic crowing. Thought he'd lost his mind.

"You were told to run, and you ran. You didn't hold me up asking questions. You stayed in sight of me. Oh, I knew where you were. Knew you were struggling. But you did it."

The hand kneaded his shoulder with affection. Oba shrugged it off.

"Arright, let's have a bite."

Jonas reached into a pack slung across his shoulder and produced biscuits and dried venison. Oba could not remember having eaten anything tastier. He chewed, swallowed, tore off prodigious amounts with each bite, washed it down with cold tea with more appreciation than he had ever felt.

The sun slanted through the fir trees, creating blue shadows and lavender snow. The sun warmed the frigid air enough to allow Oba to open the closures on his parka, throw back the hood, and feel the cold air turn the perspiration in his hair to ice. He had a rare sense of having accomplished something that was good and right. He slanted a look at Jonas, who was half-seated against the bulky pack on the sled, steadily watching him.

"What was I supposed to do, the way you took off without me? Lord knows I wasn't staying with George," he growled.

"You've got it in you, my boy! I'm sure of that. Your stamina was impressive, especially after lazing around for so many months."

Oba shook his head, bit his lip to keep from grinning. "But that was cruel," he said, low.

"Lots more will be cruel. We're in the Northwest Territory now. There's no room for coddling. You just showed me how tough you can be, son."

So now it was "son." Jonas was not his father. His father was dead, buried ruthlessly in a plain wooden box, the clods of Ohio soil covering his body where everything had been stilled by the floodwaters he had breathed in and swallowed. He carried this horrible thought like a second skin, roiled against it even now.

"I'm not your son," he said in a forceful tone.

"No, you're not. But if you were, I'd be proud of you."

Oba didn't believe that, either. Just because he'd run like some scared mutt, loping after the cunning Jonas.

THE PACE WAS slower that afternoon, with frequent stops beside the road. Now there were no small wooden houses with rusted cars in the snow, only deep, snow-covered forest on fairly level land. The air was so fresh, so crisp, it was as if a person could bite into it. The atmosphere was constantly laced with the scent of pine tar, pine needles, dead, dried leaves from the underbrush that reached above the snow.

Tiny gray birds hopped and twittered from one seed pod to another, consuming as many as possible to stay warm on bitter nights when even the stars seemed to turn to icicles. Oba had one moment of uncertainty, thinking of spending the night out here. Jonas had never spoken of the exact procedure, what would be expected of him at a time like this.

They came to a trail that veered off to the right, marked only by a wooden slat nailed to a crooked post, the letters engraved by a torch. CASSAIR TRAIL.

Jonas gave a slight nod.

"We're here. This is where we head into the real wilderness. We'll travel till sundown, then we'll make camp. You won't run on this trail, neither will the dogs, except for downhill." As he talked, he drew a heavy rifle from its sheath and laid it across the top bar of the sled.

Oba noticed how he didn't fasten it and shivered at the thought of ravenous winter creatures plowing through snow, waiting to devour soft human flesh. The jaws of slavering grizzly bears. Ravenous wolves.

"Why'd you do that?" he said, fast and loud.

"Do what?"

Oba nodded toward the rifle.

"Oh, the gun."

He said it as if that ended the subject. Oba pressed on, voicing his uneasiness about predators, grizzly bears especially, and was mortified when Jonas laughed at him, saying the bears were still in their den, wouldn't be out till spring.

Relieved, Oba walked along, his feet kicking up powdery snow, dodging branches, throwing aside underbrush. The only trail Oba could identify was a curving path of snow through trees and briars, tall dead grass and twittering birds.

Everything was white—even the sun and the sky turned white, after a while. Oba's eyes were mere slits to protect from the constant strain of light, so he felt relieved when the orange glow of fading sunlight revealed evening's approach.

The dogs were tiring, their tongues protruding from opened mouths, their steps lagging now. Oba felt the cold begin to seep through his trousers, but his torso stayed warm inside the parka's fur. Jonas was quiet now, his shoulders slumped, showing signs of fatigue.

On each side, the dense forest stretched out. As far as Oba could see, there was nothing but trees, snow, and the whitish cloudless sky.

When the sled came to a low place, and the gurgle of water beneath a thick layer of ice could be detected, Jonas held up a hand.

"This is as good a place as any."

Oba said nothing. He had no idea how one could sleep outdoors in below zero weather, with no shelter, but he figured he was about to find out. The dogs sensed a night of rest and stood quietly, their heads hanging low enough that Jonas told Oba perhaps he'd been too hard on them for the first day out. Oba looked them over, feeling nothing, and turned away.

"You gonna help with the dogs?"

"That's your job."

"Well then, you get started on the fire."

He'd watched Jonas start a few, so he figured it couldn't be too hard. He kicked away the snow, then straightened to search his surrounding for dry brush, tree bark, anything that could easily be burned. He pushed through the soft snow on legs threatening to give way, gathered what he hoped would be sufficient kindling, found matches in the metal box he'd watched Jonas pack, and proceeded to light a fire. He was proud of the hot bright burst of flame, but it faded to papery gray ashes as quickly as it had ignited. Over and over. Oba lifted his face to look around for dead pine branches.

None. Here the pines were so healthy he supposed they never dropped dead branches, and if they did, they were buried under a foot of snow. Jonas watched but went ahead driving stakes to chain the dogs for the night.

"You done real good, Flo, you old charmer," he muttered, running a hand across the top of her head, watching Oba clump back into the trees.

This time, he found heavier underbrush, a few pine branches, and a wet, snow-soaked log. He grunted with the effort of hauling it all back through the deep snow, then began again. One by one, the matches burned away, producing a tiny yellow flame, a thin spiral of smoke, before it sizzled away to nothing. Jonas finished staking the dogs, walked over to check his progress, and jumped back when Oba leaped to his feet, swore loudly, kicked the brush and logs in every direction, tossed the box of matches, and stomped off through the trees.

Jonas watched him go, then bent to the task of starting his own fire with the available underbrush, which was plenty. You simply had to know how to do it.

Oba was too worn out physically to go very far, so he sat on a snow-covered log and wished he'd had more sense than this. He could not begin to imagine the miserable cold, the frightening aspect of a dying fire and carnivores waiting in the black shadows. So he had passed the first test, but sure had failed miserably on the second.

He blamed Jonas, justifying his own incompetence by telling him-self Jonas should have allowed him to stake the dogs, overlooking the fact he'd never wanted anything to do with them. His backside was cold. He got to his feet, watching the white of the snow change into ever-deepening shadows where the firs held their branches close to the ground. A small brown creature wallowed through the snow, disappearing behind a tree.

His eyes opened wide in alarm, and he made his way back to Jonas and the dogs, staggering in his haste. He was cheered to see the sturdy orange flames licking at pieces of pine bark, looking as if the fire would grow bigger, with sufficient heat to cook a meal. Perhaps they would keep them warm during the night after all.

Jonas was singing. Not humming low, but singing lustily, the blue veins on his red forehead bulging, his mouth open wide as the words were belted out.

Embarrassed by Jonas's unabashed confidence, Oba kept his eyes averted. The words were something about an Indian girl and the moon. He blushed, clearly uneasy with this flagrant display of emotion.

Suddenly, the singing was cut off. "Did you know my wife was raised by Indians?"

"Yeah."

"No, you didn't."

"You told me."

"Did I? Well, we spent nights like this, out here in the woods, mak-ing camp, the solitude and beauty indescribable. We had nothing but each other, our love, and the presence of God. When that all gets taken away, it leaves a big, black void that comes back to taunt you from time to time."

Oba couldn't imagine his own parents living like this. They were brought up in traditional farm life, working from sunup to dark build-ing barns and houses and working the fields, the women skilled in housekeeping duties, the sewing and cooking and cleaning. They were hard workers, but they valued good homes and close community.

"I'm glad for your company."

Since Oba did not know how to respond, he merely said, "I'm hungry."

"Right-o. We'll have us a meal."

They had watery cornmeal mush and beef jerky hard enough to break a tooth. But it was food, and it filled his stomach, although he dreamt of mashed potatoes and gravy, apple pie, a warm drink.

A shelter was built by hauling pine branches, stacking a few sturdy logs against a tree, piling them on. Snow was shoveled away and thick skins laid on the bare, wet forest floor. There were more skins to roll themselves up in.

The fire blazed, sending a cheery orange light to surrounding areas. In the firelight, the dogs lay curled in the snow, nothing visible except a lump of multicolored fur, even their ears and eyes hidden as they slept.

Jonas instructed him in the ways of nighttime preparations in the woods. You left everything on, including the boots. He could dry his socks if need be, but don't sleep without your boots.

"You have to sleep with me, so don't get all polite and prissy. We don't have much choice—we need all the warmth we can get. I sleep with one eye open, so don't worry about the fire."

Oba was asleep immediately after the weight of the skins settled over him. He was too exhausted to feel awkward about Jonas being so close.

So THAT WAS Oba's introduction to the great wilderness. From time to time, he performed well, given the circumstances, but he refused any overtures from the dogs, and refused to feed them or touch them, which was a mystery to Jonas. It wasn't natural the way he avoided them, especially Flo, the most loving and affectionate one of them all.

Jonas had his misgivings, wondering if Oba would ever change.

Oba would never forget his first view of the mountains that rose like distant blue peaks covered in white, a lake nestled in the valley beneath them, fed by a wide, strong river. Everything was covered in snow, the sun creating a myriad of beautiful hues, the sky a magical canvas of blue, cotton clouds scudding on icy breezes.

It took his breath away. For a long time, he stood on the rock that allowed him to view the valley, completely speechless. Jonas stood beside him, the dogs at his feet, watching the amazement in Oba's face.

"You mean, we're going down there?" he asked finally.

"Can you imagine how far that is?"

"I dunno. Ten? Twenty?"

"Try a week of traveling."

Oba shook his head, his face full of wonder. Jonas watched as Eb rose to his feet, stretched, arched his back, then walked over to Oba and pushed his nose against his sleeve. Absentmindedly, Oba reached down and touched the fur on top of his head, then began a rhythmic stroking, smoothing back the layer of dense hairs.

Jonas looked at Eb, winking at him before turning to nestle with Sel in the deep snow.

And still Oba stood, transfixed.

"But . . . how do we get there?"

"Very carefully, down this mountain. The trail zigzags, goes around swamps and rocky places, cliffs. It's not a smooth ride. This is unsettled land. Land that's free for the taking. If you can survive out here, you can claim the land as your own.

"But how will we?"

"You'll see. You'll learn."

Oba had seen views like this in his geography book at school, but it was in black and white. He couldn't begin to describe the colors of windblown fir trees and skies so crystal blue it almost hurt his eyes. The height and the breadth and the length of this place was simply not believable.

But here he was, absorbing the wonders of unspoiled wilderness, unable to truly and reasonably say God did not exist.

CHAPTER 11

THAT SUMMER, MAY TOOK INSTRUCTION CLASS, LEARNING the rules of conduct and the way of a Godly life. There were those who shed tears upon her arrival to show a willingness to commit to the Amish church. Then there were the naysayers who sniffed their disapproval. She should know better, they said when she was outside of earshot. She would never shake the mark of her sin as long as that child lived. *Shameful woman*, they thought.

But the ministry remained unified. Where there was true repentance, there was reason for acceptance and forgiveness, and they had no reason to believe May did not bring sorrow of her past to Christ.

She gave no one cause to gossip, or to take offense at her appearance or her conduct. Naturally an obedient person, given to a desire to please others, she was more than willing to be subject to the rules of the Amish way of life. She looked forward to baptism, the water poured on her head by the kindly bishop an outward show of her inward cleansing. A rebirth.

Still she struggled when the dark times came, which were more and more frequent as she attended services that summer. As the heat escalated, so her internal struggles multiplied, sitting in a room with other applicants, the morning sun already causing beads of perspiration to form above her upper lip. The voice of the minister rose and fell, supplying the articles of their faith. Suddenly a new thought entered her mind. Had she committed the unpardonable sin that the Bible spoke of?

The room began to spin, as a nauseating sickness grasped her, a dizziness she could not control. Her heart raced uncontrollably as a very real anxiety sank its hideous talons into her mind. She had no idea what was happening; she only knew she had to regain her composure, somehow.

She looked around, her fear mounting. Did no one else feel the power of her apprehension? The minister's voice droned on as she wrestled with the fear that pushed her to the edge of her chair. Perspiration poured from her body. She reached into her skirt pocket to find the small cotton handkerchief necessary to wipe her streaming face, her hands shaking so badly she could barely do it.

Oh dear God. Help me. I honestly fear I am losing my mind.

When, how, and why had the horrible thought entered her mind? Why couldn't she shake it?

And then, just as suddenly, she thought of having left Baby Eliezer with Clara and it seemed all wrong. She could feel, in the way mothers can, that he was crying for her. What if Clara dropped him, or forgot about him while she tended to the horses? The anxiety became all-consuming. She almost got up from her seat, fled from the drone of the minister's voice, fled from the accusations in her head, fled to her son who needed her.

She did not remember what the sermons held, could not pray while she was on her knees. Her whole body ached to hold Eliezer, feed him, kiss his forehead. She should never have left him.

Could she ever be a good mother to him? The prospect was overwhelming.

Worthless. She was worthless.

WHEN SHE WAS dropped off at home, she ran to the house and scooped Eliezer into her arms, the relief of knowing he was okay and of being able to feed him so immense that she began to cry. For a while, Clara let her be, recognizing that she shouldn't interrupt the reunion of mother and infant.

Oh God, oh God. May's thoughts repeatedly made a feeble attempt at prayer, but only rose to the roof of the room and crashed back down on her head, leaving her with an inner turmoil.

The dark times had been plentiful of late, but she never experienced this cloying fear and despair. Her beloved son ate his fill and now lay dozing on her lap, and now he seemed heavy, cumbersome, a burden.

Finally Clara spoke, brusquely, impatient with May's inability to converse.

"What is wrong with you, May? You look like a scared rabbit."

"Oh, nothing."

"Whatever it is, I hope it leaves soon. What a grouch."

May did not reply to this at all, her misery too deep to allow the forming of words. She would not eat, but sat on the rocking chair, her hands loosely in her lap, staring off into space. There was no reason for the descent into fear and hopelessness. Where was the peace she should be experiencing at this time in her life? She had no doubt about her decision, had felt the transition from sinner to one who was redeemed by the blood of Christ, and this not of herself, but a gift from God.

She retraced her steps, mentally reviewing the past months, any happening that would have caused her to stumble, to lurch off the path of hope and forgiveness. She could dredge up a few months, but after that, it seemed risky to delve into her past, given the state of her mind.

She wished she could speak to Oba, then voiced this aloud.

"What?" Clara looked up from the horse publication she was reading.

"Oh, I just said, I miss my brother, Oba. I don't know what became of him."

"You said."

"Did I?"

"Yes, you told me he left before you did. He was wild and rebellious, am I right?"

"Well, yes. Mostly ruined by Melvin's treatment of him. He did not believe in God, or so he said."

Clara considered this, then put a finger to the page, turned down the corner, and laid the periodical on a stand beside her.

"So if he did not believe in God, it's hard to tell what may have become of him. You know alcohol is often what a troubled person turns to, and it causes a downward spiral sometimes for the rest of one's life."

"Don't say that, please."

Clara shrugged her shoulders. "Only speaking the truth."

The breeze lifted the white curtain at the window, then drew it back against the window screen. The air was heavy with humidity, uncomfortable.

"It's hot," May ventured.

"You don't feel good?"

"Just . . . in my head."

"What is wrong, May?"

"When we were taking instruction, the thought of having done the unpardonable sin came clearly into my mind. Clara, how do I know I can be forgiven for my past?"

Clara pondered this for a moment, then shook her head. "The only way that forgiveness reaches you is if you keep your eyes on Christ. If you constantly think of your past, of yourself, you're going to sink."

"But what is the unpardonable sin?"

"There are a variety of interpretations. Some say it's suicide, others say it's rejecting faith. I really don't know. If the Bible clearly says all sin is forgiven if we believe, that covers just everything. Everything."

Tormented, she slept very little. Eliezer cried out from his crib, his little gums red and swollen, the pain of teething pulling him roughly from an infant's blessed sleep. May no longer felt the awful suction of crippling anxiety; she only felt an emptiness, a black void before her, the fear of falling headlong, in an abstract, unattached fashion. Like a dangling sword just out of her reach, knowing it was there, but powerless to do something about it.

She moved through her days in a fog of bewilderment, never quite understanding what had occurred, this strange thought that scattered her thoughts and pushed huge obstacles in her path.

The unforgivable sin. The power of the devil. These harbingers of doom dogged her days, followed by an intense longing to see Oba, the possibility as remote and as unreachable as the surface of the moon.

Eliezer began crying interminably, pain dulling his eyes, fevers and rashes and constant diarrhea plaguing him. May felt powerless, unable to soothe him. Clara told her he'd be fine and that May had to start taking care of herself if she wanted to help Eliezer. May found no comfort in her words. What did Clara know about babies?

"You have to eat," Clara chided, from her stance at the cookstove, sausage hissing in the heated cast iron pan.

"Who can feel hungry in this heat?"

"As skinny as you are, I don't see how the outside temperature will have much effect. A good stiff breeze would blow you away."

May said nothing, hid her face.

Clara flipped the sausages, brought a loaf of bread and a pat of butter to the table, bent to sniff the butter before wrinkling her nose.

"This stuff is strong. You know, rancid. I'm going to buy a cow, make my own butter. Idy's butter isn't kept cool enough, and by the time she finally sends that lazy Sary over here, it's half gone. I'll go to Oakley on Tuesday. The livestock auction. You may as well come with me, get your mind off your woes."

"Who's going to milk the cow?" May asked tiredly, one ear listening for the wails from the bedroom.

"Who do you think? Me."

"I milked a lot of cows."

"In Arkansas?"

"Yes. The boys and I. Leviticus was too small, but Ammon and Enos did fairly well as they grew older. I'm actually quite a good milker."

"Didn't Melvin or Gertie milk?"

"No."

But he had always been there, his greedy eyes sparkling like a ravenous vulture, taunting her. Mocking her inability to escape him, knowing she was his obedient prisoner. She should have escaped before it started, should have tried to help herself more.

It was her own fault, this smudging of her purity, the ruination of her soul. The unforgivable sin. Yes, she had chosen to be with Clinton, but her life had been stamped by sin well before that.

Clara set down a pitcher of cool tea, the sides of the glass already dripping in the high humidity. May swallowed, her stomach churning at the sight of the browned sausages. Melvin had eaten so many of them. His favorite food was pork fried to a brown crisp, milk gravy, and boiled potatoes. She could hear the pork grinding between his teeth, the wet sounds as he smacked his lips.

Clara buttered a slice of bread, cut it in half, laid a crisp sausage on top to make a nice sandwich. She took a large bite, chewed, and smiled with pleasure.

"You know, May, no one makes sausages like Dan Troyer. He did a whole hog for the neighborhood last year. If you make fresh sausage patties and process them in Mason jars, it's a quick meal. It would be wonderful to have a freezer the way the English people do, but it will be a century before the Amish will allow anything like that. Too modern, too worldly. What is worldly about a freezer that keeps food fresh for more than a year?" She snorted to emphasize her point. "Some of this stuff doesn't make sense. I'd leave the Amish if it weren't for my aging relatives. I'd simply pity them too much."

"That's a good thing, Clara," May said.

"I suppose. I was born a rebel, I think. The only thing that kept me Amish was my love of horses. I'm not much for all this plain stuff, the pious expressions and the long sober faces. They all want to appear godly, which I suppose they're all better at than me."

May thought Clara didn't know the half of it. She didn't know the darkness hidden behind coats latched with hooks and eyes—wives brainwashed in the name of "submission," persuaded a wrong was right, a husband being the head of the house, the king of his domain, and therefor getting whatever he wanted.

A deep shudder wracked her thin body.

"What's wrong with you?" Clara asked, looking up from inserting a sweet pickle into her sausage sandwich.

May shook her head.

"A chill, I guess."

"Really? You got a chill on a day as hot as this?"

May smiled wearily.

Clara looked up to find a horse and buggy coming in the driveway, the horse trotting slowly, as if he knew he had almost reached his destination, and was glad of it, the sweat on his coat darkening, the harness flecked with foam.

May's eyes were large and dark, afraid of who this would be.

Clara went to the kitchen window, raised her eyebrows, said, "Hmm. Looks like Uncle Sam and Aunt Esther."

"Oh. Should I . . . you know?"

"No. You stay right there."

"I'd rather not."

"They know you're here. It would be senseless to hide."

But May was uneasy. They never had visitors, except for Betty Weaver, who never failed to impart loads of unsolicited advice, from diaper washing to the perils of pacifiers. She was always happy to see Betty, no matter how she rambled on about insignificant matters—the happiness and honesty she portrayed was like a breath of a sweet summer morning.

She went to the bathroom to check her appearance in the mirror above the sink, noted with alarm the pale clammy skin, the deep purple circles below her eyes like bruises, her eyes dark with fear and something else she could not name. She was frightened of her own appearance, suddenly, but smoothed back the blond hair, straightened the bowl-shaped covering, and went out to the living room to meet the unknown.

Sam and Esther were in their early sixties, perhaps older, but not by much, May reasoned. Both portly, the kind of physique that spoke of ponhaus, fried eggs, and *panna kucha* (pancakes) for breakfast, plenty of mashed potatoes and custard pie. Esther was short and considerably round, her white covering smashed into odd shapes beneath her too-small bonnet. But with glittering brown eyes set in rosy cheeks, her rimless glasses sitting low on her nose, May felt more at ease. Sam was of medium height, his thick gray hair cut in a traditional bowl shape, his nose protruding wondrously from between his own set of rimless spectacles, his blue eyes almost hidden in folds of flesh. But he, too, was friendly. His whole bearing exuded kindness and goodwill.

"So this is Eliezer and Fronie's May?" Esther asked. "*Ach*, I remember you so well, a little girl, so pale haired and brown eyed. And here you are with Clara. So nice of her to take you in when you needed it."

"How do you do?" May asked politely, not knowing what else she should say.

"Well, I'm doing good. I don't relish this hot weather, but then there's not much we can do about that." She chuckled as she sat in the hickory rocker, her sides bulging from the area below the arm rests. She lifted her pleated apron to find a white square of linen to mop her glistening face.

Sam folded himself on a straight chair, hiding it completely except for the legs, fixed his eyes on May's face and smiled. "Yes, Esther's right. I remember you so well. You and Oba. Where is he now? All we ever heard was the fact that he'd left Melvin and Gertie to go out in the world."

He made a sound with his tongue against his teeth, a tsk tsk sound of saying how *shaut* it was (what a shame it was).

Clara sat up straight, opened her mouth to speak, eyes flashing indignation. But she held her peace as Sam rambled on.

"I always thought so much of Melvin and Gertie. He was one to be concerned about the drift of the church. I think that was the reason he moved to Arkansas—his concern for this settlement's growth. The youth were certainly one of the factors. He just couldn't see how all the drinking and carousing could ever be stopped and didn't want his own children to be a part of it. He was also very concerned about the young girls' short dresses and wavy hair. Always one to keep the *ordnung*, although he did it in a humble way. A *deh-mütich* (humble) man."

Esther chimed in. "And Gertie was so sweet and helpful. I remember when Jonas Erb's barn burned to the ground, I think it was in June of '33. Gertie was the one who kept the meals there, organizing, letting people know who would bring what. She was a manager, one who went ahead and got things rolling. A good partner for Melvin, who was always ambitious himself."

May cleared her throat, swallowed the sour bile that rose.

Clara sat up even straighter. "That's good if you remember those times. I'm sure what you just said is all true, but the guy spiraled out of control somewhere along the line. Oba left on account of being beaten half to death."

"No!"

This exclamation of disbelief from Sam. Esther's mouth hung open, her brown eyes popped like marbles.

"Ask May."

May shook her head, her face gone gray. Clara should not be saying these things. She had confided in her thinking none of it would be brought into the open.

"He was whipped. His back is covered in scars. May used to take care of it for him."

"But . . . surely not!" Sam exclaimed, his fingers going to his suspenders, worrying the button hole attached to the button on his broadfall trousers.

"Maybe he was disobedient," Esther ventured.

"I don't care if he was disobedient or not. No one has a right to punish cruelly. Any punishing with lasting scars is too harsh."

Through all of this, May was silent. A rousing cry from the bedroom brought her to her feet; like a wraith, she disappeared down the hallway to diaper and feed Eliezer in private.

And Clara spoke. "Things went on in that house. I don't know if May has ever revealed all of it. I have my suspicions, but I'm not pressing her. My idea of the whole situation is Melvin's ambition to make money with that cotton spun way out of control, after he knew how much he could make with those black people as sharecroppers. You know how they get a small plot to grow their own cotton, in exchange for picking the landowner's. Not much different from slavery in my opinion. This all went to Melvin's head, and he figured Oba would be subject to his every whim, and he wasn't. I remember Oba; he was a child full of energy and mischief. Always had a hard time behaving in church."

Sam clapped his hands over his rounded stomach. "My, my, he was that. But do you think May is speaking the truth?"

"I have no reason to believe otherwise. May is a good girl. She's not one who would deliberately lie to cause a sensation. She was worked hard in Melvin's house. Evidently Gertie went backwards fast, after he took her to Arkansas, especially after May arrived. She became too heavy to do much, took to her rocking chair eventually. And died of heart failure."

Esther nodded. "Yes. I remember Jonas Erbs went to the funeral with the Greyhound bus."

"Well, I hardly know what to say," Sam added, his usual jovial manner disintegrating into deep concern.

Clara spoke in her take-charge manner. "Nothing we can do or say will change anything. Oba is out in the world filled with bitterness toward the plain people, and May says he doesn't believe in God. She is terribly worried about him but has absolutely no idea where he is."

May set Eliezer down in the playpen, but couldn't quite bring herself to reenter the room with the other adults. She felt a fleeting sadness at the thought of always having to hide him, always feeling ashamed.

Clara poked her head through the door. "They want to see little Eliezer."

Without protest, her usual obedience put in place, she picked him up, smoothed the blue skirt over his chubby legs, ruffled his hair into place, and took him to the living room, where, to her relief, he was welcomed with kind eyes and no judgment.

Esther reached for him, propped him on her lap, and checked him over from the top of his curly head to his little white socks, clucking and fussing like a biddy hen.

"Isn't he something? Why May, I've heard of this little colored baby and must say I hardly knew what to expect. He certainly doesn't favor you at all, now does he? But he is as cute as a button. You must be so glad you have him to remember his father."

May nodded, tears forming. She stood before Esther, thin and tired, her hands at her side, trying to take in the wonder of this woman's acceptance. Was it a good sign? A promise of a brighter future?

"So tell me, what prompted your runaway from Melvin?"

For a long moment, an awkward silence settled across the room.

Finally, May crossed her arms, stepped backward to lean against the doorframe, and spoke in a tight voice. "I'd rather not talk about it."

But Esther persisted, shifting focus slightly. "What was the father's name?"

"Clinton Brown. The son of a sharecropper. We became friends."

"But why did you leave?"

"It . . . it seemed like the right thing to do, at the time. I mean, I was guilty, but . . ."

"Yes, well. I feel sure you will see to it that this little one is brought up in a loving home, in the Lord. I hear you're joining the church, for which I was so glad." Esther's smile was genuine, her eyes kind.

Sam watched Esther with the baby, who was cooing and gurgling as she spoke to him. His eyes radiated pride in his good wife's way with the babies.

Clara caught May's eye, raised an eyebrow, and smiled. *See?* She seemed to be saying. *Not everyone will always be against you.*

Clara brought a bowl of buttered popcorn to the kitchen table, set out glasses of tea, a tray of Swiss cheese and saltine crackers. She was greeted with enthusiasm as she held up a fresh custard pie from the cooler, brought plates and knives and forks.

The snack on that hot evening was a welcome respite, an evening breeze springing up as the sun slid behind the pine trees to the west. Birds called their babies to their beds, anxious to have their fledglings in a soft place for the night. The custard pie was polished off with delight, the only aftermath a small pile of crumbs in the center of the plate. The birdcalls reverberated through the tiny kitchen, suddenly seeming even smaller with the bulk of two large people enjoying a social visit.

"Listen to those birds," Esther commented.

"I think the pine trees are a safe haven for many of them. They are alive with birds in the morning," Clara said.

"Birds are created to bring us cheer," Sam said, smiling as he leaned back in his chair, his feet comfortably thrust beneath the table.

"Which May will need in the coming years," Esther said wisely. She leaned forward, laid a plump hand on May's thin knee, gave a small reassuring pat. "My dear, when people say cruel things, always remember that they don't understand. They were not in your shoes, not once, so they have no reason to judge. And the birds will always sing."

May nodded, her heavy-lidded eyes downcast, too choked up to say anything at all.

When they took their leave, Clara flopped haphazardly on the couch, one leg thrown over the cushions, in the most immodest fashion. She laid her head on the back of the couch and said, "Angels. Like fat angels straight from Heaven. What saints! What absolute salt of the earth."

"But do you suppose they meant it?" May asked, as she gathered plates and glasses to the edge of the table.

"They're as genuine as can be. I always knew they were loving people. Their children are the same way." Clara stopped, looked at May, who had her back turned. "May, don't let the devil get you down. I know you've been wrestling with something, the way your natural energy for life has dwindled. You don't seem to have an enthusiasm for anything. Care to talk about it?"

Almost, May buckled.

She could feel her heartbeats increasing, the thought of pouring out her deepest, most shameful secret. Perhaps she was even putting Clara's wellbeing in jeopardy by allowing her to house the vilest of sinners. It was her fault, somehow. Clara would not have spoken ill of Melvin, except for May's own reports. She needed to stop blaming Melvin and Gertie for something God could very well view as her own sin.

The unforgivable one.

CHAPTER 12

By the time they'd gone a third of the way down the face of that mountain, Oba had felt weak with fear so many times he lost count. The trail was so narrow there were only inches on each side of the wooden runner, with an ice-covered rocky cliff rising up on one side and a steep drop-off on the other. Snow clung thickly on every available surface, in crevices of rock, on twigs and branches, fallen logs and piles of rock.

The dogs pricked their short triangular ears forward, whined, put their noses to the crusted snow, but never once refused to go places Jonas asked of them. Sometimes that meant going straight down, at an incline so steep it took both of them to hold the sled back, digging in their heels and hauling back with all their weight, heels dug into the snow like a balking horse. The sled inched down over, teetering on the brink, sending small snow sprays whirling into the distance like angels' wings waiting to convey their spirits.

Oba didn't think at these times about whether he believed in God or not. He was so petrified, sure they were all going to die, that he had to rely on something, anything, and so he began silently praying without even realizing it. He felt that they were constantly hovering between life and death. He would surely lose his mind if he cared too much, either way, so he didn't allow himself to think about it. With the dogs all bunched up in a tangled mass of fur, harness, and slipping feet, the sled at a dangerous sideways position and both men hauling back, he could only depend on instinct. He clung to the load when a strap broke and sent Jonas into the edge of a hard rock, his face scrunched up in pain and outrage. Tree branches whacked his face like whips. Without Jonas's strength behind the sled, it lurched and wedged itself between two rocks, jerking all seven of the dogs backward or sideways on their haunches, the lines pulled taut.

Jonas ran a hand over his red, irate face, looked at Oba and said, "Find a pole." Curt, hard words bordering on anger. Oba took one look at the seriousness of the situation and walked back up the trail, fast. To get to a tree or a fallen log required a steep ascent, through heavy snow, pulling himself up by one tree that grew erratically out of the steep incline, then another. When he finally located the tip of a sprawling, uprooted tree, he was soaked with perspiration, his thighs burning with fatigue. He kicked at the snow, uncovered a thin pine tree, then got out his hatchet and whacked at branches till he had a fairly long pole, devoid of any growth. Heaving it out of the snow, he began the downhill descent, his hand wrapped firmly around it.

When he came within sight of the sled, tilted at a a a crazy angle and wedged like a cork, he found Jonas kicking branches off a fallen tree, a small fire crackling where he'd cleared snow. The dogs were lying where their harnesses pulled them, curled up and taking a rest.

"What's with the fire?"

"We'll take an early break. I don't like the looks of those clouds. If we don't keep our strength up, we won't be able to dislodge this thing."

He dug around in the tin box that held their cache of food, melted snow in the cast iron pan, added salt, cornmeal, and a bit of flour, stirred in bacon grease and bits of dried beef, until a thick, flat pancake bubbled, which he flipped in three pieces and cooked on the other side. They ate it steaming hot out of the pan, burned their tongues and scorched their fingers, but Oba devoured it. He had no idea how they would untangle the dogs and sled lines, but he could see the wisdom in Jonas stopping to rest before they sorted it out.

Oba wouldn't have noticed this, but out here there was very little time to think of himself. Oba Miller was not that important anymore, his quick rebellion that surged through his veins at the smallest request from Jonas not always noticeable. Every hour was a serious challenge, one that required all his strength and concentration just to survive.

Jonas rinsed the pan with melted snow and packed things away before scanning the lowering sky. He scratched his chin, assessing, then instructed Oba where to insert the pole and got the dogs on their feet, cracked the whip, yelling, "Mush!"

Bravely, they flung themselves into the traces, scrabbled for a foothold, zigzagged to gain leverage, and flipped the sled neatly on its side with a grinding, cracking sound of wood on rock. Jonas hopped up and down, hollered and carried on, blaming Oba, the dogs, these rocks, and all of British Columbia.

There was nothing to do but begin the tedious task of unloading, pushing the sled across the dangerous terrain, and reloading. It was a daunting prospect, but with those clouds rolling in from the northwest there was no time to lose. Oba bent his back and went to work.

He paused long enough to take a deep breath. The air had taken on a strange yellowy sheen, with a raw odor like copper, the way a penny smelled if you held it in the palm of your hand for any length of time. He wondered about this, but seeing Jonas in his mood, he decided against questioning him. The sun was only a blur behind the increasing clouds, turning the bright day into a colder, darker version, an ominous tinge to the frosty air.

The insertion of the pole beneath the left runner was all it took. A mighty heave, calling the dogs at the right moment, and the sled was upright. Now to carry everything across the rocks and back on the sled. It went quickly, each man hurrying, a feeling of urgency as the afternoon wore on.

"I hope this trail levels out a bit. We're gonna have to make camp if it starts to snow. The thing is, we're not in a good position for wind." Jonas was speaking in a serious tone, watching the sky. He didn't mention the danger of avalanches, the deadly giving way of thousands of pounds of snow that gained momentum as it began its descent down a bald mountainside, turning into a vicious juggernaut as it gained speed.

"So what do we do?" Oba asked.

"Try to get as far down the mountain as possible. But going too fast could send the dogs and sled down over. So we'll take it careful."

Oba walked along, his eyes trained on the lead dog, Eb. You really had to hand it to that fellow, the way he seemed to pick his way over anything, lean into his traces to pull when there was a steep incline, or pick his way downhill with skill and confidence. It seemed as if dogs were more loyal than horses. Some horses would balk, throw themselves, resist dangers like this, having more common sense than their owners. But Eb seemed to be leading the way, not Jonas. Could dogs take command and go with their gut feelings?

Eb trotted now, the trail winding around an outcropping of rock, leading Flo and Sel, the two females who were right and left of him. The sled made a hissing sound as it flowed smoothly, the dogs' feet making hardly any noise at all.

Two dogs were named Jack and Buck, but he wasn't sure which was which. Then there was Sac and Arnie. Eb was magnificent, though. He was larger, stronger, than any of the others, although Jack came close. Buck was rangy looking, a bit goofy, sometimes leaning left when he should have gone right, but Jonas said he was a young dog.

The air was turning colder, the wind increasing. There was no place wider than perhaps a double width of the sled, with increasing jumbles of rock. The world below them appeared to be closer, the great swath of mountains covered in white, with jagged gashes of dark pines, a frozen lake, windswept, far below, a winding river that fed into it.

"Why aren't we making more progress?" Oba asked worriedly.

"Because this trail goes up and down, doubles back and winds around, so that you put in three times the distance. All we can hope for is a bit of widening of the trail. A nice outcropping of rock."

Hard bits of driven snow struck Oba's face. He reached back to pull up his hood, realized the value of the fur rim that circled his face. The wind bore down with a relentless force, sending snow squalls flying across their vision.

"Eb, watch it there. Oba, get in line. Our visibility will soon be cut off and we'll have to stop. If we could manage a bit of space . . ."

His words were cut off by the howling of fresh gusts of wind, turning the world into oblivion, a wall of white snow flying in a thousand directions, churning up even more snow as it ravaged the side of the mountain.

Just like that, Eb brought the journey to a halt, stopped in his tracks and refused to budge, his owner knowing all too well what this imposed. No matter the inhospitable terrain, the location of the camp, here was where they would stay.

They measured the approximate distance to the edge of the cliff, then kept their gear toward the bank away from it and spread a tarpaulin from the top of the loaded sled to the ground. Jonas worked with the dogs, loosening buckles, chaining them to the sled, fed them their allotment of frozen fish, while Oba cleared snow from beneath the makeshift lean-to. With a fire crackling away, food in their stomachs, and a steaming coffee pot set on the fire, Oba experienced a sense of what he could only describe as almost happy.

The wind and snow whipped away outside, but with a layer of it holding down the tarpaulin, the fire on the outer edge, it really wasn't too bad.

The dogs burrowed into the snow, curled up in little bundles, and went to sleep, protected by their outer layer of fur and dog hair.

Jonas, however, was as touchy as a cat in a bad mood. He was not happy with this arrangement, the way they hung on the side of the mountain. He was thinking of avalanches and plunging over the side of the cliff. He scowled at Oba's cheery face and asked why he was so happy, now that he was stuck in a snowstorm on the edge of a cliff.

"I'm glad we have shelter and a fire is all," he growled.

"Yeah, well, I don't want you stumbling off the side of the mountain when you go out during the night. Or any other time. You won't be able to see a thing."

Oba nodded, thought it very odd that Jonas was the sour one, while he found himself oddly oblivious to dangerous imaginings or the fact that anything had gone wrong.

"You know what? We have the rest of our lives to get where we're going. What does it matter if we sit here for a week?"

"Huh. You have a lot more life left than I do. I wanna build me a cabin somewhere along that river. It has to have a bit of a view, plenty of trees. We'll need trees to build it."

"You're not joking?"

"Why would I be?"

The wind roared all that night and into the next day. When the storm finally abated, the eerie calm jangled Oba's nerves. It was hard going for the dogs, the way they floundered through deep snow, but with the trail mostly downhill, they were pleased with the distance they covered.

Oba was in awe of Eb. That was some dog, he grudgingly admitted. He thought of the tick-infested hounds that lolled around the sharecroppers' houses, lazy and grouchy as wet hens. He'd always hated them, the way they bared their yellow teeth and looked at him with all that red showing from the undersides of their eyes. He'd never expected to feel this amazement for a dog. Sometimes when Eb stood on a small hill and looked out over the valley, his tail curled up over his back, his head up and ears forward, he was beautiful. There was no other way to describe it.

WHEN THE TRAIL widened, leveled out, and the greatest part of the mountain was behind them, they celebrated by baking a cake of sorts in the covered Dutch oven. They heard water, birdsong, smelled wet stones and mud, stopped in a copse of birch and cedar to make a camp, stayed for three days, washed clothes and themselves, plunged into freezing water and soaped their hair, their weary bodies, shaved, and brushed their teeth. Or Oba did; he was never sure if Jonas owned a toothbrush.

Jonas went out with his shotgun and returned with three ptarmigans, the birds plucked and broiled on a spit, salted and peppered until the meat fell off the bones. Oba could not remember the taste of anything quite like this. He tore off the tasty flesh from the bones. Jonas was tossing the bones to each dog in turn, but Oba noticed that Eb was watching only Oba, hoping to receive a token of his affection.

He glanced over, laid the bone on the edge of his plate. Jonas watched this dance of resistance from Oba, knew Eb was too smart to beg, wouldn't whine. When most of the meat was eaten, Oba had a nice stash of bones on his plate. Slowly, he set the plate in the snow beside himself, glancing sideways at Eb.

Jonas laughed to himself, but knew he'd ruin the delicate balance between the two by making fun of Oba, who was obviously being bullheaded.

Oba got up, stretched, yawned, looked at Eb in the firelight, who returned his gaze steadily, his beautiful ears two perfect triangles of attentiveness. Oba looked down at the plate, slanted a wary look at Jonas.

Jonas lifted his chin in Eb's direction. "Go ahead."

Oba hesitated, then walked over to Eb with the plate, took one bone between his thumb and forefinger and held it up high. Eb sat very still, waiting.

"Can you jump, Eb?" Oba asked quietly.

Eb got to his feet, pranced. All the other dogs did the same thing, whining now, eager for this treat. He had meant to give one to Eb and toss the rest, but how could he do that? He turned to Jonas, self-conscious with this newfound affection, not quite knowing what to do with it. Jonas grinned slowly, told him to give them each one.

"I never did this, Jonas. What keeps them from taking off a finger?"

"Hold one end, offer the other."

Quickly, Oba did this, then turned away. He felt silly, stupid. Why would he worry about pleasing a dog? They were just dogs, and he'd told Jonas he hated them all, which was the truth.

But in his own defense, things were different out here. He couldn't explain the difference, but every day, every moment contained entire books of feelings and thoughts, fear mixed with excitement and challenges so daunting you sort of went through your days pressed to the extreme. Courage was mustering up enough guts to do what had to be done, but this was more than courage. You had to stay on top of failure, really. Failure to be alert, to gauge timelines and distance, hunger and thirst, danger and safety, it was all rolled together in one element that brought a deep abiding gratitude for the warmth of a fire, and yes, the admiration and appreciation of a good sled dog. The difference a sprinkling of salt made on a bland piece of meat. The bulk of another human being to share the warmth of robes and sleeping bags, in spite of uncleanliness.

"Dogs are begging for your affection," Jonas observed.

"Sel isn't."

"Why is that?"

"She doesn't trust me."

"She doesn't know you."

"It's not that. I kicked her when we were back at George's. When I, you know, didn't want to be there."

"Do you want to be here now?"

"Where else would I be?"

"Good question."

"How long do you plan on traveling?"

"Well, spring comes late, but I've seen some signs. I figure if we head out to the lake in the next day or so, follow the river till we find a suitable spot, it'll be about right. We need the frozen ground and the snow before the mud and the black flies and mosquitoes arrive.

They're pure torture till you get used to them. Mud is a seasonal hazard, believe me."

Oba plunked himself down by the fire, stared into the gently leaping flames. Was he willing to spend his life away from civilization? Would this lifestyle be permanent? His childhood in Ohio, the transition of losing his parents and moving to Arkansas and the disastrous results, all seemed far away, a remote area in his life that had no consequences at all.

His look became dark, brooding, a scowl taking up the good humor of a moment before.

Jonas watched the young man's face, wondered what caused the change of expression. Tonight he'd displayed an interest in the dogs, but would he remember tomorrow? Over and over, Jonas told himself to take a day at a time, allow him enough rope to trust him and the dogs on his own.

"Did your parents love you?" Oba blurted out, quite unexpectedly.

"Oh yes."

"How do you know?"

"It wasn't spoken, but we knew. Home was a good place."

"Yeah, for me, too."

The fire crackled, a log fell, sending a shower of sparks skyward. Eb stood up, his hackles raised, a low growl coming from his throat. Far away, a wolf lifted its nose to the night sky, gave off the undulating call of the Northwest Territory, a call of the wild creatures who respected and feared that sound. The call died away, only to be taken up again, more voices chiming in until the hairs on the back of Oba's neck stood up, goose bumps running up and down his spine. Again the call died away, the wilderness eerily still, as if it held its breath, waiting for the next wave of lonesome sound, a sound of longing, or sadness, a strange desolation coupled by the announcement of superiority. It seemed as if the wolves howled their reign over the wild territory, let every creature know they were to be acknowledged.

"Don't you ever lose dogs?" Oba asked unexpectedly.

"No. They hold their own."

Jonas was seemingly unmoved by the wild howling of the wolves, although Oba took notice of him getting to his feet to throw more wood on the fire.

THEY TRAVELED FOR five more days before Jonas halted the dogs, held up a hand, and said that forested hill was where they would build. The river ran strong where the current was too fast to freeze over, the ice a foot thick on the quiet stretches. The river bottom was covered in round stones, beneath the layer of snow that blanketed the entire countryside. Snow-blanketed mountains rose all around them, and behind them the majestic blue sky. It was breathtaking.

In Ohio, as a small boy, there had been no mountains, only rolling hills in some areas. After he left Arkansas he had seen mountains, plenty of them, but nothing came close to these jutting peaks. They reminded him of the ragged edge of broken dishes—huge, dangerous-looking craggy peaks that stirred his blood. He wondered how far a person could go up before he perished in the cold and thin air.

How had the mountains come to be there in the first place? How long had they been there, and what was their purpose? This world of cold and snow, of raw beauty and dangerous peaks, instilled in him a sense of awe, a worshipful desire to understand. How could God drown his parents and also create this beauty? Who would ever be able to figure it out? He no longer denied God's existence, the way he had in Arkansas, but he still couldn't see how a loving God could take his mother and father away from him.

SPRING BROKE THE ice on the river and brought soft breezes that sighed through the fir trees, snow melting into soft rivulets that dripped from the bare branches. Birdsong was an explosion of sound as the dark of night gave way to purple and lavender streaks in the east, the time when Jonas was bent over the cooking fire, stirring the daily pot of oatmeal, the stuff he called porridge. Oba was thoroughly sick of it, but knew better than to complain about any food set before him.

They slept in a makeshift shelter and spent their days felling strong, tall trees that were in abundance everywhere. They dug a foundation, hauled river gravel, leveled off a spot among the trees, packed down the soil, and laid the floor. The log walls went up slowly, with Jonas being meticulous about the length and size of each log and how they fit together.

Some days Jonas took his gun and walked off to find meat, telling Oba not to work on the cabin until he returned. Oba refused to go hunting. He knew he wouldn't be any good at it, would just scare off any game. He could feel Jonas becoming impatient, could visualize the wild game running off as he slowly lowered his gun, having ruined their chances of getting a good meal. He was stupid, and it was only a matter of time before Jonas would realize it and start shouting at him the way Melvin had.

To lift a rifle to his shoulder, sight along the barrel, take aim, pull the trigger, and actually hit the target required far too much skill. It required experience, finesse. Hunting was simply too intimidating—just the idea of it made him feel weak and incompetent.

So on the days Jonas went hunting, Oba sat around camp and pouted, watched the dogs, made a pot of coffee, stared into the fire, and remembered May. He longed to talk to her, take in her sense of calm. She was so centered, so sure of her obedience, so sure of her faith and purpose in life, while he wobbled on the outskirts of his own existence, propelled by anger and refusal to comply. He needed to look into the steady brown of her eyes, listen to the soft, low voice, make him feel everything was right with his world. Would he ever see her again?

The fire crackled, threw off heat, creating color on his face, setting the coffee to boiling. The dogs sat, watched Oba, their eyes squinted at him, a few of them circling the trampled area on their chains. Sel and Flo were asleep, their noses buried in the thick fur at their sides.

He drank cup after cup of coffee, till his nerves were so taut his teeth were on edge. He thought of hitching the dogs to the sled, following the river, exploring the waiting wilderness, but he knew it would never work. Jonas would disapprove. Or would he? Jonas urged him to try new things, told him to drag logs on his own, harness the dogs, shoot a rifle.

So no, it wasn't Jonas, he supposed, but his own unwillingness to face his fear. His fear of everything. His heart dropped at the thought of making an attempt to harness the dogs to the sled, to set out on unknown terrain.

He felt trapped, on edge, so he paced around the perimeter of the camp as the dogs watched his every move, their ears alert to the voice that would ask them to walk with him. He'd made some progress in his relationship with the dogs, but he still kept them at a distance. He stopped his pacing in front of Eb and stared him down before continuing his walk.

The sun was warmer, the shafts of sunlight that stole between branches a friendly harbinger of things to come. The snow was melting underfoot, slushy and wet, creating a brown smear of wet soil where his footsteps circled the fire.

He stopped when he heard a strange buzz.

He looked into the forest surrounding him, stepped away to see down to the river. He saw nothing out of the ordinary, and still the buzzing continued.

He felt his heartbeat accelerate, the fear of the unknown turning his mouth dry. He realized the buzzing sound was in the sky, an airplane, at the same moment Jonas came crashing through the trees, his face red with exertion, his eyes wild, panting like a dog. He slid to a stop, threw down his rifle, and shouted at Oba, pointing to the sky, where the steady buzz had turned into a droning sound that steadily increased.

"It's Alpheus! Alpheus!"

Oba said nothing, merely stood with a hand to his forehead, palm down, his eyes squinting in the sun as the aircraft came into view. Jonas ran past him, thrashing through underbrush and wet, soggy snow, slipping and sliding, his arms flailing like a windmill.

The airplane dipped lower, circled, the drone turning into a roar as it circled again. Oba couldn't imagine where the plane could possibly land, but the pilot must have known the area well. Oba gasped, sure the plane would hit the treetops, wrecking the delicate gray wings and hurling the pilot to his death. But then the plane found open water, extended the floats, landed as easily as a butterfly on a blade of grass. Oba stood in disbelief, his mouth open as Jonas caught the rope thrown to him and watched the plane pull alongside the pebbled bank, the motor stilled completely, before the door was thrown open to reveal a pilot not much bigger than a child, a yellow bill cap on his head, his grin wider than the river.

Oba leaned against a tree, watched all the handshaking and back-slapping, the shouted words of greeting, and felt an outsider, yet again. He took a thorough dislike to the scrawny little man named Alpheus, his airplane, and his proud ability to land that craft on a very small expanse of water. He held his eyes to narrow slits, turned away, and left them to all the stupid backslapping.

Really, what was wrong with a quiet hello? Or a simple handshake, without all that senseless ruckus?

CHAPTER 13

As the days turned into weeks, May's torment worsened, till Clara herself realized something had to be done. She was obviously enduring a torment of the mind, some sickness of her nerves, some odd malady she felt helpless to heal.

May could not fall asleep now without the aid of comfrey tea, and when she did drift off she was rudely jerked awake by the force of her anxiety less than an hour later, to lie awake as waves of panic overtook her. She suffered this all in silence, trying always to present herself to Clara with some semblance of normalcy. She dressed in her neat pleated dresses and aprons, her white bowl-shaped covering on her blond head, caring for Eliezer as best she could.

Clara saw the lack of loving care, the ease with which she left him on the floor with his toys, the amount of time elapsing before she took notice of him. May would sit for hours, a vacant look on her face, rocking and staring into space. When she became so thin her dresses hung from her shoulders like a sack, Eliezer cried with hunger and the breastfeeding stopped.

Clara boiled milk, diluted it with water, added blackstrap molasses, and trained him to drink from a bottle, with May watching empty-eyed. Clara took her to town for a visit to old Doctor Hess, sat with her as he examined her thoroughly, found her to be underweight and prescribed a packet of pink nerve pills to be taken three times a day. May swallowed them dutifully, and continued to decline.

After that, May refused to attend services, dropped out of instruction class, and became a recluse, hidden away in Clara's house, her eyes large and frightened, full of fear and something Clara could not name.

Betty Weaver came to visit, then Erma Stutzman, but neither one knew what to say. They had seen "baby blues" and plenty of it, but this was not ordinary baby blues. They brought over pies and cookies and cajoled her into taking little nibbles, offered to watch Eliezer for a while so she could get some rest and Clara could get a break. Usually May shook her head, mumbled that she was fine.

It was during a hot August night that Clara kept dreaming of a baby crying in the distance, over and over. Confused, she awoke to the sound of Eliezer's insistent cries that kept increasing until he was quite hysterical. Alarmed, Clara swung her freckled legs over the side of the bed and hurried to May's bedroom to pound on the door.

"May! May!"

When there was no answer, she turned the knob and went in, lifted the sobbing, perspiration-soaked baby from his little wooden crib, and hurried to the bed, only to find it empty. For a moment, Clara honestly thought she might faint from fear, the thought of not having done all she should bringing a sickening remorse.

She laid the screaming Eliezer on the bed, struck a match on her thumb nail, and lit the kerosene lamp, then lifted the baby to her shoulder, patting his back, saying, "Shush, shh. Hush, little one."

She went to the kitchen to heat his milk and trembled in her slippers. Where was she? How did one go about getting help if one was saddled with a screaming infant? She coached herself to think sensibly, to take one step at a time. Give the baby his bottle, get him back to sleep. Get dressed, grab a lantern, and go for help at the nearest neighbor. Don't worry about barking dogs or stinking skunks hiding in the fencerows.

She pounded on Simon Weaver's door. When there was no answer, she went around to the back where she hoped was the bedroom window, almost stepped on a cat or an opossum, she couldn't be sure, and tapped on the window. She was rewarded by the sight of parted curtains, a bushy head emerging through the window and a guttural, "You scared the daylights out of me."

Clara didn't apologize. "I need help. May's missing."

"What do you mean, she's missing?"

"I can't find her. She was not well. Her nerves."

"Oh, that. Well, give me a minute. I'll get the boys."

"I have to get back to the baby."

With that, the screen was put back in the window, and Clara ran, her lantern swinging like a huge firefly through the night.

SIMON AND HIS boys showed up soon after Clara returned to the sleeping Eliezer. The flickering yellow wick on the lantern revealed Simon, his hair combed into obedience by a hasty attempt at decency and stuffed under his straw hat. Clara had never much noticed Simon's three boys, but now they loomed in her home as large as their father in the circle of light.

Clara told them she had no idea where to begin, but likely around the buildings. No, she had not been well. Clara was afraid for her, having dropped out of instruction class, succumbing to the voices in her head telling her she could not be forgiven. She had not been eating, needed help with the baby.

Simon took this bit of news very seriously. His eyes were wet with tears in the lantern light, and he shook his head in sympathy, before turning to the boys.

"John, you and Dan go search the barn. Take Clara's light there. Andy, you start the surrounding fields to the east. I'll take the side behind the house. If we don't find her within a half hour, we'll have to get more help. Not sure we want the cops involved just yet."

It was the longest thirty minutes of Clara's life. Frantic, she paced the house, went out on the porch, and back into the kitchen. She tried to pray, but her throat was choked with fear. She had never experienced fear of the unknown quite like this. Over and over, she felt the pressing need to know, to know this moment where she was. Someone had to find May, now.

When the men returned without May she was honestly afraid she would faint from disappointment and despair. Where had she gone? And why? Surely May would not think of doing anything that would leave little Eliezer alone and helpless in the world.

One of the boys was sent to a few more of the neighboring farms. The widow Annie came to sit with Clara, a woman of sorrow and rife with empathy. When Eliezer awoke, cried out from the bedroom, it struck Clara all over again. They might never find poor, troubled May, especially if she did not want to be found.

SIMON WEAVER'S ANDY was no stranger to helping out in the neighborhood, being a kindhearted man in his late twenties, living at home, helping his father on the large farm of 200 acres and more horses and cows than most Amish farms. There was plenty of wooded land, and then there was land that lay too close to the pond to be tillable, but there was still over a hundred acres to be planted and harvested. With the farming practices of the late 1940s, this endeavor was labor intensive, forking loose hay on tow wagons piled high and bulging, chopping cornstalks by hand after pulling off the ears of corn, still wrapped in the dry brown husks of autumn. A quick flick of the wrist, two pulls on the husk, and the golden ear was tossed on the wagon bed. Cows were milked by hand, and with a herd of twenty-one, Andy and his brothers were no strangers to hard work.

He was tall, husky, tan, and dark-haired, his eyes wide and flat, squinty-eyed, with a prominent nose and a wide smile. The smile was from his mother's side, everyone said, the way Kettie welcomed, spoke, laughed, and befriended everyone she encountered.

He'd been betrothed at twenty-one, to the county's rarest beauty, a girl with flashing good looks, an hourglass figure and fully aware of it. She'd broken off the engagement at the eleventh hour, leaving him awash in a river of loss and longing that still haunted his days if he allowed it. Some said they never thought Andy would show that wide smile again, and he didn't for a length of time. Eventually, though, the smile would make an appearance, like the sun creating a streak of light in the dark clouds, but the pain and sorrow of losing Doris never quite left his eyes.

He'd seen May in church, marveled at the talk that filtered through every conversation. She didn't look the type. Mysterious, she was. The way she was so small and pale, so gentle-eyed and timid. The opposite of Doris, for sure. And yet, here was this brown-skinned baby, proof of her promiscuous ways. From time to time, he wondered about that. Was it true that the child was hers? Well, he'd laid it all aside, May and her past, the things said about her, not wanting to get tangled up in the suffocating vines of love again. The whole thing was far too unpredictable.

When he was awakened with the news that she was missing, he couldn't help but wonder if she'd run off to go back to her world again, leaving the baby in someone else's care. But then Clara had said she was troubled in some way, although no one was saying exactly what that meant. He guessed it couldn't be easy trying to raise a black baby in the Amish community, especially without having been married. That would probably be enough to "trouble" anyone.

He had a feeling she was troubled in the way women described other women as having "nerve trouble." There were mental hospitals for the ones who lost their minds—they were housed in wards and given some kind of treatment that made them forget. Only rarely had he heard of an acquaintance being taken to one of those places, and he found himself hoping May would not wind up there. Sometimes, a person would take his own life, in the throes of deep despair, but it was never spoken of except in illicit whispers, downcast eyes, and a knowledge of having overstepped boundaries by mentioning it at all.

He thought of the pond, the large body of spring-fed water that lay between Clara's horse farm and their own. If this girl was troubled enough, she might have gone there with the intention of ending it all. He hoped not, in a vague sort of way, still not emotionally attached to any of the night's goings-on. He was tired, had gone to bed exhausted, the way they'd beat the thunderstorm getting the last load of hay in the barn. He guessed if this May was what some folks said she was, she had likely lit out for town and the Greyhound bus station. But he'd check the pond, just in case.

When he heard a splash, he thought it must be a muskrat, the way the north bank was slick with the activity of these rodents who dwelt there. There was a half moon, but not enough light to actually define what made the splashing noise, although he slipped in the dew-wet grass as he picked up his pace.

She was lying half out of the water, her hands grabbing desperately at the thin grass growing in the mud. She was coughing, spluttering the way a child will do when dipped unexpectedly in water.

He slid down the bank, went to her small form, bent over, and put his arm beneath her shoulder to lift her fully out of the water. She was dressed in a cotton nightdress, her hair matted to her delicate head, desperately coughing, gasping.

He carried her up the bank, laid her on the grass, one arm keeping her head elevated as she retched. Water poured from her nose and mouth as she struggled to breathe. He rubbed her thin back, alarmed at the protrusion of her shoulder bones. He tried to speak soothingly, telling her she was going to be okay.

She took one last shuddering breath, then began to sob, deep heart-rending sobs that wracked her whole body. She began to speak in a hoarse voice, a convolution of ragged words that made no sense. He was afraid for her sanity as she became more and more agitated. She tried to sit up, she sneezed and coughed, writhed away from him, her eyes wild with fear.

"Don't touch me." Her voice was low, horrible in its hatred and angst, her breath coming in swift, ragged outbursts. He sat back, left her to lie in the grass, curled into a fetal position, covered in mud, grass, and soaked through with the summer's stagnant pond water. The sobbing continued, so he let her go, realizing his own helplessness if she did not want him there.

How long was it? He should let the search party know she had been found, but he could not leave her here alone.

Cicadas shrilled from the locust trees, their insistent cries only adding to the sense of unreality. Crickets chirped their repetitive calls and katydids did their best to correct the dullness of their repertoire, filling in the spaces with their own chorus. A fish jumped close to shore, the splash startling in its copy of what had drawn him to May.

The sobbing eased, but the hoarse words began again.

"I didn't tell Clara. It's killing me. I can't carry this any longer. If I have to, I must surely die."

Andy listened, waited, as the sobbing continued. He had not known a person could be capable of these heart-wrenching sounds, the sorrow and pain too deep to be fully expressed. Whatever had occurred in the past must have raked its ugly claws so deep into her mind, her being, that it had driven her to the desire to die.

She sat up, steadied herself.

"Who are you?"

"A neighbor."

"Why are you here?"

"Clara has a search party out looking for you. I am the one who found you."

"I have to go to her."

She could not get up by herself, so he stood and reached for her hands. She looked up, the light from the sputtering lantern revealing her terror, her cold, genuine fear of him.

"You're not going to . . . you know. Hurt me?"

"No, of course not. Why would I do something like that? Just give me your hand, and I'll help you up."

"But you have to let it go as soon as I'm up."

"Yes."

Her hand was so small and light, so slick with mud and water and bits of grass, he could barely keep it in his grasp. When she was on her feet, she swayed, took a few steps backward, to fall back into the wet grass and lie still. Andy bent over her, asked if she needed help.

"Just let me go. Perhaps I can die here by myself."

Low and soft, the words were an expression of her wretchedness, the absolute misery which drove her to these desperate measures. Andy felt a wrench of his heart, an almost physical sensation of pity so deep it was as if he could feel her dread of continuing the journey of the rest of her life.

"Come, May. Please? They'll need to know where you are."

He bent to lift her, keeping a firm arm behind her back. She swayed again, but his strong arm supported her. When she stumbled, he drew her closer, matched his steps to hers. He felt an alarm at how slight she was, much too thin, too sick and weary.

A dog began to bark, furiously. A shout.

Andy answered with one of his own, which brought one of his brothers, who hurried off to shoot the rifle that would be a signal to the remaining men. May flinched when she heard the shot, but Andy steadied her.

Then she was in Clara's arms, who was laughing and crying, scolding, talking, telling her she was not slipping out of her sight ever again.

May cried, but silently.

Andy stood away a short distance, his hands at his sides, unsure what he should say or do.

Then he heard May begin to speak. He felt like an intruder but could not tear himself away. He heard every word and was shocked beyond anything he'd thought possible. The words were not meant for his ears, but he'd heard them distinctly before the search party descended on the three of them.

CLARA HELPED HER to the bathroom, drew a steaming bath, laid out clean towels and washcloths, a new cake of soap, and left her to undress and relax in the soothing water. May lay back in the porcelain claw foot tub, closed her eyes, and began to pray, the words like music notes sent to the heavens, words of affirmation to God the Father, words of praise, of thanksgiving for her deliverance. She could no longer carry the burden of her past alone, hidden away, where it grew like a debilitating disease, slowly overtaking any strength she had left.

For far too long she had balanced the need to appear normal with the maelstrom of what had occurred at a very young age. Right and wrong had gotten all twisted inside, until she'd believed she was doing the right thing by staying silent, by being obedient in all things. The darkness would always be there, but a brilliant light had begun to penetrate the black void, a light that had entered after speaking the truth to Clara.

He could feel God with her, and He would never leave her. Of this one thing, she could be certain. No, she had not done the unpardonable. She was not to blame. She knew that now.

The night was warm and starry, but the breeze was cooler now, so the neighbors took their time, drank coffee, kept a lighthearted conversation flowing. When May appeared at the door of the living room, wearing a heavy chenille robe, her hair caught up in a loose tie, her eyes swollen from her tears, Andy looked up to meet her large brown eyes. She met his dark gaze, and smiled hesitantly before folding herself on the arm of the couch. Clara leaped to her feet, gave her own rocking chair to her, fussed and clucked like a nervous chicken.

The widow went to sit beside her, took her hand, and spoke quietly, saying how baby blues came late for some. She related the sad story of an acquaintance who had to go to the mental hospital when her baby was six months old. She stayed two weeks and was never the same after she came out.

"Having babies is tricky. You never know when the blues will come on you, sneaky like. I think you'll be all right, though. Dena had six children in six years, this baby was the seventh, and it was too much. The fourth child was a dwarf, with heart trouble, and she was always afraid of finding him dead, which she never did. But you know, stuff like that will wear on you, get you down. So you'll be all right. I think you have it so nice here with Clara."

"Oh yes," May whispered.

"Yes, you do. And the dear child. His skin color might be a problem for a while, but folks are kind. They'll get used to it. He'll likely encounter some meanness, but take a day at a time. You'll always be welcome here."

She squeezed May's hand. Involuntarily, May squeezed the calloused hand right back, soaking up the generosity in her eyes.

Andy was the last to leave. He came over to sit near May, his bulk filling the empty space. He left a scent of moss and newly plowed soil, rain-washed earth, and waving grasses. When he leaned over to ask if she felt better, she nodded, breathed his scent, and remembered Clinton. Startled, she looked into his face, wide eyed, her brown eyes with the down-slanted edge of sorrow and pain like an arrow in his chest.

He walked home through the warm starlit night, thought of Doris with a deep, physical longing, her vibrant good looks, the sense of humor that lit up his world, taken away when trust was so complete.

What was this with May? He was honestly afraid of entanglement in any relationship, and this girl appeared full of complicated troubles. He'd always loved the flash in Doris's eyes, but this May's eyes were like a rich patch of freshly turned earth, so dark brown. Her eyes would haunt him for many days, the sadness mixed with beauty.

CLARA SAT WITH May that whole night as she unburdened the painful memories one by one. Everything. Clara listened quietly, her face flushing with anger, then turning pale with horror.

Finally, she took a deep breath, searched for proper words.

"May, you know these things happen, what Melvin did to you. Yours is not the only situation. But we do not speak of these shameful instances to others. To speak of it to folks in this community would double the amount of suspicion surrounding you already. We women are mistreated, but we don't speak of it. We carry it to our graves, but with the Lord's strength and forgiveness. I can only hope the time will come when men like Melvin have to be held accountable, but for now, we bury it. We hide it away, and if we're strong, it disintegrates into a puff of seed blown away by the wind. But not everyone can do that. There are plenty of women who suffer the rest of their lives with the consequences. I am more than glad, May, that you found the courage to tell me. To share the burden is very healing."

May nodded. "How do you know?"

For a long, uncomfortable moment, Clara was silent, then she sighed audibly.

"You know, I've always loved horses. When I was fifteen, a horse dealer came here to the farm, and well, it wasn't good. I fought worse than a tomcat. Screeched and clawed and carried on. Dat got the story from him the next week—I never said a word of course—and I got the scolding of my life. The story all twisted around. From that day forward, I turned sour and vowed to spurn all men, every single one. They're weak, unharnessed, total apes."

May was aghast, ashamed to hear these words. "Oh, but not all of them. My dat, Clinton." And she thought of Andy.

"Pshaw! You take your pick. I don't plan on changing anything. The Bible tells us clearly it's okay to be single, and single I am, and plan on staying that way." She laughed suddenly, a loud burst of genuine humor. "I have a mean eye. Any man that comes around now pays me a certain respect. Keeps his distance and thanks the Lord I'm not his wife."

May smiled with her. "Bless you, Clara, that can be a gift in itself."

MAY RETURNED TO her former self as the weeks went by. She loved her son with the same abandonment as before, stayed busy with the harvest from the garden, canning corn, green beans, and red beets. She made sweet pickles soaked in a brine made from vinegar, sugar, and spices; she baked loaves of bread and hummed while she did so. The burden had been lightened by sharing it with Clara, and the darkness was kept at bay by her faith in God.

When she was baptized in the name of God the Father, the Son, and the Holy Ghost, the kindly bishop bent over her as he dribbled water on her head three times, and tears ran unchecked down her cheeks.

CLARA SEETHED. SHE could not put May's experience with Melvin out of her mind, could not pretend to forget about it. She would never speak to the ministers on this subject. A woman bringing up the unthinkable . . . it simply wasn't done. And she knew that May would never allow her to make a fuss about it.

She didn't exactly pray about it—the will to confront Melvin was too strong. She asked God in an abstract manner whether it was all right with Him if she went ahead and traveled to Arkansas, but she didn't think He'd mind too much.

She went right ahead making plans, procured tickets for the long train ride, and told May she was visiting her elderly relatives in Missouri. She said that Simon Weaver and his boys would do all the animal and barn chores, leaving her to care for the lawn, garden, and the house. She wasn't lying outright, as she did have plans to visit them someday, just not on this specific trip.

May wondered why she was leaving now, in the middle of the busy harvest time, but being who she was, she simply accepted her decision and asked no questions. She fought back unease, thinking of staying alone at night, thinking of the harrowing nights alone in the apartment when Clinton did not return. Would Clara leave, waving blithely as she was driven away to the railroad station, never to return? She put a hand to her chest to still the beating of her heart, swallowed the ever-present fear, and began to pray, leaning on the power that was always with her.

It was Andy who strode across the fields to accompany Clara to the barn and take instruction on the care and feeding of the horses. May was in the house with Eliezer on her lap. She stood to go to the window and saw them both against the fence, forearms propped on the top rail, one foot up on the bottom rail, deep in conversation. She found Andy's profile pleasing, conjuring memories of Clinton. Was it the way his shoulders were held? The narrowness of his hips?

She didn't know, but turned away and told herself perhaps she had better restrain this kind of dreaming, as no good could come of it. Her focus was Eliezer, and he meant everything to her. It was far better to be single all the days of her life, give herself wholly to her son, than to subject him to a stepfather who would always hold him at arm's length.

Andy walked home that night without catching a glimpse of May, but he inquired about her welfare to Clara, who told him she was improving each week. She shook her head and said she'd seen more in her young life than most people see in a lifetime, then gazed out across the pasture with the stance of a falcon, keen-eyed and fierce.

Andy blinked, asked if she'd be safe at night. May, he meant. Clara assured him, but asked him to keep an eye on the place, just in case.

CHAPTER 14

ALPHEUS HAD BROUGHT SUPPLIES: ROOF SHINGLES, WIN-dows, door latches, a sink, a stove, so many useful things that Oba couldn't help but get excited as he unpacked one delight after another. There were chocolate bars, peanut butter, elderberry jam, and pota-toes. Real groceries. Store-bought cereal and pretzels, boxes of canned goods. He lifted cans of peaches, tomatoes, beans, corn, and peas. That night, they cooked and ate a glorious meal, the best Oba could remember, with little Alpheus leaning over the fire, frying, boil-ing, baking. He looked like an elf, so small and sprightly, his move-ments quick. Oba filled his plate with beef stew, something called flat bread, and a sort of warm cake with elderberry jam through it.

There was news from different trading posts, towns sprinkled along the route Alpheus ran, his small plane the means of trans-porting necessary items to the hunters and trappers throughout the region. There was talk of grizzly bear sightings, hungry bruins who left their dens in search of food, terrorizing anything in their path. Wolverines thick as beavers. Time to thin that population, for sure.

Oba listened, fought back the fear that rose like bile in his throat. What was a wolverine? Jonas never mentioned that animal. He didn't want to ask, didn't want to reveal his fear, so he listened, squinting into the fire.

"Didn't trap yet, huh?"

"Not yet."

"Hunt?"

"Nothing big."

"What about the boy there?" Alpheus grinned at him.

Oba glared back. The little man resembled a Chihuahua, that snappy little dog with protruding eyes that could stare into your own with an unsettling, yellow gaze.

"Oba? He doesn't hunt."

"He doesn't? Well, he will. He will. You can't live in the bush without learning to hunt. That, my boy, is what we all strive for. To bring down that caribou, or moose, pack out the meat, freeze it in caches, and chop off a hunk of meat when we need it. What about fishing?"

"Soon's the ice breaks. I need a boat, though."

Jonas watched Oba, uneasy with his silence, and was glad when Alpheus left, although he felt the wistfulness as he waved goodbye. He stood by the river and watched the aircraft become smaller and smaller as the distance swallowed it up.

BY THE TIME most of the snow was gone and the river ice was broken up and carried downstream by the swollen current, the cabin was complete with the roof on, windows in place, even a sturdy door with a latch. It had a small front porch and crude steps leading up to it, and Oba felt as if he had accomplished the most worthwhile project of his life.

He loved that brown cabin, swept the wooden floor with the homemade twig broom, stoked the fire in the stove, crawled into the homemade bunk lined with dried river grass, and felt at home. Every morning, now, he was up early, down at the river, baiting his hook with whatever he could find. He caught nice brown trout and crappie, cleaned them, and fried them in lard. All the praise from Jonas for his fishing prowess brought enough confidence for him to shoot at a target, and when his first shot landed a bull's-eye, he was hooked.

He ran down to see where he'd hit, pumped the air with his fist, grinned, and hooted as Jonas made his way down to see results. Jonas slapped his back so hard it hurt, but it hurt in a good way. He felt like a man, a real outdoorsman, an accomplished fisherman, and now a crack shot. He practiced relentlessly, shot so many rounds of ammunition that Jonas made him stop. Oba slapped at blackflies and grinned.

That night, cold descended on the Northwest from some unusual arctic vortex, along with strong winds laden with stinging snow and no mercy on man or beast. Oba woke in a freezing cabin, snow scraping against the window panes like sandpaper being dragged against the walls. The air was gray, the light of the sun obscured by the mighty force of the storm.

Oba was restless and paced the cabin till Jonas put him to work wiping down traps, oiling gun barrels, rubbing linseed oil on rifle stocks.

Jonas watched him work, noticing the intense concentration, the slow, methodic way he went about it, producing perfectly cleaned traps, and guns so well-preserved he couldn't have done better himself. He told Oba so.

Oba looked up, a slow grin across his face, his eyes wide. "What do you mean?"

"What I said. You're doing a great job."

"Wow. Thanks."

He was ashamed then, and lowered his head and rubbed vigorously at a gunstock that had been cleaned before. Jonas looked at the top of the blond head, his heart warming even as his chin wobbled with emotion. Someone had to give the boy a chance. He was not easy to get along with, for sure, had his bouts of silence, the times when his sullen brooding almost drove Jonas to insanity . . . until he remembered the scars on his back.

One day shortly after the ice in the river broke up, Oba had plunged into the frigid water, yelled, and then danced around on the muddy riverbank, his back was blue and yellow and gray, the white welts like latticed piecrust. Jonas turned away as Oba bent to step into his pants, his back so horribly exposed in the light of full midday sun.

He asked him that night.

"Who injured your back like that, Oba?"

"I don't want to talk about it."

"You should. Be good for you."

"How could it be good for me?"

"Get it off your chest."

"The scars are on my back, not my chest." He was trying to joke, make light of it, deliberately put the scars safely away.

"I'm serious, Oba."

"I told you. Don't worry about it. I'm not, so why should you be?"

"Did this man ever come to justice?"

"Of course not. He's Amish, very religious. There's not one man on the face of the earth who would imagine him doing anything like this." Oba's face contorted. He swallowed, got up, and stalked to the door, held the latch as if to prepare himself for flight. "It's why I don't believe in God. He drowns your parents, then allows this . . . this hypocrite to pound away with that whip hissing. Do you have any idea what some of these welts looked like? Felt like? No, you couldn't. You can't even begin to imagine the disgust that wells up in me when I think of him sitting there, his face like a sheep . . . I can't tell you. I hate him."

For a long time Jonas had been silent. Finally, he spoke, "You believe in God."

"No, I don't."

"You do. He drowned your parents, you said. Allowed this man to whip you. When you say that, you acknowledge His presence, His power. Of course God exists. How can you travel to a place like this, see the towering mountain ranges, the storms and the sun, the animals, everything, and not believe?"

Oba let go of the doorknob, came to join Jonas at the table, propped up his elbows, and rested his chin in his hands.

"I just don't know. Maybe I believe He exists, but I don't trust Him. I don't want to say I am okay with Him directing my life." Suddenly, he looked up sharply. "You know why I came out here? 'Cause I figured

He couldn't find me as easily. What can happen out here that I can't handle by myself? I mean, yeah, the trip with the dogsled and all, but that was pretty rewarding, you know what I mean? Man, those dogs are unbelievable. They don't quit. When they run across the snow, it's as if they harmonize, like the chorus of a song. They're great."

"Why don't you tell them?"

"Why would I?"

"Dogs need praise, same as we do, Oba."

"I wouldn't know what to do with praise if I got any."

Which was why Jonas was on a mission now, to build up this young man, help him see his own worth.

THE LATE SNOW was heavy, loading down the fir trees. Tree branches sagged, the weak ones snapped and thudded to the ground with a muffled whump, becoming completely buried before the spring sun began to melt the heavy layer.

The roof on the cabin held up, as Jonas said it would. There would be times when they'd need to shovel it off, but this was a test, a test his workmanship had passed with flying colors. The interior of the cabin smelled of new lumber, and it was clean, their few belongings organized on rough-hewn shelving. It was home.

Oba lounged on his bunk in the evening, reading whatever was available by the light of a kerosene lamp. Sometimes he'd half listen as Jonas talked of his past.

"There's nothing quite like it, living out here with the woman you love. We shared everything, hunting, fishing, building. She was right here by my side, loved the dogs, the cold. There were times we didn't see anyone for months, close to a year or more. We never went hungry."

His voice rambled on, but Oba heard only bits and pieces, thinking about his own future, which held no possibility of meeting anyone.

As he often wondered before, was there someone out there who would be wiling to get to know him, want to be a part of his life? How did someone go about starting a friendship, if a girl became available?

It was far easier to push the thought away, try to be grateful, content, find a new goal, hone a skill. Like hunting, trapping, fishing.

"You know you'll want to meet a girl sometime, don't you?"

"How?" Oba grunted, from behind the cover of his book.

"There are girls up and down this river."

"What? Indians?"

"They're the best."

"Hmph."

"Come on, Oba. You know, if you're not happy here, you do have the opportunity to move out the next time Alpheus flies in."

Oba didn't answer to that, mostly on account of not knowing what to say. The world he had known seemed so far away, so remote, as if it had been another lifetime. For one frightful moment, he felt adrift, unanchored as if he did not belong here with Jonas and never had. But where, exactly, did he belong?

He vowed never to return to the Amish, to banish all that from his thoughts. As far as he was concerned, that part of his life was taken away by the death of his parents. The time in Arkansas was like a bitter medicine that soured his attitude against any plain lifestyle. Right or wrong, he didn't care.

He slept fitfully that night, lay awake thinking of Jonas's words, his future brought before him in startling reality, his past fastened to his ankles like a ball and chain.

In the morning, he decided to go on his first hunt alone. He told Jonas what he planned to do, in spite of being warned about the wet snow.

"Take the dogs," Jonas said. "I'll go with you."

"No, I want to do this by myself. Prove to you I can be a hunter, now that I've mastered the art of shooting a gun."

Jonas grinned. "Don't get lost."

"There's always the river."

"You got your compass?"

"Somewhere."

He dressed in warm clothes, carried a pack on his back with an extra pair of socks, a few pieces of dried meat, ammunition.

The dogs whined when he stepped out of the door in the early morning light, but he paid them no mind. If he meant to stalk an animal, he would do it his way—he certainly didn't need a bunch of yapping dogs.

He stopped, met Eb's gaze now, saw the eagerness, the tapping of his paws as he anticipated being allowed to go. Should he? He hesitated, turned toward the cabin, then looked at Eb. He was a commanding presence, a large, well-formed animal with expressive blue eyes, and strong, obedient.

Unknown to Oba, Jonas was watching through the cabin window, and smiled at the boy's indecision. When Oba turned and walked back, he busied himself at the sink.

"Hey."

"Yeah?"

"Mind if I take Eb?"

"Go ahead." He was nonchalant, as if this was an everyday occurrence, this wanting of a dog. He turned to watch as Oba bent to loosen the chain. Jonas's eyes teared up as Oba passed a hand over the top of the dog's head, spoke a few words.

Eb cavorted with glee. He leaped and spun, rolled and yelped, before falling into step with Oba. Jonas watched them walk to the river, turn right, and make their way along the pebbled bank where the water was already melting the snow away from the rushing current.

Ah, but it was a sight to see. A young man and his dog, both in the prime of their life, setting out to face the wilderness, and Jonas knew well enough his own fears. He wished them Godspeed, felt a rising of pride coupled with concern, wondered if this was what it was like to have a son.

THE DAY WAS gorgeous, the sky as blue as a bluebird's wing, with milky clouds like wisps of cotton strands, the sun a yellow orb of gentle warmth. The snow was blinding, the mountains rising to the north in stark white beauty, crags and cliffs shadowed in purple and blue. Snow geese honked overhead, their wings beating the air rapidly as they hurried to a destination they knew about and no one else. Birdsong enriched the rippling of the river as it tumbled over rocks, the snow draped like whipped cream over them.

Oba took a deep breath and felt the pure oxygen enter his lungs as his chest expanded. He picked up his pace, his rifle slung comfortably over his shoulder, the magnificent Eb at his side. He was quite suddenly relieved and grateful to have his company. The trees and undergrowth increased and the river pushed between jumbles of huge rocks, like slabs of broken dishes, the scrubby trees clinging to rock walls as the river roared past. Ice clung stubbornly to the bank in the shade of the rock formations, a testament to the freezing temperatures, the fierce cold that could quickly snuff out a man's life.

Oba turned away from the river to enter a grove of alders, the undergrowth thinned to a comfortable level. He climbed up a long incline, through more trees, and out into an open field that fell away in front of them, revealing a panorama of untouched beauty so vast it bordered on unreality. He'd seen plenty of these sights on their journey, but had always been moving, hurrying on to their destination. Now, alone, he stood on the brink of all this beauty, this unspoiled vista creating a deep emotion that roiled uncomfortably in his chest. Awe, disbelief, a melancholy awareness of his own insignificance in a world so colossal, so limitless. And to think this was just a small part of the universe.

What was his life worth? He felt so small, so insignificant.

All around him lay snow-covered infinity. Who could know what lay beyond the craggy peaks, and beyond that? He had no idea which directions Ohio and Arkansas were from there. Where was May? Was her heart still beating, her cheeks flushed as they'd been when she bent over his back with warm soap and water?

He could not describe what he felt at that moment, only knew he needed to find her. He needed to know she was alive and well.

He opened his mouth and croaked, "May!"

The sound was piteous in the far-reaching view before him, but his heart swelled as he called her name again.

"May!"

An urgency he couldn't name gripped his soul, and he shouted her name now, shouted it over and over into the immense wilderness before him. Unexpected tears blinded his sight, as he screamed now, unleashed his despair and desperation, the lost hope of ever finding his beloved sister.

"May! May!"

The measureless primeval forest swallowed the cry of his heart till he became aware of his futile attempt at reconnection and fell to the ground crying hysterically, his chest heaving in pain. He didn't know how long he lay on the wet snow, his body wracked by his sorrow, till he felt a warm tongue like a washcloth working on his face. He sat up, groaned as he gathered the dog's head and held him against his own, his tears warm against his chilled cheeks. Eb seemed to know this mission was important, so he sat patiently as Oba kept him in the circle of his strong arms.

He breathed in a long trembling breath, wiped his face on Eb's coat, then sat still as stone, one hand caressing the thick hairs on his neck.

He began to speak.

"Okay, Eb. You win, you big old lunker, you. I don't like you. I don't like any animal. But you look at me with your eyes like blue ice in that perfectly beautiful dog face, and I have to admit, I'm glad you're here with me. Now let's go see if we can find a caribou or a moose. Just forget what I said about May. She's gone. I miss her, but she's not here. I don't know where she is right now, maybe I never will.

"My parents are dead, Eb. Their bodies are in the ground. I can't think about the flood waters, the terrible rainstorm that made that creek rise the way it did. Why didn't they take May and me along with them? Why did they leave us that night? We were left at the mercy of relatives who had no room for us. Not in their homes or their hearts.

"My mam used to tell us the story of Jesus, how there was no room for Him either. Should I go back to believing that rubbish, Eb?"

He fell silent. No, it wasn't. He knew Jesus had been born, knew, too, God had created these mountains. He couldn't *not* believe those things. He just wasn't sure God cared about him, even a little.

He stood, his sharp eyes watching for any movement, figured it should be easy finding brown or black in this white landscape. He began to walk, staying close to the tree line, with Eb plodding behind him. All morning, they drew away from the river, fought their way through heavy snow, stopping occasionally for a breather. He kept his eyes out for any large animal, especially bear and the elusive wolverine.

He was walking along a narrow gully where the undergrowth had thinned, so he made good time, winding his way up to the top of a small rise. The trees were young, more like seedlings than real trees, with deep yellow grasses waving their heads above the heavy snow. He looked up to find himself within sight of what appeared to be a heavy bundle of brown fur loosely slung across a moving mass of bone and muscle.

Grizzly!

Oba froze, fear numbing his body. He felt electrified by it, burned up by raw, agonizing knowledge of the beast's capability of tearing his body limb from limb. The bear was alone and hungry, ravenously hungry, after his winter's hibernation. A low rumble began in Eb's throat. Oba reached down to hush him. The great beast was immense, his head swinging from side to side as his paws navigated the deep snow. Crows called overhead, a warning to all lesser creatures.

Oba's mouth was so dry he could not swallow. His throat was constricted with terror, his heart pounding so hard he felt his chest walls expanding. He lowered the rifle, slowly slid the safety lever.

What was one small bullet to that mountain of flesh?

He watched through blurred vision as the bear continued his rolling gait directly into his path, his head swinging in his direction. The great beast stopped, halted in his tracks, a low snuffling coming from his slavering mouth. He lifted his head, his brown upturned nose sniffing the wind. His eyes were amazingly akin to a pig's eyes, small and oblong, without feeling. The beast rose up, opened his mouth, and emitted a blood-curdling roar, a sound so primal in its quest for food, the desperation of his hunger, that Oba was driven into a quiet zone, adrenaline carrying a certain calm to save his own life. His and the life of the dog.

He lifted the rifle to his shoulder, knowing he had a few seconds to mark the difference between life and death. He remembered all of Jonas's instructions at target practice in one flash. Always steady, take your time aiming before you fire, get those sights lined up. High up on the shoulder.

He didn't have time.

As the bear dropped on all fours, gathering his haunches for the powerful rush that meant being mauled, Oba breathed one word.

"God."

And he pulled the trigger. The rest was a blur—an explosion of sound, Eb falling sideways, the bear's oncoming rush, snow, the sound of horrible slavering and roaring. Oba raised the gun and shot again, a wild stab at self-preservation. There was a terrible growl from Eb, a whir of gray and white as the dog launched into action, his jaws open, lunging toward the grizzly and latching on to its face. Oba stumbled backward, running his back into a tree, but before he could get in another shot, a crack of gunfire came from the top of the incline.

As if it was all playing out in slow motion, the bear grunted, the loose skin folding over the muscle of the large frame as it sagged into the snow, the massive head lolling to one side as blood trickled from the gasping mouth. There were shouts, then, and Oba was aware of a small figure zigzagging through the underbrush.

He heard a volley of senseless words, the crashing of twigs and old winter grass, snow churned by heavy boots. Oba could barely breathe for the crashing of his heart. He struggled to stay upright as Eb began to bark, low and forbidding.

"Is he down? Watch it there. They're not always dead when you think they are. Stay back. Get your dog off."

Stung into action, Oba called to Eb in a choked, hoarse voice, as the tall, fur-clad figure strode up to him. He was aware of a fur parka, the hood pushed back, hair as black as a raven, a round face the color of a clean penny, huge eyes as black as night. He realized he was face to face with a young woman.

"He's down."

"Looks like it."

"Congratulations. You got him."

She offered a hand. Oba took it. They pumped up and down a few times, grinned stupidly.

"He almost had you. I was walking along the top there, saw the whole thing. About killed me with fright. I'm Sam."

"Oba."

She nodded. "Strange to see anyone in this area. You just move in?"

"Not too long ago."

"My parents and I live maybe six miles from here. On up the river. Lived here all my life. They wanted a boy, so they named me Samuel, even though I am a girl."

She blushed slightly, and Oba noticed the brightening of her eyes, the thinning of her lips as she smiled self-consciously. He didn't know what to do with all this discomfiture, this awareness of her, the beauty of that flawless copper skin, the dark eyes that created a lasting storm in his chest.

"Well," he said finally. "Hello, Sam."

And she laughed, a deep throaty sound that made Oba laugh with her, freeing his shy, reclusive self.

"Looks like we better get some help, packing this thing out," Sam said then, nudging the downed beast with the toe of her boot.

"I'll go get Jonas if you stay here," Oba offered.

"Stay here? No thanks. I'll go with you wherever you go. That there was a good reminder that bears are out of hibernation. I shouldn't have come out alone in the first place . . . but I guess it's a good thing that I did."

"All right," he said, grinning, immensely pleased.

I'll go with you wherever you go. The words played a tune in his ears.

CHAPTER 15

THE MORNING WAS STAGNANT WITH THE HEAT OF LATE SUM-
mer, high humidity causing Clara's new covering to fall flat, irritating
her to the point of distraction. Her red hair was frizzy, her covering
had become limp and sloppy, and her green dress felt so hot she
wasn't sure she'd survive the train ride.

May stood holding Eliezer, offering assurances, which were very
kind, given the sight of disarray that was Clara. She simply was not
made to be dressed meticulously, typically being at home in a barn
dress, boots, and a scarf.

"For two cents, I'd give up this trip," she shouted from the
bathroom.

"Do you have to go?" May asked.

"I do, it's been too long."

"Your aunt and uncle. Are they elderly?"

"Fairly. In their seventies."

She kissed Eliezer, waved a hand at May, and was down the steps
and out the door the minute her ride showed up, leaving a bewildered May standing just inside the screen door, wondering at her
strange behavior. It was all so unlike Clara, taking it upon herself to
visit an aunt and uncle, normally uncaring about any of her relatives,
pooh-poohing the mention of visiting a sick cousin. But then, who
could tell with Clara? She lived by her own rules, went to church when

she felt like it, and stayed home when she didn't, uncaring whether she was talked about or not.

May shrugged. She felt alone then. Absolutely alone, like a stranded person in an endless desert. Eliezer felt like a frightening responsibility, too heavy, too fragile. He might choke on his baby food, develop a fever, fall off a table. The list was long and daunting. She clutched his small round body tightly, her breathing altered as her heart fluttered. She should not have allowed Clara to leave.

She began to pray.

Dear Father, I thought I was all right. I'm not. I must have placed all my faith in Clara and none in You. Increase my faith. Help me to be brave, in the face of my fear.

The day was interminably long, dreadfully hot and humid. Eliezer was fussy, his teeth ravaging his little pink gums until they became red and inflamed. May cleaned the house when he napped.

She took notice of the darkening sky as she sat on the porch fanning herself with one of Clara's horse magazines. Perhaps there would be a cooling rain.

Eliezer lay by her feet on a blanket, cooing as he played with a string of bright beads. Finally, his pain seemed to be subsiding, which allowed for a moment of respite. In the distance, the sky turned into an alarming shade of dark gray, the flat unmoving portentous arrival of a brewing storm. She leaned forward, held the beads for Eliezer, smiled when he wriggled with delight, one chubby arm grabbing for the beads, never quite able to make successful contact. She laughed when he finally caught one end, gave a hefty tug. Oh, he was such a beautiful child, so well formed, so perfect with the soft, tightly curled black hair. She would never be ashamed of him, between herself and God; it was difficult with others, who she knew looked down on both of them for what she had done.

"Hello, May."

Startled, she looked up into the bluest eyes.

"Oh. It's you." She sat up, twisted her fingers in her lap, resisted the urge to pick up Eliezer and disappear.

"Yes." A pause. "Is this your son?"

Immediately he wished he hadn't asked a question he already knew the answer to, especially when he saw the way she flinched and turned away.

She nodded, kept her eyes lowered.

"He is a fine child."

Again, she nodded, not knowing what else to do. She bit her lower lip, moved one bare foot on top of the other to hide her chipped and broken toenails, the line of dirt surrounding them. She'd been in the garden.

"May, it's all right." His words were soft and low, filled with kindness.

She looked up.

Their gazes met. He was moved by her mixture of pride and courage, the misery and shame. She was stirred to the depth of her soul by his absolute acceptance, his kindness above all. For a long soothing moment, they were locked in a silent exchange of emotion, of admiration and the beginning of something neither one could name.

Thunder rumbled now, jagged white streaks of lightning flashing from the depth of sodden gray clouds. Starlings flew to the safety of the barn with short, choppy flaps of their awkward wings, as sparrows whirred off into the distance like frightened balls of dust. A bluebird trilled its beautiful warble, calling the fledglings to the safety of the pine box Clara had built.

"I saw there was a storm coming and figured I'd check in. Clara said she'd be away. You okay here?"

May looked off into the distance as another flash of lightning sizzled across the sky, followed by a loud clap of thunder, a rolling of monstrous sound following. He watched her face in the dimming light, the porcelain contours of her thin nose, the large, troubled eyes, so dark to be crowned by her blond hair. Her mouth like a soft rose, so vulnerable.

He had wrestled with the words she had spoken to Clara that night, wished he had not heard them. They were not meant for him, but he would never be able to forget them.

"Yes. I mean, no, not really. I'm sorry, but . . . It's just us, me and um . . . you know, the baby. But please go if you have things to do."

"What is his name?"

"Eliezer, for my father."

"May I hold him?"

Without further words, Andy bent to lift him, as sure of himself as a real father, tucked him into the crook of his arm, and sat on the porch floor, his legs on the steps leading to the walk. He lifted him up by his armpits, and Eliezer stood sturdily on his legs, his wide smile pushing up his rounded cheeks.

"Well, hi there, little man! Aren't you a sturdy little guy?" Andy said, clearly delighted with his new friend.

And Eliezer laughed outright.

"I'm used to babies. Seventeen nieces and nephews. Might be eighteen after today. My mom was off to Sarie's house this morning." He chuckled, commented on his hair. "Cutest thing I ever saw."

"Clinton's hair.

"That your husband's name?"

A stony cold silence, the crackling of the approaching storm.

"He . . . wasn't my husband."

"Where is he now?" Andy's voice had turned deeper, gruffer, his profile very serious in the developing darkness.

"He's dead."

Why this all-encompassing shock of happiness at her sad words? He felt a traitor, guilty of dishonesty when he spoke. "I'm sorry. What happened?"

"I will never know."

"Do you care to talk about it?"

She took a deep breath, realized how much she wanted to tell Andy everything. She began in a low, sad voice, from the time she left her uncle's farm till Clinton's failure at procuring a stable income to support her, the unspeakable reality of his mysterious death. The time she went to the morgue to identify his body, his beloved face.

He could hear the raw emotion, the loss, the terror of her nights without him. Knew, too, she had been driven to this by her own appalling amount of suffering. She had been through far more than most people had been in a lifetime. He told himself to stop, go slow, don't befriend her till you know, but this inner caution held as much control as a greased axle on a wagon.

"So you still love him?" he ventured breathlessly.

"I always will. No decent man would have me."

"I'm a decent man."

All conversation ceased, a heartbeat stopped.

He looked up at her, his eyes squinted into smile lines, his wide shoulders dwarfing Eliezer as he held him up.

May gave a small breathless laugh. "What should I say to that?"

"I'm saying, I am a decent man, and I would have you."

"Oh, you mustn't say that."

"Why not?"

"I'm ... not worthy. I am a single mother with an illegitimate child."

"You are also a fine Christian girl who has given her heart to Jesus, which according to my measure, is the best anyone can be."

"I have sinned immensely, running away with Clinton. The rewards of that sin was his death."

"You think that? Really?"

"I do."

Almost, he corrected her, told her he overheard her words to Clara, but a thunderous clap made conversation impossible. Andy rose to his feet as large raindrops hit the stone walk. The wind rose to howl against the maple tree, turning the leaves inside out, the pale green undersides fragile in their exposure.

He held the door for her, took notice of how small she really was. Did the top of her head reach his shoulder?

She lit a kerosene lamp and he helped her close windows as the rain was lashed against the window screens by the powerful wind. The house was uncomfortably warm, but neither of them seemed to notice, content to share the intimacy of a softly lit kitchen table in the center of an August thunderstorm. When Eliezer became fussy, she felt shy, not knowing how to tell Andy he needed to be fed.

He handed him over, told her he probably wanted to nurse, a word that made her blush miserably and leave the room immediately.

Her hands shook as she changed his diaper, her mind in a state of unrest as she fed him, then laid him on a clean diaper after he fell asleep, so small and limp, so sweet and satiated.

He was on the porch when she returned, watching the ferocity of the storm, his hands in his pockets. She was unsure of joining him, but felt the cooling breeze and stood just inside the screen door.

"Come on out, May. Feels wonderful out here."

She pushed the screen door open slowly, stepped out into a flash of blinding lightning, uttered a small "oh," and was pulled to his side by one powerful arm. She felt the solid strength of him, caught the scent of new-mown hay and cultivated earth, knew she wanted to stay there, right there in the safety of his good strength forever, but dashed that acknowledgment to the ground before the thought was completed. She, the least of all women, who would do well to remember her shame.

"A storm is a really beautiful thing, May."

At that exact moment a ball of blue lighting hit the lowest, thickest branch of the maple tree, splitting it off at the base with an earsplitting crack, like a rifle shot. It crashed to the ground, sending tremors up to the porch floor, where May stood with her face hidden against the rough chambray of his shirt, both of his arms holding her slight form against him, as he thanked the good Lord for his perfect timing.

A DISGRUNTLED CLARA rode through the heat of central Ohio with a repulsive lift to her nose and an attitude ill-fitted to her surroundings.

The railcar was packed with folks opening or closing windows according to their own version of comfort, which in Clara's view was not attainable, so why didn't everyone just shut up and sit down? It was hot and dusty, and all this getting off the seats and sitting back down was merely adding strange sweaty odors to the already foul air.

She did not relish this duty she had taken upon herself, but kept up a grim determination to see it through. When the door opened and a large black man with a tray held up by a strap around his neck approached the couple in the first seat, Clara leaned into the aisle to watch the proceedings. His tray contained egg salad, chicken salad, or ham salad sandwiches, for twenty-five cents.

His voice was husky, well-modulated, his manners impeccable as he made his way down the aisle, bowing and smiling, putting the quarters in a small leather pouch. When he approached Clara, she purchased an egg salad sandwich, acknowledged him with an air of kindness, opened her sandwich as he moved on, and glared at a red-faced kid who hung over the back of the seat in front of her.

Bold, that's what he was. Seriously, what a brat. Why didn't parents watch their children and make them behave?

"Turn around," she said, twirling a finger to show him what she meant.

He stared at her, stuck a grimy thumb in his mouth.

"Turn around. Get down from there."

He kept up his staring and thumbsucking, so Clara stuck out her tongue laden with egg salad, crossed her eyes, and stayed that way till he slid down over the seat and never reappeared.

SHE WAS SICK and tired of train travel by the time she reached Blytheville, Arkansas. Sticky and covered in gray dust, thirsty and hungry for a good meal, she was in no mood to begin a decent conversation with anyone.

Arkansas was so hot she guaranteed if you broke an egg on the sidewalk it would be fried in no time. The air was yellow and heavy and stunk to high heaven. Brick houses jammed up against one another, covered in dust and red earth and green-headed flies.

She had no idea where this Melvin Amstutz resided, but she'd never live long enough to find out if she didn't take care of herself first. So she walked off in the direction of what appeared to be the main street, her satchel clutched in one freckled, perspiring hand, her mouth as dry as sandpaper, and her stomach caved in to the point where she was afraid someone would hear all those rumblings. When she spotted a large window with "Don's Food" in circular lettering, she hurried across the street without bothering to see if there was more traffic coming, resulting in a few cars honking their horns, the occupants glaring at her, shaking fists, making ignorant remarks about the dumb Amish.

Nothing new, she shrugged, and made her way to the wooden door that scraped open to the sound of a lone sleigh bell tacked along the top. She sat down at a small table, ordered mashed potatoes and gravy, and felt better with every bite.

She spied an elderly couple, white-haired with bent backs, and decided they were likely her best bet. She approached, asked if they knew how to get to Melvin Amstutz's place, and was given knowing nods and clear directions.

She hired a taxi, sat in the back, and called out directions.

Flat. This land was as level as a tabletop. She caught glimpses of a brown river winding through the flat landscape like a snake. The whole area gave her the shivers.

She found herself feeling anxious as the taxi driver turned into the drive, although, by all outward appearance, it was a very normal Amish farm. The place was neat as a pin, the board fence freshly whitewashed, the barn in good repair, the lawn green and mowed evenly, with a beautifully kept large garden in the back.

She breathed in, let it out with a whoosh, paid the taxi driver, and yanked the car door open. She marched to the front door, looking neither right nor left, and lifted a hand and rapped smartly, her chin set in determination.

Footsteps. She was amazed to find a portly woman, dressed in blue, a white apron around her waist.

"Hello?"

"Hi. I'm Clara Yoder, from Apple Creek, Ohio."

"Yes, come in."

"First, am I at the right place? I'm looking for Melvin Amstutz."

A small sigh. "This used to be his home. My husband and I moved to another settlement, but when this came up for sale, we moved back. He's not here. Melvin, I mean."

"Where is he?"

"Here. Sit down. Would you like a glass of tea?"

Clara watched as she poured the cold tea. She noticed the absence of children despite a scattering of toys on a bench by the wall. She thought that they must be somewhere outside doing chores or playing.

"Melvin is in the mental ward of the state hospital."

Clara's mouth dropped open. "Why?"

"First, tell me who you are and why you're here."

So Clara did, but she got only halfway through before the woman began to turn pale, and then to cry. She excused herself, moving quickly to the back door. Clara got to her feet, watched as she scuttled, as fast as her portly frame would allow, to the barn, where she began calling for her husband. She returned with a gray-haired man in tow, throwing her arms wide as she spoke in agitated tones.

When the woman and her husband came back to Clara, the woman sounded desperate. "Tell him. Tell him," she said, breathing shakily as she mopped her forehead with a dishcloth.

"I'm Clara Yoder. I live in Ohio. May Miller and her son Eliezer are in my care."

At this news, the gray-haired man threw his hands in the air, speaking loudly, "*Gott sie gedankt* (God be praised)," while his wife began weeping in earnest.

"Tell us, tell us more."

They moved to the porch and Clara began to speak, feeling emboldened by these people's concern. She shared May's story, and although she tried to avoid details that would be inappropriate to speak of, the couple understood what had happened clear as day.

"No. Oh no. No." The woman threw her apron over her head, her husband reaching for her hand as he gave into his own tears.

He blew his nose, wiped his eyes, then introduced himself and his wife as Leonard and Sadie Yoder, the folks who had been neighbors when the children arrived. He told her of the suspicions they harbored, but how, as was the custom, they never interfered until Oba revealed his scars.

They'd moved on account of the ministry refusing to budge on the case, but when Melvin's farm came up for sale, they'd moved back.

"What about the boys?" Clara asked, tight-lipped.

"Ammon and Enos are out in the world. They wanted nothing to do with this community, so when Melvin was taken the state placed them with an English family in Jonesboro. We met them once and they seemed like nice folk. I certainly do not blame those boys for wanting to leave, neither do I judge them. It's a miracle if those boys come away unscathed. Levi—Leviticus—is with us. I don't know what he will say when he hears news from May. She was like a mother to him. So sweet and kind. And all the while . . ." She shook her head in disbelief.

Leonard Yoder began to speak.

"Melvin is not in his right mind. He's violent, taken with fits of weeping, he shouts and swears terrible. They try different pills, do the shock treatments, but all we can hope for is God having mercy on his soul. Losing the mind is not something we understand, so we can only pray for him. I go visit him about once a month, try to talk sense to him, talk about repentance, Jesus, the plan of salvation, but I can only hope for the best. I often wonder if he wasn't healthy in his mind for much longer than we think. He seemed to be an angry, tortured soul."

Clara's mouth was a hard slash. "It's good of you to have mercy on him. I find myself without a smidgen. May has to live with this now, for the rest of her life. She'll never forget. I hope the time will come when men are punished for this. Held accountable. I hope a time will come when women and girls can speak out, without the crippling shame. The thing that is hardest for me to bear is the sincere obedience, the spirit of servanthood May has always shown. She will go to her grave with the battle of forgiving him, forgiving herself, for as outlandish as this may seem, she will blame herself, if allowed to be alone with such thoughts."

"But these things are kept in the dark, you know. It is better for the health of the community, better for everyone involved. Especially the good name of the Amish church," Leonard said piously.

He would have done well to keep that opinion to himself, with Clara's eyes flashing hot sparks of outrage, lashing out with words he had never encountered from anyone's mouth. She made no apologies afterward, simply sat and stared at them both with eyes as cool and clear as a midsummer's brook.

An awkward silence prevailed, but the conversation was soon patched up in the way of forgiveness by Sadie doing her best to soothe ruffled feathers, bringing a refreshing jello salad and slices of walnut cake with brown butter frosting. Leonard was careful with the way he expressed himself, watched Clara with a wary eye and an unexplained respect for a whole other brand of Amish womanhood.

A shadow appeared in the doorway.

Clara looked up to find a tall, dark-haired youth standing awkwardly, his hands sunk deep into his trouser pockets.

"Oh, Levi. Levi, *komm mol* (come once). This is Clara Yoder from Ohio. She lives with May. You know, your May. May Miller."

Clara had never seen a youth with such pure gladness etched into all his features, his eyes ablaze with it, his grin as wide as his handsome face which dissolved into near tears as he remembered his companion, a stepmother figure, a friend and mentor. He said nothing at all, but Clara caught the glistening of his tear as it fell.

"Would you like to travel to Ohio to see her again sometime?" Sadie asked, to which he nodded, his eyes like stars on Clara.

Clara smiled at him, then told him if he ever came to visit, she just might keep him, the way her farm was filling up with horses and never enough time to keep everything the way she wanted.

Leviticus smiled, and when he spoke, telling her that he would love to see May, Clara was amazed at the depth of feeling in his gravelly voice.

Leonard took her for a tour of the farm, the cotton fields now turned into corn and alfalfa. Holstein cows dotted the pastures, productive milkers who were the pride of Leonard's life. Clara was smart, curious, asked him why he didn't farm cotton the way Melvin had, and was told there wasn't that much profit unless you paid the black sharecroppers unfair wages. He just couldn't justify that and stand in front of God with a clean conscience, which perked up her opinion of him considerably.

Leonard offered to take her to see Melvin, but Clara was unwilling, seeing no sense in confronting someone who was no longer responsible for the workings of his mind. He could no longer hurt those children, or any children, and that was the most important thing. At this point, what he had carried out here on earth had to be reckoned with between him and God. As Clara was driven away in the taxi, she could only breathe a prayer that God would somehow heal each of those precious children, and especially sweet, obedient May.

Chapter 16

THE WET SNOW MELTED. THE CALL OF SCRUB JAYS AND RAVENS ushered in the newborn fawns, the bear cubs, and arctic fox kits. Mud caked between boot soles found its way indoors and turned the huskies into brown, bedraggled animals who were taken to the river for a swim and a good soaping, only to be turned into mud again.

Huckleberries, gooseberries, blueberries—every green bush popped into a riot of purple berries. Grizzlies and brown bears became fat and lazy; the grasses turned into a myriad of green. Jonas hacked away at a sloping south-facing field, planted turnip seeds and beans, pumpkin and summer squash. He knew which vegetables would thrive and which would never make it through the short summer.

Her name was truly Samuel. Sam Zusack. Her parents were from Anchorage, Alaska. Her mother was an Inuit woman who married a white trapper from British Columbia and bore him one child, a girl named Samuel.

Oba and Sam were as innocent as the rising sun. They spent every possible day on the river, in the woods, where she taught him everything there was to know about the great Northwest. The days were long, with only a few hours of total darkness in midsummer, and they didn't waste a moment. They needed to stockpile all the fish they possibly could, necessary for the health of the dogs. Hunting itself was serious business, the meat from elk, moose, or caribou insurance against winter's hunger.

The first real problem they needed to tackle was the lack of a boat. An outboard motor was considered a necessity by Sam's father, a bearded man in his fifties, his hair in a long braid down his back, a seemingly permanent wad of tobacco in one cheek. Brad was tall and lean, like Sam, slower than a tortoise and about as talkative. Slow to smile, even slower to give an opinion, but easy to like, Oba hung onto every word that finally found its way out of his mouth. Jonas chuckled, mostly, when Brad was around, shaking his head in disbelief at the length of time it took for him to speak.

His Inuit wife, Rain, shortened from Rainwater, was given to chattering, chock full of Arctic lore, adept at every hunting and fishing trick known to man. No doubt about it, the Zusack family colored their world with light and laughter. It was a tremendous blessing to have human company to revel in, to enjoy, to cook moose steaks and blueberry cobblers, to sing and share stories around an outdoor fire, the sparks shooting skyward to nestle with the stars.

And Oba fell into a miserable love. Miserable on account of Sam's complete lack of interest, an innocent unawareness of the abiding love that took control of his life. When he didn't see her for several days, he was pathetic, mooning about the cabin like a forlorn hound dog, driving Jonas to yelling at him to go jump in the river. When he was with her, he was worse. She would appear with her cap on backward, her black hair a tangled mess, dressed in torn jeans and a muddy plaid shirt, her fingernails ringed with grime, alight with some new device to snare rabbits or net fish. Each time he was thrilled to see her while simultaneously feeling tortured with an unnamed desire for *more*. Finally, an amazing girl who he could see himself marrying, and all she seemed to care about was hunting and fishing. She treated him like a brother, which was the last thing Oba wanted to be to her.

Brad and Jonas spent all summer building a boat, using green lumber and the help of a boat-building manual. The art of boat building was not something acquired overnight, for sure, Oba thought, as he watched the men struggle with attaining some semblance of a bow.

"A boat needs a good shape. You can't just build a flat raft," Brad said, scratching his head in bewilderment. "But this lumber doesn't want to do what it's supposed to."

They put Oba to work, bending, holding pieces with clamps, fitting the long planks like a handclasp until spikes could be driven to hold the heaviest timbers, then bolted into place. He felt the thrill of seeing the craft come to shape, saw the outline of a genuine wooden boat, felt an accomplishment even greater than he'd felt as the cabin took shape.

They slapped at the ever-present blackflies and then got used to the constant high whine of mosquitoes as the season went on, the bites only annoying on occasion. The river gurgled over rocks and the sun shone most days as bald eagles wheeled overhead, their wingspan an amazing display of power. The dogs whined on their chains, but Jonas didn't trust them to stick around if they were let loose. He took them for long walks to keep them fit and get their energy out.

The day came when the boat was pitched and painted, the outboard motor attached and ready to go. Sam arrived with her parents and Jonas was in high spirits, a time of celebration after months of hard work.

Brad navigated the river in his own boat, which was how they usually came to visit. To trek across the untamed land would be arduous work—there was no sense spending half a day hiking to and from Jonas's cabin when they could cut around the woods via the water. The river was deep and wide, with dangerous bars of gravel that protruded along its banks, but Brad knew every twist and turn, knew where the best route would carry them along. Often, Sam would be standing at the wheel, taking instructions from her father as she brought the boat through the current, her face alight with the challenge of pleasing him, showing him she could do this as well as he could.

And Oba stood on the bank, gripped by his feelings for this adventurous, completely guileless young woman.

She hopped off the boat, turned to grab the rope, then helped tie it to a tree, watching as her father instructed her. She turned to smile at Oba.

"Hi, Oba."

"Hi."

"You ready for the big day?"

"Yeah."

She smiled again, her teeth as white as snow in her copper-colored face, her hair caught up in a braid along the back of her head. Oba's heart melted within him, knowing he would never tire of the sight of her, would always become tongue-tied and brainless the moment she stepped out of that boat. He imagined himself saying clever things, the way he would entertain her with his knowledge of the world and experiences in towns and cities she had never encountered. But when she was present, all the words seem to disappear from his mind.

All he knew when he was with her was the way she infused his entire being with light and warmth, each moment as wondrous as the next. Sam netting fish, uncaring of the cold river water, her feet clinging to rocks as surefooted as a deer. Holding a rabbit by its ears, after a quick shot, her face like a sunbeam. She could skin and gut a rabbit with a few quick strokes of her knife, shove the carcass in her backpack without thinking. Oba learned far more from her than he could ever teach her.

They created their own sense of competition. Oba was taller, more muscular, could cover more ground without tiring, and had become a crack shot, able to compete with her ability at bringing down game.

And today he would learn the intricacies of navigating a boat on the great river, a job he did not look forward to. He was deathly afraid of water, the drowning of his parents the root of his uneasiness at the sight and sound of a swift current. He had learned to enjoy swimming and fishing, but getting in a boat was an entirely different matter. But today he would have to hide every sign of his desperate timidity. He knew how Sam felt about boats, about the river—she loved them. There was no way he could let her see his fear.

The boat was handmade, heavy, with a definite lack of grace. Something about it appeared quite different from the Zusacks' craft, a factory-made outboard more than twenty feet long with a delicate bow, a wide body, and all the correct measurements. Oba viewed them both from his perch on a large rock, watching Jonas and Brad roll the heavy vessel on small logs until they reached the water, where it flumped into the river with a tremendous splash and rocked back and forth like an overfed duck. Brad and Jonas lifted their faces to the sky, howled, and then did a clumsy victory dance, clapping each other's shoulders. Rain shook her head, her flat, wide eyes squinting as she smiled, and Sam laughed outright.

She saw that Oba wasn't participating in the celebration. "Aren't you happy to have a boat on the river?"

"Yeah, I am. I'm just not a lunatic."

She frowned at him, two small puckers appearing below her smooth brow. "They aren't either," she said, only a bit stern.

Oba turned away, did not answer. She watched the mysterious face, the profile she was accustomed to seeing, the quiet way he had about him, his eyes never quite revealing anything. He was an extremely handsome young man, any girl would be sure to notice, but she could never place her finger on exactly what it was that kept her at a distance. He was a great hunting and fishing companion, a true friend in every sense of the word, but she could never bring herself to think of him . . . well, in that way.

Her mother was protective of her only daughter, had seen Oba once, said there was something about that boy, and shook her head.

Her mother was a full-blooded Inuit and had lived in the Far North all her life. She had enjoyed a simple, happy relationship with her husband from the day she married him. They lived a solitary life, which suited her very well. She felt herself lucky to be with a good man like Brad and wanted the same for her daughter.

Rain was not a mother who coddled her daughter, but expected her to learn to fish and hunt, how to keep a decent cabin, sew her own clothes, learn how to harness a dog team and drive them. She was proud of Sam and had no intention of letting some good-looking, white-haired scoundrel ruin her chances at a happy, fulfilling life.

So she watched beneath lowered lids, half her attention on the river and half on the interactions between Oba and Sam. Like a statue Oba sat, still and unresponsive, as Sam spread her hands. If Sam knew what was good for her, she wouldn't worry about him. Rain gave a small snort and turned her attention to the men who were trying to get the engine started, pulling on the rope over and over.

Finally, with a weak blatting sound, the motor came to life, causing more jubilation from the men. Sam leaped away from Oba and ran recklessly down to the water, splashing through the shallows and hauling herself onboard, from where she motioned to Oba.

Rain looked over to watch his response and was amazed to see him white-faced and apprehensive. What? Was he afraid of a boat?

"Get going, there," she shouted.

"Does the boat hold four?" he asked.

"Go find out."

He shook his head and sat on the rock as if his backside was glued to it. "You go," he said, angry now.

The motor was revved into a louder, faster gear, the rudder drew to the right, and the nose swung out into the current toward the middle of the river before moving upstream, Brad at the back, Jonas in the middle, and Sam at the bow, her face lifted to the sky as she exulted in the power of being on the water.

Rain chuckled, then lowered herself to a grassy knoll and sat cross-legged, her elbows propped on her knees, her keen eyes surveying the opposite shore for signs of wildlife. She decided to ignore Oba. If he wanted to be friendly, it was fine with her; if not, they'd sit there in separate worlds till the boat returned.

A swan gave its plaintive cry from somewhere in the deep water grasses on the opposite bank. Another answered, so Rain watched for its arrival and exulted in the grace and precision with which it landed on the faraway bank. Oba sat like a stone, giving no indication of having heard the swans or the answering call.

As for Oba, he felt like a complete failure, and he was convinced that Sam had lost any shred of respect she might have had for him.

AS THE DAYS grew cooler, Jonas grew more serious about gathering enough food for the winter. Alpheus would fly in some necessities and luxuries, but the biggest part of their food would be from the land. The old radio on the shelf crackled and sputtered, with occasional news from the outside, but Jonas knew winter was coming by the feel of the wind, the shortening of the days that would bring the sudden cold during the night.

Gradually, Oba learned to appreciate the boat. When it was just Jonas and Oba, it was easier to climb aboard. Jonas picked up on his fear but didn't make a big deal of it. He encouraged Oba gently, letting him come at his own pace. Eventually Oba got used to the idea of sitting atop the water in a craft that actually seemed perfectly reliable and waterproof, in spite of his misgivings. He learned to relax, to ignore the tilt of the boat when he cast his bait too far, or when they leaned over with the net to scoop large flashing silver char, trout, and salmon into the bottom of the boat, where they gasped and flopped about until they died.

He learned to accept the death of animals, of fish and large beautiful caribou or elk, as gifts for their survival. He learned to feel the thrill of setting his sights, pulling the trigger, and watching the animal collapse, or, if the shot was not perfect, of trailing the fresh blood till they found it. He grew confident in cleaning the animal, packing out the meat, drying it on racks or preserving it in Mason jars, knowing this would stave off hunger when winter storms prevented any interaction with the outside world.

He missed Sam when the Zusacks' visits became less frequent, but knew they, too, were intent on gathering food for winter. He thought of her every day, longed to see her with an intensity born of his love for her, but had no idea how to spark her feelings. It was better to focus on the job at hand, better to be grateful for Jonas and his easy companionship.

He no longer brooded when there was only him and Jonas. He was too occupied, too intent on the job at hand to think about his own petty feelings. Jonas could speak freely, unafraid of the dark look and curt reprisal. He watched Oba stumble from his bunk, wash his face, and brush his teeth and wondered what possessed a person to brush his teeth every day. Perhaps it was some holdover from his Amish upbringing, that teeth brushing.

He told Oba this one morning, as he was bent over the sink, plying the toothbrush as if his life depended on removing every trace of anything that might have clung to his teeth. Oba finished, rinsed the toothbrush, tapped it on the edge of the porcelain sink, put it in the stoneware mug, and set it on the highest shelf. He grinned at Jonas, a good-natured grin that made Jonas decide he was one of the best-looking young men he'd ever seen.

"The Amish? I doubt if they had much to do with brushing teeth. My mom was particular about it. Guess it stuck."

"You never say much about your mother," Jonas observed.

"No, I don't. Guess it's easier that way. It seems like a long time ago. Another world, really."

Jonas glanced up, noticed the lack of anger, of fierce self-defense, and wondered what brought this about.

"What I wouldn't give for a dozen eggs," Jonas said, changing the subject for fear of saying the wrong thing.

"Yeah. Oatmeal gets pretty boring. But if you're hungry enough, it isn't bad. We always made it with milk, though. It's creamier. Out here, a cow and chickens wouldn't last very long, would they?"

"There's some folks have them. They bring in a few chickens, a couple of calves, and raise them. It takes a sturdy barn, though, with all the predators.

"Why don't we?"

Jonas shook his head. "Too much trouble."

THE LEAVES CHANGED to astonishing shades of red, orange, and golden yellow, the grass turned brown and brittle with a lack of rain. The river ran low, revealing a wide pebbly beach strewn with driftwood. The air was frosty in the morning and the days were filled with hunting and gathering. The air surrounding the cabin was rank with the smell of drying fish impaled on lean branches strung from forked poles stuck into the ground. But their days were full to the brim, every hour taken up by a sense of urgency, a need to stockpile meat for themselves and the dogs.

Oba's eyes took on a new light, a shining from within, a sense of purpose. He didn't notice it himself, but Jonas saw the change, day by day, week by week. It seemed as if Oba thrived on challenges, was never happier than being pushed to his limits. He was dead tired in the evenings, but never sullen.

Before the first snow fell, Oba surveyed the amount of dried fish, the jars of meat, the cache built behind the cabin, and realized he had been a large part of their success. It was a new and strange perception, one that was startling in its sense of well being as he stood beside Jonas, surveying the results of their relentless labor.

"It's enough to make a man proud," Jonas said. "Thanks, Oba."

"Thanks for what?"

"I couldn't have done this without you."

"Yeah, you could."

"No. You don't understand. I couldn't. I'm not getting any younger."

Jonas didn't tell him about the awful pangs of pain from his arthritis, the swelling of his joints, the pain keeping him up at night as he changed positions to ease the discomfort. He felt the cold seep into the corners of the cabin, dreaded the worsening of the condition he knew would occur.

Oba caught Jonas's eye, grinned, but words eluded him. He had no idea how to respond to praise, but in that moment, he felt happy and like he belonged.

ALPHEUS BROUGHT IN the supplies before the river froze over. He was delighted to see them, his elfin face alight with good news and good food. Oba greeted him warmly and helped unload and sort through boxes and bags. They spent a long evening sitting around the homemade table, listening to stories from Dawson Creek and beyond. Someone—Alpheus had no idea who the man was—had found a fairly large amount of gold west of Dawson, up toward the Yukon Territory, so now there was an influx of feverish men who had more craziness in their heads than common sense. Alpheus leaned back in his chair, crossed his wiry arms across his concave chest and shook his head.

"It's almost the '50s, mind you. That stream of men in the 1800s will never be repeated, hopefully, but this is bad enough. They aren't equipped to deal with the rigors of this country. Driving into Dawson by the carload, it's a mess. The world's changing, but some things remain the same. The greed of men, the lust for gold, the unfairness of race and social status."

Oba looked up, wondering at the man's language. Some things were the same the world over, he supposed. As an orphan, you were below others, bound to cruel relatives and their expectations. There was prejudice against anyone who wasn't white. There was greed, yes, the love of money that took completely possession of someone like Melvin, turning him into an evil man who let nothing stand in the way of his goals.

The men's voices droned on, but Oba was lost in sharp memories like knives, scars twitching and searing into his back. He moved his shoulders, tried to rid himself of the sensation, but gave up and went to lie on his bunk, caught up in the throes of his past.

He felt the hot sun on his back, heard the jabbering of the sharecroppers, heard, too, the rattling of the wagon as Melvin approached, the mules on their normal hurried trot. The expectation of being called, asked to do some menial work that sent hot rebellion through his veins. He thought about the similarities between hatred and defiance, found no difference.

He simply hated Melvin, and that hatred had stayed in his heart, causing him to be miserable with the realization of it. He'd blocked out God on account of it. Told himself he didn't believe, when he knew very well there was a God. He was just terribly frightened of Him, given the fate he knew all haters deserved.

How did one go about shedding hatred?

He'd never wanted to before, never let it bother him that much. But now, listening to Alpheus and Jonas, the atrocities of men, he realized he was no better. The only thing missing was acting on his feelings. But it wouldn't take much to become violent, the way some men did, hitting with fists, drawing knives or guns.

A deep fear brought a numbing chill, then the heat that enveloped him like a fiery current. Was he, in fact, no better than a murderer, hatred blooming in his chest like a vicious growth?

Far into the night, the men's voices droned on, but Oba heard only the half of it, embroiled in his own searching, his own discomfort. If only he could talk to someone, but who would be willing to listen?

Not Sam. She was too young, too unencumbered by the severity of real life. Raised in the wilderness, free as a bird as she roamed the forests and waterways of the Northwest; she would never understand the deep measure of his pain. He knew Jonas would just tell him to forgive. But how did one go about forgiving?

He slept very little that night.

As it was, Rain proved to be the one who opened her heart to him. Arriving on the cusp of a heavy, wet snow, with Brad in tow, she had come with the sole purpose of teaching Oba how to make good bread, a staple for the long winter. She clucked and stewed, fussed at the other men and shooed them out the door.

"You can fish, set traps, do something," she said in her openly demanding voice. "Just get out and give us some space."

By then, after weeks of unrest, Oba was bleary eyed, sullen, and uncooperative. He couldn't see why he had to be the one to bake bread. Couldn't Jonas do it?

Finally, Rain stopped, put her hands to her hips, and glared at him with black eyes that sparked angrily.

"What is your problem? You have moods like thunderclouds. It's rude, and annoying."

Oba looked up, an angry retort on his lips, but there was something so inquisitive, so birdlike, and . . . he didn't know what. She was so short and dark and round-faced, like a chickadee with her snapping eyes. He lowered his eyes, shrugged his shoulders.

"Where are you from? Why are you here? I've often wondered what your story really is." Her voice softened a little. "I tell you what, let's make some tea and you can sit down and talk to me while the dough rests. Tell me your story." When only silence filled the room, she added, gently, "Pretend I'm your mother."

"I don't have a mother!" Oba shouted, his voice hoarse with exhaustion and misery. He left his chair, wheeled and flung himself face down on his bunk.

Rain was not surprised. She sat on the edge of the bunk, making Oba uncomfortable, but she did not move. She began to talk in a soothing voice, telling him her own story, one not unlike his own. A destitute family, given to alcoholism, she was given to white traders, abused, neglected, an indentured servant of sorts.

As her soft voice ran on, Oba flipped on his back, his weary eyes alight with interest. Without realizing it himself, he was actually absorbing her words, listening to her with astonishment. When he raised himself on one elbow and began to talk, she sat very still.

The bread dough rose up over the bowl, the sourdough starter vigorous beside the heat of the stove, but it went unnoticed as Oba's past was brought to Rain's ears. She was not shocked. Her only emotion was a deep and lasting empathy. When Oba twisted his body to face the wall and deep shuddering sobs came from a place within, she merely placed a hand on his back and began a rhythmic massage.

She felt the ribbed welts, continued rubbing, and waited out the storm of his weeping, her own eyes brimming as she sat beside him.

After his storm of heartbreak had passed, she began to speak gently.

"Life is not always fair. Why circumstances occur the way they do is not our choosing, but we have to deal with it the best we know how. Bitterness and anger will only dig us an early grave. After I became a Christian, I was shown the way to inner healing, and so can you."

She paused, waited for a response. When none was forthcoming, she waited patiently till Oba asked her to move, please, then got off his bunk and sat with his elbows on his knees, his head hanging low, his blond hair like a tousled halo.

"I don't know if anyone can help me. I don't know if I'm worth salvaging, with all the hate inside of me."

CHAPTER 17

THE HEAT OF SUMMER GAVE WAY TO AN EARLY AUTUMN THAT year, with a frost covering the earth unexpectedly in late September, causing housewives to lift their hands and lament the loss of the late cabbages and green beans. Farmers watched the cold rain drive against the east windows in the barn the following day, crossed their arms and shivered, then went to the house for their long underwear and an extra pair of socks before continuing the job of hauling manure onto the hay fields that had the last cutting taken off the week before.

Samuel Troyer came to visit Clara, said she'd better think about getting her manure hauled the way it was fixing to be an early winter. She eyed him with condescension and asked what was wrong with hauling manure in the snow? Nothing was quite as irksome as a man telling her how to manage her farm. It was her farm, her horses, and what was wrong with making her own decisions?

"Oh, nothing's wrong with it. It's just the fact that you have quite a pile of manure behind the barn, thought you might want to haul it before the snow flies."

"You already said that."

On his way home, Samuel wondered what it was about Clara, the way she could reduce a man to a stuttering schoolboy with her *ga-schwettz* (talk). She was just a *grosfeelichy frau* (proud woman), and mark his words, no good could come of it. Who had ever heard of a woman living alone, having so many horses in the first place? That was exactly what was wrong with the modern-day world, these women thinking they could do what men did. It all started when they allowed women to vote, that was the thing. He could see nothing good coming from women going out and getting jobs, leaving children with whoever would take them.

As Samuel grumbled on his way home, Clara's face lit up with an idea. She hurried into the house, kicked off her boots, threw her coat and scarf over a chair, and put the coffee pot on.

"May!"

When there was no answer, she went to the stairs, called again.

"May!"

"What is it?"

"Come here. I want to tell you something."

Quiet footsteps on the stairs, a finger to her lips as she approached.

"Is he sleeping?"

May nodded.

"Sorry."

"It's all right."

"Sit down. Hey, you know I have a mountain of manure behind the barn. Old nosy Samuel Troyer stopped in and thinks we'll have an early winter, then had enough nerve to tell me I should haul my manure before the snow gets too deep. So, I'm going to make a frolic for the men in the community. Next Saturday. The women can come along if they want, bring a covered dish. I'm not cooking for so many people. They can bring something."

"Oh my, Clara. You don't want the whole church here," May breathed, aghast at the thought of the whole house swarming with children. She thought of Little Eliezer exposed to all the colds and flu.

"No children. I'll make that very plain."

THE FOLLOWING SATURDAY brought a cavalcade of manure spreaders, drawn by a variety of faithful Belgians or Percherons, brown, white, or black, their immense feet lifted higher than normal, the excitement of being among so many different horses causing them to lift their heads on thick, arched necks.

The day was sunny, with a brisk October wind, but felt hats were drawn down tightly, coats were donned, and warm gloves put on to protect the hands holding the reins. The men were in high spirits as teams jockeyed for position. Pitchforks were brought out and the manure began to fly.

May stood at the sink, filling the coffeepot, her back to the huddle of talkative women, glancing out the window for one person who she could not find.

The kitchen table was loaded with dishes containing a variety of home-cooked potato casseroles, meats, vegetables, dumplings, and noodles. One by one, the lids were lifted, exclamations of praise like birdsong saturating the kitchen with shared cheeriness and love of cooking. May smiled shyly from the stove, uncertain if she was genuinely included in all this goodwill. Then she caught the eye of Hannah Weaver, a thin, dainty woman married to one of Simon's sons, Paul.

Hannah smiled, and when she saw her smile was returned, she made her way to the stove, crossed her arms, and leaned sideways.

"How's it going for you? The care of the baby and all."

"Good. It's much easier now than when he was younger. He cried when his little belly hurt, and I didn't always know what to do for him."

"Oh, I imagine. I can't think how hard it would be to be without a husband. Paul is just wonderful with Dena and Marvin."

"Is he?" May's eyes radiated happiness—what a blessing to have this young woman single her out to start up a real conversation.

"He is. I think he might have learned it from his father. I always thought it seemed as if Simon was good with the children, and I'm proud to call him my father-in-law."

May's expression was wistful, but she nodded her head, smiled shyly. "I don't know the family very well."

Here Hannah gave her a look of curiosity. "Kettie said Andy was doing Clara's chores when she went visiting. I didn't know she had relatives in Missouri or wherever she was."

"Andy? Yes, he did." She hurried away, the heat creeping into her face. What must Hannah think?

When Hannah followed her to the sink, put a hand on her waist, a touch as light as a feather, May turned her face away.

"Don't, May. Don't feel ashamed. I would be more than happy to see Andy with a nice girl, after all he's been through." She leaned closer. "I heard he was here during that awful storm. That was a very good thing."

May smiled but made no comment. Hannah couldn't begin to realize the haven she had found in Andy's arms. There, her past had been obliterated, wiped away like a message on a chalkboard. She lived and relived those moments, wondered at God's mercy. But this was hidden in her heart. She must never speak of it to anyone, knowing no good could come of it. She was not worthy of a good man's love. Would never be.

May faced Hannah after a few moments. Their eyes met and held, both smiled, then turned away in confusion.

A loud wave of laughter erupted from the rest of the women.

"May! Do you have that coffee ready?"

May smiled, assured them it would be in a few minutes, felt a wave of love and acceptance at the shouting of her name. Could it be? Could it possibly mean she, May, was a part of the community, expected to make coffee and serve it when it was time?

"May, I brought these molasses cookies. Henna Sarah brought walnut bread with frosting on it."

"That's great. I made chocolate crinkles and snickerdoodles, so we have a real good break for the men. Clara said she'll be in when it's ready."

"All right. Do you need help filling the trays?"

"No, but you can get the cream from the pantry."

"May, Eliezer's awake," Roman Annie called from the bedroom.

Here was where the acceptance would end, she thought, hurrying to retrieve her baby from his crib. She held him over her shoulder without feeding him, the boiling coffee on her mind, his little dress smoothed over his rounded backside, her hands nervously tucking in a stray part of the skirt.

Only for a moment the kitchen was quiet, with the sound of the clock's steady tick-tocking from the living room. Then Japheth Yoder's wife, Ella, trilled, "Oh, let me have him, May. He is so adorable I just can't stand it. Look at that hair."

There were a few raised eyebrows, a few frowns of disapproval, but Ella was clearly the one in charge. She held him up on her lap, his sturdy legs supporting him, his smile so easy and quick, it almost brought Ella to tears. A general hub-bub followed, with exclamations of wonder at how he had grown, what a handsome little fellow, and so forth.

Clara clattered through the door, her face as red as her scarf, calling for action in strident tones. Women hustled after her, bearing trays of cookies, the huge coffee percolator, and a stack of mugs, but May chose to stay in the kitchen, away from prying eyes.

Delicious smells wafted from the elongated wooden table. There was stewed chicken and dumplings, green beans and onions, meatloaf with tomato sauce, mashed potatoes, scalloped potatoes, and fried potatoes. Noodle casseroles with sausage and browned butter, ham gravy, and chicken gravy. Peas in a white sauce and scalloped carrots. Apple pies, cherry pies, and pies that looked like custard but had two layers, which someone dubbed Montgomery pie. Cooked cornstarch pudding, canned peaches thickened with jello, cream tapioca, and pumpkin torte.

The men piled their plates high as talk flowed freely. May listened to the uproar about the price of milk, the creamery making things hard for the farmers. But, the men agreed, as long as they could supplement their income with pigs and chickens, the mortgages would be paid.

May moved from stove to table, quiet, demure, the perfect example of a humble young woman. Eliezer was handed from one lap to another as dessert was served amid the men's praise. Women blushed as their husbands passed on some of the pies, waiting to take a slice of their wives', guaranteed to be the best. No one was shy and everyone enjoyed the company of those around them as talk and laughter filled the room. May's cheeks were flushed as she filled water glasses and served coffee with Hannah.

The door opened and he was there, filling the entrance to the kitchen amid yells from the men at the table.

"Now you show up, after we're about done!"

"No work, no food!"

"What? You have to finish up by yourself."

And so forth.

Andy was laughing, his eyes crinkled until only a thin line of turquoise blue showed through. He took off his hat, raked a hand through tousled hair, looking, looking across the kitchen, searching for May.

Her back was turned, but he recognized the slope of her thin shoulders, her white covering with the lovely blond tendrils showing beneath.

"Someone give him room."

"Sit over there, Amos. Git."

Their eyes met above the talk and the gaiety—met and held. May's cheeks bloomed like a rose in the heat of a June sun, and he lowered his eyes to his plate. A deep happiness spread through him, the knowledge she was here, and was happy to see him. He ate quietly now, without entering into the conversation. He was half listening, but his mind was far from the kitchen table and its occupants.

They had no idea how many of those around them had taken notice of their attraction. These things were not spoken of in public, except in hurried whispers between women, hands held sideways over wide grins, eyebrows arched in playful wonder.

May was exhausted after the din of the frolic. She lay in her bed, her whirling thoughts keeping her awake. What was this new and questionable acceptance? Was it only to ride the crest of happiness to be sunk into the depth of despair? The women seemingly loved Eliezer, held him and clucked over him, as if he was white. A normal baby.

Oh, but her little Eliezer was normal, too. He was perfect.

If any of them had known Clinton, they would all agree. It was only the deviation off the beaten path, the coupling of an Amish girl with a colored non-Amish. The respected order of the day had been slashed, allowing folks to judge, to become angry, to look down on upon her.

But she deserved those judgments, she reasoned. She should be grateful for the slow shift in attitudes, in spite of being mystified by it.

DOWNSTAIRS, CLARA LAY awake for reasons of her own. She had been the single one, yet again, the odd one out in a world of couples.

What if one of those kind, blustery men were her husband? Every time she looked in the mirror she knew there was not one reason why any man should ever give her a second glance. But still, sometimes she wondered what it would be like to be wanted.

She had seen it. She had caught the look between Andy and May, had thought she would be happy if this should occur. So why the searing stab of jealousy?

Andy Weaver was, hands down, one of the nicest men she had the fortune of knowing. She'd often pitied him from afar, wondering what one person had ever done to deserve the kind of treatment that hifalutin' Doris handed him. But she supposed it was the human condition, men falling for a flirtatious eye and a figure to match. And here was skinny little May and all her sorrow, and a man like Andy took to her like a magnet.

She forced herself to wish them the best.

What was wrong with her? She had never liked men, told herself she would never marry, and meant it. Perhaps it was normal to feel this way after a day surrounded by couples. Sometimes it just got tiring being so different from the others.

Well, God gave her this red hair and spotted her like a leopard with these freckles, had sent the feed man and allowed the spirit of rebellion within her, so she guessed she was who she was for a reason.

She thumped her pillow, rolled over, and fell into a deep sleep. In the morning she awoke refreshed and charged downstairs to start her day. She donned her homemade coat and her red scarf and went out to her horses, putting last night's silliness behind her.

May stood near the washing machine where she was doing laundry, appreciative of the wringer washer propelled by a gas engine. What a modern marvel! And so kind of Clara to purchase it. She loved feeding Eliezer's diapers and nightgowns, his dresses and *unnahemlin* (undershirts) through the rollers that squeezed the soapy water before falling into the rinse water. When she rinsed the clothes well, pounding them up and down in the clean water, she swung the wringer into position and fed the clothes through the wringer again, watching as they tumbled into the clothes basket, then carried them outside to peg them on the wash line where a stiff breeze caught the diapers and flapped them like white dancers, the edges taking on a bit of a freeze.

May sang as she worked, then went to check on Eliezer, who was still sound asleep in his crib. She hurried back to finish the washing before he woke. She would fry ponhaus for breakfast, fry the leftover potatoes, and make her perfect fried eggs. Perhaps *ponnakucha* (pancakes), Clara's favorite. Oh, but what if the day came when she would make Andy's breakfast? She chided herself for having those foolish thoughts, felt the blush spread across her face.

And then her thoughts turned to Oba.

Dear brother, where are you? I want to tell you about Andrew Weaver, and the dear Amish brethren who accept Eliezer and me. I wish I could see you, talk to you. Are you all right? Are you somewhere nearby and I don't know it, or are you halfway cross the world?

She prayed for Oba, asked God to keep him in His care, felt the calm that accompanied her deep inner faith. She knew if she could not have Oba, she could still trust God.

"Thy will be done," she murmured as she hung out the last apron.

Clara returned from the barn, her glowering face giving away her bad mood, threw her red scarf on the hook, and went to the stove, holding out her chapped, reddened hands.

"You know, May. I'm not ready for this. It's *blitzen* cold already, and it isn't winter yet. I can imagine the kind of weather that's waiting to break loose."

She gave a shiver, then stood even closer to the heat. "Your ponhaus is ready to flip."

May lifted a corner of the seasoned meat, replaced it, and went on with the pancakes, without saying anything about it.

"They're ready to turn," Clara prodded.

They were not as crispy as May would have liked, but being the obedient person she was, she inserted the turner and flipped the squares of ponhaus expertly. Clara frowned, watched as May tested another cast iron pan for the level of heat, then poured batter.

Everything was wrong that morning—the food, the weather, the mess those men made in the barn—till May was more than happy to see Clara don the coat and scarf again and let herself out the door and back to her horses. May worried all morning about whether she had done something wrong. Perhaps she had said the wrong thing at the frolic, but then, she'd barely spoken to her all day.

When Clara did not come in from the barn at lunchtime, May went in search of her, leaving little Eliezer on his stomach, grabbing at any available toy placed on the blanket. She was not in the forebay or in any of the stalls. Horses whinnied, shook their heads up and down, pawed at the straw, but there was no Clara in sight.

Where could she have gone?

Perhaps to the pasture in search of something. Or in the haymow. She had turned to leave, her thoughts on Eliezer, when she heard a low moan, a sound that sent a stab of fear to her chest. She clutched at her unbuttoned coat, raced back to the area the sound came from, slid the wooden latch on the gate, before taking stock of the animal that stood with his head tossed, a fiery look in his eye.

The stallion.

And then she caught a glimpse of red.

The sight of capable Clara thrown into a corner, as if someone had taken a rag doll and pitched it violently, was so unexpected and so terrifying that May opened her mouth and screamed.

The stallion tossed its head and stomped his foot in agitation as raw fear paralyzed May, but only for a few moments. The dire situation was imprinted on her mind, and she was stung into action. Keeping one eye on the stallion, she kept to the opposite wall, reached Clara, and called her name, loudly, over and over, before reaching under both armpits and moving backward.

Only a few feet, and May could tug no farther.

The stallion's nostrils quivered as he let out a ringing blast of sound, a primal call of conquest, but one that lent superhuman effort to May's slight form. She bent to the inert Clara with a renewed energy that bordered on panic, and moved backward another short length before trying again.

The stallion took a step forward, then another, his ears turning back with the equine hostility May recognized instantly.

She straightened, looked into his eyes, and with what she hoped was a command, said loudly, "Whoa."

The stallion's ears flicked forward. He stopped.

May moved Clara another short length. She looked behind her, then at the stallion, before beginning another desperate struggle. Breathing hard, she straightened before catching her breath.

"Clara. Clara. Wake up," she called urgently.

The only response was another low moan.

The stallion walked over. His face was inches away from May's head. He was a huge gray and white horse, wide in the chest, with a long well-built form. She had always admired him from a distance, but now, in this enclosed area, he was gigantic, a threat to both of them.

May reached out a trembling hand. The stallion raised his head, moving the halter away from her reach, then pivoted, exactly what she had feared. He was turning his rump to lash out with both hind feet at the unwelcome intruders invading his space.

There was nothing else to do but call out a firm "Whoa." She repeated this, trying at least to distract the horse as she began drawing Clara through the straw and manure yet again. One desperate lunge and she reached the gate and broke through. The last few feet she simply rolled Clara out of the gate's way, before closing it with trembling hands. She turned to Clara, called her name over and over, with no response.

Was she dying, here on the cold floor of the barn?

She had to check on Eliezer. She dashed through the cold, ran up the steps, heard his mournful cries as she yanked at the door.

"Poor baby," she crooned, as she caught him up in her arms. "Shh. Shh."

What to do? She had to get to Clara. She bundled Eliezer into his little coat and bonnet, grabbed a quilt from the crib, and hurried out to the barn, the blanket drawn well over his face.

The gloom of the barn disoriented her after the cold sunshine outside, so it took a few moments before she could discern the fact that Clara was not where she had left her. Clutching Eliezer, her heart pounding, she called out.

"Here."

Weak and trembling, but it was Clara, lying by a pile of hay, having pulled herself to an odd position as she tried to get up.

"Clara! I'm here. Are you all right?"

"No. Why would I be?" Her voice was like barbed wire.

"Let me help you."

"It's my leg."

Quickly, May put Eliezer on a soft mound of hay, then gasped at the odd angle of Clara's foot.

"What do you want me to do?"

"Go get someone who can get me to a doctor. He turned and it was like a gunshot on the side of my leg. He got me good. Must have kicked out with both legs, I don't know."

"I'll take Eliezer."

"Guess you'll have to. I'm not much good lying here."

May picked him up, went through the door, and assessed her situation. Simon Weaver's farm was a good half mile, but it was the closest Amish neighbor. There was a small white house closer, but she remembered hearing that the young couple there was away visiting relatives.

She started resolutely across the corn-stubbled fields, her small shoe print creating a trail through the cold, moist soil. She shifted Eliezer from side to side, her arms numb with the effort, her legs trembling from exhaustion as she pushed herself on. She climbed a wooden fence, crossed a pasture, and let herself through a gate before arriving at the back of a huge white barn. Shyness overtook her, and she hesitated, then moved past the barn, up to the yard gate.

The door opened, and Simon Weaver came out to meet her.

"Here, here. What brings you out on this cold weather? Bring the child inside quickly."

He held out his arms, and May gladly deposited the heavy bundle into his arms.

"It's Clara. She was kicked by her stallion," she gasped.

Simon strode into the house, calling for Kettie in stentorian shouts, with the poor wife appearing at the door of the washhouse with soap clinging to her hands.

"Here. Clara was kicked. You watch Eliezer, and I'll take May."

"Oh! Yes, of course. Here. Give him here." She reached for the baby, glad to settle on the creaking hickory rocker with a little one to care for. Simon wasted no time getting his team ready, and May hopped up gratefully, Clara the only thing on her mind.

The doctor was called, and soon the leg was set and put in a clumsy plaster cast. Clara was given a pair of crutches and told to stay off that foot for six weeks, at least.

Clara just glared at the doctor, as if he was responsible for the whole incident. May found herself speaking up to thank the doctor, and then Simon, since Clara was clearly not in a mood to say anything pleasant. She made sure Clara was settled comfortably with a blanket and a cup of tea before she went back to retrieve Eliezer, wondering how on earth they would manage the horses with Clara unable to walk.

CHAPTER 18

He took the dogs by himself that day.

He packed a few strips of dried meat, his rifle, an axe, and a couple extra traps he would install in strategic areas. Jonas wasn't feeling well, his arthritis flaring up in his shoulder. He told Oba to be careful, especially along the river where the ice would appear solid but was not, it being too early in the winter season.

It was exhilarating standing on the back of the sled with the seven dogs strung out in front of him, straining into the harnesses, their feet like a whisper as they hit the new snow, creating a sort of chorus, their heads bobbing as they ran. They loved to run, and it showed in the tireless lope that carried them along the riverbank. On either side, the fir trees stood sentry, guardians of the meandering river filled to the brim, ice beginning to form like islands of lace. Along the banks, the ice appeared to be substantial, but Oba remembered Jonas's warning.

He kept to level terrain as much as he could to take it easier on the dogs, but when he came to deeper forest, there were more rugged turns steep inclines that seemed to come out of nowhere. He breathed in the sharp air, rife with cold and the scent of pine and hemlock. He set the traps where he thought the area might contain a few arctic fox, or snowshoe hares, the huge white rabbits that left their clumsy footprints in soft snow.

He had never spied a wolverine, the voracious killers who fearlessly attacked much larger animals, tireless in the chase of prey, stronger than a wolf in spite of their smaller size.

He refused to let his mind dwell on grizzly bears or the smaller brown bears. He had never overcome his deep-seated fear of being mauled by one, but he felt safer as early winter blanketed the land, knowing they would be hibernating.

He stopped the dogs for a rest on top of a hill where the trees had thinned to stands of young spruce trees, dotting a greasy field with a full panoramic view of the mountain range directly ahead. He wondered why they were named the Pink Mountains, which made no sense except for the pink glow a setting sun would cast over them. He never tired of the ever-changing views of this awesome land, never tired of his forays into uncharted territory.

It was Sam who had taught him all the lore of her ancestors. They had spent hours together, hours of learning the skills of a good provider. He missed not having her with him, but knew it was best to go without her, give her time to spend days with her family, wondering where he was, why he did not show up. Or perhaps she didn't care and didn't miss him at all.

Oba was tired of the miserable existence called falling in love. What other ailment could cause someone to moon around the cabin wanting to be with another person every single hour of the day, until his life was nothing but wishing and wanting? He spent all his time dreaming up ways and excuses to run on over to her cabin, a distance that required a few hours of travel on foot. Often she would welcome him with gladness, then treat him like a little brother, or like her mother or father. He finally admitted to himself that she did not experience any of the dry-mouthed heart palpitations he did. In fact, she acted as if it spited her to quit whatever it was she was working on when he showed up at their cabin.

Once, she had been skinning a rabbit, and she went right on with her work as if he hadn't appeared at all, leaving him standing beside her as she expertly plied the long, curved hunting knife, holding it in her teeth when she needed both hands to draw the skin away from the carcass.

Her mother had made a rabbit stew, with dumplings simmered on top, full of rich gravy and savory onion and carrot. He had never eaten a better meal, he told them. Oba and Sam had walked together that evening, skipping round, flat rocks on the river, without saying much of anything. He was completely happy, a sense of lightness, a feeling of finding a lasting home. He'd watched the curtain of dark hair swinging as her strong arm pitched an expert underhand throw, sending the flat rock skipping across the slow eddies of the river.

Today he stood on the edge of a steep incline, the mountains ahead of him, the enormous blue of the sky shrinking him to a pinhead of existence. So unimportant, so small and insignificant.

Who cared about him? Who knew he was gone, remembered him?

May. Surely May wondered about him.

To leave this great country to resume his search for her was so pointless, but staying here pining after Sam wasn't much different. One was as fruitless as the other.

He thought of Rain and her preaching about God, about Jesus. Well, that was okay for her, but he was ashamed of Jesus. His name made him uncomfortable, so uneasy, in fact, that he didn't like to hear it at all. Who could ever know for sure that He even lived and died on a cross? That whole deal was completely uncivilized in his opinion, but then he guessed thousands of years ago, people were barbarians, putting someone on the cross for thinking differently than the mainstream, for healing people and all that weird stuff.

Rain had brought out his shameful emotion, though, the way he'd cried like a baby, something he wished he hadn't done.

But still. He had felt a little better inside, as if some of the cobwebs had been swept, the darkness and hatred of Melvin Amstutz no longer as powerful, maybe.

Perhaps you could deny God all you wanted, and he'd never stop trying to win you over, sending people like Rain to make you see that you weren't the only one living with pain and a searing hatred.

Suddenly the dogs burst into a frenzied barking, leaping to their feet as they all turned in one direction.

Oba froze.

Slowly, he turned, watched across the young spruce trees, the snow-covered valley of grass and saplings that sprouted from the earth. He reached for his rifle, clicked the safety off, desperately searching for the object of the dogs' frenzy.

A huge bruin moved steadily through the spruce trees, his wide head with a snout like a pig, small eyes like those of a swine, a lumbering, rolling gait with massive paws turned in, like a pigeon-toed person, his enormous shoulders jostling the loose skin so that his whole body seemed to roll.

On instinct, he called to the dogs, his only sensible thought to leave the area as fast as possible. Here was the approach of his greatest fear, a full-grown grizzly, who had foregone hibernation for reasons no one would ever know. Oba swallowed bile, felt waves of nausea accompany a powerful urge to throw up. His fear controlled every aspect of his thinking, his body responding with heat and icy chills, a heartbeat that hammered erratically, dizziness, and loss of vision. Almost, he fell sideways, but caught himself on the curved wood handle of the sled.

The dogs were going crazy. Eb was actually dragging the remainder of the dogs, tilting the sled as he leaped forward, baying, creating a terrible ruckus. Oba knew he should loosen them from their traces but could not find the strength to do it.

The great bruin stopped, lifting its large golden snout. Oba watched through vision blurred by his fear and anxiety. When the bear resumed his walk, his great head swung back and forth, his eyes focused on the dogs, who were leaping, falling over each other in their urge to attack.

Oba was trembling all over, his teeth chattering like castanets. He realized then, he felt the same thing he had so many times in Arkansas, waiting, watching Melvin approach with the whip, his large calloused hand curled around it, containing the stinging length to the handle.

A spurt of adrenaline brought a searing urge to do something, change something. He didn't know what he was supposed to accomplish, but in reality, he knew he did not need to stand alone and take this.

This time, he could defend himself, or die trying.

To compare the wild grizzly to Melvin Amstutz brought a new level of focus, a sharp instinct for his own survival. The bear lumbered on, stopped, swung its massive head in irritation, then rose slowly, ominously, on two hind feet, creating an unearthly roar that reverberated across the valley.

Oba saw Melvin. He saw him lift the whip, his face splotched with purple marks, heard the roar that came from the grizzly's mouth.

He felt the first slash, the one that always took his breath away, and he screamed and screamed. His screams rattled in a hoarse throat, before a great and terrifying calm spread across his chest. He lifted the rifle, drew a perfect bead, thought of Sam's words—high in the shoulder, the neck, or between the eyes.

Melvin. The whip. Cowering, whimpering, begging for mercy, and still the knotted end of rawhide repeatedly broke the skin on his back.

The bear would move on up the slope, his canine teeth puncture his skull, crush the bones like dry twigs, his claws rake his skin like the end of Melvin's whip.

He pulled the trigger, then again. The bear jumped, dropped to all fours and dashed to the left, rolled on one side, tried to get up, but Oba drew another shot, placed on his skull, and the bear rolled completely, his legs buckled beneath him, and he was still.

Oba babbled incoherently. He cried and sobbed and hiccoughed as he waited to see if the beast would rise to his feet once more.

He felt as if he had faced down his greatest fear, the image of his past, the deep hurt that kept him in its jaws, lived in his body, snaked between healthy muscle and bone, cartilage and blood vessels, slowly taking him down like a degenerative disease. Breathing heavily, he wiped his eyes on his sleeve, then his nose, and laid the rifle across the handles of the sled as he went to quiet the dogs.

Eb understood and laid down, but whined with impatience, his light blue eyes watching every move. The other dogs followed his lead, and silence hung over the pristine land, a silence ruffled only by the chirping of a few juncos high in the spruce trees.

Oba cried long after he'd taken his rifle and approached the bear. He tried to contain his free-falling tears, then gave up when he realized no one was there to hear or see. He stood above the fallen grizzly, knew he had aimed well, knew he had accomplished a heroic shot, knew he would be accepted as a true man of the Northwest Territory, especially in Jonas's eyes.

He also knew, in ways he could not fathom, he had shot down his greatest adversary. He might never know what became of Melvin, but somehow, he realized, the rest of his life was up to him, whether he chose to hang on to old atrocities or whether he chose to move on, even if it meant doing so imperfectly. He would always struggle, but only at times, and those times would lessen with years.

And he said, "Thank you, God."

THE COMING HOME was phenomenal, Jonas in disbelief, then unrivaled elation. They had to get to the downed grizzly before predators did, so they took the boat to the Zusacks' homestead, their sled dogs and oversized sled, knives, meat packs, and whatever the family thought they might need in case of a night's stay.

Oba was flushed with pride, too happy to care whether he was being foolish to accept all the fuss. He led the way into the deep forest, then out to the open field of spruce, just before darkness fell across the land.

Guided by the light of the moon and burning torches, the bear was skinned, cut into pieces, and packed in canvas packs. A huge fire kept predators away from the fresh meat, but they could hear snarls and the barking of foxes, wolves, and perhaps wolverines as they took to the offal thrown a good distance away.

"Them wolverines is pretty shy, but I can guarantee if there's one of 'em at the guts, there ain't nothing else. They'll kill a wolf, given the chance," Brad said, as he sat in the firelight after washing his hands in the hot water from the pot that had been hanging from the tripod.

The meat was all packed on the sled, tied down, and ready for the journey home. To travel at night would be inviting catastrophe, so they fried slabs of fresh bear meat, seasoned with too much salt and pepper. Rain laughed heartily, said it was the only way to eat bear meat.

"It's sort of tough, it is," she said, in her low, singsong voice, with the ending "it is" tacked on to most sentences. "But if we have a late spring, chunks of this here meat tastes pretty good with carrots and turnips from the cold cellar."

Oba's face shone as he lifted a seared chunk of the meat to his mouth, chewed, swallowed, then nodded thoughtfully. He smiled broadly, pronounced it delicious.

Jonas slapped his knees, laughed uproariously, and said he'd never seen it fail, the person who shot the game always tacked the delicious tag on his animal. Oba laughed outright, a full-throated gravelly laugh the Zusacks had never heard.

"Well, it is good. I mean, not like beefsteak or anything, but it's my bear, so I'll say it's delicious."

Jonas nodded, his eyes twinkling. "Works every time."

The night was cold, freezing cold, filled with the mournful howl of wolves, the sharp barking of foxes, the rustling of spruce branches as the wind began to howl after midnight. Sam rolled up with her mother, as two bodies retained the heat more efficiently, and Oba rolled in with Jonas on one side, Brad on the other. The fire was kept going, a wave of cold washing over Oba every time one of the men left the warmth of the bedroll to replenish it.

In the morning, the dogs had feasted on the bear meat and were ready to run, but the journey became difficult with the wind howling in from the north, whipping the soft snow into clouds that obscured their vision. They battled deep drifts. Oba's admiration for the two women bordered on worship, the way they moved gamely through any terrain, lowered their faces and yanked at their fur-lined parkas. Even Rain, short and squat, kept moving right along in the sled runners' tracks without complaining.

Sam was strangely silent.

Oba had tried repeatedly to catch her eye, to speak to her alone, but she shifted her eyes or avoided him altogether. A few times he'd caught her dark eyes steadily fastened on his, but she always looked away before he could raise an eyebrow in question.

As they neared home, she drew back, till Oba was afraid she'd fall behind too far, unable to find her way back. He waited till she caught up, then fell into step beside her.

"You're quiet, Sam."

"Why didn't you take me with you?"

"I don't really know. I guess maybe I wasn't sure you'd want to go. It's pretty cold. I thought I'd set a few traps along the way."

She nodded.

The only sound was the soft *shh-shh* of their feet moving through the snow, the sound of snow particles blowing across the top, the sighing of fir branches as the wind released fresh bursts of snow.

"You haven't come to the cabin in a while," she said, finally.

"Sam, you didn't want me there," he said.

"Why do you say that?"

They plodded on together, neither one facing the other. She came to his shoulder, or slightly above it, so if he did look over, he saw only the top of her fur parka.

"Well, whenever I showed up, you were always busy finishing whatever you had to do, after which you didn't seem particularly happy to see me. Just went about your business. So I figured you didn't want to be with me anymore."

"You were never happy. I don't like unhappy people. They create a bad aura. As if they have a spirit that will eventually wreck my own. Your bitterness was eating away at my own happiness."

Oba was taken aback, ashamed into silence.

Finally, he said, "I'm sorry. I didn't realize."

"Do you know I have never heard you laugh till last night?"

"But . . . I do laugh."

She shook her head. "No. Never."

"I did last night."

"Once. We'll see what the winter will bring."

"What is that supposed to mean?"

"What I said."

"Sam."

"Hmm?"

"You know I have almost no experience with girls, and right now I'm really confused. How can I be the kind of person you want to be around?"

"Either you are, or you aren't. And you weren't always. I have never seen you like last night. You were a whole other person, but I'm afraid it won't last."

"Do you care whether it will or not?"

She stopped, so his steps halted. She turned, and her mittened hands went to his parka. Oba stopped breathing, the weight of her hands like feathers on his chest, her dark eyes enormous with feeling. In all of his thoughts of her, he could never have imagined the beauty of her small dark face framed by the fur on her hood.

"Yes, I care. I haven't always because so often you were like a dead person, living because you had to, not because you wanted to." She stamped one foot impatiently, as if she were mad at him. Yet her eyes shone with much more than anger or frustration.

She was too close to him, too beautiful with her eyes lit from deep within. He had no words. His eyes stayed on hers.

He wanted to hold her, tell her of his all-consuming love, the misery of his days without her, but he remained cautious. Yes, they had spent many hours together, but not once had they come close to expressing their feelings. Instead, they had focused on the love of the wild, the learning and teaching of wilderness skills.

Oba had always loved her. Had wanted her from the beginning. Perhaps, though, it had been a selfish love, and one that could not have lasted, the way he was warped by the hatred of his uncle.

He took her mittened hands in his, looked deep into the dark perfection of her beautiful black eyes, and told her with his whole heart that he would try to come up to her expectations.

She smiled, her white teeth flashing, then turned and resumed walking, leaving Oba to follow, guided by the soaring of his heart.

AFTER THE SUCCESS of that hunt, many more followed, with Jonas and Brad teaming up to create drives along the river where moose or elk often came to drink. The Zusacks had plenty of meat for winter use, but these days Jonas was in pain much of the time, and he wasn't sure there'd be a day coming soon when he couldn't be out there hunting. He wanted a good elk or a moose—maybe both—stored away, just in case.

He never complained, never made life hard for Oba, but Oba saw the way he winced when he swung an axe, grabbed at his shoulder when his rifle kicked at an arthritic joint. The cold weather was brutal for him, and Oba found himself wishing he had a soft mattress for Jonas, even an old lumpy one like the one the Zusacks were so proud of.

Feeding the dogs, carrying water to them, all of it fell on Oba's shoulders now. Jonas found himself wandering to a window when he knew Oba was doing chores and was gratified to see him roughhousing with Eb, then playfully pulling Flo's head under his arm, laughing as she scrambled for a foothold.

Oba had changed, that was for sure. Though Jonas refrained from asking the young man what exactly had caused the shift. He knew the wilderness life would be good for him, but these days Oba almost seemed like a different person.

Wasn't that the way God worked sometimes? He came unannounced, did His glorious work in the heart, and it was only by the fruits, the change in demeanor, that mere mortals could tell. So he decided to remain quiet, ask no questions, and just appreciate the days filled with Oba's talk, his smiles, and more frequently now, his laughter.

When Oba shot a bull elk not far from the cabin, the Zusacks joined them for a butchering day. The dogs lay sleeping in their insulated coats, sated with fresh meat and bones to gnaw. Inside, Rain kept the agate canner boiling with jars of meat, seasoned with salt and pepper.

Jonas beamed from his bunk, pillows propped behind his back, relieved and happy to have plenty of meat till spring. Rain moved from table to stove, short and round, like a little teapot, whistling low under her breath or singing outright in a throaty soprano that rose to squeaks from time to time.

She set the table for five, fried the best steaks in flour and oil, boiled carrots and potatoes, opened the last can of peeled tomatoes, and called everyone in, her voice carrying like a drill sergeant's.

Jonas needed help to get to the table, for the first time. He stood for a long moment, unable to put weight on one knee, till Oba caught his eye and went to him. He knew Jonas hated being dependent on another person, so he said nothing, merely placed a hand on his own shoulder, grabbed his waist, and hoisted him to the table.

Brad observed this maneuver and told Jonas he needed a cane. "I'll make you one. Carve designs on it and everything."

Jonas shook his head. "It'll take more than a cane." He paused and looked around at these people he had come to love. "I guess we'll give thanks for our food, then I'll have to make an announcement."

After the prayer, sober faces turned to him expectantly.

"I'm getting out."

"What do you mean?" Brad asked, the shock on his face quite evident.

"What I said. I need medical attention, and that takes money. We've got our furs, and I have some money in Dawson. I need something to help bear this pain—some kind of medicine, I expect. My hip and knee are too far gone. I'll come back once I'm fixed up a little. It's up to Oba whether he comes with me or stays here with the dogs."

The food was passed with somber faces, but hunger overtook other feelings and they ate well. They changed the subject. Oba's brown eyes shone in the lamplight as he retold his story of the slain elk.

Rain mopped up her gravy with a slice of sourdough bread and tried to keep from staring at her daughter's expression. It was clear something had shifted between Oba and Sam, and here he was ready to accompany Jonas out of the bush, which she knew Sam would never do. She would never leave Brad and her.

At the conclusion of the meal, Jonas explained that he would go out with Alpheus at the end of the month. He cleared his throat, looked at Oba, and offered him the cabin, the boat, everything if he wanted to stay.

Oba shook his head. "I can't stay here, Jonas. You took me in when I needed you, and it's only right that I return the favor. I'll stay with you at least until you get a doctor and figure out what's going on with those joints."

Sam seemed to shrink smaller into her chair, her shoulders drooping and her large, dark eyes fastened on Oba's face.

"I don't want you to do anything you'll be unhappy about," Jonas said very seriously.

"I will be okay. It's just until you get some help, right? I had no idea how serious your pain is. Why didn't you say anything before?"

"I'm getting older. It's not just the arthritis. I feel short of breath. I'm getting weak."

A sober group grappled with this knowledge, but each in his own way. Brad and Rain evaluated the loss by their daughter's tremulous expression, though they felt their own sadness too. Somehow they all knew this wasn't going to be a short visit to civilization. If it was bad enough for Jonas to leave at all, it was going to take time for him to heal up enough to come back—if he ever did.

Jonas actually hoped Oba would stay, for Sam's sake, though it touched him deeply that he was so loyal.

Oba battled right from wrong, without fully understanding which was which. Should he show his dedication to the fast-declining Jonas, or stay and prove himself to Sam? Perhaps they'd only be gone a short while . . . or maybe it would be many months. Did he want to live here in the wild for the remainder of his life? If he stayed, would he always live here with Sam and her parents without knowing whether May was dead or alive?

Did he love Sam with the truly sacrificial love this lonely life would require? He breathed, "Show me" to the air surrounding the table, then smiled widely and said Rain had baked an amazing gooseberry jam cake, lightening the mood of the room enough to bring back a few smiles. Even Sam's eyes lit up a bit. She couldn't help it. His smile was contagious.

CHAPTER 19

As if May's time with Clara with her leg in a cast wasn't hard enough, a winter storm began somewhere in the Midwest, gathering force as it blew across Indiana and into Ohio, bringing winds of hurricane force and a blinding, icy snow, creating a freezing vortex unfit for man or beast.

Clara drank cup after cup of black, scalding hot coffee and fretted and worried about the horses, the barn, the roof on the barn, the barn doors, the latches on the barn doors, the water pipes, the mare about to foal, the supply of oats, the lane drifting shut. And lastly, would May please turn that spigot in the sink? It was dripping and drove her absolutely batty.

Her skin itched inside the cast. Her toes were cold. Couldn't May find a better place to dry those diapers than behind the stove? On and on she complained, till May actually wept into her dishwater.

Help arrived on horseback.

Andy Weaver rode in, put his horse in an empty stall, and fought his way to the house, where May met him in the washhouse, her eyes huge and full of joy at the sight of him. She lifted her hands to exclaim at his appearance, and he grabbed her hands and held them to his snow-covered coat, his eyes telling her how pleased he was to be here, in this house.

They entered the kitchen, flushed and laughing, obviously happy to be together, leaving Clara high and dry, stranded with her broken leg and ill temper.

"Hello, Clara!" he sang out.

"You're crazy."

"No, I'm not. I came to do your chores. Make sure the pipes are open. You should be glad to see me."

"Hmph."

"Come on, Clara, aren't you going to offer me a cup of tea?"

"May can get it for you."

May put the kettle on, then turned as Andy seated himself at the table. She brought a tin of buttermilk cookies, the kind with ground walnuts and rolled in confectioner sugar, his favorite.

He bit into one, rolled his eyes in appreciation, smiled at May.

She smiled back, withholding none of her gladness.

From the couch came the sour observation, "If you two don't quit your smiling, your faces will break in two."

Andy hid a grin. May turned her back. Eliezer chortled in the background.

"Come here, little man," Andy said, then left his chair to scoop him up in his strong arms, while Eliezer turned his head to see who had picked him up.

May waited for his face to crumple, waited for the cry that was sure to follow, but when none came, she smiled again.

Clara barked from the couch, "You better get to the barn, Andy. It looks as if this storm is nothing to mess around with." She wanted to say, *Just go, get out of my kitchen with all your flirting and carrying on. And May, stop simpering about like a lost kitten.*

But Andy took his time, drank his tea, and ate at least half a dozen cookies, with Eliezer grabbing whatever he could reach.

When he left to go to the barn, May turned to Clara. "What would be good for supper?"

"If he stays, you'll need twice as much."

"I'm thinking chicken and gravy, with fried potatoes. We haven't had stewed tomatoes in a while."

"Why don't you two just get married?" Clara asked suddenly.

"Clara! He'd never ask me."

"Think not? Well, I can tell you it's not the horses he cares about, and it sure isn't me."

May turned to Clara with a serious look on her face. "Clara, I hope if the time ever comes for me to leave this house, you will always be blessed for your kindness. I will never forget what you have done for me. You gave me another chance, a whole new life. But I don't know if I ever will. Our lives are not our own, but God's. If it is His will, I will marry someday, but I am surely not expecting that to happen."

Clara turned her head to stare out the window at the wind-driven pellets of snow, her face impassive, her jaw set. When she didn't speak at all, May was afraid she had offended her in some way, unknown to her.

When she did speak, her voice had lost its hard edge, as if the blade of her sharp retorts had dulled. "Thanks, May. I didn't deserve that. I know I've been a horrible shrew, laid up like this, but it's hard on my good humor."

"Is that all it is?" May asked softly.

"Of course. Well—" She paused, weighing whether to say more. "The other Saturday at the frolic, I felt kind of left out, the way everyone had a husband, and there was Andy, who may as well have grabbed you and kissed you right then and there. I don't want a man, never have, never will, but no matter how often I say that, I still have my moments of feeling like a . . . I don't know, an extra thumb."

May's voice was earnest when she replied. "Of course you would feel like that at times, Clara. I do understand. But with you and me, there is no difference. We marry someone if God wills it so. If not, we don't. Either way, we always have God who is in us, through us, and all around us, every day of our lives."

"But you will be blessed. Not me, necessarily. You're a much better person than I."

"Oh, that's not true. Besides, God's love is the same. He gave us our nature, knows everything about us, our inclination toward evil, our struggles to overcome it."

"You really believe He's that close?"

"I do."

"Well, He probably has a fit about how I act with this cast on."

"He knows how you feel."

"Guess so." Then she went right back to complaining about the itch under her cast, the fact that she could not take a long, hot bath, the roll of flesh around her middle that had grown since she sat on her backside all day, the brown tips on the African violet leaves, and didn't May know she was burning the fried potatoes?

When Andy clattered into the washhouse, he was breathing hard, his eyes wide with the force of the storm. If things got any worse, he said, he had no idea how he would get to the barn in the morning, and by the way, he hoped it was okay if he spent the night.

May turned to put another chunk of wood on the fire to hide the blush that rose in her face. Clara told him she'd have to sleep with May so he could have her bed, but he would not agree to that, saying the couch was perfectly comfortable. May kept her back turned until she regained a sense of calm, then served the simple, wholesome supper with lowered gaze.

As Clara predicted, the serving dishes were scraped clean, and Andy asked if the buttermilk cookies were still available. May hurried to the pantry to set the tin on the table and filled three coffee cups as Eliezer banged his spoon on the tray of his high chair.

They settled into an easy camaraderie, the three of them in the warm glow of the kitchen range, the storm scouring the sides of the house, pelting against the windows like handfuls of thrown sand. The wind moaned and the wooden siding creaked as the house withstood the storm.

Mostly, they stuck to Clara's favorite subject: horses. The buying and selling, training them, what to feed them.

"Why'd your stallion turn on you?" Andy asked.

"There was a mare . . ." Her voice drifted off.

Nothing more was said, and the subject turned to the practice of reining a horse to his back pad. Andy wondered if it was good or bad.

"Well, if it's a high-spirited horse naturally holding his head in an arc, the rein is loose when he runs, which is comfortable. But sometimes someone drives an old nag who is only comfortable running with her neck stretched out, like a cow, or a camel. Sometimes a man will rein the horse too tightly, for appearance's sake, which is really hard on the poor thing."

She was in her element, displaying her knowledge for Andy's sake, and he seemed duly impressed. May was happy to sit and listen, to watch his eyes crinkle before he smiled, to notice the breadth of his wide shoulders, the way his wavy brown hair caught the glow from the kerosene lamp.

It was shameful, she thought, her attraction to him. She must not allow herself this joy, this deep happiness when he was in the same room. But when he caught her eye and smiled, her knees turned weak with the fractured beating of her heart.

At bedtime, May took Eliezer up the stairs to her room, put him in his crib, and covered him with three quilts. Cold seeped through the wooden window frames, turning the upstairs into an ice box.

She checked the locks on each window, then crept into bed, shivering. Her feet were freezing, so she drew them up beneath her flannel nightgown and burrowed deeper into the soft mattress, thankful for the roof and walls surrounding her.

She could not remember a storm such as this, the lashing of bare branches like frenzied dancers, the wind moaning, roaring between buildings.

Andy was on the couch below her, his huge body cramped between the arms, without sufficient covers. He would tend to the fire in the cookstove and the one in the living room, so their morning would be more comfortable.

With Clara on crutches, it was indeed a comfort to have someone else in the house. May pondered Clara's words, the revelation of feeling an outsider when surrounded by couples. May had never imagined it, never in all the time she had lived with Clara.

This accident had brought out the worst in Clara, a side that reminded May of Gertie, always finding fault, her disapproval thick and suffocating. May realized how desperately she wanted a home of her own, a place filled with love and happiness, the way it had been with Clinton.

She loved Andy Weaver the way she had loved Clinton Brown. Her love ran pure and true in her veins. In her heart, she knew his kindness, his desire to do what was right and good in the sight of the Lord. She would gladly serve him all the days of her life, if he only would allow it. But Andy knew everything about her past, even the worst part of it, so it was unreasonable to imagine he would ever make a commitment to her.

Sin. Her past was riddled, pockmarked by it, like the deeply scarred facial skin of someone who had a bad case of acne. And there were the dark times, the times she was helpless under a cloud of accusation, of self doubt and doubt in God, when she wanted to end her life because of her own unworthiness.

But Andy had seen that, and still he came to do the chores, which meant he did not despise her. Oh, for a chance to be a wife and mother in a loving community that would embrace her and all her faults. Would there ever be a possibility of fulfilling this deep longing?

She drifted into an uneasy slumber and was rudely awakened by Eliezer's frenzied cry, a cry of pain, one that propelled May from her bed immediately. She felt the heat before she uncovered him, felt the fear rise in her chest. Crooning, she picked him up, feeling his burning face, anxiously attempting to quiet his hoarse cries. She took him to her bed, cuddled him to her warmth, attempted to nurse him, but he would have none of it. He needed comfrey tea from the jar in the pantry and quickly. A vinegar bath with lukewarm water. She lay listening to his soft cries and whimpers, before realizing this must be done in spite of Andy, who would see firsthand what trouble a baby really was.

She lifted her sick child, then made her way down the stairs, her feet like a whisper, but Eliezer's cries intensifying.

"Shh. Shh," May crooned, but nothing did any good.

Andy was there before her feet hit the bottom step, holding out his arms. "Give him here, May. You go get whatever you need."

Gratefully, she handed him over, then went to the kitchen, found matches to light the kerosene lamp, put the kettle on after stoking the fire, watched Andy pacing the floor with the crying Eliezer.

She steeped the tea leaves, then went to him, held out her arms.

"I'll take him," she whispered.

"Finish what you're doing," he whispered back, gently commanding. His eyes were drooping with sleep, his T-shirt white against his skin.

She turned back to the teakettle, poured hot water in an agate basin, added cold till the temperature was suitable, then poured a half cup of vinegar into it. Together, they allowed the warm water to do its work, soothing the worst of the fever raging through his small body.

May saw the brown skin, the curly black hair, winced as Andy was faced with the sins of her past. It was nothing short of cruel to be so attracted to him and simultaneously to be so sure of her inability to marry any normal, young, God-fearing Amish man.

They did not speak till Eliezer was swaddled in a clean nightgown, wrapped in warm blankets, and May held him to offer the tea. He drank thirstily.

Andy watched her, an angel in a white flannel nightgown, the white cloth tied beneath her chin, the outward sign of her inward belief, the head covering worn to bed, so prayer would not be hindered. This was the same belief his mother had always followed, as she bent over his own sick bed. It dispelled the last of Andy's reserve—he was now totally sure she had returned in spirit to the Amish customs. He caught his breath at the sight of her. He wanted to see the beauty of her blond hair undone, the white headscarf thrown to the floor, but not now. That would all come later.

She got to her feet, set the bottle on the table, then turned to carry Eliezer upstairs.

"May!" The whisper was urgent, forceful.

She stopped.

"Would you come back downstairs, please? After he's settled?"

She whispered yes and made her way up the stairs.

He met her at the bottom step, held out his arms, and she went into them without hesitation. For a long moment, they stood like this, drinking in the warmth and comfort of one another. In the soft yellow glow of the kerosene lamp, she lifted her face to find his wide, crinkled eyes searching hers.

Her hands went to each side of his face. She felt the night's growth of stubble, felt the contours of his cheeks, traced the outline of his perfect, wide mouth, before gently drawing downward. She raised herself on tiptoe, met the unbelievable softness of his mouth, a sweet yearning, a hesitation, before both surrendered to the beauty of their longing, their love.

"May. May. My sweet May," he murmured, before reclaiming the softness of her lips. "I love you," he said brokenly. "I love you so much."

She reached up to feel the tears on his eyelids, wiped them away before answering in a tremulous voice, "As I love you. But I'm so afraid you won't have me."

"Why would I tell you of my love if I didn't intend that?"

She drew closer, hid her face on his chest. "Just . . . it's complicated. My past. Eliezer."

"I love you, May. That love includes Eliezer. Your past is gone, darling. Your past is erased by the blood of the Lamb. The only way it can exist is if your doubt allows it to thrive." He kneeled down on one knee, looking up to May's surprised eyes. "If you'll have me, May, will you be my wife?"

From the depth of her fractured life, to the slow ascent from the pit of abuse and molestation, the gathering of life-sustaining handholds from the kindness of strangers, she had survived to this moment. The beauty of his words, his acceptance of Eliezer, his wide sweep of dismissal about her past . . . Her heart opened, reached out, and enveloped this indescribable joy.

"Yes! Oh yes!" she breathed, then drew him up to her willing mouth for the seal of their joint happiness and love.

A door creaked open, a throat cleared. "Ahem."

Andy released May. They stepped apart, two silhouettes against the backdrop of the kerosene lamp.

"Clara?"

"Yep, it's me. I'm freezing. You'd think with a man in the house, there would be some wood put on the fire."

"I did," May answered, already falling into her defense tactics.

"It's still cold. Didn't the storm let up at all?"

"I didn't take notice."

"I guess not. You obviously noted each other, though," Clara snorted.

There was no answer, so Clara rambled on, putting together the bits she had overheard with what she saw.

"Well, if you're going to get married, there's no use delaying it. It's time to get on with it. I figured I'd offer you the house, here, and I'd build a smaller one on the back lot. Unless of course, you plan on farming the home place. Which will it be?"

Andy was taken aback and had no immediate answer. Clara led the way to the kitchen table, turned the lamp up, and put the kettle on. The clock showed 1:15.

She flopped into a chair, threw the crutches aside, scraped another chair across the floor, and thumped the broken foot on top.

"So proceed. What are your plans?"

Andy found his voice. "We haven't reached that point yet."

May was horrified, shrank away from Clara's advances, dreaded the onslaught of disapproval.

"So what did you reach?" A mocking tone.

A few short minutes of true happiness, the pinnacle of joy, and here was the first obstacle, hard edged and damaging.

Andy sat up straight, cleared his throat. "Clara, this is between May and me. Until we're ready to move on with plans for the future, we'd both appreciate a bit of respect. Your offer is very kind and I appreciate it, but we could do without the sarcasm and mockery. Now I suggest we all go get some more sleep and perhaps in the morning you'll find a way to be happy for May."

Clara opened her mouth, closed it, then reached for her crutches and swung off across the kitchen floor and into her bedroom. May watched, felt a kind of sympathy for her, but realized Andy's refusal to accept her snide words was necessary. She told him she was grateful, and he looked at her with so much love that she got up from her chair to sit on his lap, resting her cheek against his face.

"I do not deserve a noble, kind man," she said softly.

"Oh, don't you worry, darling May. I'm not. I just won't have Clara taking away the tiny amount of confidence you possess. You don't have to put up with her jealousy."

THE STORM ABATED, the world turned into a still, dazzling landscape of white, drifts creating deep blue and lavender shadows. The sun on the glossy snow created an almost blinding brightness, causing May to squint as she held her feverish baby at the kitchen window, running water into the teakettle for more comfrey tea.

After morning chores, Andy had made his way home, riding on horseback, the horse wading through snowdrifts up to his chest. She had not wanted him to go, but knew it was necessary to see how his family was faring, and to let them know he was safe. May felt so many different emotions: the worry about Eliezer's fever, the newfound commitment of love, the staggering possibility of Andy changing his mind, Clara's jealousy that raised its ugly head like some intimidating creature lying in wait to consume her.

Clara was in the rocking chair, rocking lightly as she pushed at the floorboards with her good foot, another horse magazine held to her face. The kitchen was quiet except for the hissing of water droplets as May set the kettle on the stove. Eliezer whimpered, then began to cry in earnest.

Clara looked up. "Give him here, May."

"No, I don't want to bother you with him."

"It's no bother."

Was there a possibility of Clara wanting to make amends? Gratefully, May handed her the crying baby, met her eyes, and smiled tentatively.

"You think I'm a bear, right?"

"No, I don't."

"Sorry, May."

"Don't feel bad. It's all right."

"It isn't really."

May bit her lip to keep the tears at bay. So much had happened in so short a time.

"May, I like to sound as if I have everything under control, and I don't always."

May nodded as she steeped the tea. "You've said that before."

"It's just that . . . well, to see you with Andy brings out the worst in me. I'm a homely looking thing, you know, and no one would ever want me with this fiery red hair, a nose like the trunk of an elephant, and freckles like the stars at midnight."

May shook her head, ruefully, searching Clara's eyes for signs of mockery. "Clara, we get things all wrong in our own heads."

"What's that supposed to mean?"

"It's not about what we look like."

"That's a lie, and you know it."

"No, Clara. I'm serious. This is the way you appear to me. You imagine yourself to be the ugliest person on the face of the earth, so to hide your deep sense of unworthiness, you portray yourself as a hard-nosed individual who knows everything and is more capable than any other person, man or woman. Which you are, mostly, the way you are with owning a farm, the expertise with the horses, all of that. But you leave out a very important part."

When Clara watched her so intently, May knew she wanted to hear more, wanted to know how May felt about her.

"You forget about God, the one who directs our paths. He knows every hair on our heads, knows our lives before we are born. If there is a . . . a gentleman out there for you, he will find you. But you have to decide to let go of your armor, your denial, everything. Give it to God."

"I don't want a man."

"Then why all of the jealousy?"

"For you, May, that's quite a mouthful."

"But the truth, right? Look, Clara. I was shamelessly attracted to Andy the first time I saw him but never imagined in a thousand years I would have a chance."

A loud snort interrupted her. "With your angelic looks? Puh!"

"Remember my past? What about Eliezer?"

"He doesn't care about all of that."

"And so, if God wills it, neither will the person care about what you describe as homely looking. Besides, you know, you aren't ugly at all. God gave you those freckles, and I find them fascinating. And your red hair is stunning."

"Oh, shut up."

"Rude, rude, Clara."

They both laughed and a softening of the atmosphere followed. The sun illuminated the cozy house, bathing it in the winter light of newly fallen snow. Eliezer's fever worsened as the day went on and both women put aside their differences to hover over him, anxiously waiting for Andy's arrival in case he would need a doctor's care.

In the late afternoon, when he rode back through the snow, May met him at the door, and he took her into his arms as gently as if she were a precious jewel he might lose if he weren't extremely careful. May laughed a ringing joyous laugh, put her arms around his waist, and drew him to her with all her strength. But she did not lift her face to his, in respect to Clara, who was clearly still wrestling with her own feelings.

Moments later Eliezer awoke, hot and feverish, crying weakly, which alarmed Andy, to the point he shrugged back into his coat and hat and rode home to his mother for advice, then returned with burdock leaves and instructions on the heating of onion and woodash for a poultice. The combination eased Eliezer into a deep, restful sleep. While Andy fed and watered the livestock, Clara barked orders from her rocking chair, saying she was hungry for *oya Dutch* (Egg Dutch).

So Egg Dutch it was, with sausages and stewed crackers for the evening meal. Clara enjoyed it tremendously and softened her attitude, her eyes containing a worshipful light as she talked to Andy.

May smiled and smiled, telling herself over and over that this kind and wonderful man was hers, all hers. If there was a possibility of a heart being weighted down with too much love and happiness, then she just might be in serious danger.

When she was with him, his love made her worthy.

CHAPTER 20

WHEN JONAS DEVELOPED A HACKING COUGH, ONE THAT seemed to tear at the lining of his esophagus, and he raked a clawed hand across his massive chest every time the onslaught began, Oba became tense with worry and frustration. He pleaded with Jonas to let him radio Alpheus for help. Or to go to the Zusacks to get Rain or Brad. But Jonas shook his head, the long gray hair unwashed and greasy, his face flushed, his eyes reddened with spider veins cross-hatched across the normal white.

"I'll be okay. Just give me another slug of whiskey."

The cabin reeked of his sour whiskey breath. He weaved haphazardly between table and stove, then back to fall muttering on his bunk, passed out until a trail of spittle ran down his chin. When he soiled himself, developed a splitting headache, and rained obscenities on the desperate Oba, Oba realized it was time to take matters into his own hands.

His fingers shook like aspen leaves in a stiff autumnal breeze as he harnessed the dogs, fed them a handful of treats to get them to cooperate, then took off in the direction of the Zusacks' cabin. It was tough going for the dogs, the way they kept floundering as they broke through the half-frozen crust. It was a thing of beauty, to watch how the remainder of the dogs would hold perfectly still as they waited on the ones who had broken through. The air was cold, sharp beyond belief, the frigid intake of breath leaving him gasping and coughing as he ran. When the going was smooth, he'd swing himself up to ride as long as possible.

Nothing had ever invoked the sense of freedom, the feeling of lightheartedness, as when he clung to the carved wooden handles of the sled, the dogs strung out in front of him, their bodies moving like rippling water, tongues lolling from mouths that seemed to be smiling broadly with the joy of running. Just running headlong with that head-bobbing gait, their feet whispering across the snow like dozens of fingers on white piano keys, creating a chorus only he could hear. He was one with the land, the lovely creatures running ahead, the endless blue sky, and the air as crisp and cold as slivers of ice.

These moments created a sense of destiny, a glimpse of the kind of life he wanted to live, one in tune with nature, without being disturbed by all kinds of people that humbled his thoughts and brought anger and rebellion like a flock of irate blackbirds. Here in the North, there was calm, a vast world without the complication of other human beings.

Except for Sam, who brought a whole Pandora's box of chaotic thoughts and feelings. So she thought he was dead inside. If she only knew.

More important things to think about now, he kept his thoughts on the business at hand—getting to the cabin to summon help for Jonas.

OBA RETURNED WITH all three of the Zusacks, their faces taut with fear and worry. Rain cried openly when she found Jonas, Brad shook his head, and Sam's large dark eyes searched for answers in Oba's face. They shook him awake, shooed Oba and Sam outside till they cleaned him up, bathed the feverish perspiration from his body, dressed him in clean clothes. Rain cooked moose broth with dumplings and tried to spoon some into his mouth, without success.

She nodded to Brad, who set up the two-way radio to get in contact with Alpheus. The crackling sound as they waited to connect with someone so far away seemed like an eternity. Jonas breathed lightly, his chest rising and falling, his mouth open, as if death was imminent.

Sam cried softly. Oba went to her, slipped his fingers into hers, and held them as gently as a fledgling dove.

Brad worked the two-way radio.

Rain sat with Jonas, held his hand, then stroked his shoulder. "Come on, Jonas, speak to me. Help is on the way. Alpheus is coming as soon as Brad connects. I'm going to pray for you now, Jonas. Pray along with me, okay?"

Outside, the dogs set up a chorus, howling and leaping at their chains. Sam lifted questioning eyes to Oba. Together, they tiptoed softly to the door, lifted the wooden latch to slip outside. Immediately, they found the target of the dogs' agitation, a fast-moving wolverine, low and squat, racing across the river ice without fear of humans or howling dogs.

They stood together, watching the beauty of this elusive creature as he stopped, lifted his wide, jowly face, and sniffed, then dropped on all fours to scuttle into the fir trees at the edge of the riverbank.

"I have a hard time believing they are a vicious animal," Oba remarked quietly.

"They are. I'm amazed to see one this close in broad daylight."

After that, an uncomfortable silence lay between them, the air rife with unasked questions and absent answers. They had talked about their feelings only once, but now the prospect of being apart loomed before them both.

"Jonas. You think he'll ... ?" Sam began, stepping out on safe ground.

"Kick the bucket? I'm not God."

The old crackling sarcasm bit into Sam's delicate psyche. She winced. "I only meant to say, will he survive this, whatever it is?"

"No idea."

Sam inhaled deeply, rolled her eyes, then kicked at a chunk of hardened snow. "You certainly aren't God. Not even close."

"So what is that supposed to mean?"

"Exactly what I said. Oba, you do possess a mean streak. A nastiness runs through your veins, and when I think you have changed, it crops up again, like some menacing raven, ready to pick your eyes out."

Oba clenched his teeth, his mouth a hard slash. Here he was, out in the middle of nowhere, trying to find his way, groping forward, and this girl had just knocked him off course all over again. He took a breath, calmed himself.

"Look, let's not stand here with these petty disagreements with Jonas in a bad way. I'll tell you this. I'm going out with him when Alpheus comes. He rescued me when I needed someone, and I can only do that much for him."

Sam swung the silky curtain of her black hair and lifted a hand to push the heavy mass away from her face, a gesture Oba found mesmerizing.

"You already said that," Sam said quietly, her large, dark eyes filling with tears.

"I'll be back," he promised.

"You probably won't."

"I will."

Sam shook her head. "I honestly don't think you will. You have never forgotten your sister. What is her name?"

"May."

"Yes. I don't think you will ever find true peace until you find her, and I don't think you are cut out to live this life of isolation. I see the restlessness, the gazing off to the mountains in the south, and I feel your longing. You don't know it, but going with Jonas is more about you than about him. You want to go."

Oba shook his head. "I want to stay here with you. If you would accept me the way I am, I would stay."

"No person is enough to keep someone in the wilderness. I would never be enough. You would always chafe at the restrictions of this great land."

Oba's eyes flashed with indignation. "Sam!"

His outburst did not faze her. She looked at him, holding his gaze until he looked away.

ALPHEUS ARRIVED THE following morning.

Jonas had taken almost a cupful of the broth and was speaking with coherence, but he was extremely weak. Oba packed his black satchel, the belongings he would need to accompany Jonas to the hospital in Victoria.

The goodbyes were tearful, heart-wrenching. Jonas, in a weakened state, wept openly, only a thin shadow of the massive man charging into the wilderness with his dogs. The Zusacks would get everything—the dogs, the provisions—until their return, which Jonas told them would only be a few weeks at the most.

Oba hated emotional times such as this. He shifted uncomfortably, put his weight first on one foot, then the other, tried not to watch Rain's tears as she embraced Jonas. He hated the fact that Brad's voice was choked with tears as he clapped a hand on Jonas's shoulder. He held Rain stiffly, his face expressionless as she wept, glad to be released from her clenching hold. He looked away from Brad's searching gaze, blinked with discomfort.

Sam's eyes searched his, but it took a long time before he met the dark light in the beauty of hers.

"Goodbye, Oba."

"Goodbye, Sam."

He stepped away, turned his back. Her hands fell to her sides as she stood apart from her family, alone, watching Oba's retreat.

He didn't look back.

TO CLIMB INTO the small gray airplane beside Alpheus, with Jonas made as comfortable as possible, took a large amount of false bravery. Oba's insides were quaking at the thought of the plane's takeoff in these treacherous conditions.

Alpheus assured him there was enough open water ahead, although the conditions were certainly not favorable. If it wasn't for the fact that Jonas was so ill, he would not have attempted this flight, but a man could not allow his friend to perish without putting his own life on the line for him.

So this was what a cockpit was like. Smaller than he'd thought. Oba distracted himself by observing the dash full of round clocklike dials and numbers. Levers and buttons. A windshield. Not too terribly different from an automobile.

The roar of the engine and the noise of the propeller was much louder than he'd anticipated. He had to calm himself to keep from screaming his panic, to keep from trying to stop this metal bird that flew through the air on gasoline engines and good luck. Sweat broke out on his forehead when the plane began to move. He could sense the concentration of little Alpheus, the skill with which he eased up on one lever, pulled back on another, his small hands dancing across the worn leather tops.

The plane bucked when they hit open water, then skimmed along like a great bird. The trees on the riverbank rushed past, faster and faster, until there was a blur of green and white. He felt as if someone pushed him back into his seat, and became aware of the fact they had lifted off the water, were flying low above the treetops.

Alpheus breathed in, then let out a long, slow breath. "Well, sonny, God was with us back there. No doubt about that. Now look to your right. A sight you will always remember, even if you live to be a hundred years old."

The sight below him was breathtaking. Absolutely picture perfect. Mountain ranges, forests blanketed in pristine white, trails like the outline of jigsaw puzzle pieces, glistening rivers, with no indication any man had ever been there to ruin anything. As they climbed higher, the scope of his vision widened and broadened until he could barely fathom the immensity of this unequaled territory. And to think he had made his way into the interior running, climbing, sliding, learning about sled dogs and danger. And thrived on it.

He was aware of being surrounded by clouds, the scenery below enveloped for a short time. He wondered vaguely if his parents' souls had taken flight in this way.

What happened when someone died? He knew they did not simply turn into nothing, no matter how he had disputed God's existence for much of his life. God was real, he knew that now. He had always known it, if he was honest, but it had been easier to deny God so he didn't have to rely on anyone but himself.

And there was this thing about Jesus, in Rain's words. Well, if anyone carried any clout in that department, it was her. She was the most real of any person he had ever met. Good from the inside out. She took the saving power of Jesus Christ as her reason to be glad about many things in her life. He wondered if she'd ever said or felt a bad word about anyone. If ever anyone would convince him to be a devout Christian, a real one, it was her.

Oba heard a moan from the back.

Oba turned. "You okay, old man?" he shouted about the roar.

"My back aches is all."

Oba could barely make out the words over the sound of the plane.

The clouds outside the window had thickened, but now that they were in the air Oba felt confident in Alpheus's abilities. As long as Alpheus seemed relaxed, he would try to stay relaxed too.

"So where in Victoria do we land?" Oba asked, his words light, casual, though he had to shout to be heard.

"An airport."

"Oh, yeah. Of course."

Conversation was limited, with the roar of the engine, so Oba fell silent. The radio crackled with bits of static and jumbled voices. Alpheus reached over, lifted a black oval attached to the radio, spoke into it, words Oba couldn't understand. When he replaced it, he turned to the left and watched out the window as the light turned a shade darker, as if a thin veil had been thrown across the window.

His thoughts kept returning to his parents, for reasons he could not tell. If their souls were in flight, did they know they were going to another place? Was a soul aware of the transaction from earth to Heaven?

He guessed he would never know, until it was his own time to die. And he didn't have to know. Wasn't that what this thing called faith was all about? Not knowing, but having enough belief that you could count on things turning out all right?

His parents seemed very close, the image of them quite vivid. His father's old straw hat in summer, the way the brim was broken along the edge from his lifting it to allow the breeze to dry his perspiring head. The hat was actually blackened around the crown, from the sweat of his brow, but then, that was the way every farmer was when the temperature reached almost a hundred. "Mercury's gonna bust that thing," his father would say, laughing, as he examined the outdoor thermometer.

Those were the days they spent at the creek swimming, splashing, watching the bugs walking on top of the water. His father called them Jesus bugs because Jesus walked on the water himself. Did he really, he had wondered, then decided, yes, if his father said so it had to be true.

It was so easy back then. No complications, living in the cocoon of the Amish world. Every person was good, or so he thought. Everyone looked the same in church—white shirts, black vests and trousers, hair cut in the bowl fashion, cut off evenly around the ears and neck. Every girl or woman was dressed in the pleated skirt dress, a white bowl covering on her head, and everyone traveled in a horse and surrey. Occasionally an English person would arrive in an automobile, but they, too, were friendly, nice to him. School was a safe haven, with friends he loved, who got into mischief and were quickly reprimanded by the strict teacher he loved as well.

It was after his parents died that his world turned upside down. His mouth drew down in a straight line, his eyes darkened. Could he forgive the Amish relatives who had pawned him and May off to the Amstutzes, or would he always struggle with that? Suddenly, he was tired, so tired. He no longer wanted to face the battle of life. If he lived to be a hundred, would he ever find rest in his soul?

Should he go back to the life Jonas had shown him? If he returned to an Amish community, would he survive in the old ways and rules? Either way, the specter of his past would always bring a hot rush of terrible anger, the kind of fury that threatened his spiritual and emotional well-being.

Jonas moaned, then cried out above the roar of the engine. Oba turned, reached out a hand to console the suffering man, felt the heat through the plaid blanket. He glanced over at Alpheus, who was glaring through the windshield, the light decreasing as the plane roared on. Alpheus kept grabbing the oblong black object, which he supposed was his channel to the rest of the world through radio.

Oba felt no fear, only a sense of calm, knowing he was in capable hands with Alpheus transporting them. He realized that he liked being in the clouds, above the turmoil of his life. Too soon they would land in Victoria, accosted on all sides by humanity, a city teeming with all sorts of businesses and buildings, cement sidewalks, and streets humming with trucks and automobiles. He shrugged his shoulders to loosen them, imagined himself taking charge, staying with Jonas as he was put in a bed, doctors and nurses tending to him. He'd never been to a hospital, had no idea what to expect.

Oba berated himself for his lack of confidence. He was a man, after all. He was an adult and should be capable of handling a situation such as this. If he had conquered so much in the wilderness, he could figure this one out, too.

Alpheus reached up, yanked at the radio. He spoke a rapid-fire volley of words, words Oba couldn't make out. He peered at the one round clocklike dial, then the other. Alpheus's right hand clenched the throttle, the left stayed on the control wheel. He seemed more intense, took no time to shift attention to Oba.

Oba looked out to the right, found the blurred outline of mountain peaks, snow covered, the gray sky appearing to blend with the landscape until they became one. He thought maybe the gray sky was not a good sign, but surely Alpheus had flown through bad weather plenty of times.

The light plane bucked as Oba became aware of flying bits of hard snow pinging against the windshield. He looked at Alpheus, who was concentrating on the flight instruments, muttering to himself. He turned to Oba, his small eyes giving nothing away, except a shout accompanied by a grin that eased Oba's concern.

"We're in for a wild ride!"

Oba grinned back, but gave no indication of the sickening fear he felt suddenly, as if he was yanked to reality, made to see the dragon of danger as the small plane roared through the increasing wind.

After that shared grin, one to give a sense of security, another to cover up the dread, the situation became increasingly more frightening. The air pressure must have increased, the way his ears popped and jangled the sides of his temples as if pressed by two hands. Alpheus worked the throttle, his foot easing up on the rudder pedals, his eyes constantly going to the control dials.

Oba knew fear then, a real all-consuming fear gnawing at his insides till he felt wave after wave of nausea. He fought to keep from gagging. The smooth ride turned into a pitching roller coaster, the wings dipping one way, then another.

Jonas cried out in fear and misery.

Alpheus worked the throttle, tried to keep the plane steady as best he could. Snow attacked the windshield like millions of tiny bullets, hurled against the small plane by the force of a tremendous gale, a freak winter storm with furious intent. It was as if a giant hand kept pushing them in the opposite direction they were trying to go. The plane lost speed, was turned from side to side.

The outspread of the wing on his side pitched violently. Oba grabbed for the control board, the edge of his seat. He braced the soles of his feet, but felt as if he was being tossed like a pebble in a tin can.

"We're going down," Alpheus shouted.

"You mean . . . ?" Oba felt the color drain from his face, felt his upper lip stiffen and turn dry as the horror of death overtook him. So this was how his sad life would end, plummeting to earth, his skull crunched like . . . He swallowed back his shrill cry of fear.

"No, get below the worst. Control dials don't tell me much. Watch for the mountains."

Oba strained to see, searched desperately for signs of jagged peaks, but the only thing in his view was the gray void of hurled snow and the wind behind it.

The small plane pitched and bucked. The radio was useless. Alpheus pulled back on the throttle and his feet worked the rudders as he clung to the control wheel.

Oba clenched his teeth. He did not want to die. Their survival depended on his eyesight to help Alpheus guide the plane safely to an open field, a river. And yet he could not see anything at all. He wiped down the window, wiped a hand across his eyes, would have burned a hole through the window for better eyesight.

But there was nothing.

The hopelessness of their situation enveloped him, the realization of never making it to land safely. Did one simply give in? He had no control, was being whisked along at an alarming rate.

"I can only do so much," Alpheus called out. "If we're too low, we'll hit a mountain, possibly, and if we go too high, with this amount of wind . . ."

Oba nodded.

He was seized with the knowledge of having gotten this all wrong. The revelation was earthshaking. This was not Alpheus at the wheel at all. It was God. This was his life. He was merely a passenger with a much higher power at the controls. He could stare out that window till he was blinded by the effort, but God was still the one who called the shots.

He was shaken to the core of his being.

So this was the answer. If God was sitting at the controls, then he could be surrounded by a sea of humanity, crowded city streets, or a long empty stretch of nothing, and had nothing to fear. Here was Alpheus, doing everything in his power to save their lives, but in the end, it wasn't Alpheus who decided whether they lived or died.

He turned his eyes to the storm, searching for any significant change, but there was none.

Wait. There. There to the left of his windshield.

A brilliant light, an ethereal glow of glorious blue. Slowly, the shape of a perfect angel appeared as in a fog, then turned into a beautiful vision of a heavenly being, the diaphanous gown swirling along to the gorgeous strain of peaceful, restful music.

Oba stared, was overcome by the wonder of it. He reached out a hand to call, to let the angel know he was here, to help them in their plight, but knew the vision was a gift, one he could not have, not now.

"Alpheus," he called. "Turn left. I think we need to go toward the angel."

"What?"

"I saw . . ." He tried over and over to tell Alpheus what he saw, but his voice was impaired. He tried but could only clear his throat.

The engine was throttled down to the lowest speed, the descent as cautious as Alpheus could manage with the bucking of the plane, the howling, twisting wind. When they grazed the treetops, it threw the plane to the right, the impact as sudden as the speed of lightning. Oba screamed once, then heard a sickening, ripping sound as fiery pain shot through his body from the soles of his feet to the top of his head.

THE WIND TOOK on the primal howl of an arctic storm, the great Canadian firs bending and twisting in its power, sending the tops of snowdrifts into a solid wall of snow, beautiful in its ferocity.

In the vast forests of British Columbia, a group of trees had been sheared off, the twisted ends thrust toward the sky like a jagged yellow crown, heralding the grisly sight of the broken, mangled wings of the small aircraft. A part of the body of the plane was broken, ripped in two after being impaled by the massive trees, the gray metal strewn like a child's broken toy.

The snow made a shushing sound as it blew across the wings of the plane, one broken off completely, another crumpled like a ball of aluminum foil. There was no sign of life, no spoken word, no movement at all.

A snowy owl peered from the appendage of the nearest tree, tilted its head, and blinked at the wreckage. A sharp-eyed raven sprang from its perch, lifted its great wings to flap away into the distance, the hoarse cry from its beak ominous in its portent.

CHAPTER 21

WHEN WARM BREEZES REDUCED THE SNOWDRIFTS TO SLUSHY crystals melting steadily into the frosted ground, the earth became a sea of mud. With the arrival of March winds, the forsythia and pussy willows burst into luxurious color and the buds on the trees swelled to bursting. Birdsong escalated to a strident cacophony, the woods alive with the calls of frenzied bluebirds, sparrows, orioles, and cardinals, whose goal was the building of sturdy nests in which to raise their young.

The horse farm was alive with the greening of pastures, newborn foals dancing on ridiculously long legs, the worried mares nickering as their offspring flew headlong into an unforgiving fence. The small house with the dormers in the roof seemed to take on new life as well, as if a fresh coat of paint had been applied, with the magical backdrop of brilliant green, the border of daffodils like a soft, scented rug.

Clara walked slowly, bent over to grasp the hands of the toddling child taking uncertain steps, a smile illuminating the dark face, his tight black curls shuffling in the wind. His navy-blue skirt swirled around the sturdy legs clad in black stockings and high-top shoes. From the clothesline, May watched, smiling, as they made their painstaking journey to the barn, to show him the *gaullies* (horsies).

Her world had been transformed a week earlier, when Andy Weaver had asked her to be his wife in the most humble manner she could have imagined. Her throat still constricted at the thought, the way his true character had been revealed.

He'd told her if he lived to be a hundred years old, he would never be worthy of her, whereas she shook her head in denial as tears spilled onto her clasped hands. And when he got down on one knee, grasped those tear-splashed hands, and kissed them, she became aware of feeling redeemed, rescued by this large, strong man with the sweetest nature.

When he lifted his face and asked her to be his wife, she put one hand on each side of his face, gazed deeply into the blue, squinted eyes, and said yes. Oh yes.

She bent to his fervent kiss, his arms going around her waist, until she thought to die this way would be the highest honor. She loved him with her whole wrecked and ruined being, felt the lifting up of the past riddled and pockmarked by pain and abuse, insecurity and despair. No, she did not deserve him, but he was here now, and he was hers all the days of her life. She would lay down her life, would serve him, love him, spend her days honoring him as her husband, her friend.

The wedding was a month away, when the wind-blown tulips would sway and sing the German wedding songs along with the congregation. A breach in tradition meant the wedding service would be held in the home of the groom, with Clara's house much too small. The wedding dinner would be in the welding shop at Japheth Yoder's, just down the road from Simon and Kettie.

Western tradition differed from the eastern Lancaster tradition, where the service and meals were housed in one building. In Ohio, the service was in one home, the celebration in another, the cooks and tables prepared by appointed members. May knew of no other tradition than the western way, but would have been grateful for either one.

She sewed a new navy-blue dress, crisp white cape and apron, a powder-blue dress and pinafore for Eliezer, and counted the days until April 15th.

The plans to take over the home farm were still intact, but the Weavers needed time, a year or two, to plan and build their doddy house and move into it before Andy and May could have the big farmhouse.

So Andy had rented the Fogelsanger place, a small ranch-style home built of sturdy red brick, a green shingled roof, and a row of trimmed boxwoods like green bunny tails. There was a small red shed in the backyard, a perfect tiny horse stable with room for a few Rhode Island Red hens and a rooster.

It was the sweetest little home, like a storybook dwelling, she told Andy.

She had opened the front door, the green paint so fresh and new, to find a gleaming hardwood floor and blue plastered walls with cute rounded doorways. Knotty pine kitchen cabinets lined the kitchen walls, and the pink bathroom had multicolored tiles that appeared so soft and puffy that she had to touch them to make sure they were hard.

She had dashed from room to room, her cheeks infused with roses, her brown eyes containing so much joy, so much anticipation. No matter they had no furniture, that she had no hope chest filled with embroidered pillowcases and crocheted dresser scarves, no set of fine china and silverware. Clara had an extra table and chairs she'd bought at auction, on account of the auctioneer being unable to procure a bid. With some white paint, it would do a fine job. Andy promised her new furniture—a sofa, chairs, a bed, dressers. The extra bedroom across the hallway would be Eliezer's.

May clasped her hands like a delighted child and looked out the large bay window at the yard. She sighed contentedly. She would be a normal young wife and mother, accepted, loved in the community. Sure, there would always be the stragglers who felt pious in their judgment of her, a fornicator in the eyes of the Lord, one who would yet reap what she had sown. But May was lifted above the sordid mutterings of those who did not understand the beauty of love and forgiveness, by the blessing of a man called Andy.

THEIR WEDDING DAY dawned bright and clear, with a crisp breeze as fresh as the opening of a rose, and as sweetly scented. The rainstorm the evening before produced drops of dew like diamonds on the lawns, leaves and spring flowers embellished with crystals, the sky an azure blue dotted with lamb's wool clouds.

Clara walked with May, little Eliezer bundled on the express wagon in a box, the blankets stuffed around him to keep him safe.

Clara had forgone the traditional navy, for reasons only she would know, opting for a dress in brilliant sea green, one quite questionable pertaining to the Amish *ordnung*, but one that set off her flashing red hair and adornment of freckles. She'd put a wide band of black velvet on the sleeves, which were shortened to above her wrists.

But May told her she looked nice, which was true. Eye catching. She stood out like a peacock among a flock of domestic turkeys, but that, too, was perfectly all right on such a fine day.

Andy was waiting in his parents' kitchen, rising to his feet again and again to watch for Clara and May. His buxom mother was dressed in navy blue, her cheeks like apples, her eyes snapping with high excitement. Repeatedly, she tucked a stray hair into her crisp white covering, wiped the kitchen counter for the dozenth time, then grabbed the linen tea towel to wipe a fingerprint off the window.

"Now, Andy," she said from time to time. "Do you know the wedding vows? Do you understand your *beruf* (duty)?"

"Ya, Mam."

"Do you?"

"Ya, Mam."

"You know that you're marrying this girl in sickness and in health, and in your case, with a colored baby?"

"Ya, Mam."

"You know his future might require extra care and attention, depending on how folks react to his skin color?" She stopped, then shook her finger at him. "And don't you think of making a difference between him and your own. He is your own the day you marry May. Your very own."

"Ya, Mam."

"Oh, here comes Paul and Hannah. Hannah!" she called much too loudly.

Andy sighed, went to the mirror to check out his white collar, then turned to accept his sister-in-law's handshake and congratulations.

When May stepped through the door, hesitantly, almost shyly, he hurried to receive her. He took the windblown child and untied his stocking cap, then opened the buttons of his coat. Hannah watched as the child's hands went to Andy's face, and Andy laughing as he pulled one arm out of the coat, then the other.

Yes, things will work out, she thought.

May greeted Andy breathlessly, then sat on the bench by the kitchen door, put there for the purpose of greeting guests. With Andy by her side, her confidence grew.

They were married by an old uncle, a bishop from north of Orrville, a man with Andy's height and breadth, his white hair and lengthy beard like Moses of old, his ruddy face containing the same squinted eyes, but a voice like a bullhorn. Exhorting, lamenting, encouraging, he kept the congregation spellbound, then wept openly as he pronounced them man and wife and blessed them with the blessing of Abraham, the God of old and still the same. His voice contained all the love they would ever need, and for months, folks spoke of this wedding sermon, the way there was power that manifested itself throughout the house.

God Himself had been there.

May sat beside Andy, cut the wedding cake, received presents, experienced swirls of happiness in all colors. The china was a gift from Andy, blue flowers with green leaves on a white background, the silverware engraved with their initials. There were pots and pans, mixing bowls, a potato masher and spatulas, towels and wooden clothespins, cake pans and cookie sheets, agate roasters and bread pans.

"Oh, Andy," she breathed, her eyes like stars. "I can't take this all."

"Why not, my love? Why not?" he whispered, pressing her to his side for only an instant.

"But it's just not right. I don't need it all."

"You will," he grinned, looking at her meaningfully. "We have an entire farmhouse to fill."

Confused, she looked up at him, then smiled and blushed when she understood his words.

Clara sang louder than anyone, seated front and center, her brilliant dress drawing many guests' attention, which she enjoyed to the fullest. She felt beautiful on this day, she really did. There was just something about wearing the color no one else dared to wear that put her a step above.

As her voice soared, she felt the genuine good wishes she was supposed to feel for Andy and May. She decided it was a gift from God; really now, the way she'd struggled with jealousy in the beginning, then felt so righteous and holy, tears welled up in her green eyes. Perhaps, if she did what was right, God would bless her as well, even in her fifties, even with freckles, a hooked nose, and no chest to speak of. But she wasn't going to take just any homely old man, either.

She had her priorities, and she wasn't giving them up for just anyone.

To be living in a small brick house with green shingles and no upstairs was like playing house at home with Mam and Dat as a little girl here in Ohio. Except now, she had her very own husband and not a make-believe one, although sometimes she felt as if she lived in a world too good to be true.

Finally, her house was truly her own, with no person or group of people she needed to please, whom she served every day with no thoughts of herself. Nothing had ever been hers, not really. On idle days, she had daydreamed of her own house, her own furniture and bedding and dishes, but never had she imagined this wealth.

She had bakeware to spare. A closet in the spare bedroom contained a box with muffin tins, a tube cake pan, extra spatulas, and a few canisters to keep grease or salt or whatever a person felt like putting in them. She had extra blankets, extra towels, and twelve blue-and-white striped washcloths she had no use for except to stack neatly in the narrow bathroom closet. Oh, it was truly unimaginable, these undeserved luxuries.

She found three small soaps, put them in a pretty pink dish, and placed it on the side of the small sink in the bathroom. It matched the glistening tiles perfectly, and she stood back, crossed her arms, and inhaled deeply, allowing the pleasure of this one small thing to spread its wings of happiness around her.

And her precious child, Eliezer, would toddle from the new sofa to the chair and throw himself against the soft cushions before exploding into a joyous laugh, his small brown face lifted to the ceiling, so proud of his own accomplishments. He loved to explore his new home, as if he knew these floors and walls were truly his own.

Then there was Andy.

To live with this fine man was an honor, an undeserved privilege, one she had never dared to hope for. When she hung his large, blue chambray shirts on the line, she felt her heart sing, and when she brought them in, she buried her nose in the scent of him. She took pride in whitening his undergarments, in darning his socks, replacing missing buttons on his denim trousers.

Did ever an Ohio housewife have cleaner, softer laundry? She wondered, then giggled as she rinsed down the wash tubs. Now she was becoming *grosfeelich* (proud), and it was all Andy's fault. His praise came as easily as his breathing, a natural language for both her and Eliezer.

She cooked cornmeal mush in boiling, salted water, poured it into a cake pan and cooled it, then sliced the yellow rectangles and fried them in lard, the high walls of the cast iron pan catching most of the splatters.

When the hens produced eggs, they all had two eggs with fried mush, and May made tomato gravy to go with it. The table was set with the blue Melmac dishes, a gift from his mother, on a blue gingham tablecloth with a white vase of red tulips in the middle, the food steaming hot, the coffee bubbling in the percolator on the back of the stove.

She always looked forward to Andy's return from the farm, where he did his share of the milking each morning.

The kitchen was bright and sunny, the color in May's cheeks reflecting the red of the tulips as he caught her eagerly into his arms.

"Oh, I hope I never get tired of this," he murmured against her lips. "Never was a man blessed the way I am."

To wake up with him beside her, to gaze into the love in his squinted blue eyes, before she had to think of one other thing, was far more than she had ever imagined. She felt found, discovered. She finally had a place where she belonged, without danger or guilt. She was this man's wife, and the blessing of God united them as one, and for this she was eternally thankful.

He ate with the appetite of one who wakes early and works hard before eating. A panful of fried mush disappeared, along with his eggs and three fourths of the tomato gravy, slice after slice of May's homemade bread, before he sat back and drank his coffee, asking her where she learned to make bread like that.

"I made bread almost all my life, Andy. Gertie taught me when I was ten years old in Arkansas. Her arms weren't strong, so I learned to mix and knead it when I was a child."

Andy watched the darkness of her remembering diffuse her face, before reaching for her hand. He took her small one in both of his, then looked deep into her large, dark eyes. He smiled with the tenderness he felt.

"That was a good thing. There is never anything so awful that we cannot find one thing to be thankful for. God knew then that someday you would be my wife, and I would have a hard time knowing which was more precious, you or your bread."

May was very serious, then looked a bit confused, till he laughed, and Eliezer threw back his little head and opened his mouth wide to laugh with his father. When May saw this, she drew her hand away, then reached out to punch his arm, laughing herself.

"I thought you were being serious."

He caught her arm and drew her off her chair and onto his lap, where she snuggled against him as they shared a mug of coffee.

"I love you so much," she sighed. "I honestly think I am living without fear for the first time in my life. Thank you, Andy, for my home, for giving Eliezer a home."

"Eliezer is my son, May. I became his father the day I married you."

"Sometimes I just can't grasp that. Clinton would be proud."

"He would?"

"Oh yes. He was a humble man."

"You've said before."

"He was."

"So I'll always feel like second best?"

"No. Oh, no. Those years seem like another lifetime. There was so much fear, so much guilt. It seemed when I left the farm, my only goal was survival, a form of just . . . well, making it. You have to remember we were in the South. I was white, and we were not together lawfully or morally. I was never allowed back to the Amish, and the whole English world was so new, so hostile. It was just . . . I don't know. Not an environment to make love easy."

"Someday, you can tell me every little detail. Right now, I'm afraid you'll let the darkness grab you again. You know, even when you talk about making bread as a child, I can sense a change in you. I get worried."

"There's no need, Andy. I am all right."

"But you might not always be all right."

May smiled to herself, tucking away the concern in her husband's voice, knowing how much he cared about her. She knew with a woman's intuition there would always be the times when her past would be brought up unexpectedly, like now, and those were the times she would release another edge of the darkness. To talk about it with her husband, the one she loved above everyone else, was a form of healing.

Mysterious, yes, but still. She had never thought of the fact that God had known her so intimately at ten years of age, but of course he had. Every painful, bitter step of the way. He had been there.

SHE WASHED HER dishes in the bright kitchen, washed Eliezer's face and hands before setting him on the floor, where he lurched off toward his toys, only to stumble and fall, then raise himself back to his feet and toddle off.

After the dishes were washed, she would go outside in the brilliance of the day, take a shovel, and dig around the perimeters of the house, where the chickweed created a tangle of green mess among the spent daffodils.

Imagine, she thought. *I am the mistress of my own domain. Queen of the brick ranch house.* She lifted her arms and twirled across the gleaming kitchen floor, her small waist above the billowing of her pleated skirt, her blond hair and dark eyes radiating light and happiness. No one except Eliezer was there to see. No one could judge her as she allowed the cascade of joy to lead her bare feet in a dance of pure freedom. She stopped, put her hands on her hips, shrugged her shoulders, and let out an expulsion of air.

"Huh!" she said out loud, then put her hand across her mouth and giggled, a sound like a small schoolgirl.

She would experience joy in the summer months, she could tell. How was a person supposed to walk barefooted in her own yard, the soft breezes telling you your husband loved you, would care for you all the days of your life, without stopping to laugh out loud and go whirling about the kitchen?

Here, on this day, she would put the shovel deep into the rich soil and create a border for her very own flowerbed. She could plant dahlia bulbs if she wished, or marigolds, or make the bed wider for a lilac bush. Or a rose bush. Clara had roses and had shown her how to grow roots from a thorny switch.

She turned the soil, stopped to breathe deeply, lifted her face to watch a red-headed woodpecker perch on a tree trunk before tapping away at the loose bark.

"Watch out, Mr. Woodpecker. You'll lose your footing," she called, before he lifted his wings and flew away in short, choppy strokes.

And then, because she was so happy, she flopped on her back in the warm grass, lifted her eyes to the puffy white clouds, and began to cry. Tears ran down the sides of her face and her shoulders heaved with each deep sob as the warm breezes sifted the green poplar leaves and the small pine tree sighed as it moved back and forth.

Then she cried more, listening to the sound of the pine tree, remembering her mother's tree by the garden, when she would gather baskets of pine cones before Christmas. She wanted to tell her mother about her own pine tree, ask her what she should plant in her flower bed. She seemed very close, then. As if she could reach out and touch her.

"Mam, look at me. Can you see me?" she whispered.

The puffy white clouds did not change their appearance and the wind kept sighing in the pine tree, but May had wept her tears of happiness, the tears of love for her mother, the tears of healing from her past.

She cooked supper that evening, her face tanned from the exposure to the sun, her cheeks blooming with color. She was ravenous, so she cooked a big pot of potatoes, mashed them with milk and butter, fried pork chops into crispy, salty slabs, and made milk gravy from the drippings. There were new green beans and applesauce, with sour cherry pie and cornstarch pudding for dessert.

She hurried from window to window, watching for the familiar form of her husband, and when she spied him, she opened the screen door and ran to greet him, flinging herself into his arms, unaware of the passing motorist who turned to watch, then smiled to himself as he drove on.

Andy looked down at his beautiful wife, taking in the perfection of her, wondered how he had ever been taken in by Doris's flashing good looks.

"It is so good to be home," he murmured against her sun-kissed brow. "I never realized how long a day could become, waiting to come home to you."

Together they walked into the house, where Eliezer sat playing with his wooden building blocks. He looked up, then set himself on his feet, his little backside straight up in the air, before toddling over to Andy, who scooped him up and kissed his cheek.

"Hey, little man! How was your day?"

Eliezer merely leaned back, stared at Andy as if to say, "Why ask?"

May laughed. "He actually told you with his eyes."

The meal was served. The most pleasurable part was watching Andy eat, bent over his mounded plate as he shoveled the food into his mouth. He buttered three slices of bread, which equaled four or five bites apiece, then leaned back to give his full attention to May, who was doing her own fair share of consuming potatoes and gravy, stopping only to feed Eliezer.

She smiled at Andy.

"Marriage must be good for our appetites," she observed.

"We were haying today. That is hard work. I hope someday the Amish will be allowed to have a baler. I watch the neighboring field, the John Deere tractor pulling that wonder, popping out bales, and I must say, I want one so bad it hurts."

"Thou shalt not covet," May said quietly.

"I know. But today I did."

"It's okay. I remember haying as a child."

Together, they did the dishes, then walked around the yard to see what May had done. She heard words of genuine praise like a soft, life-sustaining rain. Andy was her beacon of light. He filled up all the empty places she hadn't known existed, so she drank in his words of love, like a person dying of thirst.

Later, they sat on the back porch, watching the swallows dip and curve through the air, calling their fledglings to roost for the night. A field of corn stretched out to the west, a verdant, rippling carpet of promise. Rains were abundant, as was the sunshine in between, the arrival of heat and humidity throughout the late summer months all the heavy green stalks would need to produce thick yellow ears of corn.

Andy's eyes squinted even more as the sun slid behind the rows of corn. May watched his profile, loved the plane of his stubby nose, the way his chin jutted out only enough to make him appear manly with the new growth, the required beard for an Amish man.

"I love you," she said softly, her heart overflowing with the beauty of possessing this man. Yes, that was the proper term. She had become one with him on the day the bishop pronounced them man and wife, and he was hers, as she was his.

What a blessed union, marriage.

She was in his safekeeping, in the circle of his care and concern, never again to feel like an outsider. She had been an orphan, never truly belonged to the Amstutz family, then lived with Clinton out of fear and necessity, her love unbalanced by guilt and betrayal. Then the months at the homeless shelter, where her strength of will had pulled her though, the uncertainty of her bus ride to her home state, an outsider. Shifted from one place to another, to Clara, bless her dear freckled self, and finally, she had found a home.

Andy took her hand, and she hugged Eliezer on her lap, thinking never had a woman been blessed such as this.

CHAPTER 22

CHARLIE HAMMER WAS THE ELDER OF THE TWO BROTHERS. Jerry was thicker, shorter like their father, and more powerful, he would be quick to tell anyone. Charlie, lean and lanky, slow and unconcerned, was just as quick to allow Jerry to run ahead, scouting out every situation, real or imagined, and then follow up with his own timeless common sense.

Their trap lines were scattered in a twenty-mile radius, more or less, considering the amount of zigzagging they did, traversing an unforgiving land beset with creeks, steep ridges, swamps, and mountains. They would leave their father at his taxidermist shop, pile the sled with enough food and gear for a week's stay. Or two, whichever suited them best.

Free as the wind, they had no timeline, no responsibilities except the gathering of furs, a veritable wealth, the way prices were escalating. Their sister Sue had begged to accompany them, but they could see no sense in allowing it, the winter as savage as they'd ever seen. Never one to give up easily, she kicked the sled and yelled at them, her face red with the effort.

"I hate when you do this to me!" she shouted, delivering another solid kick to Charlie's shin.

"Ow!" Charlie caught her arm, twisted it behind her back until she settled down. "Listen, we'd take you, okay? Except we might not have room on the sled. We're expecting a heavy yield."

"Puh. You talk like a farmer. A heavy yield, as if you were grow-ing corn or wheat." She scowled at her brothers, then marched off to assemble her arsenal of weapons, in the form of a doting mother, who appeared at the door with a few crisp questions.

"Mom, no. She can't come today. We won't have room." Jerry was adamant, not missing a beat as he lashed the load to the sled.

"She can run with the best of them, you know that." Hands on her hips, she was a figure of full-blown authority.

"It's not that, Mom. It's extra food, another bedroll. No."

And now, with the storm keeping them deep in the wilderness, over half of their traps unchecked, a sizable pile of raw furs heaped on the sled already, having to ration the food they'd brought, the deci-sion seemed smart.

It was cold. So cold, in fact, the bonfire in front of the tent did little to keep them comfortable during the night. They'd taken to getting out of bed early, dashing around in the snow, thumping their chests, stretching, anything to keep the blood flowing, to feel the tin-gle of warmth in their numb feet.

"Let's turn back after this passes," Charlie said, always the careful one, the one who thought things through.

"Naw! Come on, man. We have twice this amount out there," Jerry protested.

"How are you going to get there? This snow is going to be piled a foot high, two feet, three."

"The dogs love this. They'll get us through."

Charlie considered Jerry's view, then shook his head. "No, it's not sensible. We're turning back."

"Okay, but I'll cut a bargain. Let's check a few beaver traps at Hammond's swamp. It's only a mile or so, right?"

"I'm hungry. Our rations are low. That's going to be an extra half day, if not more."

"Think of the beaver pelts, though. You know the price is outrageous."

"Now it is. Doesn't say it will be in spring."

But Charlie gave in, after the wind ceased its mournful howling through the pines and the sound of scouring snow fell to the soft whisper of occasional flakes. A weak winter sun provided light as they fed the dogs, harnessed them, packed the load tightly, and started the slow trek to the swamp.

It wasn't really a swamp, just an overflow of the creek that wound along a low-lying area flooded over half the year, creating a perfect environment for the crafty beaver that gnawed on young saplings, building powerful homes that withstood the harshest climate. It was Jerry's favorite place, a place he never grew tired of, checking out the marvel of these clever animals' expertise in building these sturdy lodges.

It was slow going, and Charlie was losing patience as they struggled up over a rise. The sun blinded them as the dogs dropped on their stomachs, their tongues dangling as they puffed short breaths of air after pulling the sled up over the incline.

Jerry, always ahead, always the first to notice anything different, ran the back of his hand across his eyes, blinked, then gave a low whistle.

"Charlie!" he yelled, raising an arm to signal his command to hurry.

Charlie looked up, dropped the package of dried elk, and made his way to his brother, his eyes following Jerry's pointing finger.

"What is it?" he asked.

"Look at the trees!"

"What? What . . . do you think it's . . . Not a plane!" Charlie stuttered.

"That's a wing. Part of one. It's mostly covered with snow."

Charlie swallowed. There was nothing commonplace or sensible about a wreckage out here in the middle of nowhere. He had no desire to go down there. He'd never seen a corpse. He thought planes always burned, leaving a twisted mess of charred metal.

"What should we do?" he asked, all the color leaving his face.

"I'll go check it out. You stay with the dogs."

"Be careful. There could be glass or sharp metal under the snow. I'll watch."

Jerry nodded before starting the descent, his arms lifted like wings as he floundered through the snow, which was sometimes up to his hips. The lead dog whined, his ears pricked forward.

Charlie eyed his eagerness, thought perhaps a dog might be able to sniff out any sign of existence, dead or alive, so he unhooked the traces, cupped his hands around his mouth and called, "Jerry! Ben's coming down!"

Jerry stopped, nodded as the dog made gigantic leaps through the deep, loose snow. Charlie turned to hush the rest of the dogs when they set up a clamor, tugged at the traces, lurching the sled to a hazardous position.

"Hey, calm down. Calm down. He'll be back."

He watched across the blinding light of the snow, the fir trees creating a puzzle of dark and light, Jerry a squat figure standing motionless. He turned, waved an arm.

"Get down here. It gives me the creeps," he shouted.

So Charlie spoke to the dogs before floundering down the incline. Out of breath, he drew up beside Jerry. They both stood uncertainly, fear of the unknown keeping them motionless.

"I don't know about this," Charlie said finally.

"Aren't we supposed to let the police or someone else know about this?"

"I don't know."

"I don't want to see a dead person."

"Does anyone ever survive?"

"I have no idea. I can't see how it could be possible."

Jerry kicked at the snow, loosening a heavy layer off the bent body of the plane. They saw the plane was almost broken in two, the one wing crumpled like an accordion, the windshield smashed, the metal bent and twisted.

A pair of ravens flew overhead, then circled to perch on the highest branches of a spruce tree. Ben, the lead dog, lifted his head to watch them, then lay down in the snow, obedient, his nose active.

He whined, then got to his feet, his body turned toward the wreckage, his nose wrinkling, moving as he sniffed the frigid air.

He whined again, pawed the snow, then lay back down.

Jerry looked at Charlie. "He's on to something."

"Let him go."

"Ben, go. Git him."

It was all the dog needed. He made his way through the snow, pawed and scraped on the right side of the wreckage, whining in high-pitched tones. He stood back, his ears pricked forward, before piling into the snow and digging seriously. He leaped up to the side window, yelped like an eager puppy, unlike him. Jerry was the one who went over, pulled Ben aside, and stretched to look inside the front of the plane, the crumpled remains that were a twisted pile of metal. The sight that met his eyes would stay with him for the remainder of his days.

There were two bodies, in positions hard to make out. He knew immediately there was no life in either of them, the way they seemed to be broken, like hurled rag dolls, only worse. He turned away, swallowed, afraid the nausea would overtake him.

"How bad is it?" Charlie asked, his voice quavering.

"Bad."

He turned away, lifted his face to the sun, tried to steady his churning stomach. At first, he thought he heard the creaking of metal, as if the right door was swinging on its hinges. He held very still, every nerve alight to the supposed sound. Suddenly he knew what it was.

A voice was saying, "Here. In here."

He froze, heard it again. He yelled for Charlie, then yanked at the upended door, pawed and kicked, and called out. "We're here!"

From deep within the wreckage, a surprisingly calm voice repeated the fact that someone was alive. "I'm back here. I'm pinned."

"Hang on. Just hang on. We'll get you out."

Charlie was there, his eyes huge in a face the color of snow. How are you planning this, his eyes pleaded, and Jerry knew they'd need an axe, a hatchet, anything to break through. He took off up the incline to the sled, leaving careful Charlie to deal with a situation he couldn't begin to grasp.

"Are you there?" the voice called.

Weak, hoarse, it was like a man who was half dead. Charlie did not like this at all. He wasn't equipped to deal with an accident this bad. The worst thing he'd ever encountered was Jerry getting his finger impaled on a gigantic fish hook.

"I'm here."

"Can you find a way to get me out?"

"Yes. We'll get you. My brother went to get an axe."

They didn't speak. Jerry lifted the axe high, brought it down at an angle, severed the twisted door and opened a passage large enough for one of them to crawl through. It was Jerry who volunteered, Jerry with his impetuous nature, his lack of thought, which was exactly what the situation called for. He could not consider the remains of the two dead men, neither could he worry whether he was doing the right thing. There was no time to bother about details.

He became focused, sure of himself, his trapping skills honed to zero in on his target, which was the man caught between the bent frame of the plane and a heavy black object pushed far enough to keep him captive. He was young. Not much older than himself.

Jerry realized the hazardous position, caught at the upper thigh, his body twisted in a grotesque manner, his face ashen, taut with pain.

"If I could have a drink," he wheezed.

The man's eyes were dark holes. Jerry could not look, but wriggled out, yelled for Charlie, who was almost at his elbow.

"He . . . he . . . He needs water."

Charlie floundered through the snow, returned with the canvas canteen, pushed it at Jerry, wild eyed. He waited, folding and unfolding his gloved hands as Jerry disappeared.

Oba drank a few sips at a time. So thirsty. So much pain. He was cold beyond anything he had ever imagined. He thought he'd be dead by morning, couldn't know what miracle had occurred that he wasn't. Perhaps it would be best if he was allowed to go with Jonas and Alpheus. Those two good men. He'd had time to think, after he regained consciousness, but had fought the urge to sleep, drift away in warm comfort, and get all of this over with. His tawdry life. He'd laughed at the word "tawdry," but that was the best description, when he was delirious, evaporating in and out of his dreams and visions till he lost consciousness again.

"If you can lift the engine," he whispered, his throat raw.

Jerry took stock of the situation, then realized he would not free anyone without Charlie. There was no room unless he hacked away at the side of the plane, which was dangerous in itself.

"Okay, you'll be fine. I have to figure out a way to lift this thing."

When the young man had no answer, Jerry called to him but saw immediately he'd passed out.

"Hey? Talk to me. Stay with me! Don't die on me now."

Charlie called out, "How can I help, Jerry?"

Jerry knew there was no time to discuss a plan. By the time he and Charlie agreed on what to do, it might be too late. Probably it already was. That big engine block had to go. He crawled forward, grimaced as his knee caught an old man's shoe. Tentatively, he reached out to push at the flattened top of the engine block, but there was no way he could budge it. Oba moaned, then let out a blood-curdling call of unbearable pain. All the adrenaline stored in Jerry's stocky body coursed through his veins. He took a deep breath, hunched his shoulder, and threw all his weight against the wedged block. He felt it give.

He knew he had about a foot of space, enough to free the crushed victim. This time he roared with the effort of throwing every ounce of his strength into edging the engine block away.

Again, then again.

Did he have six inches? Eight?

One more time, he drove his bruised shoulder against the heavy obstruction and knew, instinctively, this time he'd be able to loosen the man's legs. If such a thing was possible.

"Charlie?"

"Yeah?"

"You have to work from the outside. We have to cut a hole on his side, where the metal isn't crumpled. Okay?"

Eventually, after what seemed to be hours, the thin blade of the hatchet sliced methodically, carefully, through the sides of the small plane. Jerry directed him from inside, and when the glaring light from the snow fell on them, Jerry saw the unconscious, mangled young man.

How long had he been trapped? If that leg could be saved, he'd eat his parka. He wondered how much blood had already been lost.

It was good, though, that he stayed conked out the way he did. Good they could move him inch by cold, painful inch through the razor-sharp opening and he didn't make a peep. Like his sister's old Raggedy Ann doll, his limbs flopping around, his head falling backward.

"He ain't old. Not like his companions," Charlie observed.

"Poor old coots. They probably never knew what hit them. Went down in the storm. Likely tried to land and folded down through the trees like an accordion. Don't see what kept this one alive."

Charlie was already on his way to the sled for the tent and bed-rolls. Jerry frantically broke off branches, twigs, moss, anything he could find above the snow, then kicked out a place to build a roaring fire. Grimly, they unlaced his shoes, felt the icy blocks of his feet, looked at each other in silence. Both shook their heads. Neither one dared remove his trousers to see the extent of his injuries where he'd been caught, imprisoned in his snowy metal wreckage.

"Poor bugger," Jerry commented.

Covered in woolen blankets, with pelts positioned around him for extra warmth, the fire as high as both of them and the tent stretched out to shelter the victim, they stood uncertainly, not sure what the proper procedure would be, when Oba called out in pain.

"Help me. Please. Somebody. It hurts. Where am I?"

The plea was heart-wrenching in its piteous mewling cry. A vital young man, stripped from his proud strength, reduced to weak cries, was more than Charlie or Jerry had bargained for. But both were soft hearted, both bent to hold his hand, rub a well-meaning palm across his shoulder.

"Look. One of us will go for help, okay? One will stay here with you. You think you can hang on for a day? A night? We don't have a radio, nothing."

"If I can have a drink of water."

And so it was decided Charlie would stay, while Jerry rushed through the wilderness for help, doing it in half the time Charlie would have.

"Now you be careful, Jerry," Charlie called after him.

Jerry swung an arm above his head, already on his way to harness the dogs. Charlie could tell by his short choppy strides he was sure of his own skill in navigating the almost empty sled with dogs keen on the trail of home.

"And don't forget food!" Charlie shouted.

Another waved arm, then Charlie turned to the tent, where Oba lay awake, his face pale and swollen, the anguish in his eyes like a dart to his tender heart. Charlie had been known to nurse puppies back to health after others had given up on them, kept a small menagerie at home, much to the dismay of his mother. So now, faced with this man's discomfort, the danger of having moved him when there were bound to be broken bones or far worse, he stayed calm, the nursing instincts creating a deep empathy.

"Okay, guy. Jerry's gone to get help. If you can hang on until he gets back, you're going to be okay." He sounded more confident than he felt.

A barely noticeable nod of his head.

"You mind if I heat some water, maybe wash the blood and the bruises and cuts?"

"Don't move me," Oba whispered. "I'm cold."

So Charlie hacked away at dead branches till he had a great pile of firewood and built up the already roaring fire.

When he checked, Oba was asleep. Charlie laid a tentative hand on his forehead, was relieved he had no fever. Not yet.

He stood, lifted his face to the clear blue of the skies, prayed for fair weather, realized he was starving. He'd take the risk and set out, hoping to secure a rabbit, a few squirrels, anything to skin and roast. He had salt, coffee, a bit of dried meat, and some flour, a pan. He could supply a scant meal with a bit of luck. He was fairly well acquainted with this remote area, having crossed these ridges and creeks before. If he wasn't mistaken, there was a small pond, like a bay of water where the creek took a wide turn, always teeming with small wildlife. They'd seen plenty of martens, fisher, and the huge snowshoe hares, the ones who provided a tasty meal.

He wondered about this turn of events, how you simply couldn't tell what would occur from one day to the next.

BACK AT CAMP, the fire crackled and burned, the tent flaps open to allow all the heat possible, which was barely sufficient. The cold woke Oba, brought him back from a deep, troubled dream, a dream that threatened him, made him feel as if he was expected to accomplish an enormous task that lay ahead of him, and he had no strength. After that, he was running, leaping, flying along snow trails, with Eb ahead of him, laughing. The sensation of power and freedom stayed with him, until he remembered the impossibility of the first dream.

He sighed, willed himself to endure the terrible pain in his legs. He could not feel his feet, had no way of knowing they were there at all. He had a sharp, tearing pain in his left side, which he figured meant cracked or broken ribs. His right arm seemed to be okay, but his left one was useless. It was hard to breathe, but since that was essential, he endured the pain that came with each inhalation.

He wondered what happened to the man who had stayed. The fire was burning lower, the cold seeping in under the bedrolls. He was just so freezing cold, so miserably, eternally cold. He tried to visualize the burning heat of the Arkansas sun, the way perspiration used to run into his eyes, drip off his nose, soak the back of his shirt and the belt on his trousers. He could hear the sharecroppers singing, the lamentations and rejoicing of their spiritual songs.

But he was still so terribly cold.

How long could a person endure pain and cold? He didn't know. He guessed as long as he willed himself to endure this, he'd survive. He wondered vaguely why he didn't die with Jonas and Alpheus. Well, those two old men were good men, likely God took them to Heaven easily. They didn't look like they amounted to much, but they had the same faith he heard his parents talk about. Heard in church, too, sitting on that hard bench swinging his legs to pass the time till his father put a hand on his knee to make him stop.

Then, in his weakened state, his spirits low with lack of nourishment and constant pain, he squeezed his eyes shut as his mouth was torn back in a grimace of unbearable sorrow. Sobs tore through his throat as he longed to be held in his father's strong arms, his mother looking on fondly. Loved. He was loved at one time in his life. He was. And then Jonas had become almost like a father to him, and now his body lay in that crumpled plane, with Alpheus.

By THE TIME Charlie returned, his tears had dried. His face seemed calm, but so deathly pale. Charlie squatted beside him, looked down on the alarming pallor, and asked if he was doing okay. Of course he wasn't okay, but it was the only thing he could think of to say.

Oba nodded, turned his face away.

"Look, I got us a nice big hare. This guy's a chunk. Don't know where he got his food, but he did all right for himself somehow. You need anything while I go skin this rabbit and get him ready for the pan?"

Oba shook his head.

"Hungry?"

"I don't know. Maybe there's a hole busted in my stomach."

Charlie grinned, glad to hear that amount of words, even a bit of humor. "We'll see," he said and patted his shoulder. "Just hang on there, and I'll get us a big fire going. We need hot coals for the frying pan."

The meal was the best Charlie could remember, the pieces of meat rolled in flour and fried with a sprinkling of salt. His spirit refreshed, Charlie became quite talkative, brought a piece of the most tender meat to Oba, who chewed painfully, swallowed clumsily, and asked for water.

He was so terribly cold.

They spent a miserable night, with Charlie getting very little sleep, replenishing the fire, awakened repeatedly by Oba's pitiful cries of anguish and pain. Finally, Charlie sat beside him, his back to the blaze of fire, and talked, trying his best to get his mind on something else.

"You know, it's a good thing that you feel all that pain in your legs. That means your back ain't broken. So where you from? You never told me your name."

Eventually Charlie slept curled up against Oba, the cold and exhaustion mercifully erased till the light from the east spread through the tent.

THE BUZZING OF the rescue plane was divine music to Charlie, but he was unsure if Oba was conscious at the time, the way he'd been slipping in and out of reality throughout the day. He stood by the tent, waved both arms in an emotional signal of welcome, cringed at the earsplitting sound and whacking of the engine as the plane descended onto the river.

Oba cried out as the two men loaded him on the stretcher. They carried him into the plane to administer to his needs as Charlie doused the fire, folded the tent, brought the sled's supplies, the furs, everything, packed up the meager utensils and cooking pots, before loading it all into the angel of rescue. Charlie noticed one of the men taking a few photographs of the mangled plane. "In case there's an investigation," the man said. "And for the newspaper."

They spoke only necessary words, to save time, everything carried out without a moment's waste. When he was lifted efficiently into the sky, Charlie looked down on the beauty of the wilderness and felt no fear. But he was ready to be back home with his parents, Jerry, and Sue.

CHAPTER 23

Oba and May grew up together, the only two children in the Eliezer Miller family, which was unusual, given the number of families with a dozen children, more or less. They never gave this much thought, however, especially at the ages of four and five, the years before they went to school, when life was one warm cocoon of love and laughter, with doting parents who lavished their affection on the two of them. There were only two, and there would never be more, so like rare jewels, they were guarded with care and an abundance of love.

Every cough or fever was tended with loving concern, cuts and bruises bandaged with precision. In a large family, most minor wounds were brushed off after a sibling examined the howling infant or toddler. Mothers were busy from dawn to dusk, their minds occupied with a thousand matters, which shifted the perspective of a scraped kneed or a bumped elbow.

May, at a very young age, was endowed with a caregiving spirit, a natural instinct to serve, to fuss over a crying baby, her eyes luminous as she ran to her mother after church, saying someone should come immediately, this baby was not happy. She looked after the baby pigs who were smallest, their larger siblings squealing greedily after a teat, making them unavailable for the littlest one. Her father would scoop him or her out of the pen, and with Oba's help, the fortunate little pig was bathed, blanketed, and fed with a baby bottle, laid ever so gently in a box, straw scattered on the bottom, a child's idea of a mattress for a poor piglet.

But Oba had no mercy on sick, mewling kittens, their eyes pasted shut with the feline plague of the untended barn cats. May would watch her brother stalk away, shaking his head, refusing any part of dealing with cats, then sigh and give up, return to her duty of scooping the skinny, sightless little thing into her arms, taking it to the washhouse for a rag and strong soap to wipe away the residue from its diseased eyes, her mother looking on with pride.

On one fine summer day in their youth, when the heat of the afternoon sun was a discomfort to them both, Oba and May flopped together in the shade of the maple tree in the back yard. The grass was turning brown beneath the tree, the rains having gone south of them for most of July and into August. Rumblings from the sky could be heard briefly, but no refreshing summer storm came.

Left to themselves, they thought up ways to pass the afternoon. Oba wanted to go to the creek, but May reminded him of the fact their mother would have to accompany them and she had to drive the horses for their dat. As children will do, they thought up ways to entertain themselves, with Oba agreeing to a tea party, but only if May provided food. Real food.

Always quick to please her brother, she ran to the house, then opened the screen door, her tiny form wrestling with heaving a small wooden chair through the opening, the door well secured by a sturdy spring.

"Oba!"

He turned his head in her direction, still lying idly where she had left him.

"Oba! I need your help!"

So he got to his feet, although a bit begrudgingly, and helped her carry the small wooden table and two chairs. She dashed back for the small square tablecloth, the one her mother had made from a flowered chicken feed sack. Hemmed and ironed, it was one of May's most beloved items. She spread it across the surface of the table, stood back to make sure it was perfectly straight before dashing back for the small metal tea set. On the outside of the cups, red and blue flowers circled the cup on a white background, but it was the saucers and the teapot that were prettiest of all. More flowers, more green leaves, and bigger.

The tea set had been a gift from her parents for her fourth birthday, an extravagance, for sure, but Fronie told herself she had only one daughter, so why not? Why not, indeed, Eliezer had echoed. The tea set was put to good use almost every day, but today was extra special, the way Oba agreed to a tea party out in the yard under this maple tree, with the yellow finches twittering among the branches, the leaves perfectly limp and straight on this hot afternoon.

Her little face was quite red from the exertion, her blond hair loosened from beneath the small black covering, the strings flapping behind her as she hurried from table to house. She brought out a glass jar of meadow tea, a plate of large pale brown sugar cookies with a dusting of brown sugar baked into them, a cereal bowl containing a cornstarch pudding, and a plate of saltine crackers with strawberry jelly to spread on them with the tiny little knives.

When everything was complete, May stood back, her little hands clasped in front of her, sighing in satisfaction. She turned to Oba, who had flopped back on the grass, watching her with disinterest, never quite understanding why someone would go to so much work for a pretend tea party. But since he was hungry and had nothing better to do, why not go about this for real? He'd be the father, and she could be the mother, but then there was only one thing wrong with that situation. She would want children, which meant a grunting piglet or one of those *grausich* (disgusting) cats she kept doctoring up.

"Come, Oba. Dinner is ready," she trilled excitedly.

Oba pulled himself to his feet, sat very seriously and put his hands in his lap, ready to put "patties down," the Pennsylvania Dutch phrase for folding hands in laps and bowing heads for a lengthy silent prayer.

"You be the dat, okay?" May asked, meaning he would be the one to lift his head first, a signal the prayer was over.

"I'm not going to be the dat today. We'll be sister and brother, like we are for real. If we do that, we won't need children."

May looked at him, her eyes big and brown, her small face the face of a promising beauty.

"Okay. All right. But you look up first."

So he did.

She poured the tea, without spilling a drop, and he helped himself to a sugar cookie, cutting it in half, then half again, so it would fit on his plate. He added a dollop of cornstarch pudding, then cut into the cookie with the side of his spoon.

"Mm. May, this is really good. Taste it."

Always eager to oblige, she followed suit, nodded her head eagerly, in total agreement.

"Oba, you would be my child, okay?"

"But I can't. I'm bigger than you."

"That doesn't matter. You would be very small. And your name is Albert."

"Albert? Whatever for?"

"Albert is a nice name. You would be at a babysitter's house, then I would come get you. The babysitter wouldn't be a nice one, okay? She would not have fed you one single thing all day. Go away now, Oba, then I'll come get you."

Oba shoveled the last bite into his mouth, then walked behind the house as May set her little table to rights. Then she smoothed her skirts and walked behind the house to find her poor, hungry child. When she reached him, she told him he had to walk on his knees, that would be much more real, so Oba did, thinking he would go along with whatever she wanted, if it meant more cookies and cornstarch pudding.

She took his hand. "Come, Albert. Poor child. Was she being very mean today?"

"Albert" nodded his head up and down, his mouth puckered into pretend self-pity.

"Well, she was not in a good mood. I'm going to have to have a talk with her, aren't I? Come, we have crackers and jelly. You want some crackers and jelly?"

"Albert" nodded, his mouth still puckered with a pretend baby face.

She tied a dishcloth around his neck, told him the bib was very nice, patted his head, and gave him a drink of tea from one of the little cups, then wiped his mouth with her tiny square handkerchief.

"Now, Albert. Would you like a cracker with jelly?"

He nodded, completely absorbed in being the child, and May performed the part of a doting little mother quite admirably. She fed him bits of cracker and jelly, alternating with sips of tea, and wiped his mouth before setting him down on the grass and telling him it was naptime. Obediently, he lay on his side, drew up his knees, and folded his hands beneath his chin, then closed his eyes too tightly, so they quivered and appeared in an unnatural sleep.

May giggled, told him to stop closing his eyes quite as tightly. He looked up at her, gave her a genuine grin, before reverting back to being Albert, who needed lots of care and attention, and May walked resolutely behind the house, where she approached the kerosene tank and proceeded to knock on the erring babysitter's door. She had a long and harried exchange with the unrepentant person, finally lifting her shoulders and saying, "*Ya vell, don.* (Oh well then.)"

As she marched away, she tried speaking in English, because the babysitter was an *Englishy frau* (English woman), and she thought she needed the last word, after all. So she shook a very small finger and said forcefully, "Well, *ich huff* all your cookies *fa-gthrots*. (I hope all your cookies become moldy.)" It would not be quite as outrageous if it wasn't poor Albert being so terribly hungry, and she having cookies to spare. Albert was *yusht glay* (just little), and who did she think she was?

Her love for Oba in real life had always bordered on worship, so now when they play acted, she was free to defend him as fiercely as her lively imagination would allow. She sat down delicately, poured a bit of tea from the flowered teapot, and sipped indignantly. She checked on Albert, who was still fast asleep, then helped herself to another cookie before carefully spreading a bit of jelly on a saltine cracker.

Oba ate everything May handed him, thought there was nothing wrong with being the child as long as he was enjoying the food. He watched May with her little black bowl-shaped covering on her blond head, and only for a moment, he thought how awful it would be to be without May. She was his only and favorite sister.

May looked up and smiled, a sweet smile of adoration. "Oba, you would fall down and hurt your leg, then we'd take you to the hospital."

"But how would I fall hard enough if I stay on the ground?"

"You could climb up on the porch roof and fall down."

"May!"

"I mean, jump down."

She covered her giggles with both hands, when Oba said he would never jump down from the porch roof.

The fall was still in its planning stage when the rattle of steel wheels became apparent. They both looked up to find their mother driving the black Percherons, a load of loose hay stacked high, bits of hay trailing after the rolling wagon. They watched as she slapped the wide leather reins, brought them down on the massive backs as she called out.

"Git up! Hi! Git on up there! Tom! Dan!"

The Percherons dug their great hooves into the dirt, their haunches lowering as they threw themselves into their immense collars, drawing the loaded wagon up the incline to the top story of the bank barn. May winced as the wide steel wheels clattered across the cement threshold before rumbling across the great wooden boards, resting on massive beams.

May sighed when everything was quiet.

"My mom is a brave person," she said, in her small, serious voice.

"Puh," Oba said. "Lots of women drive hay wagons."

"I bet not into the barn, on a hill."

"Yes, they do, May."

Emphatic as always, Oba tried to prove his point, saying Aunt Ruthie did, Alvin said she did, but May tilted her small head and stared back at Oba, completely aware that both Alvin and Oba *schnitzed* (lied). They both looked up as their slender young mother walked toward them, her face flushed with the heat of the day, her smile wide. The kind of smile that spread to her eyes and crinkled the brown into a deep line of happiness.

"Hey!"

"Mam, I'm the mom, and Oba is my child. His name is Albert. His babysitter did not give him any food. She would be English."

Fronie laughed, before sitting in the shade by the small table. "Oh now. I don't know any English people who are unkind. That is not a very nice thing to play."

"Well, then she could be Amish."

"I don't know any unkind Amish people either."

May's brow wrinkled with a perplexed expression. "Mam, maybe there could be."

"Oh, we hope not."

To be out under the maple tree on a warm, dry summer day, the world filled with love and security, life as simple and uncomplicated as the blue and black butterflies hovering over the zinnias in the garden, who could understand the shadow that passed across Fronie's pretty face?

She could hear the drone of a faraway airplane, a sound she had heard occasionally before without any adverse reaction, but today, a deep sense of melancholy seized her. A sorrow, almost. She blinked her eyes to focus on her children, shook off the sensation of foreboding, took a deep breath, and blamed it on the heat.

She was very thirsty, so she went to the pump, lifted the handle till she was rewarded by the gurgle of fresh, cool water, flowing into the tin cup that always hung from the cast iron pump by a length of string.

"Mam!"

She finished her drink, then turned.

"We still have cookies leftover. Would you like one?"

And her world turned right, revolved around her precious children, as always. She blamed the dark shadow that claimed her for a moment on her thirst. She should not have waited so long to drink from the pump.

That evening, after the children were in bed, she sat beside Eliezer on the porch swing, trying to catch a cooling breeze before entering the stifling bedroom. He reached for her hand, which she drew gently away.

A small laugh escaped her. "It's too warm for any hand holding."

Eliezer smiled to himself, then patted her hand. "I understand. It's just that I love you so much and need to show you how close I am to you."

"Thank you. I love you, too."

The chain on the hook creaked as their feet pushed against the boards of the porch floor, providing a gentle rocking motion. A tired-sounding katydid began a low-key symphony, was answered by another more energetic tone. Somewhere in the hollow south of them, a bullfrog set up his deep bass chugging, as a dog barked in a high-frenzied sound. There was no moon, so the sky was black, with a scattering of stars like broken jewels.

"Eliezer."

"Yes, dear."

"I felt the strangest sense of foreboding today, out of nowhere. It was like a sudden wave of grief, but for no reason."

He did not know how to reply to this, so he reached for her hand, without thinking. This time she let him hold it, needed the comfort.

"I heard an airplane above me, which of course I've heard before, on occasion. But I was gripped by an overshadowing sense of . . ." Her voice fell away.

"Oh, Fronie." He squeezed her hand.

"Maybe it wasn't anything at all. I thought later I was probably tired. I know I waited too long to get a drink. But I can't stop thinking about it."

"If it was something, there is no need to fret. You know God has our future planned for us, and all we need to do is keep on trusting. Sometimes, when times are hard, like now, with the money situation we're going through, we are anxious and don't realize it. You're doing a great job stretching food and clothing, everything."

And so Fronie was comforted by the sweet appreciation in her husband's voice and forgot about the dark cloud having overtaken her that afternoon. But as time went on, she realized the immensity of the feeling, the stark reminder cropping up intermittently, at times when she least expected it. With her faith as her shield, she accepted this strange phenomenon, without fear or undue anxiety.

Perhaps it was a woman's intuition, and perhaps it was a test of her faith in God, but whatever it was, it was indeed very real.

Realizing her own restrictions as a mere mortal, she kept this to herself, untroubled by it. And sometimes, for no reason at all, she gathered her children in her arms and held them as if she could never let them go. And she prayed.

She asked the Lord to keep them in His tender care, to allow them the courage and faith to meet adversity head on, to accept Christ as their personal Savior, so they could all reside in Heaven someday.

Fronie lived her life with joy and love, without understanding of the steep, rocky path that lay before her precious children. It was the way the Heavenly Father designed His perfect plan.

She watched Oba and May play so sweetly and prayed that they would always love each other. She could not have guessed the mysterious ways that God would honor her prayers and that the love between those two would be the very thing that pulled each of them through the hardest moments of their lives.

THE END.

About the Author

Linda Byler was raised in an Amish family and is an active member of the Amish church today. Growing up, Linda loved to read and write. In fact, she still does. Linda is well known within the Amish community as a columnist for a weekly Amish newspaper. She writes all her novels by hand in notebooks.

Linda is the author of six series of novels, all set among the Amish communities of North America: Lizzie Searches for Love, Sadie's Montana, Lancaster Burning, Hester's Hunt for Home, the Dakota Series, and the Buggy Spoke Series for younger readers. Linda has also written several Christmas romances set among the Amish: *Mary's Christmas Goodbye, The Christmas Visitor, The Little Amish Matchmaker, Becky Meets Her Match, A Dog for Christmas, A Horse for Elsie,* and *The More the Merrier.* Linda has coauthored *Lizzie's Amish Cookbook: Favorite Recipes from Three Generations of Amish Cooks!*

Read the Whole Trilogy

BOOK ONE

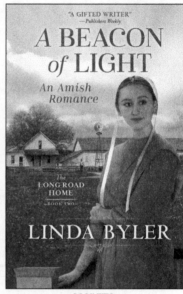

BOOK TWO

BOOK THREE

OTHER BOOKS BY
LINDA BYLER

LIZZIE SEARCHES FOR LOVE SERIES

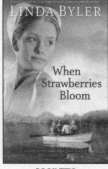

BOOK ONE

BOOK TWO

BOOK THREE

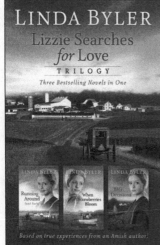

TRILOGY

COOKBOOK

Sadie's Montana Series

BOOK ONE

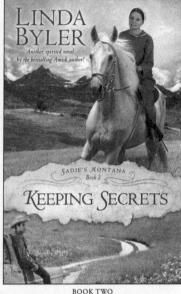

BOOK TWO

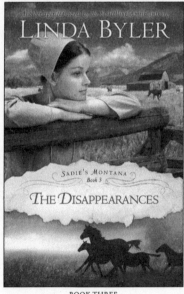

BOOK THREE

TRILOGY

LANCASTER BURNING SERIES

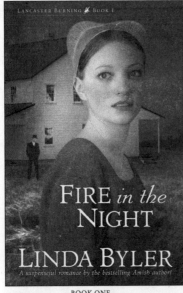

BOOK ONE

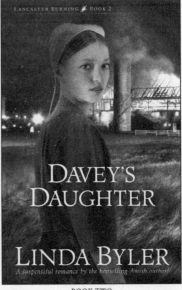

BOOK TWO

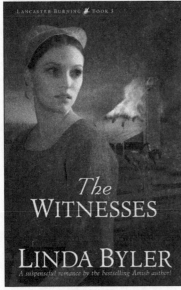

BOOK THREE

TRILOGY

BOOK ONE

BOOK TWO

BOOK THREE

TRILOGY

The Dakota Series

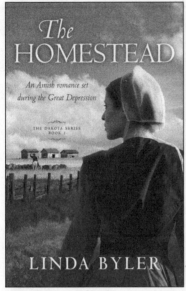

BOOK ONE

BOOK TWO

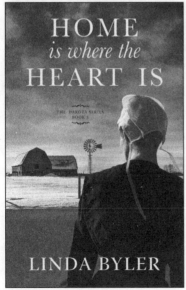

BOOK THREE

TRILOGY

CHRISTMAS NOVELLAS

THE CHRISTMAS VISITOR

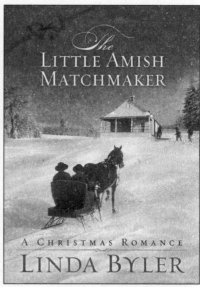

LITTLE AMISH MATCHMAKER

MARY'S CHRISTMAS GOODBYE

BECKY MEETS HER MATCH

A DOG FOR CHRISTMAS

A HORSE FOR ELSIE

THE MORE THE MERRIER

Christmas Collections

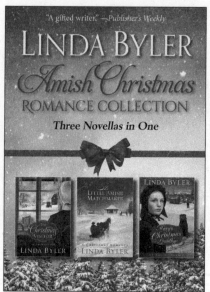

AMISH CHRISTMAS ROMANCE COLLECTION

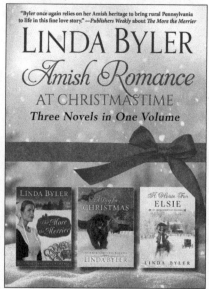

AMISH ROMANCE AT CHRISTMASTIME

New Releases

THE HEALING

A SECOND CHANCE

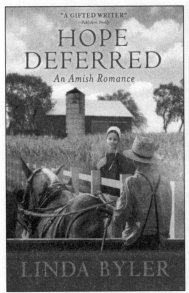

HOPE DEFERRED

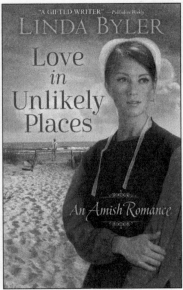

LOVE IN UNLIKELY PLACES

Buggy Spoke Series for Young Readers

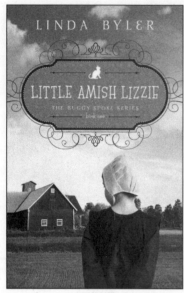

BOOK ONE

BOOK TWO

BOOK THREE